keep you to myself

BRIANN DANAE

*To the ones who never gave up and chased the light at the end of the tunnel.
It's good to see you shining again.*
- BriAnn Danae

prologue

New Beginnings… Again
Southside Kansas City – 2017

The scowl on her grandson's handsome face was one GiGi hated to see. It'd been almost permanent since she'd taken him in three years ago. Since then, she'd gotten a few smiles out of him, but not many. GiGi was sure there wouldn't be many more from this day forward.

"Synovi," she sighed, adjusting in her bed. "Stop looking at me like that. You act like I can control this, baby."

He gave her a blank stare as his jaw tensed. "A'ight, GiGi," he spoke lowly.

"It ain't no *a'ight*. Tell me how you feel."

She always wanted him to open up. Synovi hated it. There was no point in explaining how he felt. It wouldn't change the situation they were in. The situation he seemed to have been in his entire life. It was as if God hadn't given him a break since he was born. Synovi was tired of taking and failing whatever test He was putting him through.

"I'ont feel nothing."

GiGi sighed again and shook her head. "You're mad with me."

"Nah."

"Yes, you are."

Synovi shrugged. "I ain't mad at you, GiGi. There ain't nothing we can do. You in here, and I'm 'bout to go back to someplace I ain't wanted. Nothing new."

Tears pricked GiGi's eyes, hearing his disengaged tone. Already, he had pulled away, and she hated it. They'd made some progress with him expressing himself since she'd taken him in, and though minuscule, it'd been something. Now, Synovi was returning to his shell, keeping his emotions tucked away from her and the world. It was a defense mechanism he'd grown accustomed to using with ease. That barrier was thrown up like a white flag.

"I wish there was more I could do, baby," GiGi sighed, full of guilt.

Synovi saw it all over her face. As upset as he was, it wasn't with his granny. He loved her to the moon and back. Walking over to her bed, Synovi adjusted the blanket around her before kissing her cheek.

"It's cool, GiGi. You need to get better so you can get up out of here," Synovi let her know.

As hopeful as GiGi was, she didn't see that happening anytime soon. Going from living in her home of forty years to having a stroke and being in a coma for one week before being told she would be placed in an assisted living home was a lot. More than she and her seventeen-year-old grandson could handle right now. She could only pray she got better. Her nights of peaceful rest wouldn't come, knowing Synovi was yet again in the hands of some strangers.

"That's the plan, baby," she spoke just as a knock came to her hospital door.

The social worker, who Synovi already didn't like, made her presence known. He scowled her way and looked over her attire. Hair that looked wet was matted to her head, while high-water khaki pants fit snuggly around her chubby waistline. Coffee seeped from her pores as if she'd been sipping on it the second she opened her eyes.

"When you knock on someone's door, you need to wait 'til they say it's coo' for you to come in," he told her straight up.

The social worker's eyes widened. "I-I'm so sorry. I'll step out until you're ready."

"Yeah. Do that," Synovi mumbled and focused back on his GiGi.

She snickered. "Mean tail. You better not have no attitude with that lady. She's just doing her job."

"She should've knocked. That's disrespectful. You'ont play that."

GiGi could only nod her head. If he hadn't learned much while in her care, Synovi was respectful to those who respected him. Soon as someone got out of line, he was checking them. Young, old, Black, or white, he was checking shit behind his respect. His short temper was what made the smallest mishaps set him off. Not for long, though. He'd learned long ago that staying mad for hours at a time didn't change anything. It just made him madder because all his attention was focused on that one situation.

"I don't," GiGi concluded. "You make sure you call me as soon as you get to that place."

"I will. When you leaving up out of here?" Synovi wondered.

She wasn't telling him everything, and he knew it. "Right after you. Don't give me that look. I'm not lying to you, boy."

Synovi cracked a small grin. "A'ight. They bogus for not letting me stay with you," he grunted.

While she was in the hospital, Synovi shooed away every authoritative figure trying to make him leave his GiGi's side. When she woke up, she was given details of her medical condition and how her insurance would cover her stay at the living facility. Relief only lasted for a few minutes until she was informed Synovi couldn't live with her.

Not going for that, she had the doctor search for a facility that would allow him to live with her until she fully recovered. Unfortunately, none of the facilities in her insurance network allowed it. So, for now, Synovi would stay at an emergency housing shelter. While the duration of the stay was only supposed to be for six weeks, in his heart, he knew it'd be longer. Time was never on his side.

"We'll be back together again, cleaning up and listening to Anita Baker, baby. Don't you worry."

That was easy for GiGi to say. She wasn't seventeen and hadn't been bounced around throughout the foster care system. He worried so much, it could've been his middle name.

"I'll call you from the shelter's phone when I get there," he told her, grabbing his backpack off the chair.

"Okay. You still have that money I gave you?" GiGi asked.

Nodding, Synovi patted the pocket of his jeans. "Yes."

"All right. I love you, Synovi. This is only temporary."

As much progress as they'd made, Synovi still hadn't told her he loved her. It sounded foreign coming from her lips when she first told him. Somewhere in his wounded heart, he loved her, too, but uttering the words aloud hadn't come easy. There'd been people in his life he thought loved him and done the exact opposite.

Synovi wasn't quite sure how that love shit was supposed to work, but he knew it should've come naturally from his own flesh and blood. The woman who birthed him had fucked up the meaning of love long before he could grasp the true meaning and feeling.

"I hope so," Synovi mumbled, pulling the door open.

The social worker's head shot upward from her cell phone. Giving him a gentle smile, she asked, "You ready?"

Synovi's head nodded upward. He didn't want to leave GiGi, but he had no choice in the matter, like always.

Sitting in the back of her car felt like déjà vu. There'd been plenty of car rides to new homes; strangers who he didn't want to be in the care of. Feeling like a burden made him stay to himself. People weren't obligated to take care of him, even if they were getting paid. No matter how nice folks came off, Synovi didn't trust anyone.

To keep his peace and a somewhat level-head, he didn't let anyone get close enough to do him wrong. Emotionally scarred, thanks to his past, Synovi took an oath to never let anyone in and let him down. He could only hope this temporary situation was just that.

When they pulled in front of the building, distaste immediately settled in Synovi's chest. For it to be an emergency housing shelter for teens, he wondered why it was gated. *Shit feels like a prison already,* he thought as the social worker rolled her window down and pressed the silver call button.

She'd told him her name, but Synovi didn't bother remembering it. He didn't care to memorize people's names, knowing they'd be of no importance to him days from now. In this case, minutes.

"Mrs. Shimer. Social Worker from Divided," she said into the mic.

"Come on in," another voice on the receiving end said as the gate slowly opened in a screeching manner.

After what felt like forever for the iron bars to divide, they finally pulled around to the entrance. Nothing about the grounds stood out to Synovi. It was just like any other place he had been displaced at. Flowers aligned the walkway leading to the entrance, while pictures with encouraging words and business hours were displayed on the windows.

Parking and cutting the car off, Mrs. Shimer looked over her shoulder. "Ready to go inside?"

Synovi's jaw ticked as he mugged her. He'd been asked that same question more than he'd like to admit. He was never ready to, once again, be dependent on complete strangers. The shit was sad, but it was his life. Had been his life for years now.

Instead of answering her, he grabbed his backpack and opened the door. Unfolding himself from her small car gave him room to breathe. At his age, Synovi was much taller and buffer than other young teenage boys. GiGi always said he must've gotten his stature from his father, because his mother wasn't nearly as tall. Neither of them knew who he was, but his mother was nowhere near his height. Mrs. Shimer came rushing around to greet him as if she couldn't wait to get on with her day.

"Let's get you inside. Now, remember, this is just temporary until your grandmother is back on her feet. I see you didn't bring much with you, so I'll let the staff know to assist with getting you clothes from back home. Does that sound okay?"

Synovi simply gave her a head nod because what else was he supposed to say? While Mrs. Shimer handled the business side of things at the front desk, he wondered where a phone was to call his GiGi. He couldn't wait to tell her how this place smelled like mothballs and dirty bleach water. Nothing like her warm home that was filled with hints of vanilla and spice. Her place was a home… not a homeless shelter.

Shit, that's what I am, he thought, then shook his head, trying to remain somewhat positive. *For now.*

Little did Synovi know, this would be his home for more than a few weeks.

one

PRESENT DAY – 5 YEARS LATER

Light perspiration settled on Synovi's forehead as he carried a case of chicken wings through the back door of *Freddy's*. It was his fourth trip to the unloading truck and, thankfully, his last. He was not trying to spend the last fifteen minutes of his shift getting a workout in. Especially not when he should've been off two hours ago. Placing the box in the two-door refrigerator, Synovi shut it before securing the back door with a lock.

"That's the last one," he announced, coming around the counter.

Mr. Fred looked up from the cash register with a grin. "I sure do appreciate you for sticking around and helping out. One of these days, we're gonna get some more staff."

Synovi liked the old man, so he wouldn't tell him he'd been saying that for the past six months. That was how long he'd been working at Freddy's, and to this day, they were short-staffed. The mom-and-pop diner was well-known and had been around for years. Hence why the customers who visited often had no objection to the long wait times. The service was still stellar, and the food was unmatched.

"One day," Synovi concluded. He glanced at the clock and then back at Mr. Fred. "You gon' be straight here by yourself?"

"Yeah, yeah. These fools around here aren't crazy."

Every city had some crazy people, but Synovi kept his

comments to himself. He knew once he started a conversation with Mr. Fred, he'd be there another hour. The old man could talk, and clearly, Synovi was an excellent listener.

"A'ight. I'ma head out then," he let him know.

"All right, son. Don't forget to grab that food you boxed up. See you tomorrow."

He most definitely wasn't going to forget his container of food. One of the cooks, Hazel, prepared some of the best smothered turkey chops. Heading inside the break room, Synovi put his jacket and skully on before snatching his backpack and food up. Before heading back up front, he double-checked the back door to make sure it was secure. Mr. Fred and his wife had been running the diner for years with no threats or robberies, but Synovi could never be too safe.

Mr. Fred followed him to the entrance and locked the door behind him. It was later than he normally got off work, but he didn't mind. The job paid well enough and treated him the same. Synovi just wished he had his own ride to get him back and forth. Taking the bus was cool; he'd been doing it for a while, but copping his own ride was in his plans. There was no bus fare at the time, so he wasn't in any rush.

He waited at the bus stop alone for all of two minutes before it pulled up to the curb. Hopping on, he found a spot near the back and got comfortable for the twenty-nine-minute ride home. Not necessarily the home he wanted to be at, but it was what Synovi called it until he got his own spot. He had a roof over his head and clothes on his back, so he wasn't complaining. Not yet, at least.

Bidding the bus driver a good night, he made his way to Solace Place, which was right up the block. Strangely, the transitional housing building was located right next to a well-known, popular nightclub. The bass from inside poured out onto the sidewalk as the bouncer granted partiers access. A Thursday night with work in the morning meant nothing to those standing in line.

Seeing the women in their short dresses, heels that looked unbearable to walk in, and faces full of anxiousness was routine for Synovi. At his age, he should've been in the men's line opposite of them. Partying was the last thing on his mind, though. Doing a slight jog up the concrete steps, Synovi waved his access card over the reader and was granted access inside the first door. From there, the staff prompted him to give up his credentials.

"How can I help you?" one of the overnight staff, Kimmy, questioned.

"It's Synovi."

Bzzz!

The door unlocked for entry, granting him access. Stopping at the counter, Synovi grabbed the pen to sign in.

"You know it's past curfew," Kimmy said, as if he didn't know.

Synovi gave her a blank stare. "Yeah. I was at work."

"Well, Mr. K didn't know that and told me to give you this non-compliance."

Kimmy held out a sheet that stated which rule he'd broken, awaiting his acknowledgment and signature. Once you received so many non-compliance write-ups, you'd have to sit in a meeting with the director and supervisor of the program. They figured since you couldn't abide by the rules you agreed to when arriving, maybe their program wasn't a good fit.

"Tell *William* to give it to me himself," Synovi told her before walking toward his room.

GiGi would go in on Synovi if she caught wind of him addressing someone twenty-plus years his senior by their first name. Synovi couldn't care less about William and whatever he stood for. Since he'd come to Solace Place, the man acted as if him running the place gave him the right to be an asshole. Synovi didn't kiss his ass, and William had it out for him. As a Black man, Synovi wondered what the issue was.

Just the week prior, when Synovi's schedule changed to later hours, he'd given it to his caseworker, who then gave it to William. So, technically, the write-up was for no reason, and Synovi wasn't signing that shit.

"That nigga get on my nerves," he grumbled, stepping into his bedroom. *These niggas too.*

Solace Place offered life skill training in a supervised, dorm-style setting for men between the ages of eighteen and twenty-four. Some of the men battled with mental health, or in Synovi's case, lacked a place to live and were trying to get on their feet. Some of them, Synovi included, needed financial and social support to help transition them into becoming responsible, independent men.

Though it was temporary housing, a middle ground between emergency shelter and permanent housing, sometimes it didn't feel that way. At least not to Synovi. He understood having structure, but having a curfew at his age was wild. Especially when there wasn't one on the weekends.

The day he left GiGi's hospital room, nothing in Synovi's life panned out how he expected. As her health declined, the emergency shelter became his place of residence for six weeks. Since he was underage and no one on either side of his family stepped up to take him in, Synovi became a ward of the state. It broke GiGi's heart and froze Synovi's. All he knew was not feeling as if he belonged anywhere, so he got suspicious when he got too comfortable.

Once he turned eighteen, Synovi tried the community college thing, but it didn't last. Working minimum wage jobs didn't matter either, but he worked them. Apartment complexes asking for income to be triple the rent as a requirement was crazy to him. There wasn't that much overtime in the world, but he still saved what he could.

While he could've turned to the streets and become a dope or jack boy, Synovi couldn't see himself selling drugs. He'd hit a few petty licks but also knew karma was a greedy bitch, so he chilled on those. Trying to make an honest living while he was young with a hustler mentality, but with limited opportunities, was stressing him out. That and his bum-ass roommate.

"Y'all don't see this trash overflowing?" Synovi questioned as they played a game on the Xbox.

Xavier, a cat from across the hall, was the first to glance his way, while Ron, his roommate, never made eye contact. "You on trash duty, ain't you?"

"What that mean? Y'all see the shit all on the floor and just gon' leave it?" Synovi hissed, not raising his voice.

Ron waved him off. "You want it off the floor, take that shit out."

Synovi stared at the back of his head, wanting to punch him in it, but he nodded instead. "A'ight."

One thing he learned while living with GiGi was how to clean up. Every day, she had him clean a different part of the house, even if it were something as simple as vacuuming. Rooming with a grown man and living in a building with some who were dirty pissed Synovi off to no end. He didn't mind having a chore while living here; he preferred it, actually. Cleaning up behind themselves was the least they could do since they lived there for free.

Taking his food into the kitchen, Synovi tried his best to tuck it somewhere safe. Some of the men staying there had no regard for others's meals and savagely ate them. Synovi had already checked a nigga behind his food once, and he hoped he didn't have to do it again. Violence was an automatic removal from the program, and he didn't have time for that.

Stepping inside the bedroom with a glove on, he got the trash up and tied the bag. Glancing at the TV, he noticed the football game they were playing was down to the last minute. Heading out the door, Synovi unplugged the gaming device and looked at them as they hopped up from their seats.

"The fuck, cuz!" Ron thundered. "That was some bitch shit."

"You ain't gon' do nothin' 'bout it," Synovi concluded. "Next time, have the trash up off the floor. Trifling ass niggas."

Not worried about getting swung on for his disrespect, Synovi left out the room. He had to gather the kitchen and bathroom trash before showering and calling it a night. Coming out of the kitchen with two bags, he almost bumped into Kimmy.

"I'm headed to take these out and I'll be back in," he told her.

"Okay. We'll look out for you on the cameras."

Synovi pushed through the back door to an alley down the long hall and a flight of steps. It was more like a side street, yet still was dark and narrow. The one flickering streetlight didn't do much to brighten the area. Coming out here to the dumpsters would've been spooky to anyone else. Not to him, though. He liked the darkness. Some nights, when the club next door wasn't popping how it was, there was silence. Synovi came out here to clear his head. Tonight, he wasn't alone.

The woman screaming into her phone had no clue of her surroundings. So caught up in cursing out whoever she was on the phone with, she didn't notice the dark figure creep up behind her. When she went to scream, he tossed a hand over her mouth, muffling the sound. Synovi didn't think twice before dropping the trash bags in his hand and running in their direction.

A blow to the back of the assailant's head sent him stumbling, and his grasp loosened on the woman. Frantically, she jumped back as Synovi delivered the type of ass-whooping only a person with built-up anger could give out. Not only that, but Synovi's anger heightened, thinking of what would've happened had he not been out there. Men like him didn't deserve to live, but Synovi was no killer. He came real close to being one.

Slamming the man against the brick building, Synovi squeezed his neck with intent while staring him in the eyes. Before he could pass out, he let him loose and winded him even more with the punch to his solar plexus. Crumbling to the ground, the man wheezed.

"Oh, my gosh. Oh, my gosh," the woman cried out behind him. "You just saved my life!"

Synovi didn't acknowledge her right away. He wanted to deal with the creep laid out in front of him.

"Get up," he demanded.

When the man didn't move fast enough, Synovi slammed his size twelve foot into his hand, snapping his wrist.

"Aaaggh!" The man's howl echoed throughout the alley.

The woman gasped and slapped both hands over her mouth.

"Get up," Synovi commanded in a much calmer tone.

Struggling, the assaulter stood to his feet. "L-Look, man, I'm sorry. I thought she was a hooker."

"I am not a fucking prostitute!" the woman shouted.

Disgust laced her grunt, sickened that he would even think that. Even if she was a prostitute, he still assaulted her. Selling pussy or not, consent was still a thing.

"If she was, what were you going to do?" Synovi questioned. "Rape her?"

The man looked stunned by his questions but didn't answer. No answer was an answer in Synovi's eyes.

"Apologize," Synovi demanded.

"I-I'm sorry, Miss. I shouldn't have bothered you."

Too shaken up to speak, the woman just stared at him while somewhat shielding herself behind Synovi's large frame. She didn't think the backless dress that stopped mid-thigh was *that* revealing. Now, she felt naked as ever under her assaulter's gaze. She could still feel his cruddy hand groping her breast.

Just seeing him look her way, knowing he had ill intentions, made Synovi send a blow to the spot right between his eyes. They'd be black and swollen in no time. Shoving him toward the street, Synovi scoffed.

"Don't bring your ass back around here," he threatened, but meant every word.

Synovi kept his eyes on the man until he could no longer see him. While Kimmy and the other worker watched everything go down on the cameras, she called the police, not knowing the man had already been on their radar. He'd been in an altercation a few blocks up and was cuffed and in the back of a squad car before he could make it to the corner.

Flexing his hand, Synovi turned on his feet, only to be met

by the woman. She was still right up on him as if she had nowhere to be.

"Oh," she chirped, backing away some, but still in his space. "Sorry. Thank you so much for just saving me. I can't believe that just happened."

"Yeah. No problem," Synovi said, starting to walk off.

"Wait! Where are you going? I want to repay you."

Synovi kept it pushing. He didn't help her, hoping to get something out of it. He was a man. One who wasn't going to stand idly by and watch a woman get attacked.

"I'm good," he reiterated as she grabbed his arm. That made him turn and face her.

Synovi was so much taller than her, she had to lean her head back to look up at him. His gaze dropped to her hand on his arm, and she quickly removed it.

"You saved me from who knows what, and I have to repay you. It's the least I can do."

All his life, Synovi had been a good judge of character. He could read people based on the energy they gave off. This woman screamed that she wasn't a prostitute, but now he wasn't so sure. Synovi stared at her with suspicion in his eyes. Her once large curls were now loose. Wide, curious eyes stared back at him, waiting for a response. The diamonds in her ear sparkled right along with the tennis bracelets on her wrist. GiGi had a gang of real diamonds, so he knew those weren't the fake kind. The more he assessed her, the deeper his frown got. The woman caught on to what he was silently insinuating.

"I'm not a prostitute," she hissed, snaking her neck.

"I ain't say you were."

"That's how you're looking, but whatever. I was just going to give you some cash for your good deed."

Synovi flicked at his nose. "Nah. I told you I'm good."

"Who turns down money?" she exclaimed, utterly confused by him and where he even came from. "Fine. If you don't want the money, at least let me treat you to breakfast in the morning."

"Shouldn't your friends or somebody be looking for you?" Synovi pressed.

The woman sucked her teeth. "No. I'm fine."

Synovi's brows raised.

"Okay, well, I was just fine until that creepy ass man came bothering me. I just needed to step out of the club and get some fresh air. You can't even do that shit in peace without a weirdo breathing down your back. Ugh," she vented.

Synovi simply stared before he began to walk away again.

"Why do you keep walking off when we're talking? That's rude," she fussed as if she knew him.

"Talking to strange men in an alleyway isn't safe."

Her mouth fell open, and her eyes bulged. Then she chuckled, which made Synovi's nose crinkle. *What this bitch on?* he thought.

"You're not strange, though. So, are you going to let me treat you to breakfast tomorrow or what?"

"If I say yeah, will you go back inside the club?"

The woman grinned. "Sure."

"A'ight," Synovi said and walked off toward the dumpster.

"Wait! You don't even know where I want you to meet me," she said, following him. Clicks of her stilettos echoed against the concrete.

Picking up one of the trash bags, Synovi tossed it into the dumpster before doing the same with the other. Again, she was right up on him when he turned around.

Laughing, she backed up. "Sorry. I didn't think I was standing that close to you."

Synovi didn't say anything, so she continued.

"Do you know where Bistro is?"

"Nah, but I can look it up."

She clapped her hands. "Perfect. They have good mimosas. So let's meet around twelve."

Synovi gave her a head nod.

"Don't stand me up, Mr. I really do appreciate you. See you tomorrow."

Quickly, she gave him a hug. Synovi's body stiffened, and

he frowned. *Too fucking friendly*, he thought. With the walk of a model who was short as hell, she made it back to the side door of the club she'd come out of and slipped back inside. Synovi didn't make his way back up the steps until he was sure she was out of harm's way. Then again, the way she was moving, he wondered if it would remain that way throughout the night.

Walking down the hall, ready for a hot shower and his food, Synovi was stopped by Kimmy. She looked flustered as if she'd been the one outside.

"Are you okay?" she questioned.

Synovi's head bobbed upward. "I'm good."

"The police let me know he was taken into custody."

"A'ight."

"Can you stop by the office and do an incident report?"

"Yeah."

Kimmy wanted to say more and ask questions right then, but Synovi didn't give her a chance. He walked off toward his bedroom. Today had been long, and tonight's events made it seem like it'd dragged on. The perks of living in transitional housing were learning to live and go with the flow. From one day to the next, anything was bound to happen. Agreeing to meet up for breakfast with a stranger was new, though.

While he told her, yeah, just to get her back inside the club and off his back, Synovi had no idea that this night would change the trajectory of his life. Sometimes, being in the right place at the right time pays off.

two

"Look at this clean freak here," D'Marco jested, stepping inside the bathroom.

At the sink, brushing his teeth, Synovi made eye contact with him through the mirror.

Spitting, he said, "Fuck you."

Disinfectant, shower cleaner, an extendable scrubber, and cleaning gloves were on the floor in its own personal caddy. Synovi didn't care that the person assigned to clean the bathroom had just done it. These niggas were trifling, so he cleaned the shower himself.

"What you got up for the day?" D'Marco asked.

Had it been anyone else questioning him, Synovi wouldn't have replied. D'Marco was his homeboy, though, and one of the few men he conversed with outside of Solace Place.

"Work. You?"

"Court at three. Tryna talk Nikki into taking me off child support," he boasted with a smirk.

"How you gon' do that?"

For as long as Synovi had heard D'Marco complain about being on child support, which was the year and a half that he'd known him, he just knew something tragic must've happened for Nikki to decide that.

"How you think? Give her some dick and promise to get my shit together."

D'Marco laughed, but Synovi didn't find their situation comical. He wouldn't consider him a deadbeat; Synovi didn't care to know his business enough to place that label on him. D'Marco still told him, though. What he did know was that D'Marco could've been doing more for his child. From the stories he'd listened to, Nikki didn't sound bitter. She just wanted him to do right and stay on the right path. However the situation played out, Synovi hoped D'Marco kept his promises. Not just to Nikki, but to their daughter as well.

"You should be doing that, anyway." Synovi let him know, like only the real nigga he was.

"Aye, man. I'm trying. Everybody can't have their shit together like you."

Synovi glanced his way. "Nah. Don't project your shit on me. We all in here on the same shit. Some of us just take it more seriously."

D'Marco could do nothing but nod his head. "You right. Serious ass nigga," he cracked.

They stepped out of the bathroom, and Synovi almost bumped into Ron. He was half-asleep, trying to make it inside the bathroom to relieve his bladder. He missed Synovi but didn't hesitate to bump shoulders with D'Marco.

"Watch where you going, nigga," D'Marco spat, shoving him away from them.

Before a fight could break out, Mr. K made his way down the hall. "Gentlemen, gentlemen. No need for all the rowdiness early this morning."

"Tell that nigga to keep it pushing, Mr. K, 'fore I slide his ass," D'Marco spat.

"Nah, nigga. You tell me," Ron urged.

Being from two rival gangs and in proximity was never a good thing. It was rumored that D'Marco killed Ron's brother some years back. Never confirming or denying it, D'Marco kept the beef going. He wasn't confessing to catching a body, and even if he hadn't, Ron made him want to. Synovi didn't care to be friends with any of the men in transitional housing in the beginning, so when he and D'Marco became cool, he was instantly added to Ron's bad side. Synovi didn't care. No one was going to touch him or tell him who he could kick it with.

"Mr. Ronald, get to where you're going," Mr. K called out.

"Corny ass name. Ronald," D'Marco mimicked in an animated tone, making Synovi almost smirk.

"Don't you have a court appearance today?" Mr. K asked, facing D'Marco.

He waved him off. "Stay in our business."

"As it is my job. Mr. Black, I heard you got into a bit of a scuffle last night."

Synovi scoffed. "I'd hardly call it that."

"I watched the tapes and couldn't be prouder."

If he was looking for a thank you, Synovi wasn't offering one. Seeing that he wasn't going to further explain what happened last night, Mr. K continued the conversation.

"The non-compliance was shredded. You told Kimmy for me to give it to you myself?" he questioned.

"Yeah, 'cause you knew I was at work. You got my schedule last week."

Synovi hated when a mothafucka tried to play in his face, and that was exactly what Mr. K was doing.

"That's my fault. I hadn't gotten around to looking at it."

"A'ight," Synovi said.

"That's all? You don't want to thank me for shredding it?" Mr. K had a grin on his face.

He liked joking with Synovi, but it was clear the young man didn't care for him. Only, Mr. K couldn't take a hint or didn't want to.

"Nah. As it is your job, right?" Synovi questioned, but didn't care to hear his answer.

He mugged him and the black and white Puma jumpsuit he was wearing before walking off to his bedroom. Fridays were dress-down days for the staff, and Mr. K loved to show off the new pieces his wife bought him. Not in a bragging manner, but one where he was letting it be known he appreciated his wife for getting him fly.

Inside his room, Synovi got dressed for the day. He'd slept on the idea of meeting up with the woman from last night and figured, why not? She was adamant and he had some time to spare before work. Sliding on his navy blue Dickies pants, a crisp white tee over a white tank top, the button down left open that matched his pants, and white Forces, he was ready to go. After a few sprays of cologne and popping some gum in his mouth, he grabbed his phone off the charger and backpack with his work shoes from the back of the door.

Heading toward the front of the building, Synovi stopped by the main desk. Kimmy was off, and her replacement was one of the male workers and a few others Synovi actually liked, to an extent.

"What's good, bruh?" Mr. Smith spoke, sticking his hand out for Synovi to dap up.

"What's the deal? I ain't seen you in a minute."

"Caught a stomach bug, but I'm back. Hope you been staying focused."

"Fasho. Trying to, at least. You know how that goes," Synovi said, getting a head nod from Mr. Smith.

To keep things professional around the facility, Mr. K wanted the men living there and the staff to all greet each other by last names. The only one who got a pass if Mr. K wasn't around was Kimmy. Synovi called Mr. K by his first name just to get under his skin, and it always worked.

"Yeah, I do. You making progress, though. How your grandmother doing?"

The mention of GiGi made Synovi grin. That was his girl right there.

"She good. One of the reasons I ain't spazzed out in here. Talking 'bout, 'Now, Synovi. Where you gon' go if they put you out? You can't stay here'."

Mr. Smith laughed, knowing GiGi was serious. She'd called up to Solace Place on plenty of occasions to speak with Synovi whenever he didn't answer his cell phone. In his younger days,

Synovi would sneak out and stay nights at GiGi's place. He hated being away from familiarity after receiving it. Once the staff caught on, they politely let him know he couldn't stay there or GiGi would get put out. Not wanting to ever jeopardize her living situation, Synovi went back to the emergency shelter.

"That sounds like her. I'ma let you get out of here, though. Be safe out there," Mr. Smith said.

Nodding his head, Synovi adjusted the strap of his backpack and headed out the door. Greeted by the hustle and bustle of Friday traffic, he made his way up the street and to the bus stop. Passing the alleyway, he thought back to last night. Surely, if Kimmy saw what had happened on camera, he was sure the club's camera had footage as well. *They need to tighten up on their security*, he thought, standing next to the bench.

Having looked up where *Bistro* was through Google, Synovi hopped on the green route that headed to the nicer side of town. He was surprised the bus even ran in the area. When he arrived, the parking lot was packed for a Friday afternoon. He figured everyone must've been taking their lunch breaks.

Stepping inside the restaurant, he was greeted with a big smile from the hostess and divine smells wafted from the culinary staff. Complementary jazz music played at a decent volume, while the dim lighting made the atmosphere feel cozy and welcoming.

"Welcome to Bistro. What name is your reservation under?" she asked.

Synovi slightly frowned, then grumbled, "I'ont even know the broad name."

"I'm sorry?" the woman questioned.

"My fault. I ain't know this was reservations only. I'm supposed to be meeting someone here."

She gave him another smile. "Oh, that's quite okay. It's reservation-only during certain times of the day. Let's take a walk around and see if we can find them."

He gave her a head nod and followed her. Synovi's eyes danced about the fancy establishment. Chandeliers hung from the ceilings, wine glasses sat atop the tables, and every table they passed seemed to have nothing but people dressed up. Unlike the hostess with a welcoming personality, the guests gawked at Synovi as if he didn't belong there. Granted, he was extremely tall and built like a tight end who played for their hometown team, but so what? He hated when people stared at him. One lady looked as if she were going to drool at the mouth, and Synovi held his laugh in as her husband snapped at her.

"For fuck's sake, Sharon. Stare any longer, and he'll be able to read your thoughts," the husband grumbled.

"Ah. There you are," the woman from last night said as they approached the table.

She stood from her seat and quickly gave him a hug. Again, Synovi's body tensed as he looked at her shuffle back to her chair. He was grateful she didn't get a booth. He was too big for that.

"Here you are, sir. Enjoy," the hostess said politely. "Your waiter should be with you shortly."

"'Preciate it," Synovi said, pulling his chair out.

Sliding his backpack off, he placed it in the chair beside him and took his seat. Before he could even get comfortable, she started talking.

"Was the place hard to find?"

"Nah," he answered, glancing around.

People were still staring, and his nostrils expanded in annoyance.

"What's the matter?"

"You got these mothafuckas staring at me. We can eat here, too," he spoke loudly, making the older man next to him focus back on his meal.

The woman gasped before giggling. "Oh, my gosh. These people are not worried about you. You just... kinda stand out more than others. How tall are you?"

"None of your business," Synovi told her flatly.

Her mouth fell open. "That's mean."

"What is yo' name?"

She grinned. "Racquel. What's yours? That's crazy we didn't exchange names last night."

He thought the same, but answered her question. "Synovi."

"Ooh. Fancy. Are you from here?"

"I ain't from nowhere else."

Racquel smirked. "You're too handsome to be this mean. Did you not sleep well?"

"You nosey as fuck, Racquel. Anybody ever told you that?"

"Actually, they have. All the freaking time. But, like… how do you get to know things if you don't ask questions?" she queried, making Synovi almost regret accepting her offer to meet.

Racquel wasn't waiting on an answer, but if she was, their waiter interrupted the silence between them. Synovi hadn't even glanced at the menu. When he did pick it up, his top lip curled upward at the prices. This shit was not in his budget.

"Hi. My name's Paul, and I'll be your server this afternoon. Would we like to start off with any appetizers?"

"Hey, Paul. Yes, we would. We'll have the smoked salmon dip and chicken wings. Wait. Are you allergic to anything?" Racquel quickly asked.

Synovi shook his head no, not bothering to look up from his menu. He was about ready to ask if they had the chickens in the back for them to be twenty-seven dollars. He could go to the hood and cop a ten-piece with fries and a drink for twelve bucks.

"Perfect. We'll take that to start," Racquel let him know.

Paul tapped her requests into the iPad mini in his hand. "And for your drinks?"

"I'll take a strawberry mojito and water with lemon."

"Let me get a lemonade," Synovi said.

"Sure thing. I'll have those drinks out, and your appetizers should be ready shortly."

"Thanks, Paul," Racquel grinned as he made his way to service another table.

Synovi stared at her, trying to read what type of chick she was. Too nice had already been added to the list of characteristics. She gave off spoiled rich girl vibes. Her bold yet sweet perfume, straight silky hair, and the double C's on her purse screamed luxury to him. *Or a scammer*, Synovi thought. He wouldn't put it past her.

"You come here all the time?" he questioned.

"Maybe twice a week. So, yes. Why? You wanna go somewhere else?"

Synovi shook his head no. "Nah. We good. I'm just trying to figure out why you were pressed on repaying me. I was just doing what every man should've done, had they been out there."

The smile she'd been wearing faltered some. "Yeah. You'd think that. Every man isn't really a man, you know? It was just really kind of you, and I'm big on treating people the same way."

That he could agree on. Synovi took it as her being herself, so he relaxed some.

"That's what's up."

"So, how old are you?"

He gave her a deadpan stare, and Racquel chortled.

"What? I'm trying to get to know you."

"For what?" he asked dryly.

"So we can be friends. Why else?"

"I'ont wanna be your friend, shorty."

Racquel stopped grinning. A frown was now on her face. "You don't mean that."

"I do," Synovi replied just as Paul came back with their drinks. "Can I get a straw?"

"Certainly," Paul said, grabbing one from the pocket of his apron. "Your appetizers will be out in a few minutes."

Tearing the paper from the straw, Synovi's brows dipped, noticing it wasn't plastic. Racquel picked up on his confusion.

"It's paper."

"Niggas always trying to save this polluted world. It's already fucked up. Might as well keep using plastic."

Racquel hated she chuckled. She was still mad he didn't want to be her friend. "So..." she dragged.

Synovi took a generous swig from his glass. The lemonade was freshly squeezed, and regardless of how the straw came, he was getting him a cup to go.

"What, man?"

"Are you going to tell me?" Racquel pressed.

Synovi sat back in his chair. The little grin on her face made him shake his head. Racquel wasn't going to quit. She didn't care how annoyed he looked with her.

"I'm twenty-two."

Her slanted eyes widened. "That's it?" She was shocked.

"Yeah."

"You look way older. Like a grown-ass man," she mused, not realizing she said it aloud.

"I am a grown man."

"I mean, twenty-two isn't *that* grown."

"Yeah? So what you call it then?" Synovi wanted to know.

Regardless of age, he'd been grown for a while now. Life had matured him much quicker than most people his age, and he wasn't ashamed of it.

Racquel pondered for a bit. "According to my sister, it's the age where you really don't know who you are yet. Sorta just winging it until something works. Figuring out if certain friendships and jobs are for you. Or if you like this hairstyle and the way you dress. Wondering how you're going to pay your college debt off while recovering from a hangover and not trying to bring another life into this world."

If Synovi didn't know any better, he'd think she was speaking from experience. He agreed with Racquel on the just winging it part, but everything else was another person's testimony. College was a bust for him, he hardly, if ever, drank, and never slid up in a bitch without a rubber.

"What does it mean, according to you?" he asked, picking his glass up.

Racquel shrugged. "I don't know yet. I'm only eighteen."

His hand stilled. "Nah. You deadass?"

Grinning, she nodded her head. "Yep. Is that hard to believe?"

"Depends on how you look at it. From last night into today, I would've at least thought we were around the same age."

"Do I look old?" Racquel whispered.

"The fuck is you whispering for?" Synovi grumbled, then thought, *Here she go with this weird shit again.*

"Because! I know I don't look old."

"A'ight then. I should've known, though," he said, more to himself.

Based on the conversation alone, she wasn't as mature as she tried to come off. She may have dressed the part, but now, Synovi could see right through her. Racquel was young and running from something. He wouldn't ask what because that was none of his business, but he definitely got that vibe from her.

Racquel rolled her eyes as their food was placed on the table. "You shouldn't have known anything. But, now that you do, we're still going to be friends."

"And how you figure that?"

She unfolded the cloth napkin and placed it over her lap. "Because I said so."

Synovi shook his head but stayed his ass right in his seat. He wasn't going to tell her he didn't have friends; not many, anyway. She'd find out soon enough, though.

After their appetizers were almost gone, they each placed entrée orders.

Synovi loved a fire ass pasta, so he went with chicken alfredo, while Racquel ordered fries and a turkey burger. His pasta came out in a dish bowl that almost covered the table entirely. Racquel was sure he'd be asking for a to-go box, but she was mistaken. Synovi finished his meal and downed his second glass of lemonade.

"That shit was fire," he complimented, making Racquel smile.

"And that's why I'm here at least twice a week. Hey, Paul," she called out as he walked by. "Can you get my friend a lemonade to go, please? I'll take a box for our wings as well."

"Of course. I'll be right back."

Synovi wondered why she didn't ask for the bill. He'd done plenty of dine and dashes, but this didn't seem like the type of establishment who wouldn't call the cops. He didn't have time to be going to jail over some damn noodles and wings, no matter how good they were. Instead of asking, he waited to see how things panned out.

Paul came back with his lemonade to go and boxed up Racquel's wings for her. While they did that, Synovi headed to the restroom. He had work in a little over an hour, but wouldn't be able to ride the bus without taking a leak first. After washing his hands, he used the foot door opener to let himself out. Heading back to the table, he was stopped by a gentleman who was dressed down in jeans and a simple black tee.

"Was everything good?" he asked.

Synovi nodded his head. "Yeah, it was."

"Good. Come back and see us," he said, patting him on the back.

Sauntering off, the man didn't give Synovi a chance to reply. He watched him make his rounds around the restaurant and concluded that whoever he was, must've been of some importance.

"What's in the backpack?" Racquel asked as they headed out the door. He figured she'd paid for their meals, so he wasn't worried about being stopped.

"Work shoes and some other shit. Why?"

"Just wondering. Is that where you're going when you leave here?"

Synovi stopped walking since she had. "Yeah."

"Oh. Well, okay. I had a really good time eating lunch with you. We should do this again."

"'Cause you think we're friends now?"

She smiled. "We are. I don't know how many times I have to tell you that. Here," she said, holding her phone out for him to take. The keypad was already on the screen for him to type his number in.

"Don't be blowing me up, Racquel," he said evenly, keying in his number and saving it.

"I won't. I promise." She smiled, then quickly hugged him. "See you later, friend."

"Aye. Hold up," he called out, stopping her in her tracks. "'Preciate the lunch and shit. I coulda paid for my own, though."

"Pay? Why would I do that when my family owns the place?"

He tried not to look surprised, but he certainly was. Synovi understood her a little better now. Paul didn't ask to see her ID when she ordered her drink. The man who patted him on the back must've been kin, and she ate here all the time because it was free. Synovi nodded his head.

"Got it. I'ma fuck with you later."

"Okay." She grinned, walking to her car parked right up front.

The cherry red BMW coupe she was pushing was clean as hell, as if someone had washed it while they were eating. At eighteen, Synovi's thoughts were nowhere near driving a car that nice. He was too worried about where he was going to lay his head at. Not how fast he could reach one hundred on the dash of a damn BMW. Nor did he have worries about getting assaulted outside of a nightclub.

He and Racquel were living two separate lives; hers of privilege, and his of poverty. Synovi didn't see why the fuck she wanted to be his friend. What was he bringing to the friendship?

He didn't have an answer for that. Making his way out of the parking lot, toward the bus stop that was about two blocks away, he adjusted his skullcap. For Spring to have just come around, it felt like the previous season still. He overheard on the radio playing on the bus that the temperature's high would be in the fifties, and Synovi wondered when it'd get there. The wind had it feeling like the low thirties.

As soon as he placed both feet onto the sidewalk, Racquel pulled up on the side of him, rolling her window down.

"Hey! Where are you going?" she shouted.

"To work."

"I know that. It must be close by if you're walking."

"Nah. It's nowhere near here."

He had to take two different buses just to get here and was hoping it came on time so he wouldn't be late.

"Well, I'm not gonna let you walk. It's cold as shit. Get in," she demanded, sounding as if she was giving him no choice. Knowing he'd probably reject her offer, she added, "I won't speed. I promise."

Shaking his head in amusement, Synovi pulled the passenger door open. "This small ass car, man. I'd rather walk."

Racquel cracked up while he adjusted the seat. Sliding it all the way back, he removed his backpack, climbed in, and set it on the floor between his legs.

"Well, I don't normally have big ass niggas riding with me, sir. My apologies."

Synovi moved around until he was comfortable. "You ain't that much shorter than me."

"I'm not anywhere near six foot, though, so whatever. Where to?"

"Freddy's. You know where that's at?"

"The diner?" Racquel questioned, and Synovi nodded his head. "I do, but I'll have to use my GPS."

"You was asking me if I'm from here. Shit, are you?"

She laughed while punching Freddy's into her GPS system. "I am, but I use the navigation to get me anywhere. Why end up lost when I have this?" she said, pointing to the dashboard that resembled a flat-screen television.

"You got it. Long as you get me there without killing me, we good."

"Great. Buckle your seatbelt."

Synovi stared at her like he didn't want to. The car was already compact; him putting his seatbelt on was going to make him feel even more trapped. Racquel didn't care. She could be reckless at times, but having whoever rode with her fasten their seatbelt as she did was a promise she made to her parents.

"I'm not moving until you put it on. I don't care about you frowning your face up either," she said, fluttering her lashes.

Synovi shook his head while dragging the belt over his chest. When she heard the click, Racquel took her foot off the brake.

"Happy now?" Synovi grumbled.

"Yep. Now, let's get you to work."

She pulled into traffic and turned the volume up on her steering wheel. Nicki Minaj and Lil Baby's latest track bumped through the speakers, and Racquel rapped right along with them. When the song switched to some shit Synovi didn't know, he had the urge to reach up and skip the song, but he let her rock. After all, she had just gotten him a free meal and a ride.

Racquel drove like she had some sense, but also like a woman who loved fast cars and the speed they could reach. She seemed to have a bit of road rage as well, but Synovi understood. Only mothafuckas in Kansas City stayed in the fast lane to drive slow. Her annoyance was warranted. As well as Synovi's confusion when they arrived at his destination.

The lack of cars in the parking lot in front of Freddy's made Synovi glance at the time on his phone. He was fifteen minutes early, and there was only one car out front that belonged to Mr. Fred.

"You sure y'all are open?" Racquel questioned, peering around the parking lot as well.

Synovi thought they were. "Shit, I'ont know. I'm 'bout to find out, though."

As he unbuckled his seat belt, Mr. Fred was coming out the door. Climbing out, he greeted him.

"What's good, Mr. Fred? We closed today?" Synovi wondered.

"Yeah," he sighed with disappointment. "The Mrs. isn't feeling well. I had to rush her to the hospital last night. I'm not sure how long we'll be shut down, son. It's not looking too good."

That fucked Synovi up. He loved Mrs. Pat. She reminded him so much of GiGi, but gentler and smaller framed. Whenever he seemed to have a bad day, Mrs. Pat would sing her gospel songs, telling Synovi that everything was going to be all right. The meals he was able to take home were always prepared and bagged up by her when she was there.

"Dang," he mumbled, saddened by the news. "I hope she bounces back. Nobody else could stay and keep business running for you?"

"Unfortunately not, son. Not the way it needs to be run. Our kids are grown with families and live out of state. I don't know when we'll open back up, but if and when we do, we'll be sure to call you."

Synovi didn't know what to say. He'd been fired before, but had never just lost a job, and not in this manner.

"A'ight, Mr. Fred. You and the Mrs. will be in my thoughts," he told him.

He would've said prayers, but Synovi figured the ones he'd sent up hadn't been heard yet, so why would this one? Either way, Mr. Fred and Mrs. Pat would be on his mind. Shit, they had no choice but to be because they signed his paychecks.

"We appreciate that. Take care now," Mr. Fred said before walking off to his car. A clean-ass Buick Synovi had the pleasure of riding in a few times.

Stumped about being jobless now, he stood there for a second until Racquel blew her horn. She'd rolled her window down to be nosey but couldn't hear their conversation. When Synovi got in the passenger seat and closed the door, she waited for all of six seconds before her questioning started.

"So… you guys are closed," she concluded.

"Yeah, and a nigga just lost his job," Synovi mumbled as his chest tightened.

The number of applications he filled out and businesses he stopped by just to secure this one was nuts. His work history wasn't lengthy at all. If he could add the number of jobs he applied for to his résumé and make them count as experience, Synovi would be able to secure one in no time.

"Dang. I hate that. Did he say what was going on?" Racquel asked, genuinely concerned.

Synovi nodded his head but didn't go into any detail. Mrs. Pat's business wasn't his to share.

"Yeah. Damn, man," he grumbled with his mind now in overdrive.

For once, he thought he had some stability, but here life came, knocking him off balance yet again. He sat there in deep thought for a good two minutes before Racquel spoke. He was grateful for those one hundred and twenty seconds of silence.

"Look. Let's not worry about you not having a job right now. There's nothing you can do, buuut," she dragged, and Synovi already knew she was about to say some bullshit.

"Nah. Whatever it is you're about to say, I'm good on."

"So, you're too good to make some money?"

Synovi mugged her. "I look like a charity case to you?"

Confusion gleamed in Racquel's eyes and etched across her face. "What? No. I never said that. I know you just lost your job and you seem down, so I was offering a solution. That's what friends do."

"You and this friend shit," Synovi complained.

He didn't mean to snap at her, but his mind was everywhere right now. From experience, Synovi knew when someone offered you too much or helped more than he could reciprocate, things never ended well. The only person in his life who did something for him out of the kindness of their heart was GiGi. He hadn't come across another person yet to match or top her generosity and love. So, of course, he was defensive. It was all he knew to be.

Racquel's smile was back on her face. "Whatever. You're going to grow to learn that I take this duty seriously. Now, are you trying to make some money or not, nigga?"

"Aye, you better watch who you talking to," Synovi spoke calmly. He ain't give a fuck if she was feeling herself or not. He'd cut their friendship short.

"Oh my gosh," Racquel groaned. "You're really annoying. Since you won't answer me, I'll just tell you. I'm having a party tomorrow, and I kinda need someone to chaperone it and help me clean up afterward."

"On some janitorial type shit?" Synovi questioned.

"I guess you can say that."

"You paying me."

Racquel nodded her head. "Yes. Of course."

"I wasn't asking," Synovi let her know, and she snickered.

Since she was offering and he had no clue where his next source of income was going to come from, Synovi didn't think twice about accepting her offer. She was lucky he actually enjoyed cleaning up.

"Meany. Is a stack good?"

Synovi couldn't have heard her correctly. "A band for cleaning up?"

"Yeah. Do you want more?"

"Nah, nah. Shit, that's coo'," he replied, keeping his demeanor.

A thousand dollars was more than cool. So far, being Racquel's friend wasn't as bad as Synovi thought it'd be.

Synovi wasn't sure whose home Racquel was throwing a party in, but it was packed to capacity. How she expected him to be a chaperone when girls wouldn't stay out of his face, he didn't know. They were on him as soon as he stepped through the front door. Racquel had offered to pay for him a Lyft, but he took the bus instead. Even though he wasn't really a people person, there was something about observing the lives of others, while riding the bus. You never knew what action you'd come across.

The driveway and street were filled with cars when he made it to the address on his phone. Walking inside the house, Drake blasted loudly over the speakers while it seemed every person in attendance had a cup in their hand. Scanning the body-to-body living room, Synovi searched for Racquel but came up short. Making his way into the kitchen, a girl stumbled, bumping into him, spilling some of her drink on the floor.

"Sorry!" she shouted while walking off.

Shaking his head, Synovi kept it pushing. Inside the kitchen, there were food trays and people talking, but none of them were Racquel. Making his way to the backyard, he noticed the large pool and people actually swimming. It was warm, but not that damn warm out. He figured the pool must've been heated.

After five more minutes of not spotting Racquel, Synovi decided to post up in the living room. Facing the front door, he watched as people rolled up on the coffee table, sparked blunts, and took shots. He wasn't sure what the celebration was, but there was a lot going on.

"Hey. Who are you?" A caramel-skinned girl with bright red hair asked, all in his personal space.

Synovi lightly pushed her away from him. "Back up."

"You must be new around here. I've never seen you before."

Not bothering to answer her, Synovi gave her a once over. She was cute, in an 'I'd put you on one of my niggas' kinda way. She was petite, with long legs, a thin nose, and thinner lips. Not his type at all. Synovi liked his woman with some meat on their bones.

"So?" she asked after he made his conclusion.

Before he could rudely dismiss her, Racquel made her way over to him.

"You made it!" She grinned, wrapping him up in a quick hug.

"You know him?" Redhead questioned.

"Yeah, and I'm sure he doesn't want to get to know you," Racquel stated with a roll of her eyes.

Redhead scoffed. "Whatever."

When she walked off, Synovi couldn't help but ask, "She your friend?"

"A friend of a friend. Not really mine, but she's here, so whatever." She shrugged. "When did you get here?"

"'Bout ten minutes ago. You got all these young ass kids in here drinking."

Racquel waved him off. "Oh, this is nothing. Trust me. Do you want something to drink?"

Synovi shook his head no. "Nah. I'm good. I ain't too much of a big drinker."

She grinned. "Noted. Walk with me so I can introduce you to some people."

"I ain't trying to meet your friends, man," he groaned, making Racquel whip her head around. She pointed her finger at him.

"Don't be a mean ass tonight. We're here to have fun, and so are you. Now, come on."

Synovi wanted to stay where he was but knew Racquel wasn't having it. Following her through the kitchen and outside to the pool area, Racquel brought him over to a group of about seven people.

"Y'all, this is my friend, Synovi," she introduced him.

A bunch of murmured greetings were given as Synovi hit them with a head nod. One girl with a slick ponytail emerged from the water.

"Is this the guy who saved you?" she questioned, looking Synovi over as if she wanted to devour him.

"Yeah. This is my friend, Kaela."

Kaela stuck her hand out for him to shake. Looking down at her hand and then her face, Synovi didn't give her the greeting she thought he would. Slowly, she pulled her hand away and frowned.

"Rude, much?" Kaela chuckled, masking her embarrassment.

He didn't know what it was, but right away, Synovi could tell Kaela wasn't a real one. Not to Racquel, anyway. The way she asked if he was the one who saved her came off condescending, as if he hadn't done much. Before he wrote her off completely, he had one question to ask.

"You were at the club that night?"

Kaela nodded her head. "Yep. Were you? I didn't see you."

Her answer was all he needed to know. "Who the rest of these people? They your friends too?" he asked Racquel. Kaela finally got the hint and slid back into the water. She didn't know what Synovi's issue was, but she was surely going to ask Racquel when they were alone.

"Yeah. Most are associates, though."

"I can tell. You showing me off like I'm your nigga or something," Synovi voiced.

Racquel cracked up, slapping his arm. "It does look like that, huh? We're friends, I told you that. Plus," she said with a smile. "You're not really my type."

"Good. I ain't wanna be no way. Weird ass girl," he cracked, making her laugh harder.

"Shut up! But seriously. You're not ugly or anything, I'm just more into something else."

Synovi looked down at her. "You like girls?"

Eyes wide, Racquel was left speechless.

"I mean, ain't nothing wrong with that," Synovi let her know.

"I do not like girls, Synovi," Racquel hissed, finally finding her voice. She was not expecting him to say that, but her statement was vague, so she could see why he thought that.

"Aye. It's your world if you do." He shrugged.

"You see that guy over there with the locs?" Racquel bobbed her head in the direction across the pool.

Synovi looked that way, spotting the guy she was talking about. The table he and some other guys were standing around was set up for a game of beer pong or whatever was inside the cups. It was clear his team was winning. He tossed a white ping-pong ball across the table, making the shot into the furthest cup. Grabbing one from his side, he drained the cup before tossing it on the ground.

"I like him," Racquel offered.

Synovi didn't quite know what to say, so he hit her with, "That's what's up."

"And Kaela knows that, too, but she tried putting her cousin on him."

"And she's supposed to be your friend? Think you need to get some new ones."

Racquel knew he was right, but she didn't have time to dwell on that. "Yeah. Maybe. Let's go back inside."

As soon as they stepped through the door, commotion was all they were greeted with. A fight had broken out in the living room, and Racquel was not having that. Pushing her way through the crowd, she urged some guys who were just standing around to break the two men up.

"Why are y'all just standing there? Do something!" she shouted.

While everyone else was recording with their cell phones and rooting for who they wanted to win, the fight was broken up, and the two guys went outside. Synovi stood by, finding the entire ordeal shocking. A fight breaking out at a kickback where he was from led to gunshots. He was thankful it didn't get to that level tonight.

As the party went on, Synovi finally rolled himself a blunt, used his red lighter to put a flame to it, and chilled out. He didn't know what type of chaperone duty he was supposed to be on, but he wasn't going to be much of one. The weed he just smoked had him good and high. Sometime throughout the night, he spotted Racquel dancing on the dread-head, and he smirked. The expression quickly dropped when he peeped Kaela not too far from them with a scowl on her face. He'd warned Racquel about her already, so he hoped she took the hint.

By the end of the night, which was close to two in the morning, Synovi didn't see how people still had so much energy. Racquel and her friends were talking about going to a late-night burger spot up the street, and all Synovi wanted to do was lie down. Preferably with the person he was texting, but she stopped replying.

"Want me to bring you back some food?" Racquel asked, leaning all into dread-head with a drunken smile on her face. Her arms were wrapped tightly around his waist as if he were going to leave her.

"Who driving?" Synovi wondered.

"You her brother or something?" Dread-head asked before Racquel could reply.

Synovi cut his eyes toward him. "Nah. Now who driving?" he asked Racquel again.

"One of his friends. They didn't drink as much," she replied, and Synovi's nose twitched some.

"So, who are you to her?" Dread-head pressed.

"Who I am to her ain't got shit to do with you."

Racquel groaned. "Oh gosh."

Dread-head removed her arms from around him. "If you fuck with her, you ain't gotta fake y'all relationship for me. It's all good."

"Tyler, this is my friend. We are not in a relationship," Racquel explained.

"Yeah, a'ight. Yo, Kae, you and Mya sliding with us or what?" Tyler called out to Kaela.

Racquel's neck snapped in their direction so fast, it gave her and Synovi whiplash. "Are you serious right now, Kaela?"

She shrugged. "What? We're hungry, too. I didn't know getting a ride was that big of a deal."

Kaela smirked and walked right by them. Tyler's eyes followed, watching her ass in the leggings she had slid over her bathing suit. Racquel was pissed, but instead of saying anything, she watched them head out the front door, hop in Tyler's friend's ride, and pull off down the street.

"Fuck them," she hissed, walking into the kitchen. Grabbing the bottle of tequila off the counter, she drank straight from it.

From the doorway of the kitchen, Synovi just watched her. Despite her having money, a family who owned one of the nicest restaurants in town, and driving a luxury car, he wondered if deep down, she was hurting from something, too. It didn't matter how she tried to mask it with her infectious smile or bubbly personality. When she took another swig, Synovi said something.

"Aye. You gon' be sick as hell in the morning."

Racquel burped loudly. "Oh well. I'll handle the consequences when morning comes."

Synovi didn't bother to say anything else. She was grown, so he'd let her deal with the hangover he knew she would have all on her own.

"A'ight."

"I'm not going home tonight, and I'm sure the bus stopped running by now, so you can crash here," she let him know while yawning.

"This ain't your parents' crib?" The way she was partying, Synovi thought it was.

Racquel chuckled. "Hell no. My parents aren't together. Haven't been for who knows how long."

He wanted to ask more, but the way those words were spoken made him focus his attention on something else: the task he was going to get paid for. Starting at the table, Synovi began tossing cans, plates, bottles, and trash into the large can by the wall.

"You don't have to do all this tonight. It's late, and I'm drunk. I'll help you in the morning," Racquel said, grabbing two bottles of water from the fridge.

Accepting the extra one from her, Synovi nodded. "A'ight. At least turn some of the lights off and lock the doors."

Snickering, Racquel made her way around the house, doing just that. When she came back into the living room, she yawned again.

"House secured. You can take one of the spare bedrooms upstairs."

Having slept in worse places, Synovi didn't ask any questions as he headed upstairs. Racquel followed him and stopped at the first door.

"This room is fine," she told him. "Thank you for coming tonight. You being here really meant a lot to me."

"It's nothing."

Racquel gave him a smile. "Well, okay. Goodnight."

"Night," Synovi replied. She headed to the bedroom down the hall.

Pushing the door open to the bedroom he'd be sleeping in, the inviting smell of lavender flowed through his nose. Immediately, a calming feeling settled over him. The queen-sized bed was made up and looked plusher than any bed Synovi had ever slept in. Slipping his shoes off, he placed them by the cream accent chair before stepping inside the bathroom.

Flipping the switch, Synovi used the toilet before washing his hands. Grabbing a clean washcloth from the rolled-up ones on the counter, he washed his face before searching for some moisturizer inside the drawers. Whomever the home belonged to definitely had the guest room prepared. Whatever items you could think to need were organized neatly under the cabinet with labels, while the linen closet was full of toiletries and towels. The only thing he didn't see was some clean clothes.

Being the type of person he was, Synovi didn't want to just climb in the bed without showering first. Since he had no choice but to, he slipped his hoodie and shirts off before removing his jeans. Neatly, he placed them in the chair before laying his socks across them. He hated sleeping in socks and wouldn't be caught walking in them, either. He kept a pair of slides on his feet if he could.

Out of habit and wanting some privacy, Synovi locked the door and turned the ceiling fan on. Tossing the covers back, he slid inside the bed, and his body melted against the sheets. His bed at GiGi's was nice, but this one right here was next level. Between the lavender, plush mattress and silence of the night, Synovi was knocked out in no time. He didn't even mind that he had to get up and clean in some hours. Right now, he was about to get the best sleep he hadn't been able to get in a while.

four

"So, how was your trip? Did you meet anyone?" Leighton questioned.

Torin couldn't help but laugh as she pushed her truck through Sunday morning traffic. Meeting someone while at work was highly likely, but the men she came across just weren't doing it for her. They were either too lame, too cocky, thought they could fuck on the first night, or simply just not the type of man she imagined herself with. It was nice of Leighton to ask, though. As her best friend of over a decade, she'd always ask the questions Torin probably didn't care to hear or answer.

"Girl, no. My trip was fine. They loved the food like always. I was so tired, I didn't even have time to let a man find me," Torin answered.

Leighton snickered. "Of course, you didn't. Was probably in your hotel room knocked out."

"And was. Once I get in this house and shower, I'm relaxing for the rest of the day. My feet are killing me."

As a full-time chef, Torin could stay on go for days at a time. She was used to the hustle and bustle of her profession, but her body still warned her when she was doing too much. It wasn't often that her feet would swell up after being on them for hours at a time, but coming from a three-day event out of town, her babies were howling and begging for some relief.

"We can go get pedicures tomorrow. I'm off work at three," Leighton told her.

"That's perfect. I should be well rested by then," Torin replied, pulling onto her block. "I just made it home, so I'll text you later."

"Okay."

Hanging up, Torin pulled into her garage and just sat there for a few minutes. After getting into town, dropping everything off at her work kitchen, switching rides, and driving twenty minutes home, sis was beyond tired. Had a text not come through on her phone, she would've stayed right there in her car and fallen asleep.

Grabbing her black Glam-Aholic tote bag from her trunk, Torin closed it and entered her home after closing the garage. Right off the garage was her laundry room. Out of routine, she went straight for her alarm system, but frowned when she realized it hadn't even gone off.

"What the hell," she murmured, stepping into the kitchen. Her mouth fell open and her heart rate spiked seeing the damage. "I just know she didn't have a party in my shit while I was gone."

That was indeed what Racquel had done. Seeing all the liquor bottles and trash made Torin want to scream. Instead, she pulled her phone from her purse and dialed Racquel's number. Breathing heavily, she tried to keep her cool when the phone went to voicemail, but Torin had a short temper. Dialing her number again, she figured Racquel's phone must've been on DND. When it rang once before sending her to voicemail, Torin knew she had ignored her.

When a text came through from her, Torin didn't even bother to reply.

You're here?

"I'ma whoop her ass," Torin fumed, dropping her bag and purse right where she stood.

Walking around her home, she assessed every room, looking for any damage besides what could be thrown out and cleaned up. She was used to coming home from a trip to a clean home. Not one that looked like an entire college party had been thrown.

"She must've turned my alarm off without me knowing," Torin mumbled to herself while walking up the steps.

Racquel's car wasn't outside, but Torin knew that meant nothing. She sometimes stayed the night with her, so her first instinct was to check all the rooms. When she tried opening the first bedroom door, only to see that it was locked, she banged on the door.

"Racquel, open this damn door!" Torin shouted, twisting the nob before banging again. "How you gon' lock doors in my damn house like you pay bills here?"

"Man, hol' up," Synovi's deep voice floated through from the other side of the door.

"Oh, hell no," Torin hissed, removing her gun from her hip. Taking it off safety, she pushed the door open as soon as she heard it unlock.

Torin was not prepared to be greeted by all six-foot-two of the hard body that Synovi possessed. She had to strain her neck to look up at him and the glower on his handsome face as if she were in the wrong.

"Who the hell are you?" Torin questioned as Synovi backed up some.

Only a step back, leaving Torin to stare openly at his defined frame covered with tattoos. There were so many, it almost looked as if he were wearing a black shirt. They stretched from his chest to his wrists, while one even covered his right hand. When her eyes finally reached his waist, they widened a bit before shooting back up to his face.

His morning wood greeted her before he did. Synovi was still frowning and put Torin on an even higher alert. Training her gun on him, she asked her question for a second time.

"Who are you?"

"This must be your crib," he stated calmly, pissing her off even more.

"Mothafucka," Torin snarled.

Synovi eyed the gun and clenched his jaw. "That isn't my name."

"What?" Torin hissed.

"You called me a mothafucka. That isn't my name. And you can stop aiming that little ass gun at me, too."

Unbothered by her and what she had going on, Synovi walked over to the chair his clothes were in. Stuck, with a stunned expression on her face, Torin stood there watching him get dressed. She hated how she was openly admiring a stranger in her home who could possibly harm her, but she was.

Synovi's skin wasn't one of a rich brown hue, but he couldn't be considered light-skinned either. His complexion resembled her favorite Biscoff cookies that she loved dipping in a freshly brewed cup of coffee.

"So, you're not going to answer me?" She raised her voice, making Synovi stop sliding his socks on.

Looking up at her, Torin finally got a glimpse of the tattoo lining his tapered fade with deep waves. She couldn't make out what it said, but it somehow made him look even more handsome, even with that frown on his face. He was fine in a rugged way; she'd give him that. His mustache and slightly thick, chin strap beard enclosed a set of brown-tinted, plush lips while a somewhat crooked nose sat above them.

"You need to stop hollering. I can hear you just fine," Synovi told her.

Torin's mouth fell open. "I don't give a fuck about you hearing me just fine. Clearly, you can't because I've asked you multiple times who you are and haven't gotten an answer."

"A'ight," was all Synovi said.

If she thought he was going to give her some conversation by talking to him disrespectfully, she was mistaken. Sliding his shoes on, Synovi ignored her stare and walked inside the bathroom. He had to piss something terrible and wanted to brush his teeth and wash his face. Like Synovi knew she would, Torin followed him. He tried closing the door, but she stopped it with her foot.

"See, now you're just doing the most," she hissed as he stood at the toilet. "You can't be serious right now."

Shrugging because he tried to shut the door, Synovi pulled his dick out and began to pee. From where she stood, Torin caught a quick glimpse of *it* and hurriedly turned her head. Synovi wanted to laugh at the tiny gasp she let out, but she still had the gun by her side. By now, if she wanted to shoot him, she would've, so he wasn't fazed by it. After handling his business, Synovi washed his hands and searched for a toothbrush.

"Look, Mr. It's clear that you're not going to hurt me, and I should've been sent a bullet into your leg, but I haven't, so just tell me who you are," Torin said, watching him through the mirror as he brushed his teeth.

Synovi stared her down with intensity before spitting. "A friend of Racquel's."

"And she told you it was okay to stay here?"

He looked at her as if her question was a dumb one.

"Okay, well, obviously she did," Torin stated with a roll of her eyes. "Where is she at then?"

Synovi's right shoulder lifted, and he grabbed the washcloth to wash his face. "I thought she was here. I guess not."

On cue, Racquel entered the house, hollering her name. "Torin! I know you saw my text messages."

Torin sucked her teeth. She hadn't bothered to read it or the other ones she'd sent since walking into her home. Had she, she would've known that Racquel let her know Synovi was there. It was too late now; she had to find out on her own. When Synovi was finished, he went to walk out of the bathroom, but Torin didn't move an inch.

"You gon' keep me trapped in here?" Synovi asked.

"I should. I don't know who you are. Friend of Racquel's or not."

Regardless of what her mouth was saying, Torin pivoted

and walked out of the bathroom. Synovi smirked and looked at the heart-shaped ass he knew she was toting and shook his head. He could see it from the front, and watching it jiggle from the back wasn't a bad sight to see at all. Torin was thick and at the age where she loved her grown woman body. Synovi thought she was fine as hell, even with her mean mugging him.

Torin's golden honey complexion was flawless and reminded Synovi of the candy GiGi used to keep in her purse. The Werther's Original hard candies were her favorite. Torin's almond-shaped, dark-brown eyes fit perfectly with her oval face. Synovi couldn't help but lick his lips as he took in her feminine features.

Her lips were naturally plump, nose dainty, and teeth straight from having braces when she was in her late teens. She was rocking some curly bundles pulled into a ponytail at the moment, giving Synovi the perfect view of all of her.

"Hi!" Racquel squeaked. Smiling like all was right in the world, Racquel went to step inside the bedroom, and Torin shoved her backward.

"Why would you have a party in my fucking crib, Racquel? And then you leave some strange nigga in here? What if he robbed me? Better yet, what if I had shot him?" Torin went off, not giving her a chance to reply before she continued.

"I swear you do the dumbest things. A party? And then you didn't even have the decency to clean up. Giiirl," Torin dragged, trying to calm herself down.

"I didn't know you were coming back today. I thought you came home tomorrow," Racquel whined, as if her excuse meant anything.

"Well, you thought wrong."

"Aye. Y'all family or something?" Synovi questioned, breaking up their bickering.

"Sisters," they said in unison.

You couldn't have paid Synovi to guess that by their looks. Racquel's very fair-toned skin held a smidgen of melanin, leaving Synovi to assume that she wasn't one hundred percent white, but she wasn't fully black either. She reminded him of the talented star actress from the TV show *Grown-ish*, but a shade lighter with longer hair. She and Torin's make up were totally opposite, making more questions boggle his mind.

"Never would've thought," he concluded.

"I know, right?" Racquel grinned. "We have the same mommy, not daddy, though."

"Y'all mama Black?" he asked.

They both nodded, and he looked at Racquel.

"You fasho took after yo' pop's side of the family."

Racquel sucked her teeth and rolled her neck. "And what is that supposed to mean?"

"Right. 'Cause what you not about to do is talk shit about her," Torin followed up.

That almost got a smirk out of him. From the jump, he could tell Torin took no shit, and he liked that.

"You got more of they genes, that's all. Chill out," he said, making Torin roll her neck.

"For someone who is a stranger in my house, you sure are talking out the side of your neck. And, you still haven't told me who you are."

"I told you who I am. If you wanna know my name, ask that."

Torin sucked her teeth. "I don't wanna know shit about you, to be honest. Ugh. Where'd you find this rude ass nigga at?"

Racquel chuckled. "Well… it's kind of a funny story, actually."

"That shit was funny to you?" Synovi asked, with not a hint of humor in his voice.

Racquel's smile dropped. "I mean, not that funny, but how we met kinda is. He saved me."

Torin waved her hand. "Girl, I don't even wanna know. As much shit as you be into, I'm glad someone did. What we need to be talking about is who's cleaning this house, 'cause you crazy if you think I am."

"I got it," Synovi told her.

"What you mean *you got it*?" Torin asked.

"Yo' sister paying me to clean up yo' crib. But shit, if you gotta problem with it, that's on you."

Synovi walked by them and down the steps. Whether Torin had an issue or not, Synovi wasn't turning down a stack for her. Not when it was something he could knock out in no time. While Racquel stood there with a grin on her face, Torin wore an annoyed one.

"You really do anything, Racquel. What have I told you about watching the company you keep?"

"What's wrong with Synovi? He's my friend. I swear he's not that mean once you get to know him."

Torin's head tilted to the left. "Do *you* even know him?"

"Yeah. I mean, we met on Friday, but we've been hanging out since."

Torin's hands flew in the air as she walked off. "You not gon' learn until some shit really bad happens to you."

Racquel mumbled something under her breath, but Torin was out of earshot.

With a pep in her step, Torin looked for Synovi. He'd clearly made himself comfortable by the way he was going through the cabinet under the sink for cleaning supplies. For a second, Torin stood back, watching him. If he was friends with Racquel, she just knew he was way too young for her, but her body was singing a different tune.

This young man is just too fine. I need to find out where Racquel really met him. She thought as Synovi turned to face her. He caught her staring and blinked slowly, making her snap at him for interrupting her.

"What?"

"You the one staring. Ain't no need for all the hostility. I'm just here to do my job. Where you keep the extra trash bags at?"

Torin finally noticed the empty box in his hand. "I'll get them for you."

She hated how her breathing changed when she walked by him. Synovi's presence was intimidating in a way, yet she still wanted to soak it up. He kept his eyes on her until she was behind him in the pantry. Inside, she grabbed the new box of trash bags and a small bag of Xxtra Hot Cheetos.

Pulling all the cleaning supplies out that he needed, Synovi placed them on the countertop. Torin handed him the box and moved out of the way.

"You can at least tell me your name," she said, peeling her bag of chips open.

Synovi looked over his shoulder at her. "Tell me yours."

Torin rolled her eyes, popping a few chips in her mouth. "Yeah. You're definitely friends with Racquel being this immature."

His body faced her completely. "Aye. Don't disrespect me. I know I'm in your crib unwillingly, but I can leave, and you'll be cleaning this place up by yourself. The name's Synovi; not mothafucka like you assumed."

Torin stopped mid-chew. "Okay! And you can do exactly that. My sister hired you, I didn't. With your rude ass. I don't know who you think you are."

"I'm that nigga you gon' quit talking slick to, I know that. Aye, yo, Racquel!" Synovi yelled.

She rushed into the kitchen. "What? What's wrong?"

"You still gon' pay me if I don't clean up?" he asked.

Racquel scratched her head. She wasn't the type of person to go back on her word, but handing over a thousand dollars with no work behind it was kind of silly to her.

"Um. I'm not sure. Why're you trying to leave?"

"Because I told him to. He's too disrespectful for me," Torin snapped.

Synovi clenched his jaw but he didn't say anything. Going back and forth with a female wasn't his thing. Truthfully, he wasn't even this much of a talker, but Torin had gotten under his skin with the way she was coming at him. If anything, he was giving her the same energy right back. He just needed to know if he was going to make this bread or not, before dipping out.

"Torin, please just go find something to do. He's offering to clean up and you're being mean," Racquel said.

"I'm being— You know what. Never mind. Let me go find me some business before I hurt one of y'all. Since you cleaning shit, get my fridge, too, while you're at it. I'm sure some things in there could be thrown out," Torin quipped.

"You got me fucked up," Synovi sneered, grabbing the trash bags from the counter and walking out of the kitchen.

Racquel huffed. "Will you stop? He just lost his job and I'm helping him out."

"That's sweet of you, sis. It really is. You've always had a big heart. Next time, let me know some nigga is laid up in my crib, okay? Actually, don't make it a next time. Depending on how good of a job he does, that'll determine if I let you kick it over here again."

Groaning, Racquel stomped her foot. "That's not fair! What if he doesn't do good?"

"That's between you and his ass. Now leave me alone for at least the next hour. Y'all don' worked my nerves."

Bypassing the living room, she peeped Synovi cleaning up around the pool through the windows. She appreciated her sister for putting in the initiative, but goodness. Torin had come across plenty of rude men in her twenty-six years, but this one right here? She didn't know what to make of Synovi. Not that she had time to, but she was intrigued now.

Inside her bedroom, Torin stripped from her clothes and tossed them into the hamper. Popping her neck, she released much-needed tension before turning on the water for a bath. Her plans of lounging around all day had clearly been interrupted, but she hoped by the time she came out of her room, Synovi would be gone. All she wanted to do was catch up on some new books that dropped while she was working, while her foot massager did its thing.

Once the tub was full with the perfect temperature water and Dr. Teals lavender bath oil, Torin submerged herself inside. Exhaling, she relaxed and immediately felt the stress from the week leave her body.

Instead of sticking with her nine-to-five job, Torin made the decision to work twenty-four-seven. Being an entrepreneur was not for the weak, and it sometimes crippled the strong. Running a business hadn't only taught her so much about herself, but about others as well.

Torin's love for cooking started at an early age. On plenty of days, she'd be right by her mama's hip, watching her prepare their meals. Certain recipes Tracee, their mother, got from her mother. So, Torin would spend her Sunday mornings at her granny's place, learning every recipe she could while honing her cooking skills. By the time she made it to middle school and aced her culinary class, she knew exactly what she wanted to be in life. At twelve years old, she had no idea where becoming a chef could take her, but the places were unlimited.

What started out as preparing meals for her friends in college, turned into her being paid to cater events on campus, to athletes and coaches hiring her to meal prep. Even families who didn't have the time to cook every night due to work and children added her to their budget. Her love for food became a lifestyle she lived and breathed. There'd been some bumps along the way, but Torin managed to get over them and keep pushing.

After soaking in the tub, then hopping in the shower, Torin oiled down and got dressed. In a chill, two-piece gray lounge set from *MAG Co.* and some fluffy house shoes from their new collection on her feet, Torin made her way downstairs. Right away, the lavender scent she had throughout her home could be smelled. Along with that was the scent of a freshly cleaned home.

Her eyes stretched in awe and appreciation of the job Synovi had done. In just a little over an hour, he had transformed her house back into a home. Not a piece of trash was detected, the floors shined, and the pillows on the couch were fluffed. Torin made her way into the kitchen and smiled. The counters were cleaned, dishes were in the rack to dry, and the lemon-scented candle she had on the table was lit. All that shit she was talking and Torin was thinking about hiring him on full-time.

"'Cuse me," Synovi spoke in his deep tenor, easing behind her in the doorway.

Torin moved to the side, but not before getting a feel of his rock-hard abs against her arm. She blinked a few times, hoping it'd rid her mind of the nasty thoughts she was thinking. Her brows knitted, wondering how a man's sweat had such an alluring aroma. Her mind flashed to the scene of Gabrielle Union in one of her favorite movies, and she chuckled, understanding just why she wanted to lick the sweat off Quincy.

"You good?" Synovi asked, wondering what the hell she was over there giggling at. *She weird, just like her sister,* he thought to himself.

Torin cleared her throat. "Yeah. I'm fine. You did a really good job. Is this something you do often?"

Synovi heard the words coming from her mouth but couldn't make out what she was saying exactly. He peeped how thin the fabric of her two-piece set was from behind and had to talk his mans down from getting an erection, but from the front, Torin looked even better. He couldn't stop staring at her fresh, bare face.

His eyes savored her beauty before drifting downward to her perky, braless breasts and the way her nipples seemed to harden by the second. They then ventured lower, appreciating how her thighs, and dangerous hip dips, matched her ass and even more what rested between them.

That mothafucka fat, Synovi thought with a lick of his lips. The thin fabric did nothing to conceal the print of her goodies. When Torin shifted her stance, Synovi focused back on her face.

"Are you done?" Torin asked calmly. She knew he was checking her out.

"I wasn't, but you got it. What were you sayin'?" he questioned.

"I asked if cleaning is something you do for a living."

"Nah. It's not really something I do for others, but Racquel offered to pay me."

Torin didn't know if he was desperate for some money or

simply doing Racquel a favor. She knew firsthand how persistent and annoying her sister could be when she wanted something. So, she was going to go with the latter of the two.

"That's cool. I'm Torin, by the way," she said, finally introducing herself.

"I ain't ask you your name."

Synovi's deadpan expression made Torin wish she wouldn't have introduced herself. Here she was, trying to have a fresh start with him, and he was being rude.

"Well, I told you anyway, with your rude ass. You'd think after all that cleaning, it would've helped your attitude. I guess not."

"You done?"

Torin's mouth fell open. She went to speak, but Synovi cut her off.

"If you'd let me finish, I was gon' say 'preciate you for telling me, though. I'd say it was nice to meet you, but you pulled a gun on me."

"As I should've. I didn't know you," Torin sassed.

"You still don't."

She may have been mistaken, but Torin caught a slight hint of a smirk on his face before it vanished. Whether he was playing like he was mean or not, Torin knew somewhere in there, he had a soft spot. Like him, she could read people too. That trait must've skipped Racquel because she was blind to a lot of bullshit that came her way.

"What y'all in here talking about?" Racquel bounced into the kitchen, asking, breaking their staring competition.

Synovi liked a challenge; he'd been up against them his entire life. Torin was just the right amount of difficulty he knew he didn't need in his life, but would take it on, anyway.

"How you 'bout to pay me," Synovi stated, making Racquel laugh.

"Boy, you gon' get your money. Do you have CashApp?"

Synovi nodded his head. "Yeah. It's dollar sign NoviB."

"What's the B stand for?" Racquel asked, typing his name into the search bar.

"My last name."

Racquel didn't know why she expected him to elaborate more. By now, she should've known he wouldn't. About twenty seconds went by, and the chime from his phone confirmed she'd sent the money over. He hadn't heard that sound in so long, it almost sounded foreign.

"I added a little extra in there for your troubles," Racquel snickered, lightly shoving Torin.

"Don't shove me. He was the one laid up in my crib without my knowledge."

"That bed is comfortable as hell, too. So, 'preciate you for the stay. Next time, have a little more hospitality," Synovi let her know before walking out of the kitchen.

Racquel cracked up and walked out behind him, leaving Torin again, yet dumbstruck. She thought of going after him to get the last word in, but let him go. Her house was clean and she didn't have to come out of her pocket for it. Synovi's smart mouth could slide for now, but she promised if she saw him again, he was going to learn to talk to her like he had some sense.

Outside in the driveway, Synovi was already calculating what he was going to do with his money. With hardly any bills except his cell phone, he knew he could make it stretch until he found another job. Thinking of that had him irritated all over again.

"I know you aren't about to catch the bus home," Racquel said, looking up at the sky. "I'd feel so bad if you got caught in the rain."

Where there were once clear skies, it was now gray and gloomy, and most likely about to storm. Living in the Midwest would have you sick with the way the weather changed up. Racquel wouldn't be surprised if it snowed tomorrow.

"Yeah. That's how I got here," Synovi told her.

"I'm leaving, so I can drop you off."

Synovi thought about it. After all that cleaning, he couldn't front like he wasn't tired as hell, so he put his pride to the side. He wasn't too good to catch a ride, but his internal trauma of people doing for him out of pity always left him battling with accepting help. He'd let Racquel drop him off, but it wasn't going to be at Solace Place. That was pushing it.

"A'ight," he agreed, pulling the passenger door open and sliding in with ease.

Racquel hadn't adjusted the seat since he sat in it. Once she was in the driver's seat, she backed out of the driveway and pulled out of the subdivision. Synovi gave her all of fifteen seconds before she started up a conversation.

"So," she began, letting the word linger in the air.

"Say what you gotta say, man."

Snickering, she asked, "What do you think of my sister?"

"I'ont think nothing."

"Yeah right. I saw the way you were looking at her," she said, calling his bluff.

Synovi had a few thoughts about Torin, ones he was sure her little sister didn't want to hear. So, he kept them to himself.

"I'm a man; of course, I'ma look," he told her.

"Mhm. She's single if you were wondering."

He wasn't, but that tidbit of information was good to know. He didn't know why or how she hadn't been cuffed yet, but that was none of his business. If Synovi had to take a wild guess, he'd bank on her singleness being because of her smart mouth. Then again, maybe she hadn't come across the right man to check her ass. *Yeah, that's it,* he concluded.

"That's what's up."

"Where am I taking you?"

Just as she merged onto the highway, his phone vibrated in the pocket of his hoodie. Seeing GiGi's name on his screen put a genuine smile on his face. She was the only one who could get that out of him.

"What's good lady," he answered.

"You tell me. It's Sunday, so I know you better be making your way to see me," GiGi said.

"You ain't hanging with your friends today?"

"Them old heffas ain't my friends. I tell you, Carolynn

called herself trying to tell on me because she thought she smelled pot coming from my room?"

Synovi chuckled, making Racquel's head snap his way. She almost couldn't believe her ears.

"You was in there getting high?" Synovi questioned.

"On my damn porch, yes, I was. It was just that vape pen you got me. They were acting like I was out there, smoking a joint," GiGi fussed.

"Smoke inside next time."

GiGi sucked her teeth. "The hell I won't. I'ma snatch that ugly ass wig off her head the next time I see her."

Synovi laughed. "A'ight, gangsta. Don't get put out and make me cuss them folks out, lady."

"I'll try not to. You in the car, huh? Where you coming from?"

"My homegirl's people nem crib."

"Boy, what the hell all that mean? She a friend of yours?"

Racquel cut her eyes his way, hearing GiGi loud and clear.

"Yeah. She a friend," he replied dryly, making Racquel do a little dance in her seat.

Synovi shook his head. He didn't have many friends, so the term wasn't used often. He fucked with Racquel, though. After getting past her weird behavior and somewhat quirky personality, she was a cool person. Not necessarily his friend, but an associate for now.

"Ha." Racquel smirked.

"Well, you need to be coming on this way. I'm making Sunday dinner."

Synovi's stomach growled, reminding him he hadn't eaten today. He was sliding by there for sure.

"A'ight. I'ma be through there in a minute."

"Okay, baby. Tell that friend of yours to drive safely. It done started raining over here already."

He let her know he would and hung up. "My granny said don't be driving this car like you in a race."

Racquel snickered. "I'm not. You and her seem really close."

Synovi nodded his head. "Yeah. That's my girl."

Like always, Racquel wanted to know more, but that's all the information Synovi was offering up about his life. Taking a hint, she asked for directions to GiGi's place and headed that way.

"You and yo' sister close?" Synovi asked.

Racquel grinned and nodded her head. "Yes. Too close if you ask her, but I love it. You have any siblings?"

"Nah."

Truthfully, Synovi didn't know if he had siblings out there or not. He could've asked GiGi more about his upbringing, but there was no point. From eavesdropping on GiGi and the higher-ups when he was in foster care, he summed up that his parents had abandoned him. Synovi wasn't the type of person who needed every single detail why something happened or why someone didn't fuck with him. Once you showed him your true colors, he painted his own picture with them.

"Well, I guess we can share mine." She laughed, making him smirk.

"Nah, I'm good. I ain't really into sharing."

"Oooh. So you're a faithful lover. Okay!" Racquel cheered. "I know that's right."

Synovi shook his head. "Here you go, man."

"What? I'm just saying. So, you don't like sharing, but are you getting shared?"

"You making it sound like I'ma hoe or sum'."

Racquel laughed. "I am not! I'm just trying to see. It's typical for a man to say he doesn't like sharing a woman and being her only nigga, but will be screwing anything that has a vagina."

Synovi couldn't relate. He was stingy with who he shared his dick with and where he placed it. At least, that was the way he was now. In his teenage years, he was a bit reckless. Fucking his frustrations out was an outlet back then. Now, sex was the last thing on his mind. Sliding in some pussy while being broke and on a mission to live a better life wasn't on his agenda. When he wanted some, he knew who to call.

"Some niggas don't give a fuck."

Sucking her teeth, Racquel couldn't help but agree. "They don't, and it's trifling."

When they pulled up to GiGi's place, the rain she mentioned was nowhere in sight. It'd done a little something, but not what the clouds portrayed. She was out on her patio, watering the plants when Racquel parked.

"Okay, Granny! Look at her in her moo moo dress and matching scarf." Racquel grinned.

One thing GiGi was going to do was stay fly. Her leopard print threads were just one of many she had in her stash. Though her stroke had set her back some in other areas of her life, dressing wasn't one of them.

"I know, right," Synovi said. "'Preciate you for dropping me off."

"You're welcome, friend." Racquel smiled big.

"You ain't gon' let me live that down, huh?"

"Nope. You said it, not me. I'll see you later."

Synovi told her a'ight and got out of the car. Approaching the patio, he wasn't even all the way in when GiGi stopped him. Racquel waved from inside the car.

"I know she gon' get out and speak," she said.

Synovi looked over his shoulder. Racquel was already pulling out of the parking lot. He chuckled, knowing his granny didn't like that.

"Maybe next time," he said, kissing her cheek. "What's going on? When you dye your hair?"

Synovi tugged on one of her burgundy curls tucked underneath her scarf. The silk wrap her beautician gave her a week ago was now in curls, thanks to her sponge rollers.

"A few days ago. And ain't no next time. Y'all generation don't have no kinda manners. Pulling up to folks's home and not speaking."

Synovi had no rebuttal. "She younger than me, so that ain't my generation. Plus, you raised me differently."

"I sure did," she said, hugging him around the waist. GiGi

took a step back and looked at him. "Why you smell and look like yesterday?"

Synovi laughed. "I'm about to go in here and shower now."

"Yeah, you do that. I'd hate to think you were out here not washing your ass," she said, making him laugh harder.

The pot roast she had in the oven made Synovi's mouth water. After the week he'd had, there was nothing like a home-cooked meal to end it off right. Plus, he was a thousand dollars richer. Still jobless, but he was determined to have some shit in motion soon. He didn't know what, but like he always had, Synovi was going to figure it out. It was his only option.

five

Per usual, it was back to business after business was handled. Torin took one, maybe two, days off after a gig, but that was it. Her schedule was full, and she thanked God daily. There were definitely dry spells and times she felt burned out, but that didn't stop her from grinding. Putting the hard work in showed her how much staying consistent with what He had aligned for her paid off.

On a phone call inside her home office, Torin read over emails while listening to a potential client go into detail about her desired menu for her wedding in three months. The previous caterer she hired had a family emergency and recommended *Kaine's Kitchen*, Torin's business. Word of mouth was how Torin started from the ground up, but not all business was good. She learned that much early on in her career and still lived by that to this day.

"Yes, I understand you'd like three options for meats. With everything else you requested, including the budget you gave me, I'd suggest removing one from the list," Torin said politely.

"I can't take one off the menu. This is what I want," the bride huffed. "Is there a way I can finagle it in some way? Do you have a bride discount?"

Torin almost laughed. She appreciated her for asking, but the answer was no. Hell no. She wasn't going to lowball her business just to satisfy cheap people. Torin wouldn't even consider people cheap; they paid for what they wanted and what was in their price range. She wasn't in people's price range and that was okay.

The thing she didn't like was when people would be quick to pay full price for anything else, but wanted to play in her face and ask for a discount. It'd be a disrespect to her and her business if she agreed. More than anything, she preferred to work with individuals and businesses who saw things as an investment, not a fee.

"Unfortunately, I don't. Here's what I'll do. Let me get the invoice finalized for you and send it your way. Take a look at it, go over it with your husband, and shoot me an email with your decision. We can go from there," Torin let her know.

Again, the bride huffed. She was stressed as is, and Torin hated to add to that, but she'd be playing herself for the amount of money she was offering. She didn't mind working with people to provide great food and an experience, but they had to work with her as well.

"That's what I'll do. Thank you so much for even getting me in on your schedule."

"Of course, it's no problem. You have a good day."

The bride told her to do the same and they hung up. As soon as she placed her business phone down, her main cell phone chimed with an incoming text. She smiled at the name alone before opening it.

Good morning T. You still bringing them cupcakes up to the school?

Yes. 12:15 right?

Yep. I'll meet you at the front.

Torin reacted to his message with a thumbs up, grabbed her work phone, and stood from her desk. It was almost eleven, and she knew if she stayed in her office any longer, she'd be behind schedule. Before heading to her kitchen, she packed her work tote with all the things she'd need for the day and hit the lights.

Thankfully, the two dozen cupcakes had been baked last night and only needed icing. At DJ's request, Torin had baked vanilla, lemon, strawberry, and chocolate in batches of six. She hadn't gotten to put her baking skills to the test in about three weeks, but she still had it.

Once she finished making the whipped icing and placing them on the cupcakes, Torin boxed them up in clear containers. Rushing upstairs, she threw a bra on, untied her scarf, slid out of her house shoes, and put on a pair of New Balance sneakers she did her running around in. After making two trips to her garage, she was finally heading out after cutting her alarm on.

"Okay," she breathed. "Drop these off at the school. Remember to call Mia. See what that lady from the venue wanted," Torin rambled, going over her to-do list.

If she didn't, especially while driving, she knew she'd forget something. Fifteen minutes into her drive, interrupting the concert she and Jazmine Sullivan were having, her phone rang. The name displayed on her dashboard screen was one to be expected, but she declined the call for now. Pulling into the school's parking lot, Torin got lucky with a spot right up front. Grabbing the cupcakes, she made her way up the steps and into the building. She was greeted by the security guard at the front desk.

"Hey, Ms. Torin. How you doing today?" Chris asked with a sly grin.

Anytime she dropped by, he was forever hitting on her.

"I'm good, Chris. How are you?"

"I'd be much better if I could get one of them cupcakes up off ya hands." Chris chuckled, making Torin do the same.

"Absolutely not. These are for my baby."

"That grown boy ain't no baby."

Her lips pursed outward. "He's mine until I say so. Can you call him up here for me?"

"Sure thing," Chris said, picking up his walkie-talkie to call the security on duty for the third lunch shift. "Hey, Bird. Has DJ made it in the cafeteria yet?"

"Who?" a woman chirped back.

"She's new," Chris offered to Torin before holding the button down. "Mr. Cartwright."

"Ah. Yes. The young man from the basketball team with the blonde and black locs. Not yet. Want me to send him your way when he does?"

"I'd 'preciate it," Chris said, placing the walkie-talkie down. "He'll be right up."

"Thank you."

"How's your business been going?" Chris asked.

"Very good. You still looking to get on at the correctional center?"

The last time she was here, maybe two months ago, Chris let her know he was thinking about switching jobs. Working as an inner-city school security guard was cool, but he wanted something different. A change of scenery if you will. He looked surprised that she remembered, but that was one of her qualities. Even if it were a small detail about someone, Torin stored the information in her brain for later use.

"Damn. You remember me talking about that?" Torin nodded her head yes. "I was, but just gon' wait it out until the baby gets here."

Now, that was not something she'd been privy to. Chris could tell because he chuckled. Torin didn't even bother to ask; he offered his unsolicited details.

"Yeah," he started. "I got a baby on the way."

"Congratulations?" Torin hesitated. He didn't sound too excited about its arrival.

"Thank you. That could've been me and yours." Chris grinned.

Torin laughed in his face. "Never in a million years."

Chris threw his hands up. "Damn. Like that? What, I'm out yo' league?" he asked, eyeing the diamonds on her wrist and neck. He was sure they cost a grip.

She'd thrown on some light ice for the day, per usual. Diamonds were indeed Torin's best friend, and she had plenty of them, but that didn't mean Chris was out of her league. She hated when men insinuated that because of how she dressed or materialistic things. It was a turnoff. She wanted to tell him about himself, but she kept her comments to herself.

Torin's attention was now on the tall, lanky body that had just bent the corner. A huge smile etched her face, making DJ's do the same. She knew it hadn't been that long since she'd seen him in person, but his height said otherwise.

"Boy," Torin squealed, wrapping her arms around him. Her head stopped at the middle of his chest. "How are you this tall?"

DJ chuckled. "I'ont know. Prolly genetics."

"Yes, I'm sure that's it. I just can't believe it. You're not my little baby anymore," Torin pouted, poking at his arm. "And you got muscles now. I see you!"

DJ couldn't help but blush and waved her off. "Man, chill. I have been in the gym, though." He flexed, making Torin laugh.

"I see. All your hard work isn't going to mean much if you eat all these cupcakes. Who are they for anyway?"

He ran a hand across his neck before tugging at his chin hair. That was new to her too. It was like DJ had gone from the little boy who asked her to play the game with him to a young man with facial hair and muscles, yet still had the gentlest spirit. Looking at how much he'd grown made Torin emotional.

"This girl. It's her birthday, and I told her I'd get her something. She said she liked sweets, so I texted you," DJ told her.

"Oh my gosh. Not you out here using me to get you a little girlfriend. Let me find out," Torin laughed.

"Nah, nah. I already got her, but you know. Gotta apply that pressure to let her know I'm for real."

Groaning, Torin shook her head. "Lord, you really are growing up. That was sweet of you, though. I wish you would've told me. We could've gotten her some balloons."

DJ shook his head no. "Nah. Only do just enough, never too much," he said, but was serious. "At least not yet."

"Boy. Listen to you. I thought these were for a class party or something. I'm sure you'll be doing way too much real soon if you already doing all this."

"Yeah, we'll see. I had called and texted you, but you ain't respond. I know you be busy."

Torin knew she was busy, too, but that wasn't why she didn't respond. DJ wasn't any kin to her, but you couldn't tell her that. They were bonded in a way that made sense at first. Her ignoring his calls and texts was wrong, but it was also her trying to put some distance between them. That only worked for so long. She couldn't see herself not being in his life, especially not when she'd known him since he was seven. DJ was fifteen now and she'd been present for almost every milestone of those eight years.

"I do, but that's no excuse," she told him.

"I know you and my pops—"

Torin stopped him. "No. He has nothing to do with our relationship. That's on me. I'ma do better. You gon' have a girlfriend soon, so I gotta make sure to get my time in while I can."

DJ smirked, pulling her into a side hug. "She ain't gon' come before you."

"Mhm. You better get back in there before your lunch is over. And give one of those to your principal. She was so nice the last time I came up here."

He picked up the cupcakes. "She was frontin'. That lady mean as ever."

"You heard what I said, little boy."

DJ grinned. "I gotchu. Love you, T. Thank you, again. I'ma call you this weekend."

"I love you, too. And you're welcome," she said, watching him down the hall until she could no longer see him.

She didn't know where Chris had disappeared to, but she was thankful not to have to make any more small talk with him.

Back inside her truck, she started it up and pulled out of the parking lot. When she was about to call her assistant, Mia, her phone rang. Torin had declined Chelsea's call once, and she knew doing so again would make her think something was wrong, so she picked it up.

"Yes, my love," she answered sweetly.

"Torin. Do not hit me with that fake nice voice," Chelsea said with a smack of her teeth.

Fake gasping, Torin laughed. "Fake? Girl, whatever. You know I'm nicer than you."

"I'll give you that. But, what's up, man? Where you been at? I miss you," Chelsea whined, making her feel a bit bad.

"You sound like your nephew. I just left his school."

"What you was doing? Taking him some food?" Chelsea already knew her nephew and the grown man's appetite he had.

"Some cupcakes for this little girl he likes."

Chelsea snickered. "A'ight. He gon' end up like his daddy."

"Don't say that. DJ has so much more sense than Don, and we both know that," Torin fussed.

Without having to see her face, Chelsea knew Torin was on the other end, rolling her eyes. Anytime her brother's name was brought up, Torin checked out of the conversation. Not because she didn't care about Don, but because she knew anytime Chelsea brought him up, her hopes were still set on them getting back together.

It wasn't happening.

Not now, and especially not when he got out of jail.

Torin could still remember the first day they met. She was fresh out of high school and was starting college in a few months, but was enjoying her summer with her friends while she could. Her guidance counselor and mama had already told her once school started, she wasn't going to have time for anything but classes and studying. While Torin lived on the east side of the city, Leighton lived on the south side. The two claimed each other's neighborhoods had better-looking guys, so they'd always post up at each other's houses.

Don just so happened to be making a play out south that day and ran into them while Torin was walking out of the corner store.

Summer 2014

Torin's fresh sew-in swung against her back as she made her way to the counter. She'd gotten it done the day prior, with some added color, and was feeling herself. With a smile, she placed her Lipton sweet tea, hot chips, and gummy bears on the counter. Leighton swore she didn't want anything, but she grabbed her a hot pickle and a bottle of water. She knew her best friend and Leighton would be trying to dig her hand in her bag of chips.

"Hey, Ms. Lisa," Torin spoke.

"Hey, pretty girl. How you doing today?"

"I'm good. Trying to stay cool. It's so hot outside."

Ms. Lisa rang up her things, placing them in a plastic bag, while Torin used her card to pay. "I heard that. You and Leighton stay hydrated and be safe out there."

"Yes, ma'am. Have a good day."

"You too, sweetie."

Torin's pretty smile was wiped from her face as soon as she stepped out the door. Her attitude already wasn't the greatest, thanks to how damn hot it was, and the man doing a light jog into the store while looking over his shoulder, only made it worse when he bumped into her.

"Dang," Torin huffed.

Don caught her elbow. "My fault, baby. I was trying to see what pump I was on."

She eased out of his grasp and said, "It's cool," while walking off.

Don's attention was now on her long legs and the booty shorts she was wearing. Her white tank top fit like a second skin, and he fucked with the golden honey color in her hair. It made her skin pop. Not to mention, she smelled good. He rushed to the counter.

"What's going on, Ms. Lisa? Lemme get twenty on pump three."

Don was out of the store before she could even reply. "Mhm. You have a good day, too, Don."

He heard Torin talking shit before he got to her. Leighton's car, her mama's, anyway, was parked next to his on pump four.

"Almost tackled me to the ground," Torin grumbled, making Leighton laugh.

"You so damn dramatic."

"I'm for real. These niggas don't have no manners," Torin fussed and slightly jumped when Don's voice caught her attention.

"What niggas you talkin' 'bout, gorgeous?" Don questioned.

Torin knew she was kind of hungry, but the way her stomach did some weird movement had her shook a little bit. Don smiled at her with the prettiest white teeth while running a hand over his waves, all while getting ready to pump his gas. Torin was so annoyed a minute prior, she didn't even think to look him over. Now that he was up close and personal again, she licked her lips in appreciation. There was nothing like a fine, dark-skinned man with a pretty smile. His skin had the nerve to be shining at that. Don had some height to him, too, so that was a plus in her book.

His fit was fresh, almost identical to hers, with a white wife beater, Nike shorts, and fresh Air Forces on. Torin was rocking pink and white ones, pairing them with a pink Michael Kors crossbody bag.

"You," Torin sassed. "Didn't you almost tackle me?"

"And I apologized. What you want me to do, take you out to dinner and make up for it that way?" Don asked, almost losing Torin in the conversation, but she kept up with a smooth reply.

She could tell he was older, but she'd been put on enough game to run it just like he was.

"Yeah, you can do exactly that. I like steak and lobster, too. I ain't no little girl who wants a chicken tender meal."

Don smirked and licked his lips coolly. Stepping around to where Torin stood, he handed her his phone.

"Put your number in here. Be ready tomorrow at six," he told her, making Leighton smirk as she watched her friend.

"What's your name?" Torin asked, now smiling herself.

"Ladon."

She liked that. "Nice to meet you, Ladon. I'm Torin."

He stuck his hand out for her to shake. Neither of them knew that one handshake would have them locked in for life.

"Pretty name for a fine ass girl," Don stated in earnest. "I'ma hit you up later on."

"Okay," Torin said, smitten as hell already.

When they were back inside the car, the two best friends looked at one another and squealed with laughter.

"Bitch, he was fine," Leighton exclaimed.

"Right! You know me and my attitude. Once he bumped into me, I ain't care what the nigga looked like."

"I bet you glad he did now, huh? You got a dinner date and shit. I'm hyped for you."

Torin smiled, running a hand through her bundles. "I am too. I've never seen him around before. All that don't matter, though. I'ma make him my nigga for the summer."

They high-fived and laughed before Leighton pulled out of the gas station.

Torin made good on her promise and made Don her man for the summer and every summer after that for five years. What she didn't know was that he had a child who was seven years old, while Don himself was only twenty-five. She had family members who had kids at a young age, but never did she think she'd be dating a man who had one himself. Thankfully, Don's baby mama had moved on, and so had he.

They were the it couple, relationship goals, Pinterest board inspiration, and all. Torin thought it was so weird how so many people stared at them in public, or how much traffic her social media got just for being with him. In her eyes, she was no celebrity; just a regular girl who loved her man.

After being around him long enough and seeing how he moved, Torin quickly learned how deep in the streets Don was. The women who vied for his attention came in packs, and the amount of hate she received for fucking with him was annoying.

That didn't stop them from being together. It wasn't until

he got locked up, did Torin remove the blindfold from her eyes. By then, her feelings were past deep, and she thought holding him down was okay. He'd stuck it out with her through college, so Torin didn't see why she couldn't do the same.

She didn't start drifting away until those jail calls and visits weren't enough. Don made it so much easier for her when different women started posting him on their social media, or saw her out in public and felt like they needed to make her aware of their dealings with him. Torin was all for beating a bitch up for getting disrespectful, but behind a nigga she couldn't claim as being loyal to her? Never. She didn't even roll like that.

So, she cut ties with Don after writing him a letter on her Aaliyah shit. Torin cut his family off, except his son, Chelsea, and the baby mama, who she had no issues with. Everyone else, including his mama, who stayed talking shit behind her back, could kiss her ass. His uncles and cousins tried saying it was because he was in there and the women were just hoes to occupy his time and talk to, but Torin wasn't going for any of that. Especially when she knew she didn't have to.

Don approached her as a young, fly chick, and she was still that years later. He thought she was going to stick it out with him because of history and who he was, but was sadly mistaken. She humbled him quick. He may have been that nigga to them bitches he sat up and gamed over them jail calls, but she was that girl for real. Not just because of her looks, either. Torin had her shit together and had made a name for herself without having to be attached to Don's.

There were plenty of men out there who would've loved being Torin's man, yet Don had that title and fumbled it when he didn't have to. To this day, Torin hadn't been in a serious relationship. Not because she didn't want one, but because she'd literally had no time to focus on one.

Don getting locked up was a blessing in disguise because Torin was almost positive her life wouldn't have been what it was now had he not. Getting her heart broken had turned her into a beast, tapping into a different type of hustle she didn't know she possessed.

"I'm not talking about him going to jail, girl," Chelsea explained. "I'm talking about having a child all young like Don had him."

"Hell, I'm sure that felt like jail. Don was only seventeen. Don't speak that mess into the universe," Torin told her.

"You right. I'm too young to have a great-niece or nephew. What you doing, though? I miss you. You act like you be sooo busy," Chelsea complained.

"Girl, I have an entire business. Busy ain't the word. You can't miss me too much. The last time we were supposed to do something, you flaked on me last minute."

Chelsea sucked her teeth. "I told you something came up. What you doing next weekend? Let's go out. It's a day party at Juvie's."

"Since when did they start having day parties?" Torin wanted to know.

She loved their food, and the drinks were nice and strong, but she never knew of the owner throwing parties. It was a lounge-type setting, so she could see it.

"Ayo rented it out for his sister's birthday."

Torin groaned. "See. All the hood niggas gon' be there, watch."

"And I'ma be there with them." Chelsea laughed.

Ayo, a popular rapper from the city, was known to bring the town out. He had a large fan base who listened to his music from the city, but Torin was sure most people would come out, hoping to see Projex or Laurent. They were his friends and also in the music industry, having won a Grammy some years back. As much as she loved kicking it with her people, Torin knew that many niggas in one place with liquor in their system was a red flag.

"I'ma think about it, Chels," Torin told her.

"That's code for you ain't going. Ugh. You're twenty-six, hoe. Not ninety-six."

Torin chuckled. She knew how old she was. Hell, she had a birthday that was quickly approaching.

"You stay talking shit. I'ma pop out one time, and you better not start any fights."

"I'm not on that. I promise. Now, if a bitch tries me, then that's different."

Torin groaned and shook her head as she pulled up to Sam's Club. She had a few things to grab for meal prep orders. Going out with Chelsea either meant Torin was going to have one hell of a good time and a hangover the next day, or she'd be hearing about a fight they'd gotten into on social media for days.

Close in age with Torin at twenty-four, they immediately clicked when Don brought her around. They'd link up and kick it with each other's friends without Don being anywhere around. But, like she had been trying to do for a while, Torin wanted to distance herself. Chelsea felt that, as did DJ, and she wasn't having it. Neither of them cared that Torin wasn't with Don anymore and hadn't been for years; they still wanted her in their lives.

"We'll see, girl," Torin said. "I'm about to go into this store, so I'ma text you later."

"Okay. Love you, sis."

"Love you too."

The call disconnected, and Torin exhaled. Most days, Don was never on her mind. Having had interactions with two of the closest people to him back-to-back brought him to the forefront of Torin's brain. She didn't know how or when, but some boundaries needed to be made on her end. She loved Chelsea and DJ, but a small part of her knew the reason she hadn't gotten into a relationship was because she didn't want them to look at her differently. As if she couldn't hold Don down, but was with another man.

In her head, it sounded silly, and she never cared what people thought about her, but those were two relationships she didn't want to tarnish. Torin was going to have to learn that her happiness couldn't be based on the opinions of others because a mothafucka was always going to have something to say when they weren't the one making decisions.

six

Refusing to let him losing his job put him in a bad head space, Synovi had gotten up bright and early almost every day this week and headed to the library. By the numbness in his legs, he was sure he'd been there for over three hours, filling out applications. Jobs asked the most ridiculous questions just for you to get hired and not get trained or even do half the shit they asked you about. That was one of the reasons he was annoyed.

"Fuck they mean, what if you see Jim having a bad day? I'ma leave that nigga alone and mind my business," Synovi scoffed.

He wasn't going to work to make friends. When the questionnaire came back with him getting that question wrong, Synovi exited out of Google Chrome altogether. If any of the jobs he applied to wanted him, they'd give him a call. Other than that, he was done for the day.

Standing from the table, he stretched and yawned loudly. His phone vibrated with an incoming call as he walked out of the building. Synovi's nostrils flared, peeping the number, but he answered anyway.

"Yeah," he said dryly.

"Damn. What's the matter with you?" Jade snapped.

"Nothing. What you want?"

Synovi heard her moving around in the background and some cartoons before it was silent.

"I did something to you?" Jade asked, feeling his animosity through the phone.

Synovi hated when a person acted as if they didn't know they were in the wrong. He and Jade had been playing this game long enough for her to know when she had fucked up. Synovi understood their situation, but so did she. He didn't want to sound like a hoe and complain, but she always took him there. Explaining shit that was so obvious irked his nerves.

"Nah. You did what you always do: go missing. It's coo', but what's up? I ain't in the mood to talk."

Jade sucked her teeth before sighing heavily. "You know how it is. When you called me, it was almost two in the morning. Did you expect me to just roll over and answer your call?"

"You mean the same way you roll over and answer his after my dick been down yo' throat and every hole on your body?" he questioned calmly.

Jade gasped, hating when he talked to her rudely. "You do not have to go there! Don't talk to me like I'm some hoe."

"Yeah, a'ight. What you want, Jade, 'cause in a minute, you gon' piss me off for real. Is that yo' kid crying?"

Synovi didn't really give a fuck, but to see she was ignoring her child to sneak and talk to him on the phone made his mood worse than she already had. The night Racquel threw her party, Jade was the person Synovi called to come get him. She texted him earlier in the day, asking to see him, but he was busy. He met her at Mr. Fred's one evening, almost a year ago, and was under the impression she was single. That same night, Synovi fucked her like she was.

Two months later, well into their rendezvous and hotel visits, he found out she was married with two kids. Her youngest child was three. Jade had no intentions of stepping outside of her marriage and really cheating this time, but she was fed up. Married young and to a man who she believed couldn't care any less about her whereabouts and doings, she thought she'd have a little bit of fun with Synovi. One rollercoaster ride on his dick, and she was visiting the amusement park several days a week for the thrill.

When Synovi tried cutting her off, she became somewhat desperate. Yes, he was stand-offish, a little rude more than she liked to admit, and barely opened up to her, but Synovi wasn't her husband. He wasn't going above and beyond to please her. Especially when she already knew what the deal was but had sadly forgotten.

Jade sighed and handed her daughter a bowl of grapes. "She's fine. I want to see you. I miss you."

Synovi wanted to say something slick and make her miserable for not answering his call the other night, but he low-key missed her presence.

"You miss me or this dick?" he questioned boldly.

Jade smirked on the other end. "Both. So, can we make that happen, or do I have to beg you?"

"Don't do that. That begging shit isn't cute. I'm at the library on Bradshaw."

"Okay. I'ma drop the baby off to the sitter and be on my way."

Synovi pulled the phone away from his ear and checked the time. "A'ight. Don't be taking all day, either. You know how you get."

Snickering, Jade told him she wouldn't be long and they hung up. Figuring he had at least thirty minutes to kill, Synovi went back inside the library and took a seat in one of the chairs near the door. Pulling his phone out, Synovi couldn't help but smirk and shake his head at the text Racquel had sent him.

> Hey friend! I hope you're having a good day.
> Pasta and wings on me this weekend?

Knowing he didn't have any plans since he no longer had a job, Synovi figured he could kick it with her. He'd been thinking about the pasta from Bistro since they ate there.

Yeah that's coo

Yay! See you then

Her excitement humored him. Synovi considered himself a loner, and he was okay with that. It'd been that way since he was a kid. Making friends and having to leave them behind because of his home situation taught him how to not get attached, and he hoped Racquel did the same.

Quicker than he expected her to be, Jade pulled up to the library and called his phone. Not bothering to answer, Synovi walked outside and pulled the passenger door open to the silver Benz. Adjusting the seat to fit his tall stature, he climbed inside, placed his backpack on the ground, and closed the door.

"Hey," Jade spoke, staring him down.

Synovi glanced at her, eyeing her new hairstyle. "What up. You cut your hair."

Jade tucked a piece of her short, blunt-cut hair behind her ear. The fact that he noticed the change and her husband hadn't made her feel good.

"Yeah. Felt like it was time."

Synovi nodded. "That's what's up. It's nice. I see you got a new whip, too."

"Thank you. And this is my husband's. Just taking it for a spin today. What were you doing up here?" Jade asked, pulling out of the lot.

"Filling out fucking job applications."

His grumbled reply made Jade cut her eyes his way. "What happened to Mr. Fred's? They still haven't opened back up?"

"Nah. You'd know that, had I talked to you."

Him being upset with her didn't stop Jade from blushing a little. To her, it sounded like Synovi had been missing her just as much as she'd been missing him.

"Awww. You miss me," she cooed, reaching out to rub his face.

Synovi chuckled. "Move, man. I ain't miss your ass."

"Whatever you say, love. You hungry? We can stop to grab a bite to eat before going to the hotel."

Sliding with her to a hotel wasn't in the plans, but Synovi should've known better. If it were up to him, he'd slide his dick in her wherever, but Jade wasn't going for that.

"I ain't know you were trying to get a room," he said.

"Yes. I need a damn break, and my oldest is going to her aunt's house after school. It's still early, so we have time."

"Good, 'cause you got some making up to do," he concluded.

Jade didn't mind that at all. As long as she could spend as much time with Synovi as possible, she had no complaints. Even though she was married, it still felt like she was a single mother. She drove for a good twenty-five minutes before pulling into the parking lot of Bistro.

Synovi's antennas went up immediately. "Why you come here?"

"What you mean? You don't wanna eat here or something?"

Jade found a parking spot and pulled into it before parking. Paranoia crept over Synovi in a way he couldn't explain. The fact that he had been there with Racquel weeks prior for the first time, and now Jade pulled up here, had him tripping. He was used to them driving far out for the privacy she needed, but this was just too uncanny.

"We can. I'm just trying to see who told you about this spot?" Synovi questioned.

Jade's nostrils flared. His questioning was about to ruin her mood. "No one told me about this spot, Synovi. I've eaten here multiple times. We can go somewhere else since it seems like you don't want to be here."

"It's coo'. Come on."

Synovi unbuckled his seatbelt and Jade sat there. Her eyes squinted, wondering why the hell he was questioning her the way he was. When she didn't cut the car off, Synovi glanced over his shoulder at her as he pushed the door open.

"What you still sitting in the car looking crazy for?"

Jade's skin warmed from her trying to hold in her emotions. She knew it was out of line to be asking him anything that didn't pertain to them fucking, linking up, or where he wanted to eat, but she surely wanted to. Synovi held his stare and she just shook her head.

"No reason," she said, cutting the car off.

Grabbing her purse off the backseat, Jade hopped out and locked the doors before walking around to his side. Eyeing her outfit, Synovi licked his lips and almost wanted to say forget them eating; they could head straight to the hotel. Jade was rocking the hell out of some high-waisted skinny jeans, an ivory satin top from House of CB, and a pair of tan mule heels. No matter the occasion, unless specified, Jade was going to put on a pair of heels.

Sensing her attitude, Synovi lightly smacked her ass and kissed her cheek. "Fix your face."

She smirked as they made it to the entrance and he opened the door. That quickly, with a touch of his lips, Jade's attitude had vanished.

"Welcome in. Do you have a reservation?" the hostess greeted.

"No. We're just dining for two today," Jade said.

The hostess scrolled through the iPad mini before scanning the seating area she planned to sit them. "Right this way."

She guided them to the opposite side of the restaurant that Synovi and Racquel previously sat in, giving him a perfect view of the door and the other customers.

"Your waiter will be with you shortly."

"Thank you," Jade said, taking a seat.

Grabbing the menu, she scanned over it while Synovi scanned the vicinity. He already knew what he wanted. His silence made Jade look up, wondering what his issue really was.

"Are you sure this is okay? You're acting like someone is looking for you or something," she expressed in a hushed tone.

Synovi finally focused his eyes on her. Jade was a brown-skinned beauty in her early thirties. The baby weight that didn't exist on her five-foot-six frame resided in her round face, making her look much younger than she was. Her new hair-do helped boost her youthfulness. After two kids, she was still as slim as she'd always been, but they added curves to her once flat hips and gave her a little ass.

Under his intense scrutiny, Synovi was trying to figure out why she was sneaking around in her marriage. He'd never posed the question before, but here lately, he almost let the words leave his mouth. *That shit ain't none of my business.*

"Yeah, I'm straight. What you getting? I think I'ma fuck with the pasta."

"It's so good," Jade cooed.

Yeah, I know, he thought as their waitress came to take their drink and appetizer orders.

Across the restaurant, Torin sat at a table with Leighton, trying to conceal her laughter. Out of the two, Leighton always had the most ridiculous stories to tell, while Torin's were more adventurous, leaving you wishing she had more to add to them.

"Wait, what?" Torin quizzed, laughing. "You told him what?"

"I told that man he wasn't about to play Ring Around The Rosie down there. You either eat this ass or get up."

Torin's head dropped and her body quaked as she cracked up.

"Why would you tell that man that?" Torin wheezed.

"Because he must've thought it was a game or something. Talkin' about some, *I'll just swirl my tongue around the rim.* No, what you gon' do is act like you're grown and do what you came to do."

"And he didn't, so I guess that's why we're here," Torin concluded.

Leighton gave her a deadpan stare with pursed lips before cutting into her tender braised lamb shank.

"Yep. And I blocked his number right after he paid for wasting my time. I don't know why I even bother with these niggas, honestly," she huffed, stabbing a piece of meat and stuffing her mouth.

Bistro had the best comfort meals and it was just what

Leighton needed after her afternoon was ruined. The menu was plentiful of French cuisine dishes, adding a splash of American ones that kept the establishment packed. You could guarantee a full stomach and a stellar dining experience upon your departure.

"I swear, you have the craziest experiences. So, he's cut off for good?" Torin wanted to know.

"Mhmm." Leighton hummed the obvious. "Absolutely. One, it's clear he doesn't care about my needs, and two, he doesn't value my time. I'm not sticking around to list number three."

Torin's head tilted to the left. She didn't even know why she asked. Leighton was a no-nonsense type of woman. Whoever the guy was, was lucky he'd made it to date number three with her.

"I guess, honey. You're both grown, so I can see where you're coming from," Torin said.

"I'm glad you do. Now, who was this chick you said paid you late?"

Torin's eyes rolled as she picked up her glass of red wine and sipped. The bold, sweet taste paired perfectly with the roasted duck and vegetables in front of her. As much as Leighton needed this meal and girl time, so did she. Work had been stressing her the hell out.

"Someone Chelsea referred to me. She wanted meal prep for a week and then tried to act as if that wasn't what we discussed."

"I know you had that shit in writing," Leighton said.

"You know I did. She signed a contract electronically and all. I just hate that I had to practically curse her out."

Leighton thought otherwise. "I don't. These bitches don't be knowing who they can and can't play with. Why would you ever want to play with someone's source of income? Not just that, but your hard work. Did she think preparing all of that was for the fuck of it?"

"I guess so," Torin sighed. "She knows better now, though."

"And so do you. You need to start making folks pay full price up front, or we gon' start taking names and beating ass. I don't know why you work with anyone Chelsea refers to you in the first place," Leighton fussed.

While Chelsea hated to see Leighton coming, Leighton, on the other hand, couldn't care less about the girl. Her unwarranted hate came from Leighton messing with one of her friend's men. Technically, he was single and wanted to trick off on her, and Leighton let him.

That happened over two years ago, and Chelsea, along with her friend, was still salty about it. Leighton was more than a few niggas past and over him, which wasn't saying much, considering there was no deep connection. Why they still harbored ill feelings, she didn't know and would never care. What she wouldn't go for was Chelsea or whoever trying to get over on her friend.

"Just because you don't care for her doesn't mean she knew the girl was going to do that," Torin said, defending Chelsea.

Leighton smirked. "True. But, still. People be knowing how others move and still allow you to do business with them. You can't convince me otherwise."

Knowing there was no changing her girl's mind, Torin changed the topic. She didn't choose sides when it came to them, and she never let the other talk disrespectfully in her presence, either. Especially not behind a man who didn't matter.

"I know I can't. Speaking of business, I need to hire a cleaning service," Torin said.

"For your house?"

"Yes, and my business. It's one thing to clean up before I start cooking and during, but afterward, too? I don't want to do it anymore," Torin whined.

Leighton fully understood. The times she did help out with big events Torin catered, there was so much behind the scene work, she couldn't believe she had done it all by herself before hiring a few employees. Seeing how hard she worked and the hours she put in prompted Leighton to buy her friend a monthly spa pass. Those massages always came in handy right when Torin needed one.

"I tell you all the time… pay for convenience. You act like you're broke."

Torin sucked her teeth. "No, I act like I want things done a certain way. Money isn't the issue."

"So act like it then, Ms. Baller," Leighton joked. "Hire you someone for the job and take some of the stress off you. Hell, get you some dick, too. I know for a fact that'll help."

Torin chuckled. "Girl, fuck you."

"No, thanks, babe. I like dick. The long, thick kind that comes with a fat bankroll."

"Of course you do," Torin tittered while finishing her meal.

This wasn't the first time she'd thought about hiring someone to clean up her home and to help with the duties of *Kaine's Kitchen*. The task always became an afterthought once she was in the thick of whatever she had going on. While she made well over six-figures a year, Torin still hadn't learned the importance of outsourcing. It was one thing she told herself she'd start pushing for soon.

After a long day of cooking, serving, running errands, or whatever else was on the agenda, the last thing she wanted to do was clean up. Tomorrow, she planned to call Mia, her assistant, and look into some cleaning services. The additional help would be well worth it.

The duo finished up their meals, and Torin's eyes scanned the floor for their waiter. With the open floor concept inside the restaurant, she was given a clear view of the opposite side and of Synovi's table. His seat wasn't occupied at the time.

"That's how I'm thinking about getting my hair," Torin said.

Leighton's head swiveled to where her focus was. "That bob?"

"Mhm. Maybe a little longer, but that's fire."

"Hell yes. That's that grown bitch hairstyle. If you can pull that off, you a bad one."

Torin snickered, and the laughter got caught in her throat as she watched Synovi approach his seat. With saliva invading the wrong part of her throat, Torin damn near coughed up a lung as she tried clearing her airways. Her obnoxious barking garnered the attention of many diners, including Synovi's.

He hadn't recognized who she was at first glance since she had a different hairstyle than before. Torin wasn't expecting to see him out while she and Leighton were having lunch, let alone to see him on a date.

"You good now?" Leighton chuckled lightly as Torin set her glass of water down.

Her head bobbed. "Yeah," she huffed, clearing her throat.

Before she knew it, her eyes made their way back across the room. Synovi hadn't looked away. Torin wasn't going to be the one to back down from his gaze, so she held his attention. When he gave her a head nod, she waved before facing straight ahead.

Leighton's head swiveled between, watching the scene unfold. "Um, who is that?"

"One of Racquel's friends," Torin offered.

"A friend, or a friend, friend? That boy looks like a grown man," Leighton commented.

She wasn't sure how close they were, but Racquel had asked what she thought of Synovi. It was the same question she asked him about her. Torin didn't think of Synovi. Besides the fact that he had cleaned her home like a professional, she'd found him asleep in her guestroom. She hadn't even told Leighton about the incident.

"I'm guessing just a friend, and I would hope so, seeing as though he's out on a date," Torin said.

While they bickered about Synovi, he and Jade sat at their table with tension so thick, it made his head hurt. In the middle of them eating, Jade's husband called. Synovi wasn't sure what he signed up for in the beginning while dealing with a married woman, but he was in deep now. He knew Jade wasn't his, but some days, she acted like it, and he'd almost be convinced.

Then he was given a rude reminder that this was nothing more than a thrill for them both.

This ain't even my woman to be trippin' on, Synovi thought as she ran her mouth. Jade was trying to explain herself and apologize for answering his call for no reason.

"I ain't really trying to hear all that, Jade. Save that shit for your husband. I'm just here to fuck you and fulfill your sexual needs."

"Why would you think that's all you mean to me?" Jade asked.

"'Cause it's the truth. We ain't gotta sugarcoat it. That rock on your hand always lets me know what it is. It's best if you remember that, too."

Jade looked down at the pearl-shaped ring on her finger. Trying to cover it up was pointless; Synovi had peeped it the minute he climbed in the car. Hiding it wouldn't make the vows she professed before God and their family mean anything more than what they already didn't.

When the bill came, Jade pulled her card out. "I'm already sneaking around. Not answering my phone will make him suspicious."

"A'ight."

"Why are you acting so nonchalant? I'm trying to apologize."

"I'm not acting. I really don't give a fuck. You decided to step out on your marriage. All that explaining and shit is pointless because we both know what's about to happen once we leave here."

There was no need for Jade to say anything else, so she didn't. With an apparent attitude, she scribbled her signature on the receipt their waiter brought back. Digging in his pocket, Synovi pulled out money for a tip and stood up.

"I gotta take a piss. You can go to the car," he said.

"Fine," Jade huffed before marching off.

Synovi watched her walk toward the front before heading to the restroom. After handling his business, he walked out with an extra pep in his step and hoped the person on his mind hadn't left. He did have to use the restroom after drinking two glasses of lemonade, but he also wanted to speak to Torin. He would've done it with Jade around but didn't want to hear her mouth more than he already had. His loyalty didn't belong to her, but his next nut would, and he wasn't trying to fuck that up.

Torin's eyes brightened as he approached their table. She wasn't expecting him to come and speak, but she didn't let it show. Taking all of him in, Torin appreciated how good he smelled. His fresh scent engulfed her, forcing Torin to play nice since it seemed he was as well.

"Hey. How are you?" she questioned.

Synovi's head tipped backward. "I'm straight. You enjoy your lunch?"

Leighton snickered under her breath at his question. From the obviously cleared plates and empty wineglass, she had enjoyed it thoroughly.

"I did. Did you enjoy yours?"

"That's good, and yeah. I came over here to get an apology for how we met. I feel like you got off on the wrong foot with me."

Torin's micro-bladed brows dipped. "I'm sorry, what? An apology?"

"Yeah. That stunt you pulled… I found that highly disrespectful," Synovi said.

Glancing at Leighton, Torin wanted to make sure she wasn't the only one hearing him correctly. She sat up some in her seat.

"Okay… let me get this straight. I find you posted up in *my* house, in *my* guest bedroom with the door locked, and you want *me* to apologize for how I handled you? Is that what you're saying?

"That's exactly what I'm saying," Synovi replied.

Leighton chuckled loud enough for them to hear her. She couldn't believe Synovi's audacity. Torin laughed in his face.

"Oh, well, I guess we're going to stay on the wrong foot because I'm not apologizing for anything."

They stared one another down for a few seconds. This was way out of character for him, but he couldn't pass up the opportunity to let her know she was somewhat out of line. Had the roles been reversed, Synovi was positive this conversation wouldn't have been happening. What he did know was that he wasn't walking out of there without Torin offering something.

"A'ight. No apology for now, so how about a thank you?"

"A thank you for—oh. Mr. Clean Up Man." A grin jotted across her lips.

Synovi didn't take her moniker as disrespect. He'd let her have that.

"Thank you for cleaning up my place. I really did appreciate you going the extra mile," Torin spoke sincerely.

She expected him to offer a smile at least, appreciating that she expressed her gratitude, but all she received was a curt head nod. "No problem."

To calm her nerves, Torin took a sip of water. "Was there anything else you'd like me to know?"

"Nah, not right now. If I think of something, I'll let you know," Synovi said and walked off.

Torin kept her eyes trained on him before hurriedly looking away. Had he stuck around a second longer, she was going to tell him something she thought he should know, and it was nothing appropriate.

"Girl," Leighton dragged. "That young man made it his mission to let you know what was on his mind. What you do to him?"

"Pulled my gun on him," Torin sighed.

Leighton's wide eyes encouraged her to divulge the full story from all sides. When she was finished, all Leighton did was shake her head.

"That sounds like some shit Racquel would do. At least you got a free deep clean."

"Right. That's the only reason I said thank you because I hadn't before he left. Anything else, he wasn't getting."

"The fact he came over here and made his mama go to the car and wait is crazy. He could've introduced her."

Torin stared at her before bursting out laughing. "That was not his damn mama!"

"Could've fooled me," Leighton said with an impassive shrug.

While Jade was gorgeous, she applied a ton of makeup that appeared caked on. Leighton noticed it from where she was sitting and could tell she was much older than Synovi.

"You have no sense," Torin said. "You ready to go?"

"Mhm. I'm full and sleepy. I wish I didn't have to drive home."

Torin thought the same thing. They went to use the restroom before saying goodbye to a few of the staff and headed to their cars. The perks of her mother, Tracee's, recklessness guaranteed them free meals whenever they visited. Still, they left a hefty tip before leaving.

While Leighton had a nap on her mind, Synovi was on Torin's. She wondered if he was still in need of a job, and if so, she had the perfect one for him.

seven

"Oh, my gosh, baaabe!"

Jade's prolonged moans echoed throughout their master bedroom. She was hanging on for dear life at the edge of the bed while Synovi pounded into her. Her excessive shrills were warranted. The way he stroked her walls would make any woman cry for more, and that was exactly what he gave her.

"Quit all that hollering," Synovi groaned, smacking her ass. "Throw that shit back."

Taking directions as if he were a navigation system, Jade did just that. She used to be a runner at the beginning of their affair and was now fully trained to last the entire race.

Her hips wound and slickness coating Synovi's length that filled her to the brim. When his hand squeezed her hip tightly, Jade knew he was almost at his peak. His thrusts quickened, and their skin clapped loudly before Synovi removed himself from her snugness in haste.

Relieved and highly satisfied, Jade toppled over onto the bed. The light smack to her thigh interrupted the brief moment of mercy she tried basking in.

"Nah, come here," Synovi grumbled.

Jade's legs trembled, a clear sign of her orgasm still running its course as she climbed from the bed and onto her knees before him. Yet that didn't deter her from the duty she was summoned to fulfill.

Snatching the condom from his length, Synovi tossed it aside. A mixture of agitation and pleasure covered his face as Jade took him into her mouth. It wrinkled as if he were in pain, but that wasn't the case at all.

Sss.

A hiss fell from his lips as his lids lowered in pure bliss. He'd scrubbed his brain plenty, wondering why he didn't mind standing in the middle of another man's home with his wife doing the unthinkable to him. It was the head. Jade was a mastermind and was blowing his with each slurp.

Forcing her head back onto the edge of the bed, Synovi aided Jade in her superb efforts. Accommodating his girth, she stretched her mouth wide. Under his spell, her eyes stayed trained on his disgruntled facial features and lustful eyes as his body stiffened. Manicured hands massaged his balls, and before she had a chance to properly care for the pair, Synovi's semen slid down her throat.

"Hmmm," he groaned deeply.

A faulty step backward was taken after Jade sucked him clean. She smirked, watching his chest heave and nostrils flare. Licking her lips, she used the bed to help her stand.

"I told you it would be a quickie," she reminded him.

Synovi had no words. He'd heard her the first time she said it. Her home wasn't where they were supposed to be, let alone her bedroom. Leave it up to Jade to take her cheating to the next level again. Synovi had been to their home on two other occasions, but never the room they laid their heads.

Needing a few clothes for the interviews he had coming up, the duo had gone out shopping before making a pit stop. Jade claimed to have left a pair of dress shoes she'd bought for him at her house. Figuring the lines of disrespect had already been trampled over, he had no issue giving Jade exactly what she begged for, which he hated.

"Here," she said, handing him a warm towel to wipe off.

As he did so, Jade used a few tissues to pick up and discard the condom. Synovi shook his head, watching her unravel an excessive amount of toilet paper around it. Pulling up his briefs and jeans, he tossed the towel in the hamper inside their bathroom before washing his hands. Beside him, Jade did the same before fixing her hair and pulling makeup out.

"Why you looking at me like that?" she questioned.

"You about to reapply all that right now?"

His eyes danced over the products she kept pulling from the drawer. So far, he counted five, and it seemed she wasn't done.

Jade chuckled. "Yes. I was sweating. I won't take long. Promise. Just go sit on the bed."

Synovi snarled. "I ain't sitting on y'all fucking bed, Jade. Hurry up. I got somewhere to be."

"But you'll fuck me on it," she mumbled as he walked out, but Synovi heard her.

"And you let me fuck you on it. Freaky ass. Hurry up," he reiterated, smacking her on the ass for motivation.

Grinning, Jade did her best to do as he said. She hated rushing while doing her makeup, but time was of the essence. The thrill of engaging in an activity she knew she had no business partaking in made her nipples hard. For so long, she'd suppressed her urges to step out on her husband, and it felt freeing to do so. The sneakiness only added fuel to the fire.

As soon as she twisted the top to her concealer, Synovi stepped inside the bathroom. She huffed in annoyance, knowing it hadn't even been a full minute yet.

"Yes?"

"I think your husband is home," he announced way too coolly for her.

Panic rippled through Jade like a tidal wave. The alarm in her eyes was almost comical as she scrambled to get out of the door. Realization hit her, and she quickly pivoted.

"You have to hide in the closet," she hissed, just as her husband called her.

"Bae!" her husband hollered.

Shoving Synovi out of the bathroom, Jade forced him to walk toward their massive walk-in closet.

"Stop pushing me," Synovi grunted lowly.

"Hide behind his suits and stuff. I'll be right back," she rushed out.

Frowning, Synovi leaned against the island in the closet. He wasn't about to tuck himself behind a bunch of suits. His position didn't waver for all of five seconds before he pushed through the clothes and exhaled harshly.

His thoughts quickly changed when he envisioned himself losing his life if Jade couldn't get her composure together. She was too damn frantic and needed to get her lie straight; otherwise, shit was about to go left.

"I gotta leave her alone," Synovi grumbled, leaning his head against the wall.

Downstairs, Jade greeted her husband in a silk robe with a smile. "Hey, baby."

He returned her expression, eying her exposed thighs. "What's going on? What you doing home?"

Jade sucked her teeth. "I had to come home and change. Simone had me pick us up some iced coffees and one of the lids wasn't on all the way. It spilled all over my outfit."

"You don't even drink coffee," he stated with pinched brows.

Dramatically, Jade tossed her hands up. "Exactly, but I'm trying to get into them. She swears by them, claiming they give her so much energy. I could use that with the way the girls have me on go."

"Yeah, it might work. You about to shower?" he questioned, reaching out to tug on the belt of her robe.

Playfully, with her heart thundering in her chest, Jade smacked his hand away. "Yes, I am. What're you doing home, Mr.?"

"Accidentally left a flash drive I need on my desk. I got a few minutes to spare."

That's all you ever have to give, Jade thought with annoyance.

She wagged her finger. "I don't think so. I'ma gonna need more than a few minutes. I'm all yours when you get home."

He pulled her closer, wrapping an arm around her waist.

Jade melted against his broad frame and inhaled. His hugs always made her feel good, and had she not given him one, he surely would've known something was up. When he began kissing her neck, Jade pushed away, but he held her tighter.

Foreplay was her weakness. It made up for the lack of consistent dick he couldn't give.

"Silas," she whined when he gripped her ass. "Baby, you have to get back to work."

Knowing that was her spot, Silas stayed there for a bit longer before lifting his head. "You're right. Who else is going to pay for those shopping sprees you can't stop going on?"

Jade blushed. "You saw my bags?"

"I did. Did you get me some more dress socks?"

Her head bobbed. "Yes, and another bottle of your favorite cologne."

"Mine or yours, because you love it on me?" he queried with a smirk.

"Just know everything in those bags aren't just for me."

He pecked her lips, and Jade cringed inside. She just knew he tasted Synovi all over her lips. Had he tried to slip her some tongue, Jade would've passed out.

"I know. Even if they were, I don't mind. What you and Simone got planned for the rest of the day?"

Jade sighed in relief as they headed toward the front door. Stopping by the office with glass dooring, Silas retrieved the flash drive he needed, shoving it inside his pocket. As a Senior Business Analyst in IT, he couldn't afford to lose it. Accidentally leaving it at home was pushing it enough.

"I'm not sure. You know how she is on her off days," Jade replied.

"Have you all over the world," Silas said, opening the door. "Be good."

"I'm always good, baby. You know that."

Jade rubbed his chest with her left hand. Bringing it to his mouth, Silas kissed her fingers along with her wedding ring.

"Not always, but that's what I love about you," he confessed.

A pang of guilt settled in her chest and Jade quickly shook it off. "I love you, too. Have a good rest of your workday."

"I'll try. It would be much better already if you would've given me a lil' taste."

Giggling, Jade jumped away from him as his hand tried going underneath her robe. "Nope. You don't need to be speaking to anyone with me on your breath."

Like you not standing here with Synovi's nut coating your grill, Jade silently chastised herself.

"At least they'd know I had a good reason for running late," Silas joked.

"Yeah, yeah. See you later on."

"Be sure to cut the alarm back on when you leave," he said, walking to his car and climbing inside.

Jade told him she would and waved as he backed out of the driveway. She stayed planted in the window until his car was no longer visible and then rushed upstairs. Knowing Silas had to have entered the garage in order to see all the shopping bags made Jade shake her head at her sloppiness.

The only way she would've heard him enter the garage was if she'd been downstairs. Too consumed with the thrill of having sex in her bedroom, Jade had almost got caught slipping. She'd told lies before, but almost getting caught had her rethinking more than a few things.

When she entered the bedroom, Synovi was standing in the middle of the floor. He figured if the man hadn't realized she was up to no good after a few minutes, he wasn't about to be claustrophobic for no reason.

"You really just do what you want," Jade fussed.

"I'm just like you, for real. He spooked your ass, huh?" Synovi joked.

He found humor in them almost getting caught, now that Silas was gone.

Jade rolled her eyes. "Whatever. You're lucky he didn't come up here."

"Me? Nah. He's lucky he ain't bring his ass up them steps.

Your pussy wouldn't have been the only thing getting beat up in here. I can promise you that."

Synovi was grateful it hadn't come to that, but if it did, he wasn't going down without a fight. They were playing a dangerous game and he knew the consequences of their actions if they came to light wouldn't be a simple pat on the shoulder.

"Mhm. Let me finish getting dressed so I can drop you off," Jade said.

"I'll get a Lyft. Fooling with you, I'ma be even later."

She poked her head out of the bathroom door. "Where do you have to be?"

Synovi stared at her like she was crazy. "Did I put a ring on your finger?"

Jade sucked her teeth. "Now I can't ask questions? You really know how to irk my nerves. After swallowing all your little babies and spending my husband's money on you, I ask one thing and it's the end of the world."

"Sucking my dick ain't got shit to do with what I got going on. Next time, you'll know to mind your business. Your doors unlocked?"

"Mhm," Jade hummed, removing herself from the entryway.

It was moments like this where she truly wondered what she was doing and why. Sometimes, that free feeling she got came with a headache. Dealing with a person like Synovi, who didn't like to open up at all, was frustrating. He told her what he wanted her to know, and that was good enough. Jade didn't need to know his whereabouts or keep tabs on him. That wasn't a part of the agreement Synovi signed up for. Neither was hiding in closets, but here he was.

"When can I see you again?" Jade asked.

She was dressed and standing inside the garage as Synovi waited for his driver to pull up. Shopping bags aligned the sides of his feet, along with the pair of shoes they'd come to the house to get in the first place.

"I'll hit you up."

"Are you mad at me? I can't control when he comes home."

Synovi pinched the bridge of his nose and exhaled. "You can't, but putting me in a position to even cross paths with him is wild. You shouldn't have even been on that, but aye. Have your fun," he voiced with a shrug.

Jade hated when he got cold on her. "Here you go, acting like you don't care again."

"About you doing what you wanna do? Nah, I don't. Just don't include me in the recklessness next time."

"You didn't have to come upstairs, Synovi. It takes two to cheat."

"The only cheater is you. I'm single and was clearly thinking with the wrong head. Lesson learned," he said as a text alerted him that his driver was one minute away.

Jade always threw around him not caring and Synovi understood why but also didn't. They were almost a year into their affair; of course, he cared. He would've had to truly be a heartless man not to feel something for her. When he'd catch himself slipping and getting too deep, he'd pull back. She could never be his.

I'm explaining myself to a married woman, dog, he thought, shaking his head.

"Yeah... lesson learned. Can I at least have a hug before you go?"

"Yeah, man. Don't be all in your feelings about this shit. You and I both know what it is and what's it going to remain," he said, more to himself.

Wrapping her in a hug, he kissed her forehead.

"I wish it could be more. In another lifetime, I'd be rocking your last name," Jade sighed, trying to lighten the mood.

Synovi frowned. "Fuck no. I'd never wife you."

Jade gasped loudly. "Why would you say that?"

She couldn't help but laugh at his insolent response.

"Look what we doing. Your husband is better than me; that's all I'ma say. I'ma text you, though," he said, grabbing his bags off the concrete.

"Okay," Jade mumbled as he walked to the car.

Synovi placed his bags in the backseat and climbed inside. The ride back to the transitional house was silent, besides low music playing on the radio. Synovi was thankful for that and made sure to give a five-star review once he exited the vehicle.

"'Preciate you," he said, grabbing his belongings.

With limited time to spare, he rushed through the main door after scanning his access card. Getting buzzed through the second door, he gave a head nod to the main staff and headed down the hall to his bedroom. Dumping his bags off inside his closet, he grabbed the red folder near his bed and headed out.

Rushing out of the room, he slightly bumped into Kimmy, who was coming down the hall. "My bad!"

"Ms. Reid was just asking about you," she said.

"I'm heading to see her now," he shouted, walking quickly up the steps.

Every full-time staff had an office of their own. With the type of resources they provided, it was necessary. As a case manager, Ms. Reid needed privacy. Making his way to her office at the end of the hallway, Synovi knocked on her open door. Looking away from her computer screen, Ms. Reid waved for him to come in.

"Let me call you back when I get out of this meeting. Mhm, yeah. Okay, bye," she said to someone on the phone before locking it. "Hey. Come in. I was just wondering where you were."

Synovi pushed the door closed before taking a seat in one of the chairs in front of her white desk. She had gospel music playing, and the one window in her office was open, allowing a breeze to come through. Immediately, Synovi felt at peace.

Whenever they met, something about their time spent relaxed him. He didn't know if it was because she was really the only person he'd grown to trust here, but he made sure to make it to their weekly meetings.

"I'm right on time," Synovi breathed, clearing his throat. "How you doing? You left me hanging last week to get yo' hair done." he joked, noticing her fresh knotless braids that were pulled into a neat bun.

Ms. Reid chuckled. "And if I did, that's my business."

"You right." Synovi laughed.

"I know. But I'm doing better than I can express. How are you feeling today?"

Synovi pondered for a bit. The truth was, he was doing better than their last meeting, which was a few weeks ago. Ms. Reid had a prior engagement out of town the week before, so they hadn't been able to sit down and chat.

"No lie, I'm feeling like I finally caught a break."

Ms. Reid beamed. "That's a good thing. Catch me up on what's been going on, and I'll tell you what I've been working on for you."

Synovi's head bobbed upward. "A'ight. I got a few job interviews lined up."

"Okay!" Ms. Reid expressed with excitement. "And you were complaining about filling out the applications, now look."

"I ain't like it, but I knew it had to be done," he stated.

"As do most things in life. Which jobs reached out?" she asked, scribbling notes on college-ruled line paper. Later, she'd transfer them onto her desktop.

"A couple of office jobs where I'd have to talk on the phone, and the one for Ford."

She noticed the disapproval in his tone. "Uh, oh. Why do you sound like that?"

Synovi shifted in his seat. "Talking on the phones all day ain't my thing."

"A job is a job, Synovi," she reminded him. "You can't be *that* picky if you're needing a check."

They'd discussed this plenty of times when he thought about finding another job other than Freddy's. Words were powerful, and his wish for something new landed him with nothing in search of employment.

"True, but I know my worth, too," he said.

Ms. Reid nodded her head. "I don't doubt that you do. Settling is never the route to take, but settling for the moment in order to get to what you actually want… there's nothing wrong with that. You haven't even gotten the job yet, and you're already thinking negatively. Shake that off. We don't do that in here."

Ms. Reid was all for positivity and light. Things may not have been going his way, but this was a start. Synovi brushed a hand over his head and smirked.

"You be on my ass." He chuckled.

"And I'll continue to be as long as you're in this program. I want to see you win, and you will if I have any input. Now, three job interviews are what I like to hear. Do you need help with anything for those?"

"Nah. I still have my resume and everything from before. I should be good."

Ms. Reid clasped her hands. "Good. Then, we can move on to housing and discuss transportation. Are you still okay taking the bus?"

Synovi shrugged. "It's cool. Shit, it's free, so yeah. I still want my own wheels, though. A coo' reliable cash car. What I'd been saving is dwindling since I haven't been working."

"You're only paying your phone bill, right?" Ms. Reid inquired.

"Yeah, that's the only major one."

She glanced at his arm, noticing he had some new ink. "Looks like getting tatted is a bill too."

Synovi chuckled. "I'm done for a minute."

"Good. You have to go without some things that aren't a necessity right now."

She continued to talk as she wrote. Ms. Reid knew how it felt to only have a few dollars to her name and struggle to make it. As a college graduate who had to get it out of the mud with no family support, she played no games when it came to her job. She knew what the other side of hard work, prayer, faith, and discipline looked like.

She wanted Synovi to know what that felt like as well. Last year, he'd been saving up for a car and had almost reached his goal. After cashing his check one day and going into his room, the money he'd been saving, in what he thought was a secret stash spot, was missing. So was his old roommate.

It angered Synovi to his core that someone would steal from him, and he had no way of getting his funds back. GiGi had gotten onto him one too many times about not placing his money in a bank account. It took that incident for him to listen to her, but it was too late. Synovi had to start from the ground up all over again.

"Okay. We'll go over those numbers in a bit. Have you met with Mrs. Minnie about housing options again?"

"Last week. Everything she showed me was… I don't know. Dusty."

Ms. Reid chortled, holding a hand over her face. "Oh, goodness. You must not want to move out."

"It ain't that. I just want something nicer. I'm willing to wait a lil' longer for the ones she said were almost done getting built."

"Those are nice and in a good area. New shopping center, grocery stores, and restaurants."

Synovi nodded his head, liking the sound of all of that. "Yeah. That's where I need to be."

"Be sure to have her help you apply. There may be a waiting list, but it's probably not long right now."

"Bet. I'ma see if she's in her office when I leave here. Are y'all still gon' pay for the first and last month's rent?"

Mrs. Minnie said they would, but Synovi had to ask again.

"Yes. That's the plan, as long as you are able to cover everything else. Of course, we have resources if you need help, but that's why we're mapping it all out so you won't go into it blindly."

Rolling his tongue over his top row of teeth, Synovi shook his head.

"What's the matter?" Ms. Reid questioned.

"All of this shit is overwhelming. Then, me being out on my own. I ain't…" He paused and cleared his throat of the emotions that built up.

"It's okay. I understand."

"Nah. You don't unless you been by yourself all your life, trying to figure it out. I ain't ever been in a position to just be good or make it on my own. I always needed something from somebody. Mothafuckas who probably don't even care."

"I care, so let's start there. Life is rough, Synovi. You and I both know that, but does that mean we stop working hard for what we want? Absolutely not. What'd you just tell me? You know your worth? Well, act like it. Don't be ashamed of needing help. That's what I and other people are here for. Being prideful will get you nowhere, and you have places to be. Goals to scratch off this list," she said, sliding a piece of paper in front of him.

Synovi gritted his teeth, full of raw emotions. Ms. Reid always brought it out of him, and he hated it.

"Here. Look at this from when we first met."

Grabbing the list, Synovi read it over. More than half of the goals he wrote out had been scratched out, while some needed to be rewritten due to setbacks.

~~Get a job~~

~~Save $2,000 for a car~~

Get a car

Move into my new place within a year

~~Become more in tune with my feelings~~

Grow a relationship with Unique - maybe

~~Remember to congratulate myself~~

Seeing most of them crossed off made him realize maybe things weren't all bad.

"I need to rewrite the first two," he acknowledged.

"No. Keep them marked out. You accomplished those, and now it's time to set new ones. Backtracking means you're okay with the past. You've moved on from there and can't grow if you keep looking back," Ms. Reid said.

"Aye. How old are you again?" Synovi questioned. "You told me before."

"Old enough." She chuckled. Ms. Reid was almost thirty and didn't feel like it at all. "Now, write out some new goals while I call and see if Ms. Minnie can meet with you."

Synovi bobbed his head and grabbed a pen out of the holder on her desk. He had his dislikes about living in transitional housing, but having people who actually cared about his well-being wasn't one of them. Ms. Reid and every other staff weren't just there for a paycheck. Had they been, they would've quit a long time ago.

Mentally, the job itself was draining. Burnout was real, and self-care was highly suggested. The rewards from their hard work always paid off when the men met their goals and succeeded. As Synovi thought about what he needed to add, his phone vibrated in his lap. Picking it up, he noticed the unsaved number and almost declined it, but thought it might have been another job calling.

"Hello?" he answered.

"Hi. Can I speak with Synovi?" the woman asked.

"This is him."

"This is Torin. Do you have a minute to talk?"

Synovi was sure he had to be hearing her incorrectly. "You said this is who?" he questioned, voice a bit deeper than before.

On the other end of the phone, Torin rolled her eyes. She'd asked Racquel for his number and was now low-key regretting it.

"Racquel's sister, Torin. We met—"

"When you pulled a gun on me. What's up?"

Ms. Reid's head snapped his way. Her eyes squinted, and brows collided, forcing an indention to form in the middle of her forehead.

Torin sighed hard. "You're still on that?"

"I haven't heard an apology, so, yeah. I'm still on that. Is that why you asked your sister for my number?"

"Oh, my gosh," Torin huffed lowly.

She didn't know why his straight forwardness surprised her.

Their two encounters thus far should've let her know a simple conversation with Synovi wouldn't go in her favor. At least, not yet.

"That's not why, but we can discuss that later on. I was actually calling to see if you were interested in making some money," Torin said.

She had his attention before, but now more than anything.

"Yeah, I am."

Torin grinned. "I was hoping you said yes. Are you busy right now? I'd love to meet with you today and go over a few things."

"I'm wrapped up right now. What you gon' be on in a few hours?" Synovi questioned.

He loved how she was talking but wasn't jumping to be on her time. Torin glanced at her gold watch. She had a few people stopping by to pick up orders, but that was all.

"I'll be free."

"A'ight. Where should I meet you at?" Synovi questioned.

Since he was a potential employee, Torin should've met him at the main kitchen across town. No telling if he'd like her business proposal or not, Torin figured he could just come to her home. It wasn't like he hadn't been or wouldn't be all up and through there.

"You can come to my house. Do you need the address?"

"Yeah. Text it to me," he said.

"Sure thing. See you in a few hours."

Ms. Reid had hung up with Mrs. Minnie and was waiting on Synovi to explain what that phone call was about. Hearing him say someone had pulled a gun on him was unsettling, to say the least.

"You have this smirk on your face. What's going on with that?" she wondered.

"That phone call might be a job opportunity I actually like."

Ms. Reid smiled. "I like the sound of that. What would you be doing?"

"Cleaning."

A chuckle fell from Ms. Reid's mouth. "Um, you can't elaborate any more than that?"

"I don't know all the details yet. She asked me to come through in a few hours."

"Oh. Okay. That conversation sounded a bit personal. Is she a friend of yours? I know we've been working on your social skills."

Synovi tittered. "You talking like I can't make friends. I don't want them mothafuckas."

"It's okay to have at least one person in your corner that you can trust, Synovi. Don't be that way."

"You and GiGi," he offered.

"We're not your friends."

"Since when?" He smirked, making Ms. Reid shake her head.

"I don't know what I'm going to do with you. What time are you going to meet this *friend* of yours?"

He glanced at the time on his lock screen. "A few hours."

"Perfect. We can go over your savings and browse online for cars. Scoot your chair over here. We have some goals to keep scratching off, sir."

With his mood now better, Synovi drug his chair around to her side of the desk and got comfortable. Ms. Reid's words of encouragement had him ready to put some things in motion. The unexpected phone call from Torin only added to that. Synovi couldn't wait to see what she had up her sleeve, especially if it involved making money. From the looks of it, she knew how to do just that.

"You invited him over?" Leighton asked for the second time.

"The plane's turbulence must've made you hard of hearing. Yes! He's on his way here now," Torin huffed.

Leighton snickered as she walked through Dallas Love

Field Airport. "Girl, whatever. I'm just trying to see what you got going on over there."

"Business. That's all this is. You said I should hire someone for convenience, and that's what I'm trying to do."

"I did, but don't come calling me, talking about you fucked the help."

Torin snorted. "Bitch." She giggled. "I have no plans on doing anything with that boy. He's damn near Racquel's age."

"And you know this how?"

Torin's lips twisted to the side. She didn't know Synovi's age at all. She figured he had to be in the same age range as her sister. Why else would they know one another?

"Because I just do. Now, when are you returning home?" she asked, hearing a car door slam.

Rushing to the front window, she peeked out and spotted Synovi heading up her driveway. Torin tapped the screen of her phone for the time.

Hmm. Punctual. I like that.

"In a few days. I'm supposed to be back on Thursday, but you know how that goes," Leighton sighed.

She was a traveling loctician, and though it paid extremely well, it wore her out some days. Adding celebrity clientele to her list had boosted her. Yet, she wasn't about to throw in the towel any time soon.

"Yeah, I know. I'm proud of you and all that you do. Lunch plus a massage and pedicure are on me when you land," Torin let out as the doorbell resounded throughout her home.

"Ooh. He's there?" Leighton questioned giddily.

"Yes. Text me when you get to your hotel room. Love you."

"Okay. Love you, too."

Locking her phone, Torin slid it into the back pocket of her jeans and unlocked the door. Deeply, she inhaled and exhaled even more profoundly before pulling it open. No matter how much she coached herself on not getting caught up in Synovi's handsomeness, Torin failed. Miserably.

Her eyes weren't prepared to take him in as they roamed sporadically over his frame. It commanded the doorway and

Torin's entire focus. Distracted, she got lost in the lethal calmness of his eyes. *Gosh, they're dark. Haunted almost. Fucking gorgeous.* Torin's thoughts ran away from her, silently running right into Synovi.

As if he had a mic to her brain, he said, "Whatever you're trying to figure out, can we do that inside?"

"Oh," Torin chirped, stepping backward. "Sorry. Come in."

Fresh out of the shower, his natural scent and cologne filled the space and Torin's nostrils. Its intense woodsy yet citrus aroma caused her lids to flutter as she reminded herself that this meeting needed to remain strictly professional. It didn't matter how hard her nipples had just become or the flutters prancing about in her belly.

"Are you hungry?" she asked once the door was locked and she'd walked ahead of him.

Synovi's eyes dropped to her tiny waist and ass that sat up perfectly in her jeans. He licked his lips without realizing it. He chalked the action up to him being appreciative and wondering what she had cooked. The place smelled divine.

"Yeah," he replied lowly, stepping inside the kitchen.

"Okay. I'll fix you a plate. Have a seat."

Before he did so, Synovi eyed the various trays, dishes, and bowls of food. If he didn't know any better, he'd think she had just fed an army.

"You cook like this all the time?" he asked, deciding to pry into her business.

Torin glanced his way as she washed her hands and smiled. "Yes. I'm a chef."

"A real chef, or can you just cook real good?"

"Both." She laughed. "I have a culinary degree and have been doing this longer than you've probably been alive."

Synovi was going to let her slick comment about his age slide, but decided to nip her sly remarks in the bud before the conversation went left.

"If you want to know my age, ask that," Synovi spoke calmly.

Torin did want to know, and she hoped he was legal. *For business purposes,* she thought.

"When were you born?"

"Two thousand."

Synovi watched her exhale with relief, and he halfway smirked. *Yeah, I know.*

"Oh, okay. That's good."

"Yeah? For who?"

"Both of us. I mean, if you want the job I'm offering you, you have to be at least twenty-one."

Finally, he sat down, but then stood right back up. When he ambled over to the sink, Torin's breath caught in her chest at his sudden closeness. She scooted over to give him more space.

When he finished washing his hands and returned to his spot, it was back to business. "What does this job consist of? I was under the impression I was meeting you here to go over those details."

Torin stopped piling green beans onto his plate. "We will. I asked if you were hungry, and you said yes, so I'm fixing you a plate. If you want to get straight to business, we can."

The bite in her tone had returned, and Synovi loved it. It was clear she was trying to make up for their first encounter, and he appreciated that.

"I'd like to eat while doing so," he shared, watching her roll her eyes and then give him a tight smile.

"Would you also like to fix your own plate?"

"Nah. It looks like you got it taken care of. Thank you."

She smirked. "Oh, so he does have manners."

"And you found where you misplaced your hospitality."

Torin stared him down daringly. This back and forth was… dare she say, refreshing and tantalizing. *This boy better stop flirting with me.*

"I guess we're even, then," she said, placing his plate in the microwave.

Her knuckles stabbed digits four and five before pressing start. When it was done, she grabbed a fork from the drawer and hot sauce off the counter and walked his way. Synovi eyed the plate of smoked chicken wings, baked macaroni and cheese, green beans, honey cornbread, and black-eyed peas with smoked turkey throughout.

His head bowed without hesitation to bless his food, before it lifted and he reached for his fork. Torin sat across from him at the rectangular table, watching, waiting for his reaction. Synovi didn't know what to try first, but his tastebuds had a mind of their own.

Torin's hands stayed clasped in front of her as he gathered a generous amount of mac and cheese onto his utensil. Seeing the eye-widening appreciation cross his face as he chewed made her day.

"Good?" she queried.

"Fire as hell. How old are you, is the real question."

She chuckled as he tilted the red bottle with a yellow label, pouring the condiment over his beans before devouring his plate. His satisfaction and every other customer's was why she loved her profession. Cooking was done with love, and Torin had lots of it to give.

"Thank you, and twenty-six," Torin answered. "The women in my family had me in the kitchen early."

"I can tell. These black-eyed peas taste like my—" Synovi caught himself.

Torin waited. She wanted to know who her cooking reminded him of. When he continued to eat, she let it go. *Maybe that's a sore topic.*

"So, about this job position. You did an amazing job cleaning my place that day. I'd like to pay you to come by once or twice a week and do the same thing. Well, not all the house, but what needs cleaning."

"Yeah, that's coo'."

"Really?" Torin's voice spiked. She was not expecting him to readily agree, considering how they'd met.

Synovi chuckled and caught himself before it fully released. *Aww. He smiles. Gosh, it's as beautiful as he is.* Torin couldn't stay out of her head, but she was thankful her thoughts remained there.

"A few days out of the week isn't bad," Synovi said.

"It's not, but I also wanted you to work for my business. I mean, if you're up to it. I have four employees on payroll, but they're more so on the front end. Delivering meals, attending events with me, helping out in the kitchen if needed. It gets hectic some days. I wasn't sure if you had a job already, but I figured it couldn't hurt to ask. Plus, it seems like you really enjoyed it."

The intensity of Synovi's stare made Torin rewind the words she said in her head. She hoped she hadn't said anything to offend him. Staring at him for too long was crippling. Captivating. His dark orbs fascinated her to no end, leaving her wondering what he'd witnessed.

"What?" she questioned, finding her voice that sounded foreign to her ears.

"Relax."

That one word spoken in his deep tenor made Torin's body listen on command. It comforted her like a cool breeze after a muggy afternoon.

"I am relaxed," she fibbed.

"Now you are. You just talked without taking a breath as if you were trying to convince me."

"Isn't that what I'm supposed to do?" Humor laced her question.

"Nah. If I didn't want what you were offering, I would've never agreed to slide through. Nor would I be asking you to make me a second plate."

It was then she noticed his empty platter with nothing but bones on it. She laughed and stood from her seat.

"A man who likes to eat. I can appreciate that. You want everything?"

"If you don't mind," he replied humbly.

She didn't at all. Repeating her steps from earlier, Torin took him his plate and doubled back to grab him something to drink out of the fridge.

"Water, tea, apple juice, or ginger ale?" she asked.

"Are you going to eat?"

Her head peeked around the door. The curiosity in his voice sounded so sincere. She didn't know why that one question made her feel all mushy inside, but it had.

"I ate already."

"Oh, a'ight. A bottle of water and a ginger ale is coo'."

She returned to the table with his beverages and proceeded to watch him eat. The act was so intimate and such a damn turn-on. Torin hoped she wasn't coming off as a creep, but she couldn't help it. She assessed his facial features one by one, loving each respectively. Her favorites had to be the tattoo lining his hairline and the dimple in his right cheek that made its presence known when he chewed or made a particular facial expression.

Intrigued, Torin asked, "How many tattoos do you have?"

She spotted ink peeking from the collar of his shirt, inching up his neck. The ones adorning his arms held no color. In fact, none of them did. He preferred his body art etched in all black. Identical to his surname. Parallel to how he felt most days. The only race of women he dated. What people foolishly mistook his eye color as.

Synovi finished chewing and cleared his throat. "I lost count after ten."

"Which ones hurt the worst?" Torin queried.

Her interest in getting some new ink besides the few she already had was of no concern to Synovi. But he didn't want to be rude and not answer her.

"My stomach."

Immediately, her mind went to that day she saw him shirtless in her guest bedroom. She hadn't been given the opportunity to ogle his rear as she did his front side, which was a good thing. Torin had already gotten off track.

Done with her questioning, for now, Torin decided to wait on giving him the full breakdown of his position. The two stood simultaneously when he finished his plate three minutes later.

Synovi eyed her suspiciously.

"What?" Torin asked.

"What you standing for? I got it."

She moved away from the table, pushing her chair in. "Oh, okay. I'll just put this food away. Would you like a to-go plate?"

Synovi's chest tightened as she strutted toward the island. Torin was being too nice, too soon, and it had him conflicted. She'd called him over for one thing, but he was catching a different vibe and wasn't sure if he should rock with it or do what he always did: draw back.

When Torin's eyes landed on him, silently repeating the question without moving her mouth, Synovi nodded his head yes.

"Yeah. That's coo'. 'Preciate it."

"No problem," Torin mumbled softly, mind reeling.

What's his story? she thought, grabbing storage containers to pack food inside. No matter how long she'd been cooking, Torin still always made too much. With multiple meal orders a week, she always cooked a bit extra for herself and whoever in her family wanted some. Racquel and their mama being the top two on her list. Next came her neighbor, Blaise, a single mother of the cutest little girl. Torin made sure they were always good.

Out of habit and wanting to show his appreciation for a bomb meal, Synovi washed every dirty dish his eyes came across. Then, he proceeded to wipe down the table and island. Torin stood back, stunned at his efforts. He hadn't asked, nor had he been told to do so; Synovi just did what he felt needed to be done.

"Thank you for that," Torin said as they finally made their way into her living room.

Synovi sat on the couch, eyeing all the paperwork she had laid out on the wooden coffee table. For a second there, he thought she had lured him over for him to stuff his face and fill his belly.

"It's nothing. You got it all situated, huh?" he guessed.

"Not quite, but that's why we're here. I'm assuming house-cleaning or anything of the sort isn't your profession?"

"Not at all, but I enjoy it."

She loved to hear that. "Well, that's good. So, technically, you wouldn't be working for me as an employee. You'd be an independent contractor I hired for services."

"I need to set up pricing for something you initiated?" Synovi questioned quizzically.

"Yes. Unless you'd like me to throw some numbers out there. I had a few written out."

She handed him a piece of paper with the numbers, hours, and days of the week listed. Synovi scanned it over, calculating his take home pay in his head. It was much more than he'd made at Freddy's. Much more than he'd ever made at any job.

"My house is pretty big, so is one-fifty an hour fine?" Torin questioned. "We can base it off square footage if you'd like."

"Nah," Synovi said, trying to keep his composure. "I'm coo' with that. How many bedrooms you got?"

"Three. Along with three bathrooms and a finished basement. I converted it into a space for my business."

"What's the name of it?" Synovi asked.

Torin's eyes lit up as she shifted her posture. "Kaine's Kitchen."

"Catchy."

She giggled. "I know, right? I came up with it myself."

Synovi wasn't surprised by that. She had to be somewhat creative to have her own business and be successful.

"You're not going to need deep cleaning every week," he said, taking in her living room. It was tidy.

"No, but the kitchen will need it at least twice a week."

He nodded, running numbers again. "And Kaine's Kitchen?"

"Eh. That's more so on an as-needed hire."

"And how much will you need me?"

Torin's spine tingled at his question. The muscles near her hair follicles contracted, forcing the hair on her arm to rise. She prayed her nipples didn't follow suit. Torin couldn't tell him she'd need him in her space as much as she needed a new electric mixer.

Okay… maybe that's a want, but still.

"I have big events almost every weekend, and some during the week. I'll let you know in advance if it's an out-of-town trip, which most are already on the calendar."

"So, I need to keep my schedule open?" he hinted.

"Yes, that would be nice. Only if you're available. Like I said, you don't work for me, so you can decline at any time. For Kaine's Kitchen, you can come up with your own pricing. It's a bit more tedious than housework."

Synovi let her words marinate and realized she'd just basically made him an entrepreneur. The thought shook him, but he was prepared to put the work in.

"I can handle it."

"Perfect. Before we start filling forms out so that I can properly pay you, I want to apologize if I came off unprofessional. Those weren't my intentions," she sighed. "Naturally, I'm a giver and love to feed people so it was out of habit to ask you if you were hungry."

His silence smothered Torin. Unmoving, he trapped her with an intensity that made her pussy pulse. Synovi couldn't figure her out and it unnerved him. He had to go silent before he let his thoughts spill and ruin the moment.

"I make you nervous?" Synovi asked.

That wasn't the question he wanted to ask her, but it was the safest. Or so he thought.

"Does it seem that way?" Torin countered.

Of course, she couldn't just give him an answer.

"It does, but maybe I'm picking up on something else." He shrugged slightly. That quickly, Synovi had come to the conclusion of the uneasy yet magnetic energy between them. *She ain't had a man in her space in a minute. That's what it is.*

"Maybe so," Torin said, not feeding into the guessing game he wanted to play.

"I accept your apology, though. There was nothing unprofessional about offering me a meal. The shit was fire."

She blushed. "Thank you. Should we shake hands to seal this new business venture?"

"No," Synovi replied, nixing her suggestion.

He wanted to keep his distance, only if a seat between them, from Torin. Their propinquity on the cream cushions had already forced him to battle temptation. Touching her would make him lose the fight.

Instead, Synovi's limbs stretched forward, securing the stack of papers. He shuffled through them until he found the 1099 form and handed it to her. "You can make sure all the information on here is straight, though. That's all the sealing I need."

Torin cackled. "Back to business that quickly."

"That's all I'm here for."

I hope it remains that way, he thought.

eight

With one too many earring options to choose from, Jade's lips twisted in contemplation. She stepped out of their bathroom, holding three styles in her hand. This was the last touch to her outfit and she had to make it count. For once in her life, she didn't want to be the friend out of the group who was running behind because of her indecisiveness.

"Oooh, you look pretty," Skylar, Jade's nine-year-old daughter, complimented.

She was seated on a pillow on the side of their bed with a five-hundred piece puzzle before her. With more of the pieces inside the flipped over top, Skylar had no intentions of leaving her spot until every cut-out cardboard displayed what she knew would be a beautiful flower garden.

"Thank you, baby. Can you choose which earring matches best with Mommy's outfit?" Jade requested.

"The diamond tassels clash with your necklace, so not those. The diamond studs will be blocked by your hair, unless you tuck it. So, hoops it is. I'd take the necklace off, though. It's not really fitting."

Jade couldn't help but laugh at her skilled evaluation. She'd gone into detail as if she were a salesman, needed commission, and rent was due.

"Hoops it is then, my love. How's your puzzle coming along?" Jade asked, unclasping her necklace as she walked inside their closet.

"I'll be done before you get back home!" Skylar yelled, then squealed when Silas stepped inside the room. "Daddy!"

She rushed him with no worries as to if he would be able to lift her and hold Kalie, her three-year-old sister, at once. Silas was a pro at this now. Her hands snaked around his neck.

"What's going on, baby girl?" he asked, kissing her cheek.

"Nothing. Putting together a puzzle and watching Mommy get dressed."

"Where she think she going, huh?" Silas queried, lowering Skylar back onto the ground.

He knew she didn't know where his wife was trying to sneak off to, but he wanted an answer. It was Friday afternoon and family time. On cue, Jade stepped out of the closet with a pair of Macallan Slingback pumps in her hand.

Seeing her all dolled up made his heart skip a beat and his blood pressure rise. "Stepping out?"

"Hey, babe. Yeah. Simone asked me to go to this day party with her. Do I look nice?"

Silas licked his lips. " Yeah, you do. Sky, you and KK go to y'all room for a minute."

"But, Daddy. My puzzle," Skylar pouted.

"It'll be here waiting for you. I need to talk to Mommy in private."

Her lips poked out, reminding him so much of Jade, he couldn't help but smirk. With her arms outstretched, she received Kalie and walked out of their bedroom and down the hall to theirs. Silas pushed the door closed and locked it behind them.

Jade's brow raised. "Uh, oh. I'm in trouble."

"A day party at five in the afternoon, Jade? You know Fridays are reserved for us and the girls."

"It's one Friday out of the month, though, baby. Plus, I already agreed weeks ago. I'll be home by eleven."

Silas loosened his tie and shook his head. "It's not about the time you'll return. But you're just now running this by me. Had I not come home straight from work, you would've dipped out without saying a word."

"Not true. I would've called to let you know I was heading out. What's the big deal? You don't normally trip about where I'm going," she asked, sliding her heels on.

Maybe that needs to change, he thought, walking into their closet. He slipped his tie from around his neck, placing it in the hamper designated for dry cleaning. Next, went his button-up before he removed his shoes. Reaching low to place them on the shelving, a red object caught his attention.

Picking it up, a befuddled expression settled on his face. "Jade!"

His shout made her flinch and damn near break an ankle as she rushed to the closet entrance. "What's the matter?"

"Whose is this?" Silas asked, tone stern.

Jade could've pissed her pants, seeing him holding up Synovi's lighter. He hadn't realized he lost it until he blamed D'Marco for stealing it. She'd seen him spark one too many blunts with the same device. Sometimes, he just flicked the spark wheel, loving the sound and the flame it ignited.

"Oh. That's Simone's," Jade answered nervously.

Get it to-fucking-gether, she scolded.

"Why was it lying on my side of the closet?"

"Can it not be there or something? I exchanged purses, and it must've fallen out. I stole it from her so she wouldn't smoke another cigarette while I was with her."

Silas's dark-brown eyes tightened as he gritted his teeth. Tossing the lighter on the island of things filled with her clutter from exchanging purses, he turned away from her and continued undressing.

His angry dismissal of her had Jade panicking. Thinking quickly before she blew her cover, she walked up behind him. Her dainty hands slid up the front of his white tank, caressing his solid stomach. He had no six-pack, but Silas was still fit to be in his early forties. Having young daughters and what used to be an active sex life kept him in shape when he didn't have time to hit the gym.

Kissing down his shoulder, Jade unbuckled his belt. The latch on his tailor-fit trousers came undone next, and her hands inched inside his briefs. Thickness filled her hand, and Silas turned to face her. He pulled his tank top over his head, and her lips replaced the cloth. Licking his nipple, Jade felt him grip her silk-pressed bob, forcing her to look at him.

"You know I love you, right?" Silas asked.

Jade bobbed her head as best as she could with his firm grip still intact. "Mhm."

"I'll do anything for you and my girls," he confessed.

"I know, baby." She stroked his dick and tried lowering into a squat, but he stopped her.

Silas stared deeply into her eyes. "Anything, Jade."

"I know you will. I just don't want you mad at me."

Kissing her lips, Silas walked her backward until they were at the island. Turning her around, Jade gripped the cold granite and her short leather skirt pooled at her waist. Moving her panties aside, Silas rubbed his dick along her wet slit. A huff as if he were frustrated escaped him. Planting himself inside his wife had never felt better and the first stroke caused Jade to venture into an oblivious state.

"Oh, my… Siiiilas," she breathed, eyes crossing.

Jade was pleased and surprised at his rigidness and planned to cherish this moment. They didn't come often. Both on a mission to out fuck one another, Silas pounded into her with a point to prove. He was convinced she'd forgotten who the hell he was and what she meant to him. For five minutes straight, Silas gave Jade the best dick she'd received from him in weeks.

"You feel so damn good, Mrs. Lewis," he spoke huskily against her ear before sinking his teeth softly in her neck.

"Y-You feel even better," Jade moaned.

Her breaths were shaky, mimicking her legs as she climaxed. She contracted around him, milking his dick of every last drop of nut.

"Arrgghh!" Silas's head fell against her back, and his dick softened immediately after.

With fluttering lids, Jade's foggy vision focused on the red BIC next to her Louis Vuitton shades. Almost getting caught had gotten her some A1 pipe from her husband, and she wasn't mad at it.

I'ma have to piss him off more often, she thought with a satisfied smirk.

Synovi hated crowds.

Specifically, the party and kick it kind of gatherings. Being surrounded by so many people who he hoped only had intentions on having a good time and nothing disastrous, wasn't Synovi's vibe at all. Granted, at his age, it would've made perfect sense if he were interested. Even with him temporarily living next door to a club, he saw no purpose in indulging. He was too low-key. Too in his head about whether or not he deserved to be enjoying the moment.

"My nigga!" D'Marco yelled in his ear. Semi-drunk, he leaned into his boy. "This hoe is live."

It was D'Marco's idea to hit the day party. Earlier in the week after his link up with Torin, Synovi returned and gave him limited details about his new job. D'Marco wanted to celebrate.

"Aye, bruh. You secured a solid ass job. That's something to be proud about. Bottles and blunts on me." Whether he felt like he deserved the moment or not, D'Marco made sure to remind him he did.

Juvie's wasn't your typical location to host a day party, but that meant nothing to the local rapper, Yayo, and the crowd of people he and his sister, Miya, brought out. The restaurant had been transformed into the perfect setup for a twenty-seventh birthday bash day party.

Drinks were plentiful and the abundance of food available was just what the people needed to soak up their liquor. Synovi, D'Marco, and a few of his homeboys had been posted up in the large area in the back, before making their way inside. With three DJs spinning, ensuring to satisfy the spread of people's musical taste and encouraging a good turn up, the crowd vibed out to "Diana".

The late Pop Smoke's raspy voice blared through the speakers. Women's hips swayed and fingers snapped as the men bobbed their heads. The scene inside the restaurant was much chiller than the opposite side of the door, and that was exactly where Synovi wanted to remain. They found a spot near the bar and posted up, taking in the scene.

As reluctant as she'd been about going out with Chelsea, Torin was always down for a good time. Any chance for her to get dolled up and take a break from her strenuous schedule was a plus. She hardly stepped out, but when she did, she was sure to break a few necks.

"Let's go see who's all in the back," Chelsea suggested.

It took them damn near twenty minutes just to get through the entrance, secure a section, and now she wanted to leave. Torin wasn't feeling it. Whoever was meant to see her and vice versa would. If not, they could catch her another day if they were lucky.

"Y'all can go. I'm good right here," she replied.

Chelsea told her okay and that'd they be right back. She and her two other friends stepped down from the section, weaving through the congregation. Torin didn't mind sitting pretty by herself. What she didn't like was the questioning stares from men and women alike. Many recognized her as the face of *Kaine's Kitchen* and its viral videos, plus bomb food, while others associated her with her ex.

The hoes with mean mugs and screw faces had either fucked Don, wanted to, or heard about him. It'd been years and their breakup was still something the city gossiped about. Had Torin been the type to have stuck it out with Don, she was sure there'd be much more chatter around her name and not for anything good.

Thankfully, she'd made a name for herself, was highly respected wherever she went, and didn't have to slide a bitch today because she would. Along with Leighton, who'd returned from her stay in Dallas that morning.

While she could've stayed in bed all day and gotten some rest, she wasn't letting Torin hit the town alone. All she needed was at least five hours of sleep to recharge. If not that, the tequila and Red Bull in her cup would do the trick. Plus, she was sure a few of her boy toys would be in attendance. Leighton kept her a roster full of men with deep pockets who weren't stingy about going inside of them for her.

"You good?" Leighton asked.

"Yeah. She wanted me to go outside, but I'm good," Torin answered.

She finished off her Don Julio Reposado and orange-pineapple mixture before placing the clear plastic cup on the table. Going inside her designer bag embroidered with FF motif, she popped the top on her Mentos gum container, placing a round in her mouth. She didn't want her breath to smell anything like what she'd been sipping.

Sitting back, she watched as Leighton flirted with a hand-some man with creamy, caramel skin, rocking a messy bun. Men with hair you could wrap a ponytail holder around weren't Torin's preference. Leighton, on the other hand, didn't mind as long as his paper was as lengthy as his tresses. His dick, too, because the word small didn't exist in her world.

"Who don' got your ass out of the house and from in front of the stove?"

Torin's focus shifted to her left, where Vince, a mutual associate of hers, stood. His hand was wrapped around the neck of a chilled bottle. She smiled upon recognition.

"You should already know the answer to that," she said, as they embraced in a friendly hug. "What you doing out?"

"Trying to see what I can see." Vince smirked. "You know the hoes gon' pop out for any occasion."

"Clearly." Torin chuckled. "You ain't missing out on the action."

Vince was a well-known bachelor throughout the city and had been for years. The women who flocked to him knew this, yet still found themselves wrapped in his web of charm and flashiness. Torin would never understand why his lifestyle intrigued women, but she got it. It was the same one Don portrayed as if he weren't in a relationship. That was why he and Vince had been friends for so long.

From the outside looking in, every woman wanted the lifestyle men showed them they could have; not the one they actually lived. Torin thought for sure Vince would scale back after Don's trip up state, but by the looks of it, he had no plans to. The flashiness and being on the scene was what ultimately had his boy booked and sentenced.

"You probably right." Vince chuckled. "You been good, though?"

Whenever she came in contact with anyone close to Don, especially one of his niggas, they always asked how she'd been. The truth was, they knew exactly how she was living: like the boss ass woman she was. Some genuinely cared, like Vince, but Torin knew they were reporting her status to Don. Torin didn't need him checking for her unless he had a check for her.

"Yep. Your mom ordered some plates from me the other day," she said.

"Word? And she ain't even say shit. I'ma have to hit you up for a lil' something I got coming up."

Now, he was talking her language.

"Okay. Just let me know when."

"Bet. I'ma hit you up on Instagram."

Torin nodded and Vince went on his way. She was thankful he hadn't asked for her number. Between Chelsea and DJ, she knew one of them had probably given Don her new number. He hadn't reached out, per her request, over a year ago, so she was grateful for that.

"Girl, Vince is such a hoe," Leighton said, coming to stand by her.

Torin snickered. "What's new, honey? Who were you chopping it up with?"

"That nigga Nudy's fine ass. He been on me heavy ever since I seen him at the Future concert some months back."

"You know I don't care for men with hair, but he's fine."

"Mhm. Real mothafuckin' fine. You want another drink?"

Torin nodded her head. Chatting with Vince had made her sober up some. Before they could get out of the section and head to the bar, the DJ decided to turn up on them one time. As soon as they heard the piano keys at the beginning of "Pop It", the duo stayed planted where they were.

Sexily, Torin rolled her hips before putting an arch in her back and doing exactly what the song said. Her low-sitting, sleek, twenty-four-inch ponytail draped over her shoulder as she put on a show. Torin wasn't new to clubbing. She and Leighton had experienced the nightlife early in their adult years. As they ventured into their respective careers and focused on what really mattered, it became less appealing.

Right now, though, they were turning the fuck up. Almost every woman in the building had the same posture as Torin until Megan Thee Stallion's verse came on. There were certain lines you could only shake ass to, and others you rapped word for word and did both.

"Young bitch lit, you know I'ma shake sum'. If he got money, you know I'ma take some." Leighton meant every word as Torin followed up with the next line.

"Whoever I'm fucking these bitches want next. You eating my leftovers, that's not a flex," she rapped.

Bitches ain't fuckin' with me and this jewelry.

Holding up her iced-out wrist, the diamonds on her Audemars danced. She ran her fingers over the diamond Cuban link chain around her neck and smiled brightly. Torin had a healthy spending habit on kitchen appliances, house decor, and jewelry. That was okay with her, though, because she could afford it. Her jeweler, Naaziq, looked forward to seeing her face at least once a month.

The day party looked like a nightclub as everyone turned

up. Across the way, in another section of the lounge, Jade, Simone, and some of their homegirls were tossing back shots of D'Ussé. Jade was on her third one, needing to keep the high Silas sent her out of the door on. She almost didn't want to leave, but had already been assigned as the designated driver.

"I'm so mad my baby daddy and his friends are here," Simone fussed.

Jade used a napkin to wipe her mouth. "I don't know why you thought he wouldn't be. He has to keep his eyes on you," she snickered.

"And I'm trying to keep my eyes on that."

Lust dripped from Simone as she licked her lips. Jade didn't know which man she was talking about; there were too many in the vicinity. Yet, the one who caught her attention was just the one she wanted to see.

"Look at all them fucking tattoos on him. Whew. Got a bitch hot." Simone chuckled, fanning herself.

Jade almost broke her neck. "Um, no."

"What you mean no? Ma'am, you're married, not blind. You can't tell me he isn't good looking."

Actually, Jade could tell her much more about Synovi besides his looks. The thing about sneaking around in her marriage was that she had to do just that. She hadn't even told her sister that she stepped out on Silas and she'd never regretted it until this moment. Showing her hand would mean she'd have to confess about her affair, which she never planned to do. Jade was taking this with her to the grave.

She gulped the water she'd asked for and cleared her throat. "Yeah, he's handsome. Looks way too young, though."

"Not to me," Simone chirped.

Her sister's thirsty behavior had Jade ready to knock her upside the head. She couldn't lie, though, Synovi looked delectable in the clothes she'd just bought him earlier that week. The white Polo crewneck and denim jeans were simple, yet Synovi made it look like a million bucks. The white and red Pumas on his feet wouldn't be as clean once he left the function, but there were more where they came from. A single gold bracelet, a gift from GiGi, slightly dangled from his wrist and he sported a fresh haircut.

Jealousy bubbled in her gut as she noticed a few women gawk at him. They did it boldly, too, yet Synovi paid them no mind. His gaze was transfixed on the beauty making her way through the crowd, in his direction.

Torin was the type of pretty that captured your attention beyond looks. You could feel her aura as she passed you or entered your space. A few people stopped her on her way to the bar, and Synovi could've sworn he felt his heart pound a bit quicker when she smiled brightly and laughed at something he figured was beyond funny.

He looked on as she tapped Leighton, whispered in her ear, and they snickered together. Synovi wanted to know what was so amusing so he could repeat it just to see her enchanting grin.

You trippin', he thought as she and Leighton finally made it to the opposite end of the bar. From his position, Synovi had a clear view of her fit and he nodded his head at the nice switch up of attire he'd previously seen her in. Gone were her lounge, comfortable clothing. Torin figured if she was getting out of the house, she might as well show some skin and enjoy the warm weather KC decided to bless them with for the weekend.

The end of her lightly frayed denim shorts played peek-a-boo with the cuffs of her butt cheeks. Her white, backless body suit had her breasts sitting lovely, while the red, white, and blue Fendi Mania logo boots set the look off. They stopped right at her calves.

"Whoever that girl is, got him in a trance," Simone whispered in Jade's ear.

Weirdly, both sisters were still watching Synovi's moves. Simone for her own personal reasons, and Jade because… well, why the hell not? She, too, wanted to know who Torin was and why Synovi hadn't broken his concentration.

Waiting for her drink to be made, Torin aimlessly peered around the lounge. Eerily, she felt eyes on her and began searching for the culprit. Her head swiveled to the left, spotting

Synovi immediately. While his height would've been the main reason he stood out, that wasn't the case this time.

He'd garnered the attention from the ladies due to his fine ass ducking away in the corner, trying to keep a low profile. Torin couldn't help but chuckle at the relaxed scowl she was sure he didn't know he was rocking. It was so damn sexy, she had to lick her lips.

"Oop. Ain't that your lil' friend," Leighton jested.

"Mhm. I'ma go speak."

Leighton sipped her drink. "He looks like he doesn't want anyone in his space."

"Anyone but me. I'll be right back."

Saying excuse me more than a few times, Torin finally squeezed through the crowd , until she stood directly in front of Synovi. It took everything in her not to bury her face in his chest and latch on to him like a newborn to a tit.

Why does he always smell so good? My God!

Regardless of his minimal funds, Synovi never lacked on his appearance or hygiene. That was one thing he would never sacrifice. Plus, he knew how to make shit stretch and last. He smelled of Boss Hugo Infinite and marijuana. The mixture was intoxicating and had Torin feeling tipsier than the liquor in her cup.

"Hi," she beamed.

Synovi chucked his chin upward. "What's good?"

"I wasn't expecting to see you here."

"I wouldn't expect you to see me anywhere."

Torin shifted her weight to one side and pursed her lips. "We being mean today, or do you still have manners?"

Synovi smirked and her clit produced a heartbeat of its own.

"Nah. I ain't trying to be mean to you. Who you here with?"

Torin looked over her shoulder for Leighton. She was still in the same spot with Nudy back in her face.

"My best friend. You?"

"Couple niggas I'm coo' with. Thought you had a lot to get done before Easter on Sunday," he reminded her.

Torin's eyes brightened. She'd mentioned having to do so much to prepare for the holiday and the influx of orders she'd received. Plus, other engagements.

"Not you remembering I said that and calling me out." She chuckled.

"I don't forget much. Only things that don't matter."

"Oh. So, I matter to you?"

"You can try to."

His answer was more honest than she needed or expected. It damn near made her want to take a step back from him, but she was stuck in place. In his presence, planted, captivated by his allure. Torin felt like a goofy for not wanting to move.

"I'll remember that for later. You not drinking?" Torin asked, noticing he didn't have a cup in his hand.

"I don't drink like that."

"So, what do you do?"

"Torin."

The way he lowly grumbled her name made her body shudder. She giggled as her frame literally quivered in front of him.

"Boy, don't say my name like that. I almost forgot I promised to keep things professional between us." She laughed, and Synovi put an end to the sound immediately.

"Promises can be broken."

Torin blinked twice and thirstily searched for her straw with her mouth. She missed it a few times, too focused on Synovi staring at her. *Those damn eyes.*

"Relax. I'm just fucking with you."

Yeah, okay, she thought and swallowed the lump that formed in her throat.

"Mhm. What are you doing when you leave here?"

"You nosey like your sister. Y'all must've inherited that trait from y'all mama."

Torin sniggered. "Actually, I got mine from my daddy. Thank you very much. What'd yours give you? Impatience?"

"I wouldn't know. Never met the nigga."

"Oh," Torin exclaimed. "I'm sorry to hear that."

"Don't be. Why you wanna know what I'm doing, though?"

Glancing to her left, Torin noticed Jade still staring at them. She peeped her the minute she invaded Synovi's space, and she'd been tuned in since. Torin was seconds away from walking over to their section and asking her what the issue with her eyes was, but then it hit her.

"Your mama has been mean mugging me since I walked over here," she joked.

Synovi frowned. He knew his mama hadn't brought her ass to a day party and she couldn't even handle her responsibilities as a parent.

"What?" he pressed, following where she was looking. His nostrils flared when he noticed Jade crazily staring them down. "That ain't my damn mama."

"Could've fooled me." Torin chuckled and focused back on him. She made Synovi do the same as she used her index finger to turn his head. Whoever she was, clearly had an issue, but that had nothing to do with Torin.

Jade saw red. Actually, red and blue lights as she struggled to contain her anger. She was sure she'd be going to jail if she acted on her urges and smashed a bottle across Torin's head. Since she couldn't do that and cause a scene behind a man who wasn't her husband, she pulled her phone out to send him a text.

> Really, Synovi? You just gon' have that bitch in
> your face like that while I'm right here.

Her leg bounced as she waited for him to acknowledge her message. Feeling his phone vibrate, Synovi grabbed it from his pocket, glanced at the screen with no expression, and slid it back into its place. Jade chuckled angrily and stood up from the couch.

"Where you going?" Simone asked.

"To speak to someone. I'll be right back."

Out of the corner of his eye, Synovi saw her walking in their direction. Jade's eyes were trained on him, and the look he gave her made her stop dead in her tracks. She'd never seen him look at her with such disgust since they'd met. Synovi wanted her to walk over to them if she had the guts. He was going to ignore her ass like she claimed her husband did.

Taking the hint, Jade pivoted and headed toward the restrooms. "Why would he embarrass me like that?" she hissed as angry tears filled her eyes. "And who the fuck is that bitch all in his face?"

Jade didn't have an answer to either question, but she promised she'd be getting one before the night was over.

With his mood almost ruined completely, Synovi gave his attention to Torin, who still hadn't left his side. He didn't know what it was about her, but he didn't mind the way she seemed to insert herself into his life. So far, it seemed she was in it for the better.

"I'm not taking a shot, man," Synovi said as the bartender went to fetch two shots of tequila.

She'd gotten him to move away from the wall and sit with her at the bar. They'd been there all of ten minutes and she was trying to get him to loosen up.

"My name isn't man, and okay, fine. Glad to know you're not easily influenced." She chuckled.

The glasses were slid in front of them with two lime wedges on a saucer.

"You taking both?" Synovi questioned.

"If I take both, you'll be driving me home."

It was a joke, but obviously Synovi didn't find humor in it. "Good thing I know where you live."

Torin eyed him before picking up one of the glasses. Tossing it back, she grimaced and stuck her tongue out.

"Whew. I'm giving this other one to Leighton."

She swiveled in her seat in search of her. Whatever she and Nudy were discussing had them in a deep conversation before he realized Torin was trying to get his attention.

"Yo' girl calling you," Nudy said, nodding his head Torin's way.

Leighton looked behind her and said, "Let me go see if she's good."

"A'ight. I'm 'bouta head out. You straight?"

She smirked. "Always."

Watching Nudy's back as he maneuvered through the crowd that parted and made room for his departure, Leighton confirmed what she already knew. *I'ma run that nigga's pockets for sure.* It was the only logical thing to do since he'd taken up her time. Fair was fair.

"Leigh. Come take this shot," Torin said as she approached them.

"Oh, lawd," Leighton tittered. "You know I've been drinking clear. Why didn't he take it?"

"I don't drink," Synovi answered.

"Good to know." Leighton tossed the shot back with ease and didn't frown at all. Instead, she smiled and said, "I'm guessing you two made up from the stunt she pulled."

Torin playfully rolled her eyes. "Let's leave the past in the past, shall we? That's old news, right?"

When she turned on the barstool to face him, Synovi couldn't help but nod and agree. "Yeah. Time to give her somethin' new to talk about."

Torin hated she couldn't decipher the true meaning behind his words. She was grateful he was talking, though, so she'd listen to whatever he had to say. It didn't matter if it made sense or not.

When commotion from the back patio tried making its way inside the lounge, Synovi hopped up from his seat. He was already stuck in a corner and didn't want to be there if the fight escalated. Sensing his urgency to head out, Torin climbed from her chair as well, stumbling in the process. Synovi's eyes met her glossy ones.

"Where yo' keys at?"

"My purse."

"Hand 'em here."

He'd asked her to do one thing while he did another. Pulling her through the lounge and gang of people who decided to stay until shit jumped off, Synovi glanced around to see if he could spot Jade and D'Marco. Her eyes were on him like he was her prey. It was eating her alive, not knowing who Torin was or what she meant to him.

Nodding his head toward the exit, Jade took that as him wanting to speak to her, so she began gathering her things to head out as well. The truth was, Synovi was motioning for her to leave before things got crazy. She had more to lose if gunfire erupted.

"Aye, boah," D'Marco called out to Synovi. "You good?"

"Yeah. I'll get up with you niggas later on."

D'Marco gave him a head nod and they slapped hands before parting ways.

"How do I know I can trust you to drive her home?" Leighton quizzed as they finally made it through the crowd and outside.

The front of the lounge was still packed with partiers as well as the parking lot. Thanks to daylight saving, the sun wouldn't set for another hour or so.

"You can't. Just know you'll see her later," Synovi said, making Leighton dramatically place a hand on her chest.

"Well, excuse the fuck out of me." She laughed. "Torin, you sure he's all the way together up there?"

Playfully, Torin ran a hand over the back of Synovi's head, loving his soft waves. "Feels like it, but we'll see. You leaving?"

"Girl, yeah. About to see what Nudy is on."

"Okay. Be safe. Love you."

Leighton told her she loved her, too, and headed to her car. She was stopped multiple times by a few people, so the journey there took longer. Back inside the club, Jade tried to convince her crew to call it an evening.

"Come on, y'all. We should leave," Jade suggested.

Simone waved her off. "Girl, we're good. You see security getting the situation under control. If you trying to get back to your husband, just say that. We'll find a ride home."

The group chuckled, but Jade took that as her opportunity to ditch them. Silas had been so far removed from her mind since spotting Synovi, it wasn't even funny. As she made it outside, Jade's head scanned the parking lot for the duo. Spotting them walking toward a coke white Range Rover, she sped her walk up.

"You don't really have to drive me home. I'm fine," Torin said as they made it to the passenger side.

Synovi unlocked the car. "Get in."

"Are you always going to be this bossy?"

Before he had a chance to tell her yes, Jade yelled his name. "Synovi! Really?"

Torin drew her head back. "You sure that ain't your mama calling your name like that?" She chuckled.

His jaw flexed as he watched Jade approach them. He gave her the silent treatment, wondering why she decided to put on a fucking show. Pulling the door open, he bobbed his head for Torin to get inside. When she didn't move, he exhaled and used his manners.

"Please get inside. Let me handle her."

"I know you hear me talking to you!" Jade screeched. "Who the fuck is she?"

Torin climbed in the seat and licked her lips. "I only got in here because I don't know what type of situation you got going on and I am a little tipsy, but know this. If you don't handle her, I will."

When she patted her purse, Synovi got the hint immediately. He handed her the keys, shut the door, which was his nonverbal reply, and walked around to the front of the truck. Steam was practically emitting from Jade as she stood there with her arms crossed.

"You look ridiculous. Go back inside," Synovi said with disgust, but so calmly, it enraged her even more.

"You think being disrespectful in my face is cute? I let you slide—"

"You let who slide?" he challenged.

Jade took a step back and Synovi took two forward.

"I don't owe you no fucking loyalty, a'ight? I'm tired of having this conversation with you. Yeah, I care about you but you pushing it with this territorial shit. You are not my bitch, Jade. Stop embarrassing yourself."

Her eyes watered at his harsh words, and she shoved him in the chest. "Fuck you," she spat angrily. "Fuck you, Synovi. If you cared about me, you wouldn't be leaving with her. Who is she? You told me you were single."

He didn't care to answer her first question. "Why you out here wildin' like you don't belong to someone else?"

"Because I love you and my feelings are hurt, okay?" Jade hissed. "That's why."

Synovi drew his head back. With a shake of it, he put some distance between them. "Nah. You talking crazy now."

Inside her truck, Torin rolled her eyes and pressed on the horn. "Wrap this shit up, buttercup!" she yelled, even though they couldn't hear her.

"What the fuck did she say?" Jade growled, trying to walk around to the passenger side.

Synovi snatched her back so quickly, she almost caught whiplash.

"She can come around here if she wants to." Torin smiled behind the tint.

"Is you fucking slow?" Synovi hissed through gritted teeth. "Take yo' ass back in there."

She jerked out of his grasp. "If you get in this truck, we're done."

Synovi almost laughed but there wasn't shit funny at the moment. Jade had pissed him smooth off with her antics. He gave her a once over, wondering how shit between them even got to this point, and pulled the door open. Torin had already started her truck up.

"I guess we're done."

With that, he hopped in and pulled off as soon as Jade jumped back out of the way. Dumbfounded and even more furious than before, she stood in the parking lot, staring at the back of the truck as it pulled onto the main street. Her moment of disbelief was interrupted by a group of women that had been searching for parking.

"Are you saving that spot for someone?" the driver yelled out the window.

Jade walked off, leaving them to it. She couldn't believe Synovi had pulled this on her and she wanted nothing but revenge. It was stated that it was best served cold and she was about to remind him just how chilly it could get.

nine

Torin had so much to say and she thought about being quiet, figuring what he had going on was none of her business, but the liquor… it was on her ass and she had to say something. Their entire fallout reminded her too much of her and Don's, and it triggered memories.

"So, my assumptions were right," she said.

Synovi exhaled. "Whatever you assumed, I can guarantee it ain't the truth."

"Okay… so put me up on game, then. Is that your girlfriend?"

"No."

His answer came too swiftly to be a lie. Torin chewed on her bottom lip.

"An ex?"

"Never been in a relationship with her."

She blew out a deep, exaggerated breath. "You make it so difficult to hold a conversation with you."

"You can always be quiet."

Torin's mouth open and closed twice before she laughed. He'd said it like his suggestion was the only option.

"You're telling me to be quiet in my own vehicle?"

Synovi glanced her way. "I considered it. You can do what you want."

Having no comeback, Torin took his hint and kept her mouth closed. It was clear he needed some time to think and she was going to give him that before they'd be the next ones arguing. Propping her arm onto the console, she let the weight of her head rest on her hand. When they came to a red light, Synovi looked her way again.

She so damn pretty. Mean mugging and all.

"You got an attitude?" he asked, noticing the glower on her face.

"Nope. Just thinking."

So was he. His mind was in a million and one places, specifically the scene they'd just left. Jade made him get completely out of character and that wasn't the type of person he was. Raising his voice and putting his hands on women wasn't how he moved. Even if it were just a tug of her arm, and shove to his chest, Synovi was reevaluating everything. If they couldn't communicate without landing hands on one another, they didn't need to talk at all.

The car ride to Torin's crib was quiet and she was grateful for that. Her mind was on all the food she had to cook and meals she had to prepare. Thankfully, she had most of the big stuff out of the way and would spend all day tomorrow making sure she didn't touch a pot or pan come Sunday.

Leaning his way, she pushed the button to open the garage and Synovi pulled inside. When they got out, he followed her inside. Now that they'd exited the truck, Torin needed to get some things off her chest. Turning, she went to speak and bumped directly into his chest. Synovi hadn't realized how close he'd been walking behind her.

"My bad," he mumbled, catching her around the waist.

Torin was disgusted with the way her body reacted whenever they came in contact. It screamed for her to feed into his subtle advances, but she couldn't. The voice inside her head wouldn't let her. She eased out of his embrace.

"It's fine."

"You were going to say something."

The contemplation was written all over her face. She rubbed her lips together and sighed.

"I don't like awkwardness," she stated.

"Okay."

"And you're making things awkward between us."

"Because I suggested you be quiet?"

Torin noticed a hint of a smirk in the corners of his mouth. Rolling her eyes, she turned and walked away. She didn't have time for this shit. It was more than the request he'd made, and he knew it. A full grin covered Synovi's face as he followed the sway of her hips deeper into the home. He couldn't understand how she was toting so much ass and had no waist. Some women were just born that way, and Torin was one of many in her family.

Gotta be genetics. That shit is crazy, Synovi thought to himself.

"It's rude to walk away from someone when they're talking," he said, taking a seat on the couch.

"You were done talking. I'm not you."

When he chuckled, her head snapped his way.

"Why are you laughing right now, and I'm trying to be serious? Act your age and not your dick size, please," Torin quipped.

Those peculiar, intense eyes of his shifted her way, and Torin gulped.

"Any mention of my dick shouldn't come from your mouth unless that's where you want it to be."

Torin couldn't be offended even if she tried. The tight smile on her face told Synovi everything he needed to know. She absolutely wanted to slide him into her hot mouth and calculate his size.

He's giving big dick energy, I know that, Torin said to herself.

"Whatever," she mumbled.

"Nah. Not whatever."

"Exactly, so if I ask you something, can you give me an answer?"

Her question in regard to another question he hadn't heard yet made Synovi's head spin. All his life, he felt like he'd been interrogated. *How did you get into the system? Why didn't anyone in your family take you in? What makes you so closed off? Ready to go inside?*

The words echoed through his mind, causing him to exhale. Thanks to his GiGi, life, and Ms. Reid, he'd learned to tap into his emotionally intelligent side. Not just his own, but others as well. Synovi could tell Torin was struggling to figure him out, so he decided to give her a bit of insight.

"You can ask me whatever you'd like… my answer depends on my comfortability," he said.

Torin nodded her head. "Okay. That's fair. I said you were making things awkward because you hardly share anything about yourself with me. In the truck, when I asked about that woman, you refused to answer. Well, you answered me but didn't offer anything else. It's clear y'all have history."

Synovi stared at her lips and blinked slowly. "Ask me your question, Torin."

Her name falling from his lips wasn't agitating, but it damn sure didn't resonate like when he spoke it at the bar.

"Who is she to you and what do y'all have going on to make her think it was okay to walk up on us?"

"Her name is Jade. At the moment, we got some shit going on that should've never started, but that's over with as of today."

Torin couldn't help but say, "She must be cheating or something."

"Yeah… on her husband."

Her mouth fell open and eyes stretched. *That* was the last thing she expected him to reveal. Stunned, she scratched her scalp with the tip of her nail.

"You knew she was married?" she questioned.

"No, not at first, but the deed was already done."

"And you kept sleeping with her after you found out?"

Synovi shrugged. "Yeah. Why would I stop? I can't care more about her marriage than she does, and it's obvious she doesn't."

Torin shook her head, not liking the excuse he gave. "Because you probably keep giving her a reason not to care."

"So, it's my fault she's fucking around? I'm the bad guy?" he scoffed.

"You're technically not the good one. A person is going to cheat whether someone convinces them to or not. So, no, it's not your fault. But you're condoning it. You need to leave that woman alone and she needs to leave you alone. It's obvious she caught some deep feelings for you. Hell, I don't blame her."

The last sentence was meant to be said in her head. Thankfully, Synovi ignored it and kept the conversation flowing. He hadn't told anyone about his affair with Jade, and finally being able to vent felt more than good.

Somewhere in his mind, he'd convinced himself that what they were doing was okay until it wasn't, like today. Or like the time they almost got caught. Or whenever she couldn't answer his call or wouldn't respond to his text for hours. There were a plethora of things that could remind him that, though he cared for her, Jade would never belong to him because she was someone else's.

"Ending a situation almost a year in is wild," he said with a light chuckle.

"Not really. I mean, unless your feelings are involved too."

She hoped they weren't. Torin wasn't sure she could take him breaking that to her, but she'd understand. Feelings were bound to be caught the more time you spent with someone. It was almost inevitable. Synovi couldn't front. His feelings were involved, but not how Torin thought.

Sensing his apprehension, Torin walked over to him. Standing between his outstretched legs, she peered into his eyes. *He's hurting. I can feel it all over him.*

"They are, aren't they?" she asked.

Synovi gave her a single head nod. "Not how you're assuming they are. Imagine getting used to something, and then one day, it's no longer there. No warning, no explanation. Just gone, not giving a fuck how you feel."

"I wouldn't like that at all," Torin said softly, relating way too much with his words.

"No one would. That's why when people have good things, they hold on to them."

"People hold on to the good things they *know* they can keep… not have to give back."

The profoundness of her statement made Synovi's chest tighten. It'd taken him until this moment to grasp the concept of letting things go that weren't made for him. Not just things but places, people, situations, and even past traumas.

Belonging to someone or something, feeling wanted, had him cemented in place for so long, that shit with Jade was normal in his eyes. He was used to chaos, and she was feeding it to him like a drug. Synovi needed to shake his addiction and go cold turkey.

Torin stepped closer and ran a hand over his cheek. "You're too good of a person to share with someone else. Don't settle for that because it feels good. Eventually, it'll hurt."

"Sounds like you know all about that," he said.

"Unfortunately. I'm healed now, though. I don't want you to go through the same thing. It gets ugly and lonely."

He knew it did and appreciated her for the heads up. With the conversation much too heavy and seemingly over, Synovi placed his concentration on a better distraction from his tormented thoughts.

"You hella thick, but don't have no stomach for real. You got a BBL or something?"

Torin chortled at the confusion and lust covering his face. She didn't have a six-pack or anything, but she could grip some stomach fat and had a few back rolls.

"Nothing against my girls who go under the knife, but does this look like it was made on the table?"

She gripped her ass and wiggled it. Synovi's dick jumped beneath his briefs and he sat up straight. His long arms stretched, allowing inky hands to trail up her thighs and around the back of them before savagely gripping her meatiness. He made her cheeks bounce a few times and smirked.

"Nah. It doesn't feel like it at all."

Placing her hands on his wrists, Torin gave him a stern stare. "I don't think you touching my ass is very professional, Mr. Black."

"Neither is having your pussy in my face, but here we are."

When he bit his bottom lip, it took every ounce of restraint in Torin not to lift her leg and hump his fucking face. She tried to scoot back but he kept his hold on her.

"Right. My apologies. I'm going to go start meal prepping."

He couldn't help but give her ass a slap before reclining on the couch.

"Really?" Torin asked. "You're so mannish."

Synovi smirked. "I'm a man, baby. But my bad… professionalism. Got it."

Torin bobbed her head and slowly moved away from him. He kept his eyes trained on her and chuckled as her walk sped up once she was a good distance away. Torin wasn't sure how their conversation changed so quickly, but she wanted no parts. She enjoyed the feel of his callous hands way too much.

Instead of throwing caution to the wind, afraid the current would land her right on his dick, Torin busied herself in the kitchen. First, she made a stop in her laundry room to change out of her clothes and into something more comfy. Pulling her orders up on the iPad, she cut some music on and washed her hands.

Pickup and drop-offs started tomorrow morning, and she prayed everyone was on time. The ones who were going to be late had already rescheduled, and she appreciated that. Time was money, and she didn't have any of it to waste.

"You got something I can eat in here?" Synovi asked, walking into the kitchen.

So emerged in her duties, Torin had forgotten he was even there. She chuckled, thinking of herself, but kept it cute.

"Um, yeah. It should be some leftover salmon alfredo rolls in there. Some Caesar salad, too."

Synovi's stomach growled as he walked around the island

to clean his hands. He hadn't eaten since earlier in the day and was starving. Pulling the glass container from the fridge, he glanced around at all the cabinet doors.

"Plates?" he questioned.

"They're in the cabinet behind you or there are some paper ones in the pantry."

Synovi pulled the cabinet open to neatly stacked shelves of glass plates. "I'll use one of these. Thank you."

"Mhm," Torin mumbled as she continued mixing her dressing. "No problem."

He warmed his food up and took a seat at the table. Torin looked his way just as his head bowed in prayer. Regardless if anyone witnessed him or not, Synovi always gave thanks. Some days, he didn't know where his next meal would come from, so he was grateful.

When he finished, he lingered by the sink, not knowing where to put his dirty dishes. She had both sides occupied.

"You can just set it to the side. It'll get washed with everything else," Torin said.

"A'ight. You need help with anything?"

She glanced around the kitchen. There was always something to do. "Can you grab the order slips from the printer and assemble them across the table, please?"

"Yeah. Does it matter which ones go first?"

"No, they'll all be done at the same time."

Getting on his duty, Synovi grabbed the papers and lined the table with them. When he was finished, Torin gave him another job, and before they knew it, night had come. While she finished up, Synovi had gone into the living room to watch TV. Between his long day, the food, and the coziness of her home, he was knocked out in no time. Torin didn't even realize it until she called his name and was greeted with light snores once she made it to him.

Assessing his handsome face, she wondered what life Synovi had lived before now. Their conversation from earlier was still weighing her heart down. It ached for him. He hadn't opened up that much to anyone outside of the two women he knew he could trust.

Grabbing a fluffy throw blanket from one of the wicker baskets, Torin gently placed it over him.

Stirring in his sleep, Synovi stretched his limbs and popped the bones in his fingers. His body felt rested but tense at once, and he knew it was because of the jeans he had on. Whoever could sleep in denim was a menace to society, and that was exactly how he felt. His eyes peeled open, and the presence of light was missing, except for the television.

His head swiveled, searching for Torin, but he didn't see her. Tossing the blanket, he stood and extended his arms upward while yawning.

"Damn," he grumbled. "I was knocked out."

Downing the bottle of water he'd left on the table, Synovi headed into the kitchen and trashed the empty plastic bottle. Torin had cleaned it, leaving out what she'd need in the morning, ready to go.

Back in the living room, he grabbed his phone off the couch and peeped the time. It was well after midnight, and he needed to get back to his side of town.

Tapping on the Lyft app, he went to request a ride, but paused. Torin was going to have to let him out and lock the door. He wasn't leaving her spot unsecured and without notice. Heading up the stairs to her bedroom, he bypassed the guest room he was fond of and went down the hall. It was the only door that was slightly cracked open.

Torin lived alone, but she never slept with her bedroom door completely closed. In case she needed to hear or see something, she wanted to be able to stare out into her hallways rather than wonder what awaited her on the other side.

Entering the room, Synovi walked over to her side. She was knocked out, lying on her stomach with one leg bent and damn near touching her chest. Her foot stuck out from under the comforter. The digital alarm clock offered minimal lighting to the room, but the perfect amount for Synovi to see how peaceful she seemed. He almost didn't want to wake her.

"Torin," he whispered.

She didn't budge. Synovi gave her leg a slight nudge.

"Torin," he spoke a smidgen louder.

Finally, she shifted. "Hmm?"

"I'm 'bouta leave. Come lock the door."

"What time is it?" she mumbled.

He eyed the red digits. "One twenty-six."

"It's late."

He knew that.

"Yeah. Come on. Get up."

"Just stay. It's too late to leave."

Synovi ran a hand over his head. Spending the night, hell, falling asleep, hadn't been in his plans. *Neither was arguing with Jade and bringing Torin home,* he thought, and exhaled.

"You coo' with that?" he questioned, wanting to make sure. He didn't want to wake up to another gun being pulled out on him.

"Hmm?"

Her hum sounded agitated this time around, so Synovi let her be. He hated he didn't have a change of clothes he could put on, but he was about to hop in the shower, regardless. It had been a long day, and lying down without cleansing his skin was out of the question. Heading to the guest room, Synovi cut on the shower inside the bathroom and began to strip.

His shower refreshed him, giving him a bit of energy. Grateful for the stocked cabinet of bath essentials, Synovi brushed his teeth and lotioned down when he finished. Wrapping a towel around his waist, he grabbed his clothes and flicked the light off. He contemplated for all of two seconds on which bed he was about to lie in and made up his mind.

Entering Torin's bedroom, he was surprised to see her phone screen lit up and her on it. Her halfway opened eyes greeted him.

"You up," he acknowledged.

"No," she grumbled, turning over. "My sister called and interrupted my sleep."

"I thought I did when I came in here," Synovi admitted.

Torin frowned and then wiped her eyes. Her lack of clear vision before caused her to miss a bare-chested Synovi and a white towel covering his jewels.

"You came in here?"

He chuckled lowly. "Yeah. I told you to come lock the door, and you told me it was too late to leave. I went to hop in the shower."

Torin yawned, not remembering any of that. "Oh, okay."

"You got an extra pair of too big basketball shorts or something lying around?"

She didn't even have to think; the answer was no. "No, there's brand new boxers in my dresser, though. And before you ask, they're mine. I like to wear them sometimes."

Synovi was most definitely about to ask some questions. He knew she was single, thanks to Racquel readily offering up her relationship status, but that didn't mean she didn't have a nigga somewhere.

Placing his clothes on top of the dresser, Torin let him know which drawer they were in. Pulling a pair out, Synovi dropped the towel without an ounce of shame and slid them over his ass. They fit perfectly, thanks to Torin loving them a bit baggy on her. After folding his towel, Synovi walked around to the other side of the bed.

Torin's lips poked out, wondering what he was doing, but she had no words. Neither did he, until he pulled the duvet back and slid underneath it.

"Bed feel good as hell," he acknowledged lowly, feeling his body sink into its plush yet firmness.

Do I say thank you? Torin asked herself.

She was too worked up to say anything, let alone ask a question. Rolling over, she grabbed the cord to her charger and connected her phone. She had to be up in less than six hours and wanted every minute of sleep. At least that was what she thought she wanted until she felt Synovi's body heat against her back and warm, minty breath against her neck.

"I just wanted to tell you thanks for earlier. That conversation we had was needed," he said.

Torin rolled onto her back. "I could tell, and you're welcome."

Her chest heaved as he hovered over her. Rubbing her lips together, she wondered what he was thinking, but didn't have to for long.

"You even pretty with this bonnet on," he said.

Torin blushed. "Thank you."

"And I love your lips," he said, rubbing his thumb across her bottom one.

Her tongue glided across it just to taste him. "Synovi, I don't think—"

"Fuck being professional. Come here."

His hand latched around her neck, and his lips smashed into hers. She'd never lost her breath and bearings so quickly. Their lip lock wasn't rushed, but it was needy. The hunger she felt for Synovi bubbled in the pit of her gut with a vengeance. There was no more denying her attraction to him.

Synovi knew he had to really be feeling Torin because he didn't kiss. The act was far too intimate, and he liked getting downright nasty with it. He never placed his lips on Jade, leaving that task to her husband, but Torin was a different story. If she'd let him, Synovi was going to leave his mark on every inch of her frame.

Starting with her pussy, he couldn't wait to taste. His hand crept between her legs that Torin spread without a fuss. Sticking his hand under the band of her panties, wetness coated his fingertips as he toyed with her clit. Their kiss turned sloppy, damn near desperate, when his fingers sank into her.

It was as if he craved to connect them in other ways than his digits gliding inside her pulsing walls. The way she moaned into his mouth, sucked on his tongue, and whimpered as he drug his teeth across her bottom lip before sucking on it brought the beast out of him.

"We're not supposed to be doing this," she whined.

"Then why is this pussy so wet?"

Synovi kissed her neck, weakening the resolve she tried holding onto. Torin's back arched as he pulled an orgasm out of her in record-breaking timing. Using his free hand, Synovi lowered the tank top she was wearing and gripped her breast before suckling her nipple. Torin hadn't felt a man's touch in so long, she was losing it.

"Mmm, Novi," she moaned, chopping and screwing his name.

He kissed down her stomach, licked her thick thighs, and spread them before placing a kiss on her lips.

"Turn over," he commanded in the sexiest voice Torin ever heard. It made her want to do whatever he asked.

It was thick, like his dick that pressed against her leg as she rolled over. Synovi licked a trail down her back and kissed each ass cheek before spreading them. His tongue glided there, too, before he lifted her hips, positioning her on all fours.

"Can I taste it?" he asked lowly, placing the most delicate kisses down her slit.

Torin snaked her body, rubbing herself across his juicy lips. "Yes."

Synovi devoured her. Rolling his tongue over her stiff clit, he flickered it, making Torin gasp. He savored the exquisite taste of her, pulling her clit into his mouth and staying there. Long fingers sank into her greedy pussy. The foreplay had Torin's spine curling.

"Ooooh… damn, boy," she moaned, gripping the sheets so hard, her knuckles popped.

Synovi applied straight pressure, suckling hard before smacking her ass cheek. "You got some good pussy on you, baby. Gotdamn."

His groans of appreciation had her leaking. Dripping. Making a fucking mess all over his face and her bed. Sloppily, he sucked and licked on her pussy for eleven minutes straight, making Torin damn near shove her head through the headboard.

Lifting, he used all four pads of his fingers to rub her clit in a quick manner. "Mhm," he hummed as she lightly squirted. "There you go. You got all this built-up tension and need a nigga to drain you of it."

His head dipped, and his mouth was back on her. Torin smacked her hand on the bed as if she were in a WWE match and calling it quits. She was ready to tap the hell out! There was no quitting with Synovi. He'd been told at an early age that quitters never win, and he hated to lose. The only Ls he wanted right now were Torin's sweet lullabies as she cried his name out.

"SYNOVI!" she shrieked, giving him exactly what the fuck he wanted.

Synovi ate her pussy as if he were trying to detach it and all the juices it came with from her body. Torin's legs trembled, and her heart raced at an unhealthy rate. *This nigga is about to give me a heart attack,* she thought, breathing hard as her stomach tightened. He stayed planted between her legs until he'd made her cum two more times.

Torin sniffled as his tongue lazily lapped her juices up from her thighs and center. He needed to come lick the wetness from her face, too. There were tears of satisfaction and nervousness decorating her heated cheeks. A man who ate her that good was not to be played with. Synovi had just sucked her soul from her body and digested it.

Pleased beyond measure, Torin clapped her cheeks and grinned. She could fall back asleep just like this, but getting some shut-eye was the least of her worries right now. The warmth of Synovi's dick gliding over her slit was. Reaching between them, she let her hand travel, curious of his length. Her eyes widened when she stroked him for much longer than she was anticipating. The steep curve to the right was going to make Torin lose every good part of her mind.

"You playing with it; gon' show me what you can do on it," Synovi spoke huskily.

With pleasure, Torin tapped him against her clit before easing him inside her. Trying to anyway. His thickness was charting unfamiliar, snug territory. Synovi's body shivered at her tightness, and he exhaled so rough and loudly, Torin felt his breath on her back.

"Damn, hol' up," he grumbled, caught off guard.

"Mm, mm. Let me feel alllll this dick," Torin cooed, sliding back and forth.

Her arch was so deep, he couldn't help but fall into a daze as she threw her ass back. Her wetness and sweet moans were the only sounds Synovi heard. Slow and steady pumps had her head spinning. When he thrust deeper, wrapping a hand around the front of her neck and pounded into her like he was upset for her shit being so good, Torin screamed.

"Oh, my Goooood!"

Synovi yanked her ponytail, making her scream in ecstasy again. "I'm sure He hears you. Shut up and take this dick." The gruffness of his voice in her ear chilled her spine.

Synovi reached depths inside her walls that had Torin losing it. She couldn't believe he was doing her body like this. Then again, she could because, of course, a nigga like Synovi delivered *this* type of dick. She thought it was so unfair that he thought he had to settle for a taken woman. Jade didn't deserve this pipe anymore and Torin was going to make sure she never sampled it again.

When he pulled out of her, Torin began to protest but was quickly shut up when he swooped her up, placing her on her back. Rubbing the underside of his dick along her center, he tapped his girth against her pearl, before pushing inside of her.

"Uuuh," Torin wheezed, scooting away.

Synovi gripped her thighs, bringing her back to him and further down his dick. "No running, okay? Be a good girl and handle this dick."

"O-Okay," she answered with an erratic head nod and shaky breath.

Pushing her legs back, Synovi stroked her so properly, Torin wanted to fight. She wanted to line every bitch who'd ever received him up and slap them hoes blind. His handsome face held a scowl, revealing the pleasure coursing through his veins. Torin felt herself become wetter, as if that were possible.

"Yeah… let me open this tight little pussy up," he groaned, loving how her walls hugged him.

Torin's eyes rolled, and her mouth fell ajar. The way he was talking to her, talking her through it, drove her insane. Synovi wanted to stay inside her forever but knew he wouldn't last much longer. Leaning his weight on her, Synovi pumped his hips and kissed her lips.

"Tell me sorry," he mumbled against them.

Her eyes were squeezed tight as another orgasm approached, but popped open at his demand. Stubbornly, she simply stared. Disliking her refusal, Synovi hit her with strokes so vicious, then painfully slow, Torin had no choice but to apologize.

"I'm sorry," she whimpered just as her walls did, raining down his shaft.

"Uuggh… I'm cumming!"

This one knocked her off her axis and into another universe. Spinning, free-falling, not wanting to be caught, Torin's entire body shuddered. She groaned hard, biting the flesh of Synovi's neck, and held him tightly.

"Fuuuck," she cried.

Her shrills, the way she clung to him, and the neediness he felt had Synovi cumming right along with her. In an instant, he pulled out and released against her sheets.

"Mmmmm," he grunted, squeezing her thigh.

With heavy breaths, Synovi rested between her shoulder and neck. Relaxed, he knew he'd be knocked out in minutes. But, he had to get up and so did she. They weren't sleeping in a wet spot.

"Oh my gosh," Torin sighed lowly when he walked into the bathroom.

He came out with a steaming towel and wiped between her legs. Because he couldn't help himself, Synovi placed a kiss on her swollen lips and protruding clit once more. Torin watched him the entire time and shook her head.

He looked up at her with a smirk and those sexy eyes she wanted to gaze into forever. "How professional was that?"

Torin had no energy to laugh, but the content smile on her face was good enough for him. When he walked back into the bathroom, vibrations from his phone against her dresser came from across the room and caught Torin's attention.

Her first mind was to tell him it was ringing, but the part of her who had just been thoroughly fucked said otherwise. "Find someone else to call," she mumbled.

"What chu' say?" Synovi questioned.

She shook her head. "Nothing."

He slid his boxers on and held his hand out. "Come on. Let's go sleep in the guest room."

Torin grinned and struggled to stand up. "Okay. Let me use the bathroom and grab some panties."

"For what? We not finished. I'ma need to feel you when I wake up."

She stared at him like he was crazy. "Synovi."

He licked his lips and spanked her ass. "What I just say?"

"Fine. No panties. But don't be mad when I blame you for how tired I am in the morning."

"That's coo'," he said, cupping her sex and gently massaging it. "You need to let her breathe, anyway. I know she sore. Throw on a big t-shirt."

Torin couldn't help but chuckle at his crazy, yet serious requests. She finished handling her business in the bathroom and came right out. Opening her dresser drawer, she grabbed a big t-shirt that stopped mid-thigh and put it on before sliding her feet into her house shoes.

Synovi kissed her neck as they walked out the door and down the hall. In fresh sheets, Torin laid on one side of the bed, thinking he'd want his distance. Synovi eliminated her doubts and the space separating them, pulling her body against his.

"You still running," he said, rubbing her back.

Torin sighed. "I'm right here."

"This where you need to stay."

"I don't know about you and all these demands, Mr. Black." She giggled.

"Keep saying my name like that, and I'ma give you a few more that'll leave you hoarse."

Torin gulped and shut right on up. She needed her voice tomorrow and the day after. Now, any time after that, Torin was game. They fell into a comfortable silence and were both drifting when Synovi placed a sweet kiss on her forehead.

Torin smiled. "Goodnight."

"Goodnight," Synovi replied sleepily.

This was about to be the second-best night of sleep he'd had. Ironically, its location was in the same spot as the first best night. Only now, the person experiencing it with him made it much more enjoyable.

$$ten$$

Leighton just knew when she answered Torin's call she had to have misheard her. She was sure that the turbulence she spoke of before had temporarily affected her hearing.

"I'm sorry. What'd you say?" Leighton questioned, humored.

"I fucked the help."

The cackle Leighton let out made Torin grin and shake her head. "I know that's mothafuckin' right! I told you you'd be calling me, but I didn't think it'd be this soon."

Torin sighed as she weaved through traffic. "I know, right? I'm mad I even had to call you."

"Don't be mad, pooh." Leighton laughed. "Now, how was it?"

"I'm sprung," Torin admitted with no shame or hesitation.

Leighton pulled the phone away from her ear. "Excuse me?"

"Sprung, a dummy, foolish, goofy. T-Pain's daughter. How else do you want me to explain it?"

"Oooh, bitch," Leighton murmured. "Un, un. You sure?"

"Yes. Pretty positive." Torin chuckled. "No, seriously, though. I can see it getting to that point."

The fact that she'd been having these thoughts for more than a few days and hadn't been able to shake them was foreign to Torin. Synovi really had her head gone. Waking up to him on Saturday morning, talking all day Sunday, having movie night on Monday, and cooking tacos for him on Tuesday had to be considered sprung. Torin didn't know what else to label it.

"And this is after one time?" Leighton could believe it, but still, she needed some type of proof.

"No. Four times," Torin whispered.

"Torin!"

"I knoooow. This is crazy," she whined. "But it's so good."

Leighton sucked her teeth. "Obviously, if I'm just hearing about it. Lil' sneaky heffa. You hopped on it right after the day party, huh?"

"Not immediately. Some hours later." She giggled.

"Has the man even started servicing you... well, clearly." She giggled. "But has he started doing his job?"

"He has, and I have no complaints," Torin let her know.

"Well, that's good. I'm happy to hear you have someone to clean up, and you're getting that back blown out. It was getting a lil' dusty down there. I almost started calling you Charlotte," Leighton snickered at her own joke.

"Charlotte? Who's that?"

"Charlotte's Web."

When the name registered, Torin giggled. "Girl, whatever."

"Besides being sexually satisfied, do you like him? Is he someone you can see yourself dating?"

Torin didn't hesitate to tell her yes. Honestly, she wasn't sure how things escalated so quickly, but they had, and she enjoyed his company.

"I do. At first, he was kind of closed off, but he's opening up."

Synovi was still guarded, but their daily conversations and visits were breaking the shield some. There were certain topics that came up between them over the days, and he hardly had any input on them, but Torin didn't push. She knew whatever it was holding him back would be revealed when he was ready.

"That's good. We don't like emotionally unavailable men. And he's how old?"

"Younger than us, but trust me… that doesn't matter. He is very mature."

"Okay," Leighton cheered. "Take up for your man. I ain't mad at you."

Torin snickered. "You really make me sick, I swear."

"I know, but you love me."

She did, dearly. Leighton had been her best friend for over sixteen years and knew her better than anyone. So, that was why she was apprehensive about what she was about to say next.

"There is one thing, though." Torin sighed heavily.

"Oh, lord. He has a baby? I mean, kids are cool, long as the baby mama is dead."

"Girl!" Torin choked on a laugh. "Shut the hell up."

"What? We don't have time for baby mama drama. You remember what we had to put up with from DJ's mama before she moved on."

Torin frowned. She remembered like it was yesterday. Though Candice was cool now, there'd been plenty of days where she and Torin exchanged words and fists behind Don's messiness. She couldn't understand how Torin's fresh ass, as she liked to call her, snagged her balling-ass baby daddy.

Candice would start petty beef with her for no reason, and Torin would never let someone bully her. Especially when she was just trying to love her man. If she knew then what she'd eventually found out, Torin would've saved every breath she spewed her way. Don eventually sat them both down and explained to Candice that Torin wasn't going anywhere, lying straight through his pearly whites. He could've saved his speech and sat her down with the other hoes she found out about.

"He doesn't have any kids," Torin clarified.

"Okay, so what's got you second-guessing already?"

"I don't think he has his own car," Torin voiced. She didn't just think it, she knew.

Leighton kissed her teeth. "Oh, well. Hang it up, buttercup."

"Having a vehicle isn't the end all be all, Leigh."

"This is true, but why in this day and age would someone not have a vehicle unless they can't drive or live in a state where public transportation is the main means of travel? Make it make sense."

Torin couldn't, and that was what was bothering her with Synovi not opening up. On the days he came to her house, he was either dropped off by a Lyft driver and picked up, or he was pulling up in an older model Ford Fusion.

Of course, Torin didn't hesitate to ask if he was driving some chick's car to her crib, and Synovi reassured her it wasn't. Yet, he never said the car was his or belonged to someone else.

"There are plenty of reasons why. Financial setbacks, car wrecks, a medical condition. You never know. Plus, he's young. Not everyone is in the position to have their own set of wheels," Torin said.

"Of course, they aren't. Shit happens. Life is a trip. I'm not discrediting that those situations don't occur because I've been there and know people who have and are today. What I want to know is why it's a concern for you. You wouldn't have brought it up if it weren't."

"It's not solely about the car… just his background. I'm not really sure I know what I got myself into with him. Like, who is he really?"

Torin's question was asked more so to herself. She'd been trying to figure Synovi out from day one and couldn't. Asking Racquel was of no use because she knew the bare minimum, and Synovi had already told her the same things she did.

"I don't know, T. But it looks like we need to do some digging. You aren't in that deep yet. It's never too late to let him go on about his business."

Leighton's suggestion sounded good, but Torin knew her. She knew the tug on her heart had much more to do with the person Synovi was and not what he had between his legs. Letting him go wasn't an option unless she absolutely had to.

Torin sighed. "You're right. We'll just see how it goes. I'm about to get some community service hours in, though. Call me later."

"Okay. I have four more heads and a house visit, so I'll text you."

"Okay."

The two hung up and Torin pulled into the parking lot. She'd been up since six with a racing mind and she hoped it'd take a break for just a few hours so she could think straight. Being out in the field and giving back to the community always seemed to do the trick.

"What up, bruh?" D'Marco said, posting up in the entryway of Synovi's door.

Synovi looked up from the text message Torin had just sent him. "Shit. What's good?"

"Nothing at all. They got me working the overnight shift today. If you need my whip again, you can use it."

Although Torin had jump started Synovi's cleaning services, he still accepted one of the jobs he got an interview for. It was through a temp service and part time, but paid weekly. They were currently in a two-week training course and would receive a hefty sign-on bonus once they completed it. Any money Synovi could pocket was good in his eyes.

With his new business venture came expenses. Cleaning products weren't cheap and he needed a lot of them. Figuring out how he could budget better to save and still make money was the conversation he and Torin were having. She was all for making her money work for her.

What was supposed to be him just cleaning up at her main kitchen location turned into Synovi attending two big events she had earlier in the week. Seeing her in her element, on her boss shit, motivated him on an entirely different level. That and the fact that D'Marco had been letting him use his car.

Lugging his products on a bus or in back of a Lyft wasn't

going to work and D'Marco knew that. Synovi wanted his own ride but until then, he appreciated his boy for looking out.

"They be switching up y'all schedules like that?" Synovi asked.

"Yeah. It's peak season, so they got us working crazy shifts and some overtime. Got my baby mama trippin', thinking I'm lying."

Synovi chuckled. "It wouldn't be the first time."

"Whatever, cuz. When I be telling the truth, she wanna accuse me, so why not tell a lil' lie here and there?"

"Aye. That's between y'all. They let us out of training early today, so I'ma slide to GiGi's crib. You tryna come through?"

"Hell yeah. She cooking? Tell her I got some gas for her." D'Marco laughed.

"You trying to get her kicked out," Synovi said, standing from the chair he was sitting in.

If anything, GiGi would get herself kicked out. It wasn't illegal to smoke marijuana in the city, but the facility she lived in had certain rules. Rules GiGi hated following some days. Other than that, she didn't give them a hard time at all. Almost all the staff loved her and always asked where her grandson was.

"She'll be good. Let me grab my keys right quick," D'Marco said, heading to his room that was on the other side of the building.

"A'ight. I'ma be in the front."

The duo split, and Synovi made his way to the front. Forgetting he hadn't hit Torin back, he pulled his phone out. Noticing the incoming call from Jade, he shook his head. The night at Torin's, he'd left his phone in her room on purpose, knowing the type of time Jade would be on, and he was right.

When he retrieved it the next morning, he had eight missed calls from her and a bunch of texts that made no sense to Synovi. There weren't any typos in them or anything, but the fact that she had asked to come and get him so they could make up was ludicrous. He was going to give it a day to clear his head and think over cutting her off completely, but Jade didn't give him any time.

Before the day party fiasco, Jade would go days without reaching out, but suddenly, she was blowing his line down. Synovi had had enough of her dramatics.

"Yeah?" he answered when she called a second time.

"Are you seriously ignoring me?"

"We're on the phone talking now. What up?"

Jade couldn't believe her ears right now. "I haven't spoken to you in days and you won't return my calls."

"That ain't nothing new, Jade. I been busy."

"Busy? Since when are you fucking busy? It's not like you have a job."

"A'ight. Anything else?"

Synovi remained calm. He could've burst her bubble and talked bad to her for trying to clown him, but he let her have it.

"Look, I'm sorry. I shouldn't have said that. I'm just frustrated and don't understand what I did wrong. Do you not want to do this anymore?"

He hated the way desperation seeped from her tone. It made his brain jumble and the spot he had in his wounded heart for her soften. The same thing he told Torin he didn't want done to him, was exactly what he was doing to Jade. Leaving her hanging, confused, and unwanted, without a warning.

She's not yours! he thought angrily.

Leaning against the wall, Synovi closed his eyes for a brief moment. He never felt like he had a say so in what direction his life went. To have to choose between staying where it felt good for now or leaving to be where it would remain good had Synovi conflicted.

"I take your silence as a no," Jade said softly.

"It's not that. Let me—"

"Ah. Just the person I wanted to see. Let me introduce you to someone."

Synovi's eyes opened at the sound of Mr. K heading his

way. His eye twitched as he kept a neutral expression. Right now wasn't the time to be trying to introduce him to people.

"I ain't really in the mood," Synovi said, still holding the phone to his ear.

It could've fallen from his hand when the person behind Mr. K stepped to the side, making themselves known.

"Synovi?" Torin questioned with familiarity and uncertainty in her voice.

He stiffened in shock as confusion siphoned through him at her appearance.

"You know him?" Mr. K questioned.

Synovi waited. Their eyes locked on one another, and Torin's heart pounded. She didn't know what was going on.

"Yes. He's my… um. We sort of work together," she let out, and Synovi's throat tightened.

He didn't know what answer he expected her to give, but that wasn't quite it. Still, it was better than saying she didn't know him at all. That was his fear.

"Hello?" Jade said, trying to ear hustle.

Without a thought, Synovi hung up in her face and slid his phone into the pocket of his Nike shorts.

"Really? I didn't know that, baby girl," Mr. K said.

Synovi's head drew back. "This you?"

He didn't take Torin as the fuck with an older, bald man type, but obviously, he couldn't judge a book by its cover.

"What was that?" Mr. K questioned, and Synovi didn't know why.

His question was for Torin, as his cold eyes seared into her. Picking up on what he thought this was, Torin laughed nervously.

"Um, no. This is my dad. I'm here to clock some community service hours."

It was then that Synovi noticed the pan of food in her hand. It'd been overlooked, thanks to Torin taking up every ounce of space in his brain and sight.

"I ain't know you had a daughter," Synovi said, keeping his

cool. "As uptight as you are, wouldn't even think you had a woman."

Torin giggled and Mr. K glared at her.

"That's funny to you? I'm not uptight. Just about my business, young man. Now, tell me... how do you know my baby? That temp job isn't in her field."

"She can tell you."

Because if I do, I'ma get kicked out of the program, Synovi thought and hit Torin with a smirk that ruined her panties.

"Daddy, Synovi has a cleaning business. I'd been looking to hire one and we just happened to run into each other," Torin explained.

Mr. K looked surprised. "Really? This is my first time hearing of this entrepreneurship. I like that. I like that a lot. We'll have to talk about it more later on. I have to get to a meeting across town."

He kissed Torin's cheek and stepped Synovi's way with his hand out. Synovi's eyes dropped and he gripped it firmly.

Mr. K leaned in so only he could hear him. "I'm warning you. She's off limits." He spoke lowly before retreating, sporting a smile.

Fake ass nigga, Synovi thought, flicking his nose. His top lip curled and his eye twitched again. "Yeah, a'ight. Don't be late to that meeting 'cause you trying to run shit. She's in good hands."

Mr. K glared at him with a tight jaw. "Torin, save me some of that pasta. I should be back in a few hours."

"I already did. Drive safely."

Mr. K told her he would and headed down the hall after giving Synovi one last glance. He pumped no fear in Synovi and he should've already known that. When they were finally alone, Synovi walked over to her. Torin held her breath, thinking he was about to go off on her, but he did the complete opposite.

"What up?" he spoke and kissed her lips before grabbing the pan out of her hand. "Why you ain't make that nigga carry this?"

Torin was so smitten, her face warmed. "Hi. And because he's clumsy as all get out."

"Clown shit."

"Um, yeah. So, are we going to address the elephant in the room?" Torin asked.

Synovi nodded his head. "In a minute. Walk to the kitchen."

Bossy ass.

She led the way and entered the dining area where food was being served. Though Solace Place had a culinary staff who prepared meals, some days, different organizations brought meals in and served. It'd been a while since Torin had been able to come volunteer around the place, but she had some free time today. Plus, she didn't want it to get too late in the year when her schedule got ridiculous and she couldn't.

"Torin! Girl, is that you?" Mrs. Cannon, the head cook, questioned.

She'd been there since the place opened up and had no plans to leave. Every month, she'd remind the staff that even when she retired, she'd still volunteer.

"Hey, Mrs. Cannon. How are you?" Torin asked as they hugged.

"I'm blessed, baby. You're looking gorgeous as ever."

"Hell yeah, she is!" one of the men shouted. "Come here. Let me holla at you."

Torin shook her head at his outburst. Synovi glanced the guy's way.

"Aye. If you wanna keep eating off that plate and not through a straw, watch your mouth and keep them bulged ass eyes off her."

"Now, Synovi," Mrs. Cannon fussed with a giggle and swatted his arm. "You know he's missing a few marbles."

"He gon' be missing a few teeth in a minute," Synovi grumbled.

His jealousy had Torin weak in the knees. "Stop," she whispered.

Synovi waved her off.

"I only see your face about three times a year. You must not have any orders today," Mrs. Cannon said.

"I don't. I'm going to spend a few hours up here. Is that okay with you?" Torin grinned.

"It sure is. But you may have to check with Mr. Meany here," Mrs. Cannon said, hugging Synovi around the waist. "He thinks he's the boss around here."

"Is that right?" Torin smirked.

"Mhm. Boy needs to get some employees of his own 'cause we aren't it."

Synovi chuckled as she let him loose. "You stay fussing at me for no reason."

"Always out of love. Now, don't you go bothering Torin. She's a good girl."

"Yeah? That's exactly what a nigga like me needs," Synovi said and she smacked his arm.

"I bet you do. Come on over here so I can fix you a plate."

Synovi pushed Torin toward the exit. "Put me one up. I'll be right back."

"Mhm. I'm watching you!"

Torin couldn't help but snicker as they headed out of the kitchen. Greetings from staff who hadn't seen her in a while didn't conclude until they were outside of the building. Pulling a lighter from his pocket, Synovi took a seat on the steps and flickered the spark wheel. Torin stood on the flat concrete in front of him, waiting. She knew he had something to say.

"You remember what happened the last time you stood in front of me like this," he said.

Torin quickly took a seat next to him. "Right. So, um. Is this where you stay?"

"Yeah. For now."

She didn't like his dry reply. "Why'd you say it like that?"

"Don't act clueless. Your pops owns the place, so you know exactly what type of nigga you dealing with."

"And what kind is that, hmm?" she pressed, grabbing his chin to make him face her. His discomfited eyes made her heart ache. "One who's trying his best and just needed a little push?

One who is making a way even when it probably seems like there isn't one. Don't play with me and speak down on yourself. There's nothing to be embarrassed about."

"I just feel like I should be further in life at my age," Synovi grumbled. "Feel like I don't have shit of my own."

"You have drive and determination. Some people don't find that and tap into it until years later in life. Your journey isn't everyone else's," Torin preached.

Synovi swallowed hard. "Did you know this is where I stayed?"

"No. Of course, I didn't. How would I have known that?"

"Shit just ain't adding up. It's weird. First, I meet your sister on some dramatic-ass superhero shit."

Torin snickered and he kissed his teeth. "Sorry. Go ahead."

"Then, I meet you. You put me in a position to make some serious money and help me out, then fuck me like you trying to get taken care of for the rest of your life."

"I am." Torin grinned.

"Can I finish? You want a nigga to open up to you so bad and keep interrupting me."

Torin fell all over him and laughed. "Oh, my gosh. Okay, okay. For real. I'm listening. No more talking."

Synovi huffed. "Thank you. Ain't no way, Mr. K yo' daddy. Shit is too coincidental. I'm just saying, it looks mapped out. Y'all got something against me?"

"No, Synovi. Sometimes, God places the right people in your life at a time you need them the most."

She witnessed the frown set into his handsome features. Looping her arm through his, Torin laid her head on his shoulder.

"I find that hard to believe. The only right person He ever gave me is GiGi. What about all the other folks I needed?"

His thoughts ventured back in time to those dark moments. The lonely instances where crying, snapping out, fighting, and losing his mind had once been all he knew. Synovi had come so far, battling and pushing through his own mental hold it was hard not to revert. Especially when, for so long, he had nothing promising to look forward to. When you finally get something of value worth keeping, obtaining it is no longer the hard part —keeping it is.

In Synovi's case, his peace had one foot in the door and the other on the pavement, ready to make a run for it. This time, he was up for the chase.

"I don't know who any of those other folks are, but it's clear they weren't meant to be anywhere near you. They added no value to the man you are and don't deserve to live inside your head and play a role in the man you're becoming. Fuck 'em."

Synovi smirked at her trill reply. "Straight up, huh?"

"Absolutely. Any and everything you need is already yours. It's going to make its way to you and stick. Trust me on that," Torin stated with finality.

"A'ight. I'ma hold you to that."

"You better. At least now I won't be surprised if you tell me no about staying the night with you," Torin joked.

"Knowing me, I woulda used somebody else crib like it was my shit."

Torin cackled. "Oh, my gosh. That is sick. You had no intentions of telling me?"

Synovi stroked the hairs on his jaw. "Yeah, but not anytime soon. Was just gon' keep you guessing until I moved into my own place."

"And the car you've been driving?" Torin asked.

"My homeboy D'Marco's. He been letting me use it."

Torin's heart warmed. "That's so nice of him. I'ma ask my daddy if he knows some people who can get you one."

"Nah," Synovi said, shaking his head. "I'm good."

"But I—"

"I said I'm good, Torin. I'ma figure it out."

She huffed and stood from the steps. "Fine. You don't have to get all pissy about it. I was just trying to help."

Synovi pulled her to him and onto his lap. He kissed her neck and rubbed her kitty through the leggings she had on. Torin clamped her legs shut.

"Novi," she whined, burying her face into his chest.

"I appreciate you. Don't think I don't. All I know is how to figure shit out, so don't be offended, a'ight?"

Her head bobbed as his thumb circled her clit that emerged and greeted him. "Okay," Torin breathed hard.

"A'ight. Now gimmie a kiss."

Her lips were on him before he could finish his sentence. Synovi rubbed all over her, caressing her soft body, knowing it was exactly what she needed. When she pulled away, Torin wiped the corner of his mouth and grinned.

"You got me in front of my daddy's business showing out."

"Kaine's Kitchen and Mr. K. I never thought to put two and two together," he said.

Since being at Solace Place, Synovi had never heard anyone call him by his last name, just Mr. K.

"Nope. People really only know we're related if they know us."

Her phone vibrating in the crossbody purse she was wearing disrupted their conversation. Grabbing it, Torin noticed the familiar number and did her best to mask her shock. Quickly, she locked it and placed the phone back inside her purse.

"Dodging calls?" Synovi questioned.

"Scammers. They've been calling all day. I need to block them."

"Yeah. 'Fore they record your voice and be trying to scam me." Synovi chuckled.

The main door to the building opened, and D'Marco stepped out. "Damn, nigga. I ain't know you were out here cuddled up."

Torin stood from Synovi's lap, and he was up right behind her. "Stay talking shit."

"You know me. What up? I'm D'Marco." He introduced himself because Synovi sure wasn't going to.

"Hey," Torin spoke.

D'Marco glanced Synovi's way, then back at her. "I'ont get

your name? Wait. Ain't you the one who was hugged up with him at the day party?"

Synovi shook his head as Torin chuckled.

"That would be me. I'm Torin."

D'Marco gave her a big smile. "Pleasure to meet you. Glad you got this moody ass nigga to cheer up."

She hugged Synovi's side. "Mhm. Me too. I'ma let y'all go, though. Call me later?"

Synovi's head bobbed once. "Yeah."

D'Marco stood silently before catching the hint. "Oh, my fault." He laughed. "I'ma be in the car, nigga."

As soon as he walked off, Synovi pulled her to him and tongued her down so fucking nasty, Torin panted when he broke their lip lock. She stared at him, no longer having to wonder where he came from. Synovi was not of this world and was fucking Torin's up majorly and in a good way.

"You couldn't do that with him standing here?" she asked.

"No. Now go inside. I'll see you later."

Torin chuckled as she ascended the steps. Making her ass bounce, she squealed when he slapped it hard. "Oooh, okay, Boss. Whatever you say."

Synovi smirked at her silliness and waited until she was inside before heading to the car. The giddy grin on Torin's face was wiped smoothed off when her phone rang again, and she saw the same distinct number roll across her screen.

"What does he want?" she whispered.

She let the phone roll to voicemail and stared at the black screen. Don had no reason to be calling her. Especially not now. He was the last person on her mind and Torin wanted it to stay that way. In their time spent over the last four days, Torin let Synovi know about their past relationship, but only small details. She failed to mention that he was in jail.

Honestly, she saw no need to reveal that information. The only people who mattered to her from Don's family were Chelsea and DJ. It wasn't like they'd be around each other, so she saw no need to spill Don's business. Her only hope was that whatever he was calling for had nothing to do with them making amends because that ship had sailed, crashed, and drowned right along with all her feelings for him.

Had Synovi known GiGi was going to put him to work as soon as he entered her crib, he would've smoked first. He'd only been there for a little over an hour and had already changed her curtains, cleaned the inside of the stove, and deep cleaned her bathroom.

"I hope you know you're paying me," Synovi joked, flopping down on the couch. "I was coming over here to chill and eat."

"I don't know why you thought that. I told you I needed you to do some stuff around here," GiGi fussed. "Had you come over when I asked instead of lying up under that girl who can cook, it wouldn't be that much to do."

GiGi knew all about little Ms. Torin and the moves she was putting on her grandson's heart. Synovi had to express his feelings about her to someone, and who better than the woman who knew him best?

Chuckling, D'Marco said, "Tell him, Granny."

"You hush. 'Cause your Black ass ain't lifted a finger. Ain't good for nothing."

D'Marco cracked up. "Dang. So, that means you don't want me to leave you this?"

He held up a baggie of weed and shook it.

"Now, see. I didn't say all that. Gon' head and hand that here," she said, holding her hand out that was covered in shiny rings.

Synovi shook his head in amusement. "I thought you were okay with the pen I gave you?"

She stuck the baggie in the pocket of her capri pants. "I am. This is to sell."

"Man, nah!" D'Marco fussed. "How you gon' get me like that?"

"You can't out-hustle a hustler, baby. I just taught you something." GiGi chuckled.

A knock came to her door, and Synovi stood to answer it, but she swatted him away.

"I got it. It probably ain't nobody but Carolynn's nosey ass, wanting to know what we're doing."

"I thought you ain't like her?" Synovi laughed.

"I don't!" GiGi hollered, pulling the door open. "Oh, my. Look who decided to come and visit their mama."

Synovi's entire body tensed. Eyes darkening and mood mimicking it, he flexed his jaw as his mama entered the home. He couldn't recall the last time he'd seen her, and that was sad. They lived in the same city, from what he knew.

Walking inside, she placed grocery bags on the counter. Shock covered her face when she rounded the corner and saw him.

"H-Hey, son," Unique stuttered.

Synovi hit her with a head nod.

Her timid smile was always present whenever they were around one another. "It's nice to see you. Who's your friend?"

"I know you better open up your mouth and speak to your mama," GiGi scolded, staring Synovi down.

"What up, Unique?" he grumbled.

"He gave me a head nod, Mama. It's fine," Unique said, defending him.

"No, it ain't. Not in my presence. I done told him plenty about showing you respect."

D'Marco shifted uncomfortably in his seat and stood. "I'ma step out on the porch and spark up. Granny, you good?"

"Mhm. Enjoy it yourself," GiGi said.

Synovi wanted to get up with him but he knew GiGi would chew his ass out. Not because he couldn't smoke, but because she expected him to hold a conversation with his mama. His animosity for Unique wasn't a secret. Synovi despised her entire being and couldn't shake the feeling of betrayal, no matter what.

"So," Unique began. "How have you been, Mama?"

GiGi sat next to Synovi on the couch and grabbed the remote off the table. She turned the volume to the TV down and placed it back.

"Better. This knee of mine been giving me some problems, so I'll probably get surgery on it soon."

Synovi frowned. "You ain't tell me that."

"I was planning on it. You know I was going to tell you."

"Well, that's good. I was just bringing you some groceries by. They had blueberries and strawberries on sale at Benny's. There's some can goods in there too."

GiGi nodded. "Thank you. Benny's ain't too far from here, no?"

"Nope. About ten minutes. Right over there on Walsh."

"Hmm. Synovi, where's that place you're staying at? It's about ten minutes the opposite of Walsh, ain't it?"

Synovi cut his eyes her way. GiGi knew exactly where he was staying and the address. Hell, she knew the fax number and Ms. Reid's by heart.

"Yes."

"Your mama need to gon' head and make her way over there one day. My boy got him a nice room and the staff real nice," GiGi bragged.

"Nah. She good. We can't have visitors," Synovi said dryly.

"Since when?" GiGi wanted to know.

Unique chuckled sadly. "It's okay. Maybe we can meet outside of there. I'd love to catch up with you."

Synovi licked his lips and sat up on the edge of the couch. "Tell me this, Unique. When the last time you saw me?"

She swallowed the rock in her throat. "March third of last year."

"Girl, how you remember that damn date?" GiGi blurted.

"You can remember a date, but not that you have a fucking son?"

Synovi's voice was so cold, it made Unique's heart stop.

"Now, Synovi," GiGi sighed.

"Nah, Granny. 'Cause she sitting up here like everything is all good. Dropping off groceries and shit. When the last time you did something for me? Bought me anything, huh? You don't know 'cause you haven't. A nigga could've been dead, and you probably wouldn't have known if GiGi didn't tell you."

Unique shot to her feet with tears in her eyes. "I tried my best to take care of you! You don't know what it's like being a single mother and struggling with no family! Yes, I failed you, Synovi, and I'm so, so sorry. I beat myself up every day about letting the system have you, but I wasn't mentally or financially capable of taking care of you. I wish I could change the hands of time and go back and beg God harder to have mercy on our lives. You didn't deserve to suffer from my inabilities, and I'll never be okay with that."

Synovi stared her dead in the eyes. "You shouldn't. You never came back for me."

The heaviness of his statement and the truth behind it stilled the room. It was no secret that Synovi had been in and out of the system and was a product of neglect. Her daily struggles through life itself caused it.

To some, Unique was unfit, but she hadn't been a bad mother. Nor was she trying to neglect Synovi. Leaving him at home by himself some days to run the streets was what she thought was okay. That was until she'd done it one too many times and a neighbor called to report her.

She didn't always have a babysitter and the family support was nonexistent. When the social worker came to the home, Unique couldn't prove to them that the environment she and her son lived in was safe. Not just physically, but mentally, Unique was a danger to them both. So, instead of getting her resources, they took him.

That was the beginning of a never-ending cycle that forced Synovi into a system that did more harm than good. Unique barely had help to begin with, and after trying to battle the courts, the leasing office, the man she owed for her car note, going to parenting classes, all while not having her son, it was hard. She couldn't see the end goal and had no energy to keep fighting for him, even though she really wanted to.

While the majority of kids are in the foster care system due to abuse and negligence, many are also there because of false reporting. Unique didn't understand how they wanted her to follow these guidelines, meet every requirement, and not provide her with adequate resources. It'd make any already struggling single mother go insane.

"I tried," Unique said pathetically.

"Quit saying that. When you try at something, the outcome changes, even if only a lil' bit. When GiGi got hurt, I couldn't even come stay with you. You wanna know why? 'Cause even after all them years to get right, you were still unstable, living with a nigga who was knocking yo' fucking head through the wall. You ain't try to leave him yet, I see."

Synovi was so mad, his hands were shaking. The bruises on Unique's neck that she tried hiding were visible as day. That was why he held animosity toward her and would continue. She couldn't leave a man who shouldn't even be considered one. Synovi felt that as a parent, no matter the circumstances, he should've been able to call on her for anything. Unique had somewhat gotten herself together and, in his eyes, said fuck him, so the feelings would forever be mutual.

"Mama, I'ma go," Unique said, wiping at her wet face.

GiGi just shook her head. "You can't keep running from your problems, child. Your son is right here pouring his heart out, and the first thing you wanna do is leave?"

"What am I supposed to do?" Unique cried.

"Figure it out and love on him! He's giving you the chance to fix y'all's broken relationship, and you're not taking it. Go hug him right now."

Unique's lips trembled. "Mama."

"Go hug him!" GiGi shouted.

Synovi had never heard her raise her voice like that in his life. Unmovable, he stayed seated as Unique walked toward him. Her eyes, the same oddly colored ones as his, stared at him with apprehension so thick, fog appeared before them. There was a shiny glint of fear and deprivation there as well. Unique missed her baby. Her motherless child. She was alive but dead in his eyes, and it crushed her soul.

The closer she got, the iller Synovi felt. There was a boulder sitting on his chest, and his stomach decided to start break dancing. He wanted to stand. Let her know that this was okay. That he, too, needed to feel her. To feel something other than unloved.

"Can I?" Unique asked meekly.

Synovi nodded, and she shoved her nerves aside and stretched her arms. Only then did Synovi find his footing. He reached for her like only a child does when their mothers were the only ones who could soothe them. Unique fell into his embrace, and the tension between them began to melt as they hugged one another tightly. As hard as he tried to hold them in, Synovi's tears rapidly filled his eyes, blurring his vision.

"I'm sorry," Unique blubbered against his chest.

She soaked his shirt with tears that she'd never stopped crying. Beside them, GiGi patted her face with a tissue. This moment was what she'd been praying for more than anything.

"I love you," Unique confessed, hugging him tighter. "I never stopped."

Neither did I.

Tongue-tied, Synovi remained quiet. His palm rested against her head of loose curls, pulling her into his chest. It was going to take him some time to feel anything but hurt, but this was a start. One where he hoped ended for the better this time around because he was tired of starting over in life.

<h1 style="text-align:center">eleven</h1>

Torin remembered why she didn't go out shopping with her mama and sister. The older Racquel got, the more expensive she became. Not only that, but she had to go into every store and browse every aisle. Torin didn't mind spending money on her, but sister girl's feet were tired.

They'd been to two outlets, one mall, and now they were at Target. A place Torin did not need to be with her love for everything in it. Racquel wasn't the only one to blame; Tracee was as well.

"Racquel, you have ten minutes, and we're heading to check out," Tracee said.

"We haven't even been in here that long," Racquel groaned, folding back one graphic tee after another.

Torin pushed her basket past them. "I'm going to grab me a bottle of wine."

"For you and that friend of yours?"

"Leighton is out of town," Torin confirmed.

Tracee gave her a gentle smile. "Not her."

"Ma, please." Torin laughed, walking away. "Can a girl not want to spend some time alone?"

"You could, but I know you're not. He sounds like a nice young man."

"Let me guess, Racquel told you?"

Tracee stopped her basket near the sunglasses. "Nope. Your overly excited father did. I'm not sure why William thinks it's okay to call me about everything he has going on, but he does."

Torin snickered lowly. "You know he thinks you're still his listening ear."

"That's what he has a wife for."

There was no disdain in her tone at all. Tracee and William had a good relationship for years. William had always wanted to get married and had even proposed. They were engaged for years and never tied the knot because Tracee couldn't see herself married. She wanted a child, though, and that was where Torin entered the world.

She was her parents's pride and joy, and William thought that maybe once Tracee had her, it'd changed her mind about walking down the aisle. It hadn't. They officially called it quits when Torin was five, and Tracee gave birth to Racquel three years later.

She'd met Racquel's father, Rinaldo, at a fundraising event and dated for five years. Like William, Rinaldo wanted to marry her as well, but Tracee declined. Neither man slacked off on their parenting and had each girl, and sometimes both, more than Tracee did at one point. She'd been adamant about the life she wanted for herself and stuck to that. Not all women wanted to be married, and not all wanted to have children.

"Indeed," Torin agreed.

She liked her dad's wife, Kenya, but that was as far as it went. They married when Torin was twenty and grown. She felt like Kenya could've been more supportive of everything William was involved in. Yet, she never saw her contributing to the growth of their family legacy.

As much as William did around the city, Kenya opted out of being in the spotlight with him. She never came to volunteer at Solace Place, didn't attend events, and kept to herself. That was the reason Synovi didn't even know he had a woman.

Tracee's ear wasn't the only one William talked off; Torin had been subject to his venting as well some days. As his child, she listened but reminded him that his marriage was exactly that: his. There was nothing she could say that would change the person Kenya was or who he married. Torin wasn't sure if he was in it for the love or the comfort, but if he liked it, she loved it.

"Are you going to keep this guy a secret like the last one?" Tracee asked, not letting up.

"The last one? You're talking about the guy I went out on two dates with who couldn't stop bragging about himself and how much money he had long enough for me to place an order?"

Tracee chuckled. "Well, since you put it that way. I would've kept him a secret, too."

"Exactly." Torin laughed. "He was nothing to write home about. I want you to meet Synovi, though."

"His name. That's really nice. Sounds powerful. Kind of boss-like."

Torin giggled. "Mhm, same thing I said. I think you'll like him."

"I like them all until you don't."

"That's why you're my girl. Now, where is—"

Torin stopped her sentence short when she saw Chelsea walking down the aisle that contained shampoo and conditioners. Her eyes squinted, hoping they were playing tricks on her.

"What's the matter?" Tracee asked, just as Racquel rolled up on them.

"I think I'm tripping, but let me make sure."

Pushing her basket in the direction she saw Chelsea going in, she turned down the aisle. Her eyes hadn't been playing tricks on her at all.

"Hey, Chelsea."

Hearing that familiar voice, Chelsea turned to greet her with a grin and a hug. "Sis. What's up? Hey, y'all," she said, waving behind Torin. "What you in here buying?"

"Nothing much. I didn't know you and her were cool," Torin said, eyeing a chick who made it very well-known that she messed with Don.

"Oh, girl, yeah," Chelsea chirped like it was no big deal. "She does my nails."

That was news to Torin, and it showed. "Oh, for real." She chuckled, somewhat amused, yet felt the sting of betrayal zap her chest.

"Mhm. Why you looking like that?" Chelsea asked.

"No reason. The next time you talk to your brother, tell him to stop calling my phone. We don't have anything to discuss."

That finally got the girl's attention. "You're his ex, right?"

"You know exactly who I am," Torin said calmly.

Chelsea frowned. "Whoa. Hold on. What's the issue?"

"You're calling me sis, but kicking it with someone Don messed around on me with. That's crazy to me."

"Y'all aren't together. I don't see how me hanging with her is a problem."

Torin nodded her head. If Chelsea didn't understand the problem, she wasn't going to solve it for her.

"You can hang with whoever you want. Just don't include me in that."

She and Chelsea had plenty of conversations about this exact girl and others who spoke on her name. They'd even exchanged a few heated words with Chelsea right there by her side. It wasn't about her no longer dating Don; it was about Chelsea's loyalty. Torin didn't play that two-sided, fake shit. She either rocked with her or she didn't. She couldn't care less about the girl.

"You for real right now?" Chelsea asked, stunned.

Torin rotated her cart in the other direction. "Yep."

With that, she headed out of the aisle and to checkout. Racquel shook her head at Chelsea and followed her sister. There was a thin line between people knowing what they were doing and just being weird. Chelsea was tittering on both sides of it in Torin's eyes.

She was too far up on game to act as if Torin didn't have a reason to be side-eyeing her. They'd shared laughs about girls who did what she was doing. It made no sense, and though she was hurt by her actions, Torin chalked it up as her finally being able to cut one tie that needed to be snipped long before now.

"Well, that was interesting," Tracee said as they pushed through the sliding doors.

"She was standing there looking crazy," Racquel added. "Are you okay? I know you guys were kind of close."

Torin unlocked her truck and opened the back. "Yep. It is what it is."

Tracee and Racquel looked at one another and sighed. When Torin got in one of her moods, they knew to stay clear of her. Thankfully, they were done with their girls's outing for the day and getting dropped off at their respective vehicles shortly.

Torin played music the entire ride home while Racquel talked to one of her friends on FaceTime. When she pulled into the driveway, Tracee didn't get out right away. She didn't know what it felt like to have someone wound her heart that she never thought would, but she could empathize with her. Friend breakups were shitty, and sister-like ones were harder.

"You're not okay with what happened back there, and you don't have to be," Tracee said.

"I know, Mama. It just caught me off guard. I'll be good, though. You always told me to stop trying to hold on to things I knew I was supposed to let go of before they hurt me. That relationship was one of them."

"As you get older, you'll start to see that all my preaching back then wasn't in vain. I know you'll be fine, but when you're not, I'm a call and drive away."

Torin leaned over and hugged her. "I love you."

"I love you, too, my sweet girl. Save all that good heart for someone deserving. Let me get on home so I can relax. You girls wore me and my pockets out today."

Cutting her truck off, Torin pushed her door open and laughed. "Don't blame me. That was all your youngest's doing."

"What about me?" Racquel asked, walking out of the garage with a raspberry granola bar and fruit cup in her hand.

She'd just come from inside the house in search of a snack. "When you'd start buying these? They're fire."

"Those are Synovi's."

"I told you, Mommy!" Racquel squealed.

Tracee popped her head from the backseat of her car. "Told me what?"

"She's been letting my friend sleep over here. Y'all be doing the nasty?" Racquel whispered to her sister.

Torin chortled. "Shut up."

"Mind your business, Racquel, and grab your stuff. Your sister is grown, and I'm sure he is, too."

"Exactly. And stop calling him your friend. His only friend is me."

Racquel fell over in laughter. "Oh. He's definitely over here doing something to you," she said, eyes full of tears. "I hope he's wearing a condom. I am not ready to be an auntie."

"I wouldn't mind a grandchild. Y'all are lucky I haven't given y'all a sibling yet."

"Mommy!" they both squealed with disgust on their faces.

"Please, okay. Kill the visual," Torin groaned.

Racquel fake gagged. "No, seriously."

Tracee shrugged. She was still living her best life. "I'm just saying, but your sister is right. I hope you're being smart unless you want to raise a child right now."

Torin gulped, not liking where this conversation was heading. "I am. I still have a few more goals to hit before I bring a little baby into this world."

"Whenever you decide, I'll be here and ready. I need someone else to spoil besides myself and you two," Tracee said before kissing Torin's cheek. "I had fun today. We'll have to do this again in a few weeks."

"Oh, no, ma'am." Torin laughed. "I spent way too much money today. Catch me next month."

"Sure thing. Racquel, are you coming over for dinner or stopping by your dad's?"

She looked up from the text message she was typing. "I'm right behind you. See you later, sis. Let me grab my stuff."

The sisters hugged, and Torin retrieved her bags from the back as well. She waved as they pulled out of her driveway and then went inside the house. Toeing her shoes off right at the door, she popped the bones in her feet and sighed. Today had been long. Shopping always exhausted her, but she loved it.

Laying out on her couch, she pulled up FaceTime and tapped Synovi's name. They hadn't talked since earlier in the day, and she missed him. It'd been two weeks since she found out he lived at Solace Place. Synovi thought it would've put a strain on their relationship, but it'd done the complete opposite. The two were damn near attached at the hip and getting to the money together.

He'd completed his training and worked part time at an answering service company. It was easy money, and the old women there loved him. When he wasn't taking messages, he got his hands dirty and made things sparkle after events and at Torin's crib. She'd had so many in the past few weeks, Synovi couldn't keep up. Some of her new clientele was because of him.

Whenever he came to work with leftovers or a freshly prepared meal, someone always wanted to know where he got it from. He started leaving Torin's business flyers on the counters and giving out her social media information. She'd been booked twice already for luncheons with the company, and three people requested the meals she served weekly.

"You miss me?" Synovi questioned as soon as he picked up.

Torin laughed. "Um, hello. How are you?"

He smirked. "What's up, Love? You done tearing the mall down?"

"Yes, finally. I got you some things."

Torin couldn't hold water with him at all. While shopping, she told herself she'd just wait until he got there to show him his things. Here she was, blabbering away. Whatever way it was presented to him, Synovi was appreciative.

"Yeah? I got something for you, too," Synovi announced.

"Ooh. What is it?"

He put his mouth closer to the speaker and whispered, "This dick."

Torin cracked up. "That's it?"

"Shit, that's a lot."

Her body trembled. "Oh, I know. But for real. What'd you get me? I'll take the first gift forever."

"You was gon' do that regardless."

Cocky ass nigga.

"But it's a tattoo appointment with Lito," he said.

Torin's jaw dropped. "What? He's booked until next year."

"For everyone else, not for you."

"How did you manage to snag an appointment? You must know him personally?" Torin guessed.

Synovi nodded his head. Carlito, best known as Lito, was a highly sought-after tattoo artist with a demanding schedule and was the only person Synovi let tat him. It hadn't been that way when he first fell in love with the needle at fourteen, but Carlito inked him once, and it'd been a wrap since. Torin fell in love with the inky mural on his chest and mentioned wanting more. So, Synovi made it happen.

"I do. We grew up together."

Carlito had been a ward of the state as well. His journey had been slightly different from Synovi's, but their adversities bonded them for life.

"I can't believe this. I'm so excited." Torin grinned. "Thank you so much. When is the appointment?"

"He told me to let him know when you're available, and he'll squeeze you in. What you doing this weekend?"

"We have the Mother's Day event, remember?" Torin questioned.

He'd forgotten all about it. The holiday wasn't one of Synovi's favorites, but he always made sure GiGi was thought of. With Unique now back in his life somewhat, he couldn't help but wonder if getting her something would be appropriate.

"I forgot, but a'ight. Just let me know, and I'll tell him," Synovi said.

"Okay. Where are you? Because yes, I do miss you, and I want to hear about your day."

Synovi licked his lips and glanced out the passenger window of D'Marco's car. "I miss you, too, Love. I'm with this nigga Marco, but I'll be through there. You need me right now?"

Torin nodded and sexily hummed, "Mhm. Right fucking now."

"Where you need me at?"

She opened her mouth, stretching her tongue out. Torin wanted him so deep down her throat that the tip of him tapped at her heart. Possibly knock some sense into it because she was sure it was telling her she loved Synovi already.

It's way too soon, she thought, with her brain trying to convince her otherwise.

Synovi's eyes lowered and filled with lust. "You such a freak. I'ma give you exactly what you want when I get there."

She smirked. "Okay. Be safe with whatever you're doing."

He flipped the camera around, showing her his location. Reassurance. He knew she needed that. Synovi wasn't out here on shit but her and chasing a bag. Anything else was irrelevant. Torin wanted to believe that, she really did, but Jade was still in the picture. She may have been slightly out of the frame, but her presence still lingered.

"We at the store, and this nigga taking all day. Aw, never mind. Here he go right now. I'll be there in a minute," he confirmed.

Torin told him okay and hang up, although she didn't want to. She placed a hand against her chest, hoping to calm the swarm of butterflies that traveled from her stomach. The raw emotions she was experiencing shook her world up, and she let it. With Synovi, she had no choice. He tended to cause that effect wherever he went.

"Dog," D'Marco stressed, pulling out of the gas station lot.

"Listen. I know you trying to get shit out the mud and all, but I think I got a better idea."

Right away, Synovi knew it was something illegal. He wasn't trying to get caught up in anything that could possibly cost him his freedom, but he'd listen just in case he were wrong. Ms. Minnie had called him into her office earlier that week and let him know he'd gotten approved for the new apartments.

He was on the waiting list and wouldn't move in until the middle of next month, but it was a start. A damn good one, and he needed all the funds he could get his hands on. Getting a car was still on his to-do list as well. They'd pulled up to a few used car lots, but Synovi wasn't trying to get stuck with a lemon. It'd be just his luck to put his money into a whip that broke down right after he bought it.

"I'm listening," he said.

"I was in the store and overheard some young niggas talking about a stash house not too far out the way."

Synovi glanced his way. "And you wanna do what? Run up in that bitch?"

"Yeah. nigga." D'Marco laughed. "That's an easy lick. On God."

"I ain't fucking with it. How you know it's some real money in there?"

Synovi didn't mean real as in non-counterfeit, but authentic, like it was worth the risk. He wasn't running up in there for no pocket change.

"Why wouldn't it be? Niggas ain't talking for no reason, but I hear what you saying. I'ma have somebody sit on them and find out."

"Nah. You do it. If this shit legit, we the only ones profiting from it," Synovi stated.

He wasn't breaking bread and doing dirt with someone he didn't know. Clumsy shit like that would get him jammed quicker than he could blink.

A mischievous grin covered D'Marco's face. "Bet."

twelve

Normally, when Synovi accompanied Torin to her events, he played the back and made himself useful as needed. That hadn't been the case today. The Mother's Day Brunch event Kaine's Kitchen was vending was packed. One of the employees whose spot was usually next to Torin's had to be filled. They'd caught a cold and couldn't make it.

So, Synovi was there in their place with his customized business shirt on. At the last minute, Torin went to get his name embroidered on the front. As a growing business that would continue to make an impact, it was imperative that Torin made anything with her name attached to it stand out. Customized everything with *Kaine's Kitchen* on it did just that.

"This line ain't let up yet," Synovi said, watching as a few more people joined.

Torin smiled and scooped out a serving of garlic mashed potatoes. "I know. That means people are talking."

Seeing almost everyone walk around with an olive green plate and gold fork in their hand would always make her day. Some people had even come back for seconds. Torin opted out of bringing drinks since she knew there'd be other vendors in attendance serving them. She wanted every business to make a profit.

Rita, the woman who put on the event, had one mission in mind when creating it: to honor her late mother and show gratitude to all the mommies out there. Even those who were no longer alive, she wanted to let them know they were appreciated. The city had shown up and out to support, filling the gymnasium.

"Who's the cook of this good plate of food?" a man asked with a bright grin.

Torin smiled. "That would be me. I'm glad you're enjoying it."

"I most certainly am. You see I'm back for another serving. The misses ate up the first plate." He chuckled heartily.

"As she should've. You knew better than to only grab one, to begin with," Torin joked. "Let her know this one is on me, and Happy Mother's Day."

She didn't think his smile could get any bigger. "Aw, man. Thank you for that. She's going to be happy since she's eating for two. We're on our second child and can't wait until he gets here."

"Congratulations!"

This was why Torin loved what she did. Not just because of the food that brought people together, but also because of the stories she heard and the people she met. She'd come across people from so many different walks of life, it only encouraged her to keep going. So it was easy for her to uplift those around her. Especially those who wanted to see her succeed.

When they got a small break between meals, Torin discarded her gloves and went to wash her hands before going into her travel bag. Pulling the rectangular cardboard box out, she walked over to Synovi. He was lightly bobbing his head to the music floating through the speakers when she tapped his arm.

"What's this?" he questioned.

"Open it and see."

Torin rocked a grin the entire time he peeled the box open. Puzzlement covered his face before recognition replaced it.

Grabbing one of the cards from the deck, he scanned it before looking up at her with disbelief in his eyes.

"Yo, what?" he questioned skeptically. "You got me some business cards made?"

"I did. I knew this event would be a great opportunity for you to make some connections and get more business, so yeah."

Torin didn't know if he'd like the idea, but she was all for expanding. There was never a time she wasn't thinking of ways to be a better version of herself and wanted the same for those around her. She and Synovi were a power team right now, and she wanted him to take his entrepreneurship to the next level. Starting with one of the most important aspects of growing a business: letting people know it existed.

The white, sixteen-point card-stock, square-shaped cards were designed and printed through a local shop in town. Torin wasn't sure what colors to go with initially, but chose yellow and black. She figured Synovi could change it if he wanted something else.

The front had *SB's Cleaning Service* in bold, embossed font. She kept it simple, with no design. He flipped the card over and read the back while smirking. It had all of his contact information listed and Torin had even added that he had a website coming soon.

"Man," he said with a shake of his head.

"You like it?" Torin was a little nervous.

She was used to getting the ball rolling on ideas, but didn't know if all of this was overwhelming for him. That was not what she wanted him to feel at all.

"I love it."

Stepping closer to her, Synovi pulled her in close. His warm breath and soft lips brushed against the shell of her ear, and Torin could've melted where she stood when he whispered in her ear.

"Thank you for these. I can't wait to suck your pussy dry and really let you feel my appreciation. You're a blessing, Love."

Like always, her body snitched on her as it caught a chill. If not for his words letting her know he was thankful, the stiffness behind his jeans was a dead giveaway. Something about Torin wanting to make his life the best it could be made Synovi's dick hard and his chest tight. She was after his heart and he was ready to hand it and whatever else she wanted right over.

"You're welcome." Torin panted once he put distance between them.

"I'ma go pass these out. Y'all good?" he asked.

Torin glanced down the table at her comrades for the day. Racquel and Leighton were laughing about something and she knew they were more than likely joking about the men who were here with their baby mamas. They'd already noticed a few who were out doing the family thing, but had been in each of their inboxes recently. All had been left on read and laughed at like the joke they were.

"Yeah, we should be good. Once we run out, I'm gonna do some shopping."

Synovi dug in his pocket and pulled out a one-hundred-dollar bill. "Here. It ain't much, but I'm sure you can spend it on something in here."

Torin leaned his way and quickly kissed his lips. "It's more than enough. Thank you."

He eyed her for a few seconds more before walking off. Torin made eye contact with Leighton and Racquel and they were childishly poking their lips out, blowing kisses her way.

"Grow up," Torin told them in laughter.

The only kisses she wanted were Synovi's.

As he walked around the gym, Synovi tried shaking the edginess he felt spreading. It was a gut-swirling reaction he'd experienced once too often. Having to put himself out there, in hopes someone would want to take a chance on his business, was a struggle he vowed to overcome. The similarity between doing so and how he used to feel while in foster care was one and the same.

Your fear of rejection will keep hindering your success if you don't just do it.

Synovi spoke those words to himself and exhaled before walking over to a group of women. He'd already spoken to them when they came through the line and figured one more conversation wouldn't hurt.

"Excuse me, ladies. How was everything?" Synovi asked politely.

One woman with an extremely curly afro answered him first. "Delicious! If I wasn't trying to watch my figure, I'd go get another plate of that sweet chili salmon."

"Mhm. Sure would. It was everything. Did you or your girlfriend make it?" Another woman with locs that were fancily twisted in an up-do inquired.

Synovi smirked. "She did. Kaine's Kitchen is her food business."

"Ooh. I'ma have to hire her," Curly Afro said.

"Speaking of hiring, are any of you interested in getting your home or business professional cleaned? I just started my own cleaning company, and I'm looking to add a solid group of customers to my roster."

Fancy Locs looked at their other friend, who was blushing and rocking a silk press. Synovi had just swooned the hell out of them and hadn't said much.

"Y'all hear this, young man? Respectful, charming, and has a solid business proposal. Let me see one of these cards."

"Me too. I was just telling my husband we need to hire someone because I'm tired, okay? Gotta clean, cook, clean again, throw ass back, give the kids a bath and some mo' shit," Curly Fro said, holding her hand out for a card as well.

"Girl, he is not trying to hear all that," Silk Press said, taking a card.

"Chile, please. I'm sure he don' heard worse."

Synovi only smirked as he watched them read it over. When their heads nodded before placing the cards inside their purses, he knew facing his fears wasn't that bad after all.

"Let me not put mine up yet. I'm giving this to Tim right now," Curly Fro said. "Thank you, sweetie. I pray your business reaches a level of success that blows your mind."

"Thank you for that. I hope y'all enjoy y'all's Mother's Day," Synovi said.

They watched as he walked away and Fancy Locs smiled. "If he didn't have a girlfriend, I'd call Elise up here right now for him," she said, speaking of her daughter.

"Okay. A handsome, young, working man that likes to clean? They're not making them like that anymore," Curly Fro said. "Let me call my son and tell him to get off his ass and go cut the grass or something."

The women cackled and continued to enjoy every minute of the event. Synovi made his rounds around the entire gym floor, leaving his business cards on tables of other vendors and introducing himself to more people.

When he finally made it back to their table, Synovi was all out of the business cards he'd taken with him. A content grin was on his face, leading Torin to believe that things had gone well.

"Look who made it back," she joked. "How was it?"

"Nerve-racking, but I think I got a few potential clients," he said, sitting down. "I got you some, too."

Torin grinned widely, showing all teeth. "That's so good, baby. Watch your cell be blowing up soon. We need to get your website up and establish a schedule so things can flow smoothly. Ooh, I can't wait."

Her excitement and readiness to help him stirred Synovi's entire soul. He'd never met a woman so selfless in his life besides GiGi.

"You think it's gon' take off?" he asked.

"I know so. From my lips to God's ears. Watch and see."

Synovi couldn't do anything but nod, hoping Torin made him a believer.

Torin couldn't help but wonder how she'd gone so long without intercourse before Synovi. She wasn't dating much and did have a busy schedule, but she still wondered how it was possible. The way she craved the feeling of him inside of her, igniting a flame that only he had a match to, was uncanny. There was nothing or no one that could stop her from receiving him and the tongue-lashing he delivered at an irrationally unhurried pace.

Synovi woke her up to it. There was no way he could continue to rest and not satisfy his craving for her at three in the morning. Hours when she stretched in bed before clinging to his chest for more of him. He didn't plan on going anywhere but between her thighs.

Slow burning.

Air gasping.

Eyes crossing.

Legs quivering.

Toes curling.

Those were the type of orgasms he gave her. Synovi was an attentive lover, and Torin was sure he had some type of mind control over her at this point. She always wanted more, and he'd always give it to her. The shit was unhealthy, yet she kept indulging. Gluttony was a sin, and she was a proud sinner, promising to repent when the day broke.

"Ohhh, my gooosh. B-Baby," she whined, rubbing his head.

The motion only encouraged him to proceed. Synovi handled her pussy with care and expertise. He was only reciprocating the love she gave to him tenfold.

"You know how good you taste?"

Synovi wasn't looking for an answer; he was simply making a statement. He'd long ago cleared the curiosity of how Torin would melt in his mouth like kids's favorite cheesy puff chips. She instantly coated his tastebuds, making Synovi suck on her clit harder.

"Ummm hmmm," he hummed, mouth full.

Synovi was disrespectful with it, knowing he shouldn't try to speak when he had her in his mouth. Torin was his favorite fucking meal to eat.

"Come heeeere," Torin moaned. "I need to feel you."

At her beck and call, he lifted, and so did her legs. Synovi placed her left ankle over his shoulder, kissing the spot where her anklet dangled. Torin stroked his length as he continued to make love to her toes with his mouth. The fact that he massaged her foot while doing so was crazy to her.

Fucking multitasker, she thought and lost her breath as he slid inside of her. The sensation of him stretching her walls and sucking on her toes made her heart skip a beat. She came immediately.

"Noviii!"

He pumped into her. "I know, Love," he groaned.

Synovi felt it too. Their connection was solid. Unwavering. The way she gripped him had Synovi's head spinning. He squeezed his eyes tight, releasing her foot before pushing her legs back. Exposed fully, Torin gave him access to her whole heart and body. Synovi kissed her with so much passion as she held onto his neck.

This was that three-in-the-morning sex that created babies and connections so deeply, there'd be no coming back from either.

"You just gon' keep cummin' on this dick, huh?"

"That's what you want me to do," Torin moaned.

Damn right, he did. It was made for her to do just that. Torin grew wetter, feeling him thicken. Lovingly, she rubbed his face, staring him in those eyes she couldn't get enough of looking at. Wordlessly, they commanded her every time.

"I'm cumming," she whimpered. "Uuuh, baby."

Synovi's nostrils flared, and his jaw flexed. His eyes fluttered as she contracted around him.

"No. Look at me. Look how good you make me feel."

Torin was fucking his head up. Synovi peeled his eyes open, watching her unravel through slits. He dug deeper as she circled her hips beneath him.

"Fuck, Love," he grunted, pulling out of her.

Torin stroked out his release, loving how he felt throbbing and dripping onto her sensitivity. She rubbed him over her clit before sliding him back inside. Still hard.

"I'ma fuck you up," Synovi grumbled against her lips.

Torin smiled and pouted when he removed himself once more. With a huff of pure satisfaction, he rolled out of bed, and Torin slowly exited behind him. Her strides were slow, and Synovi looked on with concern as she lowered onto the toilet with a frown.

"What's the matter?"

"My stomach hurts. You be too deep."

He thought something was really wrong. Smirking, he cut the water on and grabbed a towel. He cleaned himself off, and Torin did the same once she finished peeing. Sex permeated the air as he pulled the sheets off and replaced them. Torin stood by sleepily, letting out a yawn every thirty seconds. Once the bed was covered with fresh sheets, the duo laid down and she resumed her spot right underneath him.

"Are we in a relationship?" Torin asked out of the blue.

It was random, but she wanted to know what they were doing. The way he'd just fucked her, she had no time to sit around wondering if Jade or anyone else was receiving the same treatment.

"We can be."

Synovi's answer was simple. Torin's next question wasn't.

"Okay. Do you still talk to that married woman?"

"Yeah. I don't have sex with her anymore, though."

"Oh, okay. Well, I think you need to figure that out. Whatever it is."

Her body lightly bounced as his chest vibrated with laughter. "A'ight, Love."

"Why do you call me that?"

"What? Love?"

She nodded her head and rubbed up and down his stomach. "Mhm."

"'Cause that's what you are," he replied with ease. "That's what you feel like."

Torin didn't know what to say. He'd given her a one-of-a-kind compliment. She didn't want to mistake his words for him saying he loved her, so she took them at face value.

"You've never felt this before?"

"Nah, so it's easy to identify."

She hugged him a little tighter, always knowing what he needed at that moment.

"What about you?" he countered.

"Been in love? No. Loved a man? Yes."

It was crazy to think back on her and Don's relationship and how much she overlooked. Honestly, Torin didn't know if it were love or infatuation now that the smoke had cleared.

"I think him having a son that I was close to helped play a role in that as well," Torin added.

"You was playing step-mama young as hell." Synovi laughed, making her do the same.

"No, I really was. No one could tell me anything either. Just young and dumb."

"We all been there. Shit, I feel like I'm just now exiting that stage of life."

"You're young, though. We both are. We can make mistakes."

He cleared his throat of sleep. "There's a difference between being young and not knowing better and just doing dumb shit."

"Like fucking a married woman," Torin offered.

Synovi laughed heartily. "Man. Change the subject."

"Hey, you brought it up." Torin chuckled and quieted. "Have you spoken to your mom?"

He was not expecting her to ask that. Surprisingly, Unique had been reaching out to him, and Synovi let her. She knew he was of age now, and there were no classes to teach her how to parent anymore, so she was doing what she felt was right. It was a slow process, but slow motion was still motion.

"Yeah. She called me earlier today. Still talking about the flowers and chocolates I got her last week."

"I know she appreciated that. I'm glad you both are trying."

Synovi couldn't lie; he was glad too. Having one parent he could now claim was something he'd always wanted.

"Yeah, she bet' not fuck up and go missing again. She'll be dead to me for real, then."

Torin knew to give people grace in all situations, but she wouldn't preach that to him. She hadn't been abandoned and left in a world alone. When Synovi's stomach rumbled in hunger, she tittered.

"You worked up an appetite."

"Hell yeah. You gon' fix me something to eat?"

"What you want?" Torin asked.

Whenever the conversation came up about fixing a man some food in the wee hours of the morning, Torin stayed mute. The way Synovi had her feeling, she'd build that nigga a boat to get to the island she built him, where only they were welcomed. She couldn't relate to the girls who wouldn't. It was whatever for her man because she knew he brought that same energy.

"I'ont know, but I'm starving. Let's go down there and see."

Torin lifted and climbed from the bed. Tossing her robe around her naked frame, she slid into her house shoes while Synovi slid on some shorts. She grabbed her phone off the dresser, and they headed downstairs.

While Synovi searched the fridge, rubbing his stomach and yawning, Torin frowned at her phone screen. They'd gotten in early from a gig, showered, and fell asleep earlier than usual on a weekend. Torin hadn't checked her phone in hours, and seeing all the notifications and missed calls made her panic.

She didn't know who to call back first: Leighton, her mama, Racquel, or her assistant, Mia. Her skin heated as she scrolled through her text messages filled with screenshots.

"What the fuck," she hissed.

Synovi looked her way. "What's up?"

Torin ignored him and kept reading the screenshots from Facebook, Instagram, and Twitter. There were even a few from her website. In all of her years of being a chef, Torin had never gotten a bad review about her cooking. If she did, it hadn't been brought to her knowledge or made public. So, to see someone not only bashing Kaine's Kitchen but her name as well had her furious, but concerned.

"What you looking at that got you breathing all hard?" Synovi asked, glancing at her screen.

"Someone posted pictures of food they ordered from me, claiming there was hair in it and it was undercooked. They left bad reviews on all my social media pages and my website, basically dragging me all over their pages."

"You know who it is?"

"Yeah, and you do, too," she said, holding the phone up to his face.

Seeing Jade's profile name and the disrespectful things she was saying about Torin had him seeing red. Grabbing the phone from her, Synovi scrolled through the comments to see what people were saying. He expected to see everyone bashing Torin, but they were doing the opposite, claiming that Jade must've gone to the wrong Kaine's Kitchen. Or that she had placed the hair in the food herself and was trying to go viral.

Other comments weren't necessarily bashing Torin, but businesses in general, saying how you couldn't eat everything people cooked, and how Jade needed to get her money back. The shit was messy and right up Jade's alley. Synovi had been spinning her for weeks. Ignoring her calls hadn't been enough because she kept blowing his line down. Instead of blocking her, he let Jade experience what he had when dealing with her.

When Torin asked if he still talked to her, he hadn't lied. He had plans to do so and end things, but hadn't gotten around to it. It was obvious Jade wasn't trying to let him go and was going to great lengths to get his attention. She had it now and Synovi hoped she knew what to do with it.

Locking her phone, he slid it into his pocket. "I ain't letting you read that shit," he grumbled, walking back over to the counter.

"Give me my phone, Synovi."

Torin tried reaching in his pocket, and he pushed her hand away.

"Move, Love. For real. You and I both know that whatever she posted is fake and reading it just gon' piss you off even more. Fuck her."

"Oh, so now it's fuck her all of a sudden? She's trying to ruin my name and you won't even let me clear the air and check a bitch?"

Synovi looked her in her angry eyes. She was ready to fight, and he knew it.

"No, I won't 'cause she's my problem that should've never become yours. I'll handle her."

"You said that the first time, and now look. Looks like you ain't handle shit," she hissed.

Synovi rolled his tongue over his teeth and pinched the bridge of his nose. "We both can't be pissed off right now. When I get angry, I really take it there and I'm trying to remain calm for you."

"Do you think that's what I want to hear right now? This old, worn pussy ass hoe trying to make me look bad and you worried about me staying calm? Nigga, please. You wanna handle something, drive me to that bitch's house."

Synovi didn't mean to laugh, but it slipped out. "I'm not driving you over there. It's damn near four in the morning."

"So? I'm sure you've been over there at that time of night, now it's an issue."

"You mad right now and trying to be funny, so I'ma ignore that," Synovi said.

"No, what you should've been doing is ignoring her. She coming for me all because you don't want her anymore. That's not my fault. Oooh!"

Torin paced her kitchen, slamming her right fist into her left palm. This was the type of shit she thought she'd gotten away from after cutting Don off. Never did she think Synovi would bring this messiness into her life, especially with a woman who was rocking another man's last name. Torin couldn't stand hoes like her.

She stopped pacing for a second and it hit her. *My business phone is in my purse.* When she walked swiftly out of the kitchen, Synovi was on her heels. His long legs reached her in no time, and he swooped her up from behind just as she grabbed her purse off the couch.

"Nah," he grumbled, wrapping her in a bear hug, already knowing what she was going for.

"Synovi, let me go. I'm not fucking playing."

"You not about to give these mothafuckas a show. Think about everything you've built Kaine's Kitchen and yourself up to be. You wanna tarnish that all over some fake reviews and lies?"

She hated that he was right. Breathing hard, she squeezed her eyes shut and counted down from ten. Her heart was thundering in her chest so hard, she thought she'd pass out.

"Relax," Synovi spoke gently into her ear. He kissed her neck and pulled the purse out of her grasp. "Fuck her. She just jealous 'cause you can cook and she can't."

That got a laugh out of her. "Shut up. I'm not supposed to be laughing. I'm mad."

"And you can be mad right in this house and off that phone, but I ain't letting you jeopardize anything yo' name attached to behind this broad. If I tell you I'ma handle her, believe me."

Sighing, Torin decided to let it go for tonight. Tomorrow would be a different story, and Synovi couldn't keep her in his grasp forever.

"Okay. I'll let you handle it, but can I just post one thing?" Torin asked.

"What?"

"If I tell you, you're going to say no. And if you say no, I'ma handle her myself."

Synovi bit her neck. "That ain't no even exchange."

Torin laughed and squirmed. "Yes, it is. You want me to do

one thing with your bossy ass, and I want to do something else. At least I asked. I only did that out of respect, but I can do what I want, Synovi."

"Man, whatever. Grab your phone, Torin."

"Torin!" she screeched, reaching inside his shorts. "What happened to Love this and Love that?"

"That ain't who you are right now."

She snickered and finally grabbed her device from his pocket. She had to dig deep, thanks to its depth. Synovi rested his chin on her shoulder and looked as she pulled up the Facebook app. Tapping on the spot that asked, *What's on your mind?* Torin typed out her thoughts so quickly. When she said she had one question to ask, she meant exactly that.

"Man," Synovi groaned. "No. That's messy as fuck."

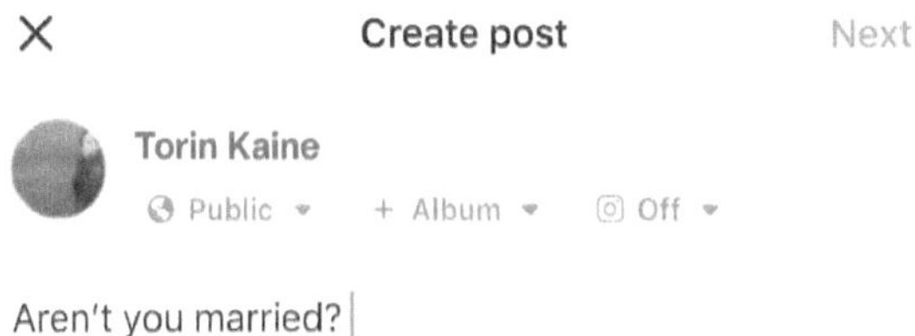

She typed out, *Aren't you married?* ready to air Jade the fuck out. It wasn't her fault she was tripping over some dick that never belonged to her in the first place. Since she wanted to take things to social media, Torin could too. Erasing the status, Torin locked her phone.

"Ugh! Fine. I'll let you handle her, but this is the last time I'm letting you, so get it right."

Synovi spanked her ass. "I will. Now come fix me a sandwich."

When he walked back into the kitchen, Torin remained where she stood. Though she couldn't stand him for it, she was thankful Synovi hadn't let her wild out like she wanted to. One bad lapse in decision-making could've turned things disastrous before she could smooth them over the right way. The Torin Kaine way that handled situations with poise like a grown woman.

"Love!" Synovi shouted, snapping her out of her thoughts.

Torin pivoted and headed his way. "You want mesquite turkey or smoked ham?"

thirteen

If it wasn't for bad luck, Synovi wouldn't have any luck at all. He just knew things were going too well for too long in his life. That never happened. Technically, the situation he was witnessing wasn't his, but it affected him tremendously, and it was only day one.

After weeks of using D'Marco's car to get to his cleaning gigs and temp job, Synovi was going to have to find a new means of transportation. Nikki, D'Marco's baby mama, had sliced three of his tires, broken the windshield, busted out the headlights, and stole the battery from underneath the hood. She'd done all of this while on Solace Place property, not giving a single fuck about the sirens in the distance.

"You keep taking me as a joke, and I'm done with your ass! You going right back on child support, liar!" Nikki screamed, chasing him around the parking lot with a bat.

D'Marco juked her, making her almost break her ankle. "Man, stop! I ain't lying! You trippin' for no reason! I told you Synovi had my whip."

"Fuck him!" Nikki screamed. "I know I saw a bitch in your car, D'Marco!"

Synovi's eyes widened as he stood idly by. "Damn. I was just trying to go to work."

He knew his boy was lying and wanted no parts. Nikki

swung the bat so aggressively, he couldn't help but wonder if she played softball in her teenage years. When it connected with the back of D'Marco's leg, making him trip, Synovi rushed over to them.

"Give me this shit," he spat, snatching the bat out of Nikki's hands.

That didn't stop her at all. She pounced on D'Marco, fighting him like he was a bitch off the street who'd disrespected her. When the police swarmed into the lot, she hopped up as if she hadn't just been drilling his head in.

"Ma'am, step away from him and put your hands up," a woman officer shouted.

"Y'all need to be taking him to jail! He's the one in the wrong!" Nikki said, but did as she was told.

The woman officer pulled her away from D'Marco but didn't cuff her. Thankfully, none of them pulled their guns out either. They were trying to de-escalate the situation as best and quickly as they could. Lover spats were common, and they got it under control within twenty minutes of being on the scene.

"Give me my bat," Nikki told Synovi with her hand out and too much grit in her tone.

"Nah," he said before tossing it over the fence he was standing by. "Go get it."

"Officer! Did you just see that?" Nikki fussed. "Y'all gon' let him just trash my belongings like that?"

The woman officer shook her head. "You didn't need it, anyway. Let's go. Get in your vehicle and go home."

Nikki mugged Synovi and D'Marco as she marched to her car that was parked crookedly in the lot. "Y'all think I'm dumb, but I know what I saw. That's okay. Just be ready to come up off them good Ford paychecks every month, *baby daddy.*"

D'Marco childishly flipped her off. She swerved out of the lot, not caring that the cops were right there.

"I can't stand that bitch. Look at my car!" D'Marco fussed.

Nikki had gone crazy with no remorse. Spotting a chick climbing out of his back passenger seat made her spazz out.

What made it worse was that she gave him a day to confess, and D'Marco said nothing. They hadn't even spoken because he'd broken his phone at work. When he went to try to get it replaced, they were talking crazy numbers, so he left.

He honestly didn't know where she was getting her information from because he'd been trying to do right by her. Now, they were back at square one.

"I gotta get me a rental right quick. I got a job up north in two hours," Synovi said.

"Where your girl at?" D'Marco asked as they headed inside the building.

Torin and her staff were an hour away, catering at a corporate event one of the women from the Mother's Day Brunch hired her for. Even if she was in the city, Synovi didn't feel right asking her for anything at the moment. He still hadn't handled the situation with Jade, and until he did so, he was treading lightly with his needs from her. She'd give him a ride or let him use her truck, no questions asked, but like Synovi always did, he'd figure it out.

"She busy. Man, damn. Let me think right quick," he fussed.

He headed toward the storage closet where Mr. K let him store his cleaning supplies. Ever since that day he called himself introducing Torin to Synovi, they'd been on good terms. They were never on bad ones in Mr. K's eyes. He saw the potential Synovi had and showed him tough love in a way he wasn't used to seeing. Torin let her daddy know that she and Synovi did more than just work together, and Mr. K couldn't do anything but accept it.

As Synovi grabbed his things from the closet, his phone rang with an incoming call from his mama. She was doing her every-other-day check-in before she got off work. Placing the bag down, Synovi answered her call.

"What up, Unique?"

"Hey. What you got going on?" she asked with a smile.

"Too much," he sighed.

He was still battling with opening up to her. Unique understood that and kept the conversation flowing before she got in her feelings.

"Oh, no. I hate to hear that. Is there anything I can do to help?"

A tingling sensation Synovi never felt coursed through his body. Hearing those words from the one person he always wanted to assist him was sobering like a mothafucka. He cleared the emotions from his throat. He wanted to tell her yes, but the thought of her letting him down would crush him.

"Nah. I'm good."

"I know I abandoned you in the past, and I failed you as well, but please don't shut me out. I want to build a relationship with you. What can I do to help?"

Exhaling, Synovi told her the dilemma he was in. To his surprise, letting her know what was going on with him lifted the weight he felt crushing his chest.

"If you can't make it, I'll figure it out," he said.

"No, I can come get you and take you. I get off work in twenty minutes. Will that be enough time?" Unique asked.

"Yeah. You need the address?"

"No. I've had it for a while. Was just scared to use it. I guess today is the day."

Synovi scratched the back of his head, not knowing if he should feel some type of way about her already having his address. Instead of harping on it, he let it go. Starting anew meant not letting the past hinder you, and he wouldn't let it.

"I guess so. I'll see you when you get here," Synovi said.

"I'll call when I'm outside."

Hanging up, he slid his phone into his pocket and continued to gather his supplies. Setting everything outside the door, he went to his room to change clothes. While most of his nights had been spent at Torin's, getting a pass from Mr. K himself, Synovi still kept most of his things here. It wasn't much, but the valuables he'd cherished over the years were tucked away.

He couldn't wait to move into his new spot and finally be able to claim a home as all his. Figuring out how to make it work was paying off, and Synovi told himself to stick it out for a little while longer. Feeling his phone vibrate again, he grabbed it and frowned.

Jade hadn't returned any of his calls for a few days, reminding him of their situation. There was no longer one, and she couldn't take it. The statuses she made, reviews she posted, and stories she tagged Torin's business in had all been deleted. Removing them wouldn't make the screenshots disappear or the disdain he had for her.

"The fuck you want?" Synovi answered calmly.

The way his voice boomed through the Bluetooth in her car startled her. "That's a rude way to answer the phone after ignoring someone for days."

"You lucky I answered. What, your husband ain't around to get on your nerves, so you wanna work mine?"

Jade gritted her teeth. "Don't worry about my husband. He and I are good."

"Best news I heard all day. Fuck you calling me for, then? I don't want you."

His words punched her in the gut.

"What? Why would you say that?"

"C'mon, Jade. Don't sit on this phone and act dumb. You know what you been on, and I ain't fucking with you. You're supposed to be grown, and spreading lies about someone's business is childish as fuck."

On the other end, Jade snickered. She'd had one of her cousins place an order under their name for her and had it delivered to their house.

"Oh, so she's why you've been moving strange. That bitch must be sucking your dick real good for you to be up her ass the way you are."

Synovi gritted his teeth. "Call her out of her name again and I'ma let her pull up on you and teach you about respect."

"Respect! That hoe can't teach me a damn thing. What she needs to do is lose some weight. All that nasty ass food she be making got her big as a house," Jade sneered.

Like I said, jealous 'cause she can't cook. Synovi hadn't found much of anything funny in a long time. There was no joking when life was hard, and you were broke. But now? Oh, right now, Jade was fucking hilarious. He wished Torin was here so they could crack up at her together.

"A'ight, man." Synovi laughed. "Anything else? You holding my line up. Go work it out with your husband and figure out why that nigga can't keep his dick up. I'm tired of doing his job."

Jade's mouth fell open. "You disrespectful mothafucka! Wait until I—"

Synovi hung up in her face and grumbled, "My name ain't mothafucka."

Fuming, Jade pounded her fist into the steering wheel. In all the time she and Synovi had been creeping around, he'd never once spoken to her this crazy. At first, she could take him ignoring her, but Jade was losing it. She didn't know what else to do and thought trash-talking Torin's business would do the trick and make him realize what he was missing, but it hadn't.

Silas had been up her ass while she moped around, missing Synovi, and she couldn't stand it. That was why she wasn't at home now. He kept finding reasons to be in her space, and Jade was sick of him.

"Why does he think it's okay to just cut me off like this?" Jade asked herself.

She stared out of the windshield with her eyes fixated on Synovi as he exited Solace Place. Her cousins's car she was driving for the day was unrecognizable to him, and that was what she needed. Following him again was going to be a breeze.

The first time had been a bust, thanks to D'Marco. The woman Nikki saw climbing from his backseat was her. Knowing Synovi had been driving his car, she followed him to the shopping center, where he tried to get a new phone. While he was inside, she slipped an air tag underneath the driver's seat and almost got caught when security spotted her.

The only way Nikki found out was because her friend was the security guard. She'd only told Nikki what she saw, and that was enough to make her wild out. Jade thought her damaging D'Marco's car had ruined her plans to track Synovi down, but his figure-it-out attitude had her now trailing his mama.

"Where are they going, hmm?" Jade hummed, turning the corner seconds after them.

Unique was driving like someone was chasing her and was pissing Jade off as she tried to keep up. Weaving in and out of traffic, she'd forgotten all about the little person asleep in her backseat.

"Mommy, you speeding," Kalie said in her tiny voice.

She'd woken up from a nap and was holding on for dear life in her car seat. Jade glanced at her through the rearview.

"I'm sorry, baby. Mommy is going to be late. Watch your iPad."

Kalie mumbled an okay and grabbed her iPad off the seat. Jade was tripping big time, chasing down Synovi with her daughter in the car, but all sensible thinking behind him had vanished.

When they finally made it to their destination, Jade waited until they pulled into the parking lot of Dryft Rentals before doing the same. She turned the opposite way and came down another lane before parking and ducking low.

"And now, we wait," she said with a grin.

Pushing the car door open, Synovi climbed out and began removing his supplies from the trunk. He was glad his slim vacuum fit in her trunk because the backseat was a mess. Not filled with trash or anything, but with junk that didn't belong. He was used to seeing it in Torin's truck and stayed cleaning out what didn't belong.

On the drive there, he reserved a rental and just needed to

verify a few things and pay. It'd be a little extra since he didn't have his own car insurance to put down, but Synovi was fine with that. You had to spend money to make money, and he wasn't missing out on it because of a mishap.

"Do you want me to wait on you?" Unique asked.

"Nah. I should be good. 'Preciate you for picking me up and dropping me off."

She smiled. "Of course. Thank you for allowing me to."

"A'ight. I'ma head in here."

"Okay. Talk to you later."

Unique's smile didn't leave her face. She waited for Synovi to place all of his things outside of the main door and go inside before she backed out. Him answering her calls was enough for Unique, but to have him trust her for a ride and show his gratitude had her over the moon. It was baby steps, and she'd gladly take them.

Synovi was grateful the agent he worked with didn't take all day to get him in some wheels. He was even more appreciative when he found out they were running a special and he was given a discount if he rented for three or more days. Knowing he'd need the transportation and having the money to pay for it made Synovi feel blessed as ever.

"So, you taking a trip somewhere?" the agent asked as they headed out the door to do a walk-through of the rental.

"Nah. Just need it for work," Synovi said.

"Nothing wrong with that. You got in on a good week. Prices have never been this good. We're heading over here to the silver F-150. You'll be able to get all of your supplies in there."

Synovi nodded his head and went to the gun on his hip when he noticed someone quickly walking toward them. He didn't carry one at all until GiGi gave him some protection once she found out he was going all over the city to clean up. Protection was just what he needed it for dealing with Jade's deranged ass.

"Yo, what the fuck," Synovi mumbled as she stormed up to them.

"Yeah, nigga. You thought I was just going to let you get away with talking to me any kind of way?" Jade shoved him in the chest. "You can't just toss me aside when you feel like it. I have feelings too!"

Synovi took a step back. "Aye. You really on some nut shit right now. You followed me here?"

"Yes! And I would've followed you wherever else you were about to go until you talked to me!"

The agent stood there, confused as Synovi was. He realized now that he needed to study his surroundings better. Or get a restraining order. Jade was on some fatal attraction mess and Synovi wanted no parts.

"Man," he groaned. "I already told you what was up. What do we have to talk about?"

"I told you I loved you and you just changed up on me. Got with this new chick and act like what we had never mattered."

Synovi had to choose his words carefully. "It did at one point, but honestly, Jade… you knew this wasn't going to last. You're fucking married!"

"I know that! Quit reminding me!"

In the midst of their screaming match, a silver Benz sped into the parking lot and damn near hit both of them. Synovi noticed the familiarity immediately and shook his head. When Jade's husband stepped out of the car, leaving the driver's door open, Synovi knew right then he was going to have to shoot his ass if they got to fighting.

"So, this is what you've been doing, Jade?" Silas said, tone laced with disgust and a type of anger Jade had never heard.

While she'd been caught up on tracking Synovi's whereabouts, Silas had been tracking hers. He knew there was a reason she'd been moving sneakily, claiming she was with Simone all the time and hiding her phone. Silas decided to see what had her forgetting she was married. He was too late, trying to install cameras, so he put a tracker on her car.

The number of times she'd visited Solace Place in a week, hoping to catch Synovi, was unsettling. A quick Google search of the place let Silas know everything he needed to know, except who Jade had been having an affair with. And now, he knew.

"Baby," she uttered, looking as if she were about to throw up. "W-What are you doing here?"

"No. What the fuck are you doing here, meeting this bum?" Silas spat, glaring at Synovi.

"Aye, man. Address your wife and watch your mouth and everything will be good around here," Synovi said.

Silas stepped his way, only to be shoved back by Jade. "Lil' nigga, what you say?"

"Silas, please! We weren't doing anything!"

"Y'all must think I'm slow. Especially you!" he hissed, yanking out of Jade's grasp. "All this sneaking around you been doing, lying about being with Simone, and wanting to enjoy your freedom. The whole time, you've been cheating on me with… with a homeless mothafucka."

Synovi pinched the bridge of his nose. "You got one more time to disrespect me."

"Or what? You can't do shit for my wife! You live in a housing facility, don't have a car, barely got money to your name, and wanna get buck with me?"

Jade pulled his arm. "Silas, that's enough. Let's just leave."

"No. Let's stay right here and discuss how you've been cheating on your very wealthy, loving, dependable husband. My man, get this on video," Silas told the agent who was already recording.

Hiding her face in her hands, Jade cried softly.

"Nah. Don't cry now. You weren't crying when you were spending my money on this broke ass boy," Silas spat.

"Heard them broke niggas got the best dick." Synovi shrugged, making Jade pop her head up so quickly.

Now, why did he have to go and say that?

"What'd you just say?" Silas asked through gritted teeth.

Synovi tugged his sweats up. "You heard me, bitch ass nigga. You talking real slick to a *broke boy* who done been all through your crib, nutted on them hundred dollar sheets, know where you get your clothes dry cleaned and fucked your wife like the slut she is. Broke or not, you and I both know why she cheated on your cornball ass. I been busting her lil' ass down for months, something you can't do."

Jade's scream echoed through the parking lot as Silas rushed Synovi. Ducking from his first swing, Synovi connected his punch, sending a body shot before getting hemmed up. Silas could've walked away and taken his wife's infidelities to his therapist, but Synovi had hit a sore spot. Having erectile dysfunction in his early forties was humiliating for Silas, especially with having a wife who was such a sexual being.

Not just that, but he couldn't satisfy her how she needed. Jade had checked out of their marriage long before now. She'd only cheated just now because she was deprived and craving something her husband couldn't give her. Other than that, there was nothing wrong with their marriage that she knew of.

"Stop! Oh, my gosh! Someone, please break them up!" Jade's yells went unheard.

The agents on duty were women and the man recording wanted no parts. When Silas placed Synovi in a headlock, cutting his air supply, Synovi reached for his gun. It was a struggle to get to it. Jade beat on her husband's back, screaming to let him go. Synovi floated in and out of consciousness and knew he had passed out when he heard another set of shouts that sounded like his mama.

How she get back here? Synovi thought, lids fluttering.

Unique noticed he left the key fob to one of the buildings he cleaned in her passenger seat and had to turn around. Thank goodness, she had.

"Let my son go!" Unique screamed, pointing her gun at Silas.

She, too, was strapped at all times.

Breathing like a raging bull, Silas lowered his arms. Synovi fell onto the concrete, gasping for air. He wheezed as his vision began to return. Unique held her gun with shaky hands and vomit burned the lining of her throat as she stared at Silas. She'd just gotten her son back and was about to lose him again.

It wouldn't be the first time *he* was the cause of their separation.

"Y-You… it's you," Unique said, trembling.

Silas frowned and cleared his throat, eyeing her suspiciously. "What are you talking about, lady? Put the gun down."

"No!" Unique shouted. "No! You know what you and your friends did to me!"

Jade inhaled shaky breaths and wiped her face. "Silas, what is she talking about?"

"He knows exactly what he and his two friends did to me twenty-three years ago," Unique said. Tears ran down her face as she stepped closer. "Isn't that right, Omar?"

Now alert, Synovi held onto the wall and stood to his feet. "Yo, what's going on?"

"Ma'am," Jade began, trying to move Silas back but he didn't budge. "I think you've mistaken him for someone else."

Unique's head shook from side to side. "No, I'm not. Omar and his friends raped me twenty-three years ago. This man's name isn't Silas or whoever else he'd been going as."

"Oh, shit," the agent whispered just as a gang of police cars swooped onto the lot.

Unique stepped closer. "You raped me and were the only one who didn't use protection. You knew I was pregnant and threatened to kill me if I told anyone."

Silas or Omar, whoever he was, shook his head. "You have me mixed up, lady."

"No, I don't! You abandoned me and my child! My only fucking son!"

"Ma'am, lower your weapon!" policemen shouted.

Synovi couldn't breathe as he watched the scene unfold.

"You took my life away from me, and now I'm going to take yours," Unique said coldly, before pulling the trigger.

A single bullet entered Omar's chest, penetrating his heart. His eyes bulged as he fell on bended knee and looked on as Unique took a bullet to the leg. She grinned with delight as she fell and Synovi rushed to her side, applying pressure to her wound.

Unique smiled up at her handsome son with the most alluring eyes she'd ever seen. When he was a baby, she stared at him all day, wondering how she'd brought something so great into such a fucked-up world. Synovi was her baby, and she'd go to war with anyone for him, including the man who impregnated her and left her for dead.

"Unique, what the fuck did you just do?" Synovi fussed.

"I just killed your father."

fourteen

Synovi stepped inside Solace Place with a headache so brutal, it blurred his vision. The last five hours of his life had him questioning his entire existence. He already felt like he didn't belong in this world or mattered to anyone, and now he knew why.

A product of rape.

The thought made his stomach flip and his head pound harder. "Fuck, man," he grumbled.

His lagging footsteps carried him down the hall, toward his room. After sitting with Unique at the hospital before she was cuffed and carried away, Synovi only wanted to be around love. His, Love. Today's events were too much for him to handle right now.

"Hey, Synovi!" Kimmy said excitedly.

Her smile dropped when she noticed his ghosted expression. His dark eyes reflected a tortured dullness of disbelief and agony. Synovi didn't have the strength to even give her a head nod as he kept on walking.

"Whatever it is, it'll get better!" Kimmy shouted to his back.

For the life of him, Synovi wondered when. People had been telling him that his entire life and shit never did. And if it had, it only lasted for a moment. He had never been able to enjoy something good without it getting snatched away. As soon as he thought he had Unique back in his life, the system… the grimy fucking system that'd rather imprison a sexual assault survivor than her abusers, had snatched her away again.

Stepping inside the room, Synovi did his best to ignore Xavier and Ron. He didn't know why they chose to sit up and play the game in their space rather than the game room, but he'd mind his business today.

"Aye, look who it is," Xavier said, turning Synovi's way. "Mr. Clean Up Man. You think I can get a job with you?"

Synovi pulled clothes from the shelved closet and continued to ignore him.

"This nigga don't hear me talking to him?" Xavier asked Ron.

"Probably not. You know he ain't got it all up there. Heard he takes meds."

Xavier laughed loudly. "That makes sense. Look at him. Aye, mothafucka!"

Synovi's hands paused from folding the shirt in his hand. Clenching his jaw, he turned around to give Xavier the attention he was looking for.

"That's not my name."

"Yeah, well, whatever it is, you heard me ask you a question. You slow or something?"

Feeling his eye twitch and pulse thump, Synovi told himself to calm down.

"I ain't in the mood today. So, just play that fucking game and leave me alone."

"Yeah, a'ight, mothafucka," Xavier grimaced and turned back around. "I think yo—"

Before the word could leave his mouth, Synovi erased the space between them and had the shirt wrapped around his neck. He'd been giving him way too many warnings, and sometimes, you had to choke a person out for them to understand that you weren't to be fucked with. Synovi had so much anger built up inside of him, strangling Xavier wasn't enough.

His fists slammed into his face repeatedly as he blacked out. He delivered every punch with thoughts of his past covering Xavier's face like it was taunting him.

For every time a foster parent denied him food, to the kids on the playground who teased him about his clothes. The social worker who asked if Unique was on drugs because they had no food in the fridge. The last blow Synovi delivered before he was yanked off was for Omar. The man he wished he could get revenge on the most.

"Synovi! That's enough!" Mr. K yelled, restraining him in a tight hold.

Coming to, Synovi breathed roughly and eyed the bloody mess before him. Xavier lay out on the ground with crimson decorating his now unrecognizable face. Synovi held his breath, thinking he'd murdered him, and released a relieved exhale when Xavier groaned and rolled onto his side.

"Get off me," Synovi spat, yanking out of Mr. K's grasp.

Snatching his bag off the bed, he went inside his closet and gathered anything of value to him before slugging it over his shoulder. There were so many concerned and confused faces in the hallway, but he didn't care to address any of them. For once, Synovi didn't have any answers for people. They could figure the situation out and handle it on their own like he'd been doing his entire life.

Hopping in the rental truck, Synovi pulled out of the parking lot and headed to the only place he knew there was peace at. For years, he'd been searching for it, only to keep coming up short. He received the short end of every stick that was held out to him for rescue.

It wasn't that way with Torin, though. She sent a boat with a life jacket to save her man from drowning in the same waters that kept trying to take him under. Torin wasn't letting this world wash away Synovi's existence if she had any say so. It needed his light, even when all he saw was darkness.

Leighton had never seen Torin this discombobulated before. She sat on her couch with her phone in her hand, waiting for someone or anybody to call her back. After getting back in town from her corporate event, she called his phone, only to be greeted by his voicemail. She knew he sometimes worked in areas where there was no reception, but not hearing from him for hours was unusual.

"I'm about to call GiGi," Torin said.

"You have his granny's number?" Leighton asked incredulously.

"Nope, but I know what living facility she stays at. I'll call up there."

Torin had already called Solace Place, and though they weren't supposed to, they let her know he'd left out hours ago. Torin was losing it.

"I'm sure nothing bad has happened to him. Let's turn on the news real quick."

Torin stopped searching Google for the living facility's number. "Why do you think he'd be on the news? Don't say that."

The tremble in her voice made Leighton's eyes misty. "I'm not saying *that*. Let's just see what's on it."

"No. You can turn it on, but I'm not."

Something—she didn't quite know what—in her gut told her that if she flipped that TV on, she'd get all the answers she was looking for. Sighing, Leighton did it for her. Torin busied herself dialing the number listed for GiGi's place of residence. She couldn't help but glue her eyes to the screen, though her ear was listening to the automated system's prompts.

"Please press five if you'd like to hear those options repeated."

Torin zoned out.

"We're here on the scene at Dryft Rentals that is still taped off as a homicide investigation. As of right now, the only information we have is that a Black male died on the scene while another victim, a young woman, was injured and taken to the hospital. Names have yet to be released, but our team will be following the story and be sure to update the community as more details roll in. Cole, back to you at the station."

Leighton looked over at her friend, and the distraught look on her face made her click the TV off. "Torin, they haven't confirmed any names yet."

Her mouth opened to speak and quickly closed due to the loud knocks at her door. With wide eyes, she pivoted and rushed to open it. When she pulled the door open, Torin didn't give Synovi a chance to enter. She wrapped him in the tightest hug she could muster.

"Oh, my gosh, baby," she breathed out. "I thought something happened to you."

When she didn't feel him reciprocate her energy, but instead stood stiffly, Torin pulled back. Wet, dark eyes that were void of life stared back at her. Panic settled in Torin's chest.

"Hey. What's the matter? What happened?"

Synovi choked on a cry as words he'd never uttered before to anyone escaped him. "I need you, Love. I'm hurting so bad right now."

Torin embraced Synovi right there on her doorstep as he fell into her and wept. His cries rocked the depths of her soul, forcing tears to slide down her face. Synovi's body crumbled, seemingly like his world, and Torin was right there to pick him up.

"I got you," she cooed softly, rubbing his back.

Synovi hoped she did because he didn't have himself.

Forty-eight hours.

Two thousand eight hundred eighty minutes.

One hundred seventy-two thousand, eight hundred seconds.

That was how long Synovi had been ducked off inside Torin's bedroom. Her blackout curtains hadn't been opened once, the main light hadn't been flicked on, and Synovi had only moved from the bed to piss and to take a shower twice. Other than that, the other side of those four walls hadn't seen him.

His phone had been ringing off the hook, but he wasn't in any type of mental space to speak to anyone but Torin. Even she was only getting a few words. At the most, she received head nods and mumbles. Synovi had been the most vocal when he buried himself deep inside of her, trying to escape his reality.

"GiGi's calling again," Torin said, watching his phone light up and vibrate on the bed.

He was laid out on his back right beside her. You'd think he was at peace with the way his hands were planted behind his head. His eyes were closed, but when he opened them, you knew Synovi was everything but tranquil. A disturbance like none other lingered in his orbs and in his heart.

The phone stopped ringing for a few seconds and started again. GiGi had given him time to think, but now she needed to hear his voice. Even if it were dry and uninterested in what she had to say, she had to make sure her baby was okay. Torin had been texting her to keep her updated, but that wasn't enough anymore.

"You want me to answer? She called back," Torin said, and was surprised to see his head nod.

Any other calls that came through, he shook his head no, so she was happy to see him finally acknowledging someone besides her. Swiping the screen, she placed GiGi on speaker.

"Hey, GiGi."

"Hey, my girl. Y'all still over there laying up like vampires?" GiGi asked.

Torin chuckled and glanced at Synovi, who still had his eyes closed.

"Yes. A little sunlight is peeking through, though."

"Well, tell that grandson of mine, who I know can hear me, that sunlight is a good source of vitamin D and he needs it. Hiding out isn't going to fix things, Synovi."

He didn't say anything, and GiGi continued.

"We've been through worse, baby. You can't let what you had no control over break you. All them muscles you got and you over there acting weak like I ain't raise you," GiGi fussed. "We're fighters."

Torin kept her eyes on him, searching for a change of expression to cover his face.

"And what I tell you about not speaking when someone is talking to you? I'm 'bout sick of the disrespect."

"What you want me to do, GiGi?" Synovi asked curiously.

His voice was void of emotion and baritone deep. The extra rasp behind it due to the lack of sleep and hydration stirred Torin's core.

"First, I want you to get out of that bed and stop thinking the world is ending. Second, remember who you are and what obstacles you've already faced and conquered. You gon' let this one hold you back?"

Synovi grunted, hating that she was asking him for an answer.

"Huh? I don't hear you. You gon' let the sins of your parents stop you from being great?" GiGi repeated.

"No."

"Well, act like it then! If God isn't punishing you for them, why do you think you should be? Get your tail up. If I have to take this shuttle over there with Carolynn's behind, I will."

"I thought you didn't like her," Synovi said.

"I will today to make sure you're out of that bed. Try me and see. And Torin, don't be over there babying him, letting him boss you around. Pop that titty out of his mouth!"

Torin covered her mouth and giggled. "Okay, GiGi."

"Okay, nothing. I'm calling back in twenty minutes after I

smoke my pen, and it better sound like y'all are alive over there. Done stressed me out on this nice day. Now, bye!"

GiGi hung up on them, and Synovi finally cracked a grin.

"I guess we need to get up," Torin suggested.

Stretching his body, Synovi opened his eyes. Exhausted by life, he just stared at the ceiling. The blades of the fan were what his mind and life felt like. Round and round at a high speed, never giving him time to think clearly. It remained on a continuous cycle and Synovi needed someone to flip the little black switch so it and his life could go the opposite direction. It had to be better that way.

"I have so many questions," Synovi said.

Torin didn't know if he wanted her input or not, but she offered it, anyway. "We can talk about it if you want."

While he got a few hours of sleep yesterday, Torin crept to her office to pull up the news article from what she and Leighton watched on the news. Finding out that the husband of the wife you were sleeping with was your father and also your mother's rapist was gutting. Torin thought she was reading some of the articles and comments wrong, but she hadn't been.

When GiGi confirmed it, shocked herself by the revelation, Torin wanted to beat every person's ass involved, except Unique. In her eyes, Mama did what the fuck she had to do. Offing Omar was the only option. Not just for her sanity, but for Synovi's peace. Unique hadn't thought twice before pulling the trigger, giving Omar exactly what she thought he deserved.

"It's fucked up how I got here, but you know what made it worse?" Synovi asked. "The fact that he had two daughters. I don't care about him not providing for me or being in my life anymore; that shit doesn't matter. He brought two beautiful ass girls into this world and who knows what he's done to them."

The thought angered Synovi and made Torin's stomach recoil. She'd been thinking the same thing.

"It's sad," she mumbled.

"Sad as hell. And there I was, just fucking his desperate

wife." He chuckled, and Torin rolled her eyes. Not at him, but at the fact that she couldn't beat Jade's ass.

"Life is crazy. I've never been the one to say something couldn't happen to me, but this? Maaan, you couldn't have paid me to believe this was how my story ends."

"It's not ending," Torin said, climbing to her knees. "This is the beginning of you taking back control of every situation you've had no say so over. I know you're hurting and things don't make sense, but they never will if you sit in your sorrows. You've worked so hard to get out of that dark hole; why do you want to go back there?"

"It's all I know," Synovi sighed.

"There's no love there."

Synovi sat up in the bed. Those four words slapped him across the face. "There's no you there, either."

Torin gave him a smile and rubbed his cheek. "Exactly. So, quit trying to escape to a place you don't feel wanted."

Pulling her onto his lap, Torin straddled him. Rubbing her thumb across the ink along his uneven hairline at the moment, she kissed his temple. Synovi hugged her around the waist and exhaled.

"No more darkness," he mumbled.

"Say it with your chest," Torin said, making him chuckle.

Synovi stuck his hands inside the back of her shorts. His hands rested against her ass and his head against her chest.

"The only dark hole I want to hide out in is inside of you."

Torin snickered. "That sounds… oddly romantic."

Synovi laughed. "It's the truth, though. Even when I'm inside of you, I know you gon' bring a nigga to the light, no matter what."

"So, I'm light, too, now?"

"Light and Love… the only thing I need."

Torin pulled back and kissed his lips. "You need a tooth-brush, too, but we'll get to that in a few minutes."

She squealed when Synovi rolled them over and began tickling her stomach. Torin hadn't gotten up to use the bath-room in an hour, so her bladder was full and about to explode.

"Okay! Okay! You gon' make me pee on myself!" Torin shouted with tears in her eyes.

"Say sorry first."

She poked her lip out. "I'm sorry."

"Nah. Apologize for how you handled me when we met," Synovi clarified.

"You still on that?" Synovi went to tickle her again, and Torin screamed. "Stooop! Okay, I'm sorry for pulling a gun on you, even though you deserved it. No one told you to be in my house uninvited."

Synovi gave her a blank stare. "You ain't have to say all that."

Cracking up, Torin pushed him off her. "Yeah, yeah. Let me up. I need to pee and go to my office."

Doing as she so rudely asked, Synovi moved to his side of her bed. He watched as she walked into the bathroom and smirked before calling her name. "Love."

"Hmm?" she asked, turning to face him.

"Thank you for being here. I 'preciate you like crazy."

Her heart warmed. "I love you, too."

She spoke the words with so much sincerity and ease, Synovi believed every word. "Since when?"

"Day four." Torin chuckled.

He frowned. "What that mean?"

"It's an inside joke, but know it's real. Now, what do you want for dinner?"

Synovi sat there with a grin on his face. Hearing her tell him she loved him and knowing she meant it, didn't terrify him like he thought it would. When he told her she was love, Synovi meant that. That was all he ever felt when she was near and the only thing he wanted to receive from her. In due time, he'd exchange those words as well and not just mean them, but understand how much power they held.

Torin had brought him out of that dark place and Synovi wanted to do nothing more than give her what she deserved… some light, too. She couldn't be the only one illuminating the world. It was time for them to shine together.

fifteen

In the heat of the moment, worrying about the consequences of his actions was the last thing on Synovi's mind. On any other day, he would've been more conscious about choking a guy out and pummeling his face until he felt satisfied. In his eyes, Xavier deserved the ass-whooping, and Synovi was ready to give him another one for deterring his plans.

With a stern expression, Synovi eyed the staff that sat around the round table in the meeting room of Solace Place. Whenever you were called in here, it wasn't for anything good. Synovi knew that when Ms. Reid called him, he should've just asked what was up instead of torturing himself by being in the hot seat. She claimed his presence was needed, but obviously not.

"The decision to go ahead and terminate you from the program was unanimous," Mr. K said.

Synovi had nothing to say, so he didn't. Instead, he let his eyes do the talking for him. The pain lingering in them compressed Ms. Reid's heart, forcing her to look away. After all the work they'd put in, she couldn't understand how or why Synovi would let words get to him. Her confusion when she received the call about the incident was warranted, but more than anything, she was disappointed.

It wasn't just about the words Xavier said, but the time he

said them that set the ticking time bomb off inside Synovi. He was tired of giving folks a pass, thinking they could talk to him in any kind of way. Treating him like he wasn't worth anything wouldn't fly either.

"Do you have anything you want to say?" Mr. K asked.

"Nah," Synovi said clearly.

Mrs. Minnie spoke up. "Regarding your housing situation, we're no longer paying the first and last month's rent. You'll still be able to move in on your respective date, but Solace Place will have no contribution."

Synovi let out a chuckle of disbelief. "So, that's it? I'm just left hanging?"

"Once you're terminated from the program, all resources besides what has already been provided stop. If you're still in need a year from now, you can reapply for housing assistance. Not for a spot here, unfortunately," Mrs. Minnie explained.

Pushing the rolling chair he was in closer to the table, Synovi rested his palms against it. "A'ight. So, let me get this straight. Since I'm no longer in the program, I'd be eligible for outreach services, right?"

"Under certain circumstances, yes," Mr. K said. "In your case, you were terminated due to violence, and that isn't something we can just sweep under the rug and still reward."

Synovi gritted his teeth as his head bobbed upward.

"A'ight."

He wanted to say more, but the lump in his throat wouldn't allow him to. Synovi knew there was no one to blame but himself for his actions, but for them to look past all he'd accomplished and brush him off was disheartening. This moment gave him a harsh reality of what Unique must've gone through.

"You don't have anything to say? No explanation for your actions or anything?" Mr. K asked. He wanted to give him a chance to express why things had transpired how they had that day.

"Is it going to change the outcome of this meeting?" Synovi asked.

"Possibly, but you gotta give us something. You can't just tell us you had a lot going on that day as an excuse for you beating that young man up the way you did," Mr. K griped.

Synovi's top lip twitched. "It wasn't an excuse. I beat that nigga up 'cause he deserved it. Whether I had a lot going on or not, this meeting would turn out the same, so fuck it."

"Synovi," Ms. Reid sighed.

He shoved back from the table and stood. "It's coo', Ms. Reid. I see how it is. I take full responsibility for my actions and gotta live with that. I 'preciate everything you and the staff have done for me here, but I guess it's time for us to part ways."

Deep down, Synovi knew this was just the push he needed. Torin was right about his life just beginning, and it started long before this meeting. He wasn't looking for sympathy, so they'd never hear why he'd spazzed out the way he did. Life was taking him on yet another journey of figuring it out, and that was exactly what he planned to do.

Ms. Reid couldn't just sit back and let him leave without properly saying goodbye. Standing to her feet, she followed him out of the office and toward the front of the building. Synovi stopped in his tracks, hearing her heels click along the tile. She released a deep sigh of worry once in front of him.

"You're going to be just fine."

Her words were a declaration of promise, spoken strongly and with emotion.

"You think so?" Synovi questioned.

"I know so. Don't look at this situation as a setback, only a setup for something much greater. You are going to receive all the things God has in store for you. This just wasn't one of them."

Synovi couldn't help but give her a grin. "Don't start preaching."

"'Cause you know I will." Ms. Reid chuckled. "I'm serious, though, Synovi. I know that whatever reason you got into that fight was truly because of a bad day, but don't let that one bad day ruin the rest of your life. Remember everything we discussed, and know that you can always call me if you need to."

"A'ight, I will."

"Is it okay if I give you a hug?" Ms. Reid asked.

Synovi opened his arms. She hugged him tightly, making Synovi feel like he could break down, but he stood tall and held his emotions in. When they pulled away, Ms. Reid's eyes were watery.

"Man, I know you ain't crying," Synovi said.

"No. There's just something in my eye."

He knew she was lying, but let her make it. Ms. Reid looked at Synovi as a younger brother she just wanted to see win in life. Her heart ached for him like an old wound on a rainy day. No matter how long ago the scar had healed, on those gloomy days of downpours, it'd remind you it was still there. In Synovi's case, he was the wound that wouldn't heal completely, forcing Ms. Reid to hate rainy days.

"Yeah, a'ight." Synovi chuckled. "I meant what I said, though. I 'preciate you for everything. Even the extra shit you did that ain't in yo' job description."

"Of course. You don't ever have to thank me. It's what I'm here for. Serving my purpose the way He'd want me to."

Synovi nodded. He couldn't wait to be that confident in knowing what he was placed in this world to do.

"I'll be in touch," he said.

Ms. Reid nodded, watching him walk away and out of Solace Place for the last time. The moment was bittersweet, and she said a quick prayer for him before returning to the meeting room. All chatter ceased as she entered and retook her seat.

"Don't stop talking on my account," Ms. Reid urged.

Mr. K cleared his throat. "Did he tell you anything?"

"No. Just that he was thankful, which wasn't surprising, but considering the circumstances, you all wouldn't have even gotten that from me."

"The rules are the rules, Ms. Reid. You and everyone at this table knows that," Mr. K said.

"And rules can be adjusted. Can they not?" she countered, staring him in the eye.

They'd done it before, so she wanted him to lie.

"Yes, they can, but violence doesn't fall under that umbrella. I'm sure Mr. Black will figure it out."

"He shouldn't have to!" Ms. Reid shouted, making everyone's eyes widen. "You come in here some days with a bad attitude and not wanting to be bothered, but do we just ignore you and tell you to figure things out? No! We give you grace and help you. That's what makes this organization run. The beauty of community and understanding. That's what makes men like Synovi trust us enough to help him. But the first time he does something that could be overlooked and discussed more, we forget all his hard work. Just throw him back out there to the same streets that never have or will care about him. Is that what Solace Place is about now? Is that our mission?"

Stunned, Mr. K sat there, letting her words absorb. That wasn't their mission at all.

"If he didn't want to be back out on the streets, he should've thought about his actions first," Mr. Miller, one of the transitional house managers, said.

With a mean mug and a wave of her hand, Ms. Reid rudely dismissed him. "Your input no longer matters, so save it."

"Are you upset that we made him leave or that his funding for housing isn't covered?" Mrs. Minnie questioned.

She hadn't wanted this outcome for Synovi either, but she was a play-it-by-the-book employee. Right was right, and wrong was wrong. Her position wasn't one where she could move off emotions like Ms. Reid's was, but she understood her frustration.

"I'm upset that as a Black-owned organization, *knowing* what our Black men go through daily, we're moving as if their lives don't matter. As if this world hasn't made them want to fight for their place in society for decades. As if a Black man who runs this place doesn't know what it feels like not to have anything. So, no. I'm not just upset about him having to leave or that his housing won't be covered. I'm pissed off because, for once in his life, Synovi felt like he could depend on somebody, and we failed him. I don't care about him fighting or any of that because, at the end of the day, if any of you were in his shoes, you'd be fighting to keep your head above water as well."

Ms. Reid stared all of them down, daring them to utter a rebuttal, but no one made a peep. Her point was made, and her heart still ached. That was okay with her, though, because she knew standing up for the voiceless, like Synovi, would force some change to take place. She'd never feel bad about speaking up for herself or others in their absence. Integrity was foreign nowadays, and Ms. Reid would forever be the reminder that it existed.

He'd never get used to receiving collect calls from Unique.

Calls, in general, from her had taken some getting used to. Hearing her say her name through the phone before the automated voice gave her clearance left a ringing in Synovi's ears. It reminded him of the social worker who had to grant Unique permission to interact with him as if she hadn't given birth to him and knew him better than anyone.

"How is it in there?"

Synovi didn't know what to say, so he asked what he thought would keep the conversation flowing.

"A mess, and this may sound crazy, but I'm happy to be locked up," Unique said.

"Really?"

"Mhm. No more abusive relationships. I'm safe in here. I'm sad our relationship has come to a standstill again. Are you mad at me?"

Synovi shook his head from side to side. Her question was one he hoped she didn't ask because he didn't quite know how to answer. All he knew was that being mad at her for protecting him would never be the case.

"Mad at you for how everything played out or because you think our relationship is over?"

"Both. Things ended before you could get some answers," Unique said.

"I'm not mad. If anything, I feel like this brought us closer."

Unique pressed against her chest, hoping to calm her racing heart. She could never talk to Synovi and not feel like she was panicking, hoping she didn't say the wrong thing.

"I do, too, even though I'm in here. They're saying it's voluntary manslaughter, but I beg to differ."

"Who is they?" Synovi asked.

"The women in here and the judge. I told a few why I was in here, and they said that, but I can claim self-defense because you were being harmed."

Synovi knew her charges would be up in the air as soon as Unique was taken from the hospital. Like him, Unique had acted in the heat of the moment when killing Omar, but wanted to fight it. No mother could stand by and let someone choke their child out unless they honestly didn't care about them.

The fact that she shot him after he released Synovi would be argued in court if the case went to trial. If not, Unique wouldn't care either way. Omar was one less waste of a man walking this earth.

"Yeah, you could swing it that way. Shit is just crazy," Synovi sighed.

"I know it is. I'm sorry for bringing more drama into your life and disappearing, leaving you to pick up the pieces. That's not fair, and I'll understand if you want this to be our last call."

Synovi could tell she was trying to remain strong, but the shakiness in her voice was a dead giveaway.

"You can call me. I forgive you for all those times you weren't there. Physically and mentally. You were battling against something much stronger than I ever knew."

Unique squeezed the phone in her hand just as tightly as her eyelids. She'd been waiting so long to hear those words.

"Thank you," she said, sniffling. "All I ever wanted to be is a good mother."

"You did your best. I do have a question, though."

"You can ask me anything," Unique told him.

"How did you know?"

Unique's mind went back to that day, and her body warmed. If she could, she'd unalive Omar all over again.

"You never forget the face of a man who did what he did. Plus, the scar on his forehead. I put that there. You'd think it would've been a daily reminder of what he did and that he'd off himself, but I guess we can't all get what we want in life." Unique chuckled.

It was a trauma response, along with other things. There were no guidelines when it came to trauma responses or a grieving period. For someone who consistently battled with one traumatic event after the next, Unique learned to live on autopilot. Naturally, her brain buried the incident, forcing her to have to deal with every other curve ball life threw her way.

Even with years passing, she hadn't fully processed what happened to her until she saw Omar standing there. It was as if every bad memory her brain tried to protect itself from came to the forefront. For Omar to start going by a totally different name, procreate with Jade, and marry her was sick. For so long, Synovi wondered why his father wasn't in his life, and now he knew why.

The permanent scar in the middle of his forehead was from Unique slicing him with the single razor blade she kept on her. It'd fallen out of her mouth, and she clung onto it, waiting for the perfect opportunity to use it. Omar took her last, making the men he was with call his name in jealousy because he was the only one who hadn't put a condom on. Unique hated that she remembered that small detail before, but was glad she had.

Through all her struggles, setbacks, misfortunes, and confusion, she promised that if she ever saw the men who violated her, vengeance would be hers. Omar just so happened to be the first victim.

"I hate that happened to you," Synovi spat.

"I do too. I don't regret you, though. I never have and never will. You were the reason I kept going because there were many days I'd think about what happened and not want to be here. Selfish of me to try to leave you, huh? It ended up happening anyway."

Her voice was so sad, Synovi couldn't help but change the subject.

"The past is the past. We can't change it," he said.

"You're right. But how do you feel about all of this? I know it's a lot."

"I'ont feel not—" He began, then stopped.

That's the same thing I told GiGi back in the day.

Synovi had come so far with tapping into his emotions, he didn't want to sugarcoat it with Unique. That was the part of growth he realized came easy once he faced those fears.

"I feel like what was meant to happen did. Ion't know how shit played out this way, but I learned to stop asking questions. If you asking about me feeling some type of way about that nigga being gone… nah. Shoulda took his wife with 'em."

Unique giggled. "Now, see. I'm not going to comment on that. I hope you're through with her. A married woman, son?"

Synovi cracked a grin, and it felt damn good to do so. "Aye. What can I say? You birthed a handsome young man."

Unique smiled. "That I did. So, tell me, what does the future look like for us? I want to be included in whatever you have going on."

He was happy to hear that and hoped she kept her word.

"We keep moving forward with making our relationship grow. I can't say what the future looks like right now, but know it ain't gon' involve you in there and us speaking over this phone."

Her mood picked up even more. "Oh, really? I'd like that. I'ma have to get me a good lawyer and go from there."

Synovi's mind was already on getting her one. He didn't

know how he'd do it, but knowing Unique was behind bars wasn't sitting right with him. When he went up to the hospital after she was shot, Synovi didn't know policemen would be posted outside of her room or that she was cuffed to the bed.

Someone posting bail for her was out of the question and beyond what their bank accounts could provide, so Unique had to sit. That was quite okay with her. In her mind, she planned to prove her innocence. Not just to the judge but to whomever else had doubted her. The only thing Synovi hoped was that it didn't get that far.

When the automated system alerted them of having one minute left, they wrapped their conversation up and hung up. Synovi sat with a blank face, not knowing how to feel. All his life, he felt like he'd been parentless, and now it was even more profound. Honestly, he wasn't even claiming Omar. He hadn't all this time and wouldn't start.

The only thing on his mind right now was how he could get some more money to his name. He was grateful to still have his housing, but everything was expensive. Every time he turned around, something cost. With lawyer fees now added to the equation, he dialed up D'Marco.

"Yo, yo," he answered.

"What that play looking like?" Synovi asked.

He told himself hitting a lick would be the last resort, and this was exactly what it was.

sixteen

Jade had no idea grieving could be this hard.

It'd been two weeks since her husband's death, and it still hadn't fully hit her. As best as she could, she tried to wrap her mind around the man she thought he was. The man she thought she knew. Not only was she grieving his death, but their entire time spent together.

Their marriage had all been a lie. She'd been having an affair for almost a year now, but that didn't matter. Not when she was now a widow, and her daughters were left without a father. Jade would've never thought this was how things would turn out.

"Mommy, you sad again?" Kalie asked.

Jade didn't realize warm tears had coated her cheeks yet again. Hurriedly, she brushed them away.

"Yes, baby," she replied softly.

Her throat was sore, and her mouth was dry from barely eating. The bags underneath her eyes were so heavy it looked as if she wore a permanent squint. Merely a shell of herself, Jade hadn't moved from her sister's couch in days. Staying in their home wasn't an option right now, and she wasn't sure if it'd ever be one again.

Kalie wrapped her little arms around Jade's legs, which were tucked underneath a blanket. "No more sad."

Sniffling, Jade hugged her back and kissed her forehead. She wished her hugs could fill the gaping hole in her heart. Unfortunately, nothing would. As Kalie bounced off to go find her sister, Jade stared off into space. She wasn't focused on anything in particular, but the flashbacks in her head were enough to keep her distracted from reality.

She tried pinpointing a time within their relationship and in their marriage when she missed the signs. Jade wasn't sure what signs she should've even been looking for, but there had to be something. Each time she thought about how he kept a secret like that from her, saliva filled her mouth. Jade was sick to her stomach, knowing Omar had been lying to her for all of these years.

That wasn't even the kicker that had her ready to croak; Synovi was her late husband's son. The same young man she'd been having an affair with and professed her love to. Despite being heartbroken, she was disgusted. Anger unknown to her settled in her chest whenever her heart wasn't bleeding.

"He's my girls' brother, and I was having sex with him. Oh, my God," Jade groaned, pulling at her hair.

It was a hot mess, just like her life. She hadn't done anything to it or cared enough to make herself look presentable. The people who had come by to give their condolences just wanted to be nosey, and that was the reason she and the girls were crashing at Simone's crib.

"I need to run to the store right quick," Simone said, walking into the living room.

Her eyes scanned the area her sister had basically turned into a bedroom and disaster. She knew nothing about grieving the loss of a spouse and just let her be.

"Okay," Jade mumbled.

"That means you have to keep an eye on the kids. I'll be gone for at least fifteen minutes."

"I said okay," Jade repeated.

Shaking her head, Simone took a seat near her feet. "Look at me," she said, grabbing her hands. "What do you need from me? I can't say I know what you're feeling, but I want to help you feel better than what you are."

Jade shrugged. "I don't know how to feel or what to think, Simone. I'm a horrible person, and the reason my husband isn't here anymore. Had I just left him alone, all of this wouldn't have happened."

"Silas, I mean Omar, is the only one to blame in this situation."

Jade snatched her hands away. "What? How can you say that, and he's dead?"

"I know you're grieving, so I'm not going to go there with you, but we both know what I mean."

"No, I actually don't know. Enlighten me, please," Jade begged.

Simone sighed. She wasn't trying to take it there with her sister, knowing how much of a vulnerable state she was in, but the reality of the situation was because of Omar's actions years ago.

"Not only did he rape that boy's mama and who knows how many other women, but he went on about his life like he hadn't ruined hers."

"You're going to believe some rape allegations from a woman who literally came out of nowhere?"

"What does she have to lie for, Jade? Especially about something like that?"

Simone was confused. The video the car rental agent recorded had been posted on every social media outlet. When she watched it, seemingly desensitized to the recording, Simone knew right away who the liar was in the video. The spooked expression on Unique's face when she noticed Omar, was a dead giveaway. If not for that, then the way he looked when she called his real name was.

"Women lie on men every day. You and I both know that. If it were true, why didn't she shoot him somewhere so that he could prove to her he wasn't who she thought he was? She didn't have to kill him."

Tears reappeared in Jade's swollen eyes, and Simone felt

bad. Regardless of the facts she was trying to make her understand, Omar had still been her husband. It was clear she was going to ride for him even in death, and Simone didn't have to respect that, but she'd accept it for now.

"You can't tell a woman who has been sexually assaulted how to handle their abuser. C'mon now. However you look at it, you're not the one to blame. Let's say he didn't rape her. Let's just say he was a deadbeat, and she wanted revenge. Does that still make what Omar did okay?"

Jade frowned. "Whose side are you on?"

"Yours, always, but be for real, Jade! Men do some fucked-up shit to women all the time! You act like Omar, or whoever the hell he is, is exempt from that. He's not. That man had been lying about his damn name, so you can't sit here and say that deep down, you believe he was innocent. His family even reached out and said how he wasn't all the way put together."

Jade's eyes widened. "His family? They reached out to you?"

"Yes, and I looked through your phone. You never found it weird that we never met anyone from his side of the family except one or two people? Hell, were they even related to him?"

Simone had received so many messages from people regarding the situation, she had to turn her phone off for a few days. Jade wanted to cut hers off as well, but knew she couldn't. Too many important decisions had to go through her. Some of Omar's family members messaged her and said that Omar hadn't been around the family in years. Not only because he didn't want to be but because they wanted nothing to do with him.

According to some of his family, Omar had a history of weird behavior. None of them called him an abuser, but a thief and a manipulator were mentioned. Simone didn't know what to take from those messages, but she did know that people weren't reaching out to them for no reason.

When Jade and Omar got married, it wasn't anything extravagant. He'd convinced her that a courthouse marriage was okay with him, so she went along with it. He splurged on their honeymoon, so Jade was OK with that. She never questioned him about his family once he told her they didn't claim him. Omar told her this sob story about his family shunning him and how he hadn't heard from them in years.

When Jade went on a rampage on her social media pages, which she never posted on, Omar was the one who made her delete them. There were too many eyes on her page, and he didn't need his family somehow getting in her ear about who he was. They hadn't been able to before then, considering he blocked them all on Jade's social media, but he could never be too careful.

"I didn't. Everyone doesn't have a family they can depend on. You're sitting here disrespecting me and my marriage as if what a random person says in your inbox holds weight," Jade spat.

"Did I disrespect you, or did I say something you found disrespectful? There's a difference," Simone stated.

"It doesn't matter. I know who Omar was. I'm not accusing him of anything I have no proof of."

"And I guess that's where we see differently. Had you not been infatuated with his son and blinded by the idea of what y'all could've been, maybe you could've seen the person you laid down next to every night for who he really was," Simone said, standing to her feet. "I'ma get the girls dressed and take them with me. Call Mama to see if you can stay at her place. I love you and know you're going through a lot, but before I let you tarnish our relationship, I'd rather you leave."

Jade couldn't formulate a sentence as Simone walked off and down the hall to her daughter's room. Their conversation had taken a turn for the worst, and Jade wasn't prepared for it. She hated to hear the truth or what people claimed was the truth. Hearing details about her husband's life and witnessing it for herself was where she was struggling. Unfortunately, Omar wasn't here to defend himself, and Jade hated that she had to live with the what-ifs for the rest of her life.

"Why would you do this?" She cried, snatching her phone

off the couch. "Why would you just die and leave me here to question everything?"

Betrayal, the same kind Omar felt seeing her with Synovi, wafted over her. She had so many questions and none of the answers she received sufficed. Jade knew she could reach out to someone, though. Going to Synovi's name in her contacts, she tapped on it before tapping the blue phone icon. She could hear her heart beating through her eardrums as the phone rang.

"Hello there!" A chipper man, who sounded nothing like Synovi, answered.

"Um, is Synovi there?"

"Sydney? No, ain't no Sydney stay here. You must have dialed the wrong number," the man said.

Jade pulled the phone away from her ear and read the number to herself. *He changed his number. What the fuck!*

"Hello?" the man questioned.

"I'm sorry. I must've dialed the wrong number," she said.

"No problem. You have a good day now."

Jade hung up the phone with a feeling of defeat. The one person she thought she could go to for some answers had removed himself from her life without her knowledge. It was absurd to believe Synovi would want anything to do with her, and he'd already decided he wouldn't have a relationship with his sisters. At least not anytime soon.

There was no way he could look them in the face and try to build a bond with them, knowing his mama had killed their father. The reason behind his demise was even more heart-breaking to try to explain. Some relationships were better left alone, and Synovi found that out the hard way. His affair with Jade caused a snowball effect that hadn't seemed to let up on its momentum yet.

A small part of Jade's mind told her to let him and whatever they had go. Even with cloudy thoughts, she knew there was nothing else for them to discuss and was almost glad Synovi had taken the first step to cut ties. If she had it her way, Jade would've continued to be a pest in his life and probably much worse now with everything that had transpired.

She stood from the couch, feeling the need to stretch and get some fresh air. She was wearing two-day-old pajamas and smelled like it. Stepping onto the front porch, the first thing that caught her eye was a bouquet. Her head shot upward, wondering who'd found out where Simone lived and that she was there.

Not spotting anything unusual, she picked up the vase and carried it inside. She placed it on the counter and plucked the folded letter taped to the side of the glass. It wasn't the type of letter that came from the florist. This note was handwritten on plain white printer paper with the logo from Omar's job printed at the bottom.

I always knew that day would come back to haunt us and Omar. I just never saw it going this way. My condolences to you and the family. – Marc

Jade jumped back from the table as if it were on fire. She couldn't believe what she just read.

"What's wrong?" Simone asked, walking into the kitchen.

"H-He did it," Jade whispered.

Simone glanced at the flowers before snatching the note out of her hand to read. Her eyes darted over the three sentences, and her jaw dropped before her eyes popped back up to Jade.

"This is from Marc, Marc?"

Jade's head bobbed forward twice.

"His best friend Marc that worked with him?" Simone questioned.

"Yes," Jade hissed, feeling her throat tighten.

She couldn't believe that men, as Simone said, did such a fucked-up thing to a woman. But they had, and now she was left to deal with the horrible nightmares of what she considered the best life.

"Wow." That was all Simone had to say, while Jade had many more words to offer.

"I-I'm sorry for calling you a liar. I can't... I can't believe I was married to a ra—" Jade said right before she rushed to the sink.

The contents spewing from her had to come from a hidden compartment because she hadn't eaten anything in days. Simone looked on and shook her head, knowing there'd be plenty more of those days to come.

This entire situation is sick, she thought.

<h1 style="text-align:center">seventeen</h1>

Synovi was used to doing manual labor. At this stage in his life, it was expected. What he wasn't used to was going from building to building, advertising himself to different businesses that may need his services. He'd been out all day, leaving his cards and flyers everywhere, and promised this was his last stop before heading back to Torin's crib.

"Thank you for dropping in," one of the women of the suites he was at said. "Make sure you reach out to the other businesses around here. You never know if they may need your help."

"I'll be sure to. Y'all have a good day," Synovi said, opening the door.

Starting a cleaning service let Synovi know there was a market for everything; you just had to find your audience. Once word got around about his exceptional cleaning, his books began to fill up. Sticking to her word, Torin created a website for scheduling and clients to leave reviews the day after Mother's Day.

Synovi made sure to block off hours he knew he couldn't work, which were when he was at his answering machine service job. With things looking the way they were, he thought of quitting and going full time with cleaning. The only reason he still clocked in every week was the thought of needing an income to fall back on if this didn't work out.

As he made his way to Torin's truck, Synovi was approached by a man dressed in black jeans and a Dolce and Gabbana tee. Now alert more than ever since that day at Dryft Rentals, Synovi's hand inched toward his gun. He didn't feel threatened, but never knew what people were on nowadays.

"Yo, my man. What's that you were handing out?" the man asked.

Synovi held out one of his flyers. "My business cards and flyers."

The man quickly scanned it over and nodded his head. "SB's Cleaning Service. You know what's crazy? One of my potnas told me about y'all, and I forgot to reach out. You clean a few of his Airbnb properties."

"Aw, yeah. Ayce and his brother, Aseer," Synovi confirmed.

"Yeah. I'm looking to hire you if you want to take on larger commitments."

Synovi nodded his head. "I'm willing to. What'd you have in mind?"

"The suites behind you. I own them."

Glancing over his shoulder as if he hadn't just come from them, Synovi nodded and faced him. Admiration showed throughout his eyes.

"These are brand new," Synovi acknowledged.

"Yeah. A couple of months old. Instead of having my tenants do a deep cleaning of their shops every week or as needed, I added it to my budget. It's the least I could do."

Synovi fucked with that. "That's love. What's your name?"

"Bostyn Crenshaw," he said, sticking his hand. "You may hear a few people address me as Boss, though."

"Synovi Black," he said, shaking his hand.

"Bet that. I'ma lock your number in and hit you up to schedule a meeting sometime next week. That coo'?"

"Yeah. I'm coo' with that. Good looking out," Synovi said.

"I should be the one thanking you. I'll be in touch," Bostyn said before walking toward the building.

Synovi stood in the shopping center's parking lot, marveling over the number of businesses. Reading the sign that displayed each name, his eyes lowered until his count stopped at twelve. A whistle as if he'd just struck gold flowed from his lips as he grinned.

"Twelve suites, once a week? Shit, I might be able to quit that job after all," he said before hopping in the truck.

Once he made it to Torin's crib, Synovi let himself in through the garage. Since getting exited from Solace Place, he'd been staying with her until his move-in date at the new apartments. Torin didn't see the harm in letting him stay with her. It was like he'd spent the night the day of the day party and hadn't left yet.

Even though living with her was temporary, Torin took full advantage of the situation. She didn't know how much she missed a man's presence in her space until Synovi filled it. If she had it her way and didn't want to see him branch out on his own, Torin would gladly let him move in.

"Love," Synovi called out, walking through the kitchen.

There were still dishes in the sink and a mess from her orders earlier in the day. Synovi found that strange because she usually cleaned up behind herself. When he entered the living room, Torin was knocked out on the couch with a blanket pulled over her head. Synovi could hear her lightly snoring, and he knew his baby must've been exhausted because that was the only time she snored.

"Love," he called out again, pulling the blanket back. Kissing her forehead, Synovi frowned.

The back of his hand replaced where his lips had been before they drifted to her neck. Torin was burning the hell up. Not caring that she was asleep, Synovi felt all over her body trying to indicate what was wrong. All that touching woke Torin up, making her groan in discomfort.

"Novi," she said hoarsely.

"Yeah, baby? You got a cold or something? You burning up."

Torin tried clearing the phlegm from her throat and fell

into a coughing fit. It sounded as if she were barking before a gruesome sneeze escaped her. Another one quickly followed, and Torin clasped a hand around her neck. Her throat was on fire.

"Ugh," she groaned with wet eyes. "I don't feel good."

"What's hurting you?" Synovi asked.

"Everything."

Reaching into his shorts, Synovi pulled his phone out and called the first person he could think of who would know what to do.

"Don't you be calling me now," GiGi fussed, answering his call.

"I was gon' call you back when I got to the crib."

"Mhm. What do you want?"

"Torin is sick. What medicine do I need to go get her?" he asked.

On the other end of the phone, GiGi grinned. "A pregnancy test."

"GiGi…" Torin got out before damn near coughing her lungs up. "That's not necessary."

"Well, grab one, just in case. You got some Whiskey over there?"

"Yeah, we do," Synovi said.

They'd gone out to buy a bottle the week before so she could learn how to make green tea shots. They got lit in the house before playing a card game called Talk To Me Nice. Leighton bought it for her, claiming she'd need it to spice up her and Synovi's relationship.

"Good. I know she has some of everything else there to make a Hot Toddy," GiGi said.

"Yeah, but I need to get her some medicine too. What if that doesn't knock it out?"

Torin rubbed her eyes. "It's fine. I'll just sweat it out."

"Be quiet," Synovi said. "Now, what I need to get, GiGi?"

Had she not felt horrible, Torin would've smirked at his bossy ass, telling her to be quiet. She listened, though, because even talking exerted so much energy. Working nonstop for over a week straight had caught up to her. Torin blamed her sickness on the change in weather and her work overload. She hadn't listened to her body telling her it needed a break, so it took one for her.

"A'ight. That's it?" Synovi said, fingers hovering over the list of things to get in his notes app.

"Yep. Now if none of those work, take her to urgent care. I'm sure it's just a cold, though. That girl needs to sit down somewhere. It's okay to rest, child. You think I made it this far without telling people no and looking out for me?"

"We ain't trying to hear all that." Synovi chuckled. "Ain't nobody tell you to get hurt so you can't work."

"Boy! Shut your behind up." GiGi laughed. "Go get my girl her things. Call me when you get back; my show is coming on."

"A'ight. Thank you."

They hung up, and Synovi locked his phone. Leaning over her, he rubbed a hand over her head and kissed her lips out of habit.

"Don't do that," Torin fussed. "You'll catch what I have."

"So what? I'ma run to the store right quick. You good until I get back?"

Torin nodded, and Synovi eyed her once more before leaving out the same way he came in. He'd never even seen her sniffle unless she ate something spicy, so he was trying to keep his cool. Synovi's mind started wandering, thinking of all her orders and events coming up, and he made a mental reminder to check her schedule when he returned to the crib.

The only thing Torin remembered before falling back asleep was Synovi kissing her lips. Even through her haze of illness, she knew that had only been about ten minutes ago, if that. So, the knocks at her front door jolting her from her sleep were maddening. Confusion plagued her mind as to how he'd returned so quickly.

"He has a key and my truck," Torin whined, not bothering to move from her spot.

When the knocking continued, she angrily tossed the

blanket off her feverish body and slowly stood. Not bothering to check if it were Synovi, Torin unlocked and opened the door, ready to curse him out.

"Why didn't you—" Torin's strained words got caught in her congested chest. She could hardly breathe, and the person standing before her snatched what little air she had left.

"What's up, T? I'm home," Don said, rocking the biggest grin.

Torin wanted to pass out at seeing Don standing on her porch. She should've known those phone calls she received weeks ago were to inform her of his impending release. The thing was, Torin didn't care, and that was why they'd gone unanswered. Why he decided to pop up unannounced was crazy to her.

Don's muscular frame with bulging muscles showed that jail had done his body exceptionally well. Speckles of gray were spread throughout his fresh haircut, and his black beard was thick and neatly shaped. His dark brown skin had aged some, but still held a nice glow. Torin didn't care to know when he'd gotten out; all she knew was this shouldn't have been a place he ever thought about coming.

"You need to leave," she said, voice croaky but stern.

The cough drop she popped before lying down, thinking she only had a sore throat, hadn't soothed a damn thing.

"Damn. I ain't welcome here anymore? Can't even get a welcome home hug?" Don asked.

Torin cleared her throat. "Absolutely not. I don't know why you chose my home of all places to come."

"Cold world." Don chuckled. He looked behind her and inside the house. "I can't come in?"

"Don," Torin sighed. "We have nothing to talk about. Go home to your son and let me live my life peacefully, like I've been doing."

"I let you do that while I was locked up. You don't think we have some unfinished business?"

Torin released a disbelieving sigh. "You can't possibly think we do. I told you what it was the minute I found out you'd been playing me all those years. Nothing has changed."

"Nah," Don disagreed, stepping closer to her. "A lot has changed. Why you ain't go see DJ off for prom?"

Torin took a step back, placing some distance between them.

"Really? That's what you want to talk about?"

"Yeah, 'cause my boy ain't do nothing to you. What happened to all that *I'll always be there for DJ* shit you used to talk about? You couldn't even show your face?"

Torin coughed roughly into the crook of her arm. "No. For what? DJ and I talked the entire week leading up to that day and on FaceTime once he was dressed. My presence was not missed, trust me."

Don smirked. "Ah, okay. I see what this is. You mad 'cause my girl was there."

"Your girl?" Torin laughed and grimaced at the sharp pain it delivered, but she couldn't hold that in. "My absence has nothing to do with her or anyone else in your family that runs their mouth about me. You, of all people, should know I don't care about what you have going on. I wish the same could be said about you."

"Then, you cut my sister off 'cause they coo'. That's fucked up," Don said, shaking his head.

Torin rolled her eyes. If Chelsea wanted to report everything to her brother, she could've at least kept it real with him. Torin didn't cut her off for no reason. On the day of DJ's prom, Chelsea posted pictures of everyone in attendance, including Don's girl. She seemed to be close with everyone in his family, which let Torin know she'd been around them long before she ran into them at Target.

She didn't care to do a deep dive into why Chelsea moved how she did; Torin simply cut ties. Popping up to see DJ off to prom wasn't a priority to her, and it hadn't tarnished their relationship. She was sure Don just wanted something else to harp over.

"You and your sister are delusional. DJ and I are good, so

if that's what you stopped by for, you can leave now," Torin said.

"It's crazy how you treat my son like he's yours, like we weren't supposed to have one of our own." Don's gaze turned cold.

"What?" Torin coughed.

"Yeah… you thought I'd never find out about that abortion you got?"

Rubbing her eye, Torin shrugged. "I mean, it's clear you know now, so where do we go from here?"

Don gritted his teeth. "You really that fucking heartless to kill my seed and not tell me?"

"Tell you for what? So, you could've lost your cool while you were in there? I should've known Chelsea would eventually say something."

Torin shook her head. The only people that knew about her abortion were Chelsea, Leighton, and her mama. There was no way he thought Torin was keeping a child after he got locked up and she discovered his unfaithfulness. A fool she wasn't.

In an upset rant about how Torin was treating her, Chelsea accidentally let it slip that she'd gone to terminate her pregnancy. Don didn't believe her at first, but he recalled his mama asking him if he'd gotten someone pregnant because her dreams had been way too vivid with fish in them. He brushed it off, knowing he'd been cheating on Torin, but he didn't think she'd get an abortion.

"She should've said something sooner," Don hissed. "After all the shit we went through, you do that?"

"Don," Torin sighed. She was over their conversation and him. Her head was pounding, and her mouth was dry as hell. "Let's leave the past in the past… that includes us."

"Nah. I ain't going for that," he said as Synovi pulled onto the street.

Seeing her attention shift behind him, Don glanced over his shoulder. Synovi pulled into the driveway and hopped out with two bags in his hand from Walgreens. Torin rubbed her forehead, trying not to seem alarmed, but she was. She still hadn't told Synovi her ex was locked up, and now he was on her porch, trying to claim what was his.

"What you doing up?" Synovi questioned, strolling up the walkway.

Torin nervously cleared her throat. "An unwanted guest was knocking on the door."

"Yeah? What's good? You need help with something?" Synovi asked, sizing Don up.

Don chuckled. "Nah, not from you. I'm sure Torin doesn't mind helping me out. You know how it is when a nigga fresh out of jail and trying to get that old thing back with their ex."

"Nah," Synovi said, brushing by him. He bumped his shoulder just to test his gangster and lightly pushed Torin back before standing in front of her. "I'ont know shit about that. Never been the type of nigga to lose something worth keeping. Feel me?"

Synovi's audacity angered Don. He could tell right away that Synovi was younger, and for some reason, that pissed him off more. It wounded his ego to know Torin had moved on without him and honestly didn't care. His fists balled at his sides, and Synovi eyed them. He wasn't in the mood to fight Don's big ass, but he had something hot on his hip if he wanted to take it there.

"Yeah… a'ight. You got it," Don grumbled.

"I know I do," Synovi said with pure confidence.

He wasn't threatened by Don's appearance at all. What he disliked was Torin not telling him who he was. They stared one another down with murderous glares, daring the other to make a move. Knowing he wasn't trying to violate his probation so soon, Don took his loss. That was his best bet because Synovi was ready to give him an L either way.

"T, I'll be seeing you around," Don called out, walking down the steps.

"Ugh. I hope not," Torin mumbled.

Synovi stood in the doorway until Don was in his car and

down the street. Walking inside the house, Torin expected him to slam the door and curse her out, but he did none of that.

"Come take this medicine," Synovi said, walking by her.

Torin blinked a few times before following behind him. She sat on the couch beside him and watched as he pulled everything out of the bags. Two bottles of orange juice, a pack of Sudafed, Vicks VapoShower tablets and rub, cinnamon sticks, and a box of flu and cold nighttime hot liquid therapy were piled onto the table.

He had to run to Walmart for a few other things, and thankfully, it was only two minutes from Walgreens. Synovi didn't want to think about what he would've pulled up on had he done so minutes before he did.

"Don't take these until you eat something," he said, grabbing the Sudafed from her hand.

"He just popped up over here," Torin explained.

She saw him flex his jaw and sighed.

"I should've told you he was in jail, but I didn't feel like that mattered."

"He was the call you ignored that day."

Synovi wasn't asking her a question. He hadn't put much thought into her ignoring what she said was a scam call until now.

"He was, and it's been that way for years. I want nothing to do with him."

"Good, 'cause shit between y'all been a wrap, and it's gon' stay that way. Nigga thinks he 'bouta pop back up and do what? Take you from me?" He chuckled lowly. "He can try."

Torin didn't know what to say, so she stayed quiet as he read over the instructions for the drink.

"I'll be right back," he said before standing and going to the kitchen.

With her head against the back of the couch, Torin listened as he filled the kettle with water from the fridge and started it. Minutes later, he returned with an orange mug, a silver spoon, and a bottle of honey. He popped the top on the plastic bear bottle and squeezed a generous amount onto the spoon before holding it to her mouth.

"Here. Take this."

So bossy, she thought, but opened her mouth.

"GiGi said, taking a spoonful of honey will help clear up some of that mucus."

"Okay," Torin mumbled, rolling her dry tongue around her mouth.

Synovi opened the packet and poured its contents into the piping-hot mug. He added a cinnamon stick after stirring it and handed it to her.

"You let him know you're mine?" Synovi questioned.

Torin blew the liquid and sipped it. She sighed before saying, "I didn't get a chance to."

"So, what was y'all talking about?"

"He asked about DJ and why I didn't attend his prom gathering."

"DJ is his son, not yours. That's what you should've told him."

Torin coughed harshly. "Don't do that."

"Do what? Tell you the truth? He thinks you owe him some loyalty and explanations, and you don't. Your relationship with his son was the only thing tying him to you once he got out. Nigga was holding onto hope for no reason," Synovi sneered.

Torin told Synovi about the run-in with Chelsea at Target without saying too much, and he told her that sooner or later, she would have to let go of everyone tied to her ex if she wanted him out of her life. It was just some advice he'd given her, not knowing Don would pop up out of prison, demanding answers.

"So, I'm just supposed to cut DJ off because I no longer deal with his father or auntie?" she questioned.

"People hold on to the good things they *know* they can keep… not have to give back."

Torin couldn't do anything but sip her drink as Synovi hit her with the exact words she'd told him. There was no rebuttal because he was right, and she knew it. It'd been time for her to let DJ go, but Torin didn't want to and figured there'd be no issues since Don was locked up. With him out, she knew what she had to do.

"You're right. I'm sorry I didn't tell you he was in jail. You don't have to worry about him."

Synovi stared her in the eyes. "It's not him I'm worried about."

When he stood up, Torin panicked. "Wait… where are you going?"

"To start the shower for you, Love. Can I do that?"

Torin swallowed her emotions. "Yes, sorry."

"And stop apologizing. Finish your drink."

She tucked her lips as he gathered the trash on the table and took it to the kitchen. He maneuvered around the house with a neutral expression, making it hard for Torin to read his true feelings, but she felt them. He was worried Torin would realize he wasn't worth keeping and dump him to the wayside like everyone else. Synovi couldn't tell her that, though, and he didn't have to.

When she was done with her drink, feeling slightly better, he came back down to get her. Synovi walked behind her, up the steps and down the hall to her bedroom. The steam from the shower had already begun to fog up the bathroom, leaving the scent of the VapoShower tablet on the shower floor in the air. Torin inhaled, hoping at least one of her nostrils cleared up soon.

As she slowly stripped from her clothing, leaving them in a pile at her feet, Synovi sat on the toilet seat. His head was down, and thoughts were everywhere. He was angry, but felt he didn't have a right to be. *Everyone has a past,* he thought.

"You're gonna sit in here and watch me?" Torin asked.

His head lifted. "Yeah. Make sure you don't pass out. See if it's too hot."

She pulled the shower door open and climbed inside, not caring about putting a cap on her head. Her neck and face were warm, but the rest of her body had chills, so the hot water felt amazing.

"It's fine," she mumbled.

Taking a seat on the wooden bench inside, Torin sat there for a few minutes, letting the eucalyptus and essential blends of the tablet work their magic. Whatever was in the liquid concoction she drank, had her body so relaxed. After three minutes of silence and her not moving, Synovi broke the quietness.

"You need me to wash you up?"

He'd never done anything so intimate, but he was willing to for her. Synovi watched her through the glass as she shook her head no.

"I got it," Torin replied softly.

She wanted to invite him inside with her but was somewhat grateful he declined. The tears glossing her eyes didn't stop her from washing up as quickly as her weakened limbs would allow her. Synovi cut the water off when she finished and grabbed her heated towel from the electric towel warmer.

"Thank you," she said as he dried her off.

A bow of his head was Synovi's response. She didn't have to thank him. Torin tucked the towel and stepped inside her bedroom. A nightgown with pockets from Walmart and a pair of long, thick socks was laid out on her bed. Synovi helped her put the gown on and pulled the comforter back so she could get in bed.

"I'ma put this on the bottom of your feet, then put the socks on," he said, holding up the jar of VapoRub.

Torin nodded and laid back against the pillows. Not only did he apply the ointment, but he added a foot massage as well. The firmness of his strokes felt so good that they lulled Torin straight to sleep. Synovi slipped the socks on and covered her with the comforter. After washing his hands, he returned and stood beside the bed. Torin looked so peaceful as she rested, despite not feeling her best.

Synovi didn't realize that watching someone sleep could make his heart contract the way it was in his chest. It'd been doing that a lot lately, and he knew it only meant one thing. When something foreign enters your life so unexpectedly, it's easy to detect how it changes you. It rearranges the wires in your brain, forcing you to think, see, act, and feel differently.

Torin was that foreign thing, and Synovi couldn't believe she'd broken through almost every barrier he'd tried to keep up. He could only prevent the inevitable from happening for so long. Done admiring his sleeping beauty, Synovi leaned forward and kissed her forehead. His kiss lingered as his eyes closed.

Damn. This gotta be what love feels like, he thought.

Wanting to do for someone who did for everyone else was just the half Synovi felt for Torin. Falling for her wasn't in the plans, but he was in too deep to turn back now. Torin had him immersed, floating freely in all her light and love. Waves of Torin crashed into him, and instead of flowing with them, Synovi had the urge to fight against them.

It was a battle, and the thought of swimming back to shore for safety hadn't crossed his mind in a while, but today it had. Drowning wasn't an option, knowing the only person who could save him might be liable to go under as well.

eighteen

"A'ight. You see that nigga right there… he the one I overheard in the store," D'Marco informed.

Parked on the opposite side of the street and a little way down, Synovi kept his eyes on the man walking inside the house with a duffle bag by his side. He'd contemplated hitting the lick all week, and the time had finally come. D'Marco did his part, keeping track of the foot traffic going in and out of the house, and now it was time for Synovi to do his.

He glanced down at the gun on his lap and heard GiGi's voice loud and clear. *This is only for your protection. Don't let me find out you're out there using it for anything but that.* Synovi knew she'd have a fit if she knew he was going against her word. But sometimes, life forces you to break the rules.

"Yeah… I see him. He the only one in there?" Synovi asked.

"Nah. It's normally one other person who be in there around this time. I'ont know the layout of the crib, but we should be able to get in there and make a smooth escape."

Synovi bobbed his head. "Bet."

It was his off day from the answering service job and broad daylight. He hadn't slept well in the last few days and knew that probably wouldn't change after today, either. Running up inside a trap house with ski masks and guns drawn wasn't anything to play with, and Synovi couldn't help but wonder if he was making a dumb decision—more than anything, a desperate one.

Since pulling up on Don at Torin's house, Synovi's mind had been playing tricks on him. One minute it was saying Torin was in his life because that's where she wanted to be, and the next, it was telling him he wasn't good enough for her. Synovi had heard plenty of cornball men talk about what a woman brought to the table, and he couldn't help but think that if she wanted to, Torin could bring another man other than him.

He'd returned to that dark hole he promised he wouldn't crawl into again. This time, it felt like there was no light because Torin was trying to give it away. Instead of sticking around her crib trying to convince her that no one deserved her radiance but him, Synovi left. He called Racquel over to watch her sister, and he checked in every hour to see how she was feeling. Synovi gave her the space she never asked for but felt like she needed, which Torin didn't find fair at all.

As he stared out of the window, he wondered if leaving had been the best thing to do. So caught up in his own world, Synovi wasn't aware of his surroundings.

"Aye. You don't hear me?" D'Marco said.

It wasn't his words that broke the trance Synovi was in; it was the insistent patting against his arm that did. He glanced his way.

"Nah. My bad. What were you saying?"

"You don't see all these fucking FED vehicles?" D'Marco hissed, ready to reverse down the street.

Hearing those three letters, Synovi's head snapped back to the house. "Yo, what?" He murmured with wide eyes.

An army of blacked-out vehicles had swarmed the street, and policemen with vests and helmets on hopped out with guns drawn. The duo looked on as the door to the house was blown off its hinges by a battering ram. Synovi had heard of homes getting raided before, but never had he witnessed one in real time. They would've been brought out in handcuffs, too, if they'd gone in two minutes before.

Synovi ducked his head low and squinted, not believing the scene in front of him. When D'Marco put the car in reverse, ready to get the hell out of there, Synovi told him to hold on.

"Ain't no way," he mumbled, seeing a familiar face being dragged through the lawn. "That nigga just got out."

Caught up at the wrong place and definitely the wrong time, Don shook his head as he was taken to the back of an unmarked vehicle and placed in the backseat. Being in jail hadn't taught him anything, and violating his probation after only being out for less than a week was a dumb move. Don wasn't supposed to be around any illegal activities, but he was on a mission.

Getting checked by Synovi wasn't something he was going to let go of so easily. It sounded good, but Don still felt like he had a reputation to uphold. Needing answers and some background on who the nigga was that was laid up over his ex's crib, Don slid through the hood to get some answers and lace a few of his boys' pockets with money to catch Synovi slipping. Little did he know, he'd be the one getting caught up.

D'Marco slowly reversed down the street and drove like he had some sense out of the neighborhood. Neither spoke until they were on the highway and were sure they weren't being followed.

"Damn!" D'Marco shouted. "I knew we should've hit their shit sooner."

"Nah," Synovi denied. "We would've put ourselves on the radar for something worse than a petty lick."

"You might be right, but fuck it. You knew one of them getting carried out?"

Synovi clenched his jaw just as his phone vibrated. "That big dude with the beard is Torin's ex."

D'Marco looked his way and shook his head. "Guess you ain't gotta worry about him."

I never was, he thought before answering his ringing phone.

"Hello."

"What's going on? Is this Synovi?"

"Yeah, this is he."

"This Boss. We ran into each other a couple of days ago outside of my suites."

Recognition registered, and he nodded. "Aw yeah. What's good with it?"

He'd forgotten about their encounter and hadn't anticipated his call. Synovi learned early in the self-employment business that everyone who said they wanted to work with you didn't always follow through. He didn't look at it as them not supporting him, but more so as the people who needed his services would either hit his line or his website.

"Everything right now except our meeting. I need to get one in with you before the week is up. Are you free on Friday at three?"

Synovi jogged his brain, thinking of his work schedule and other appointments. "Yeah, I am."

"Bet. I'll have my assistant send you a text with my office address," Bostyn said.

"A'ight. 'Preciate you for tapping in," Synovi said humbly.

"Fasho. I'll see you on Friday."

They hung up, and Synovi couldn't quite pinpoint the emotions he was feeling. Going from one extreme to the next, he told himself that the rollercoaster he was on was only just reaching its highest altitude. A few hesitant minutes from hitting a lick had saved his life, while one phone call was about to change it for the better.

"Who was that?" D'Marco asked nosily.

"This man who owns some suites over on Ellison."

"Those brand-new remodeled ones? Them hoes nice."

Synovi nodded his head. "They are. He wants to meet with me about cleaning them."

"Fucking right," D'Marco said in a hype manner. "That's gon' be some good money right there. Shit, you need my help?"

A chuckle fell from Synovi's mouth, but he was thinking the same thing. "Probably so. What you gon' do, quit Ford?"

"Man, I'll quit right now. My nigga got his own business I wanna contribute to. Tell me my start date, and I'm putting in my one-week notice."

"I thought it was two weeks?" Synovi smirked.

"You heard what I said, fam. Our goofy asses were about to get jammed up trying to rob somebody, and you 'bout to be on a come-up."

"Yeah?"

"Yeah, nigga," D'Marco spoke with booming sureness. "Watch and see. Good shit be happening to good people. Sometimes it just takes a lil' minute to reach you. You know… after all the bad you don' been through wears off." He chuckled, humored by his mashup of words. Synovi didn't crack a grin.

His words seemed too true to take jokingly. While Synovi loved seeing D'Marco's excitement and was thankful for his support, Torin was the only other person he wanted to experience this high with. He hadn't even gotten a chance to tell her about Bostyn's proposition. Synovi needed her at his side for this meeting, and he was trying to figure out how he could make up for his absence.

He thought about it and shook his head, axing the idea. *Needing her is what got me going days without seeing her now.* Confliction resided in his chest. Synovi had never been so certain and unsure about a situation or person in his life. His mind and heart were playing a game of tug of war, and both were winning.

Delivered.

Torin read over the third text message she'd sent Synovi today. The blue bubble was taunting her, daring her to send another in hopes that he'd respond. Swiping right on the screen, her text thread moved, displaying the times to the texts she'd sent him, and her nostrils flared. It'd been exactly two hours, and still nothing.

The hours that had gone by weren't her biggest issue. It was the days. Five long, agonizing days had passed since he left her crib, and he hadn't returned. Her calls had gone unanswered, and being ignored was the quickest way to get cut off by her, but Torin was trying not to take it to that extreme.

Her heart wouldn't let her.

The chokehold Synovi had on her mind, even in his absence, wouldn't allow her to just give up on him… give up on them. Knowing her actions played a role in why he'd gone missing, Torin took responsibility for them and did what she hoped would bring him back.

"So, everything is still running smoothly. I'll let the staff know you'll be back in full swing Monday," Mia, her assistant, said over the Bluetooth system in her truck.

Distracted by her thoughts, Torin zoned out of the conversation she was having while driving. "Okay. Thanks so much, Mia."

"You don't have to thank me every time I do my job," Mia giggled. "It's what I'm here for. I'm glad you're feeling better."

"Me too. I will definitely start listening to my body more. Being down for that long was torture."

"Oh, trust me. I could tell," she said, making them chuckle.

Torin didn't know what getting rest meant until she had no choice but to do just that. Thankfully, Tracee stepped in and filled her orders while she was down, and her team took care of everything else. Having a mother who taught her how to cook and cared about her business just as much as she did, was a blessing.

Their numbers may have been small, but they always made it work. While they all told Torin to stop calling and texting them, trying to see how things were going, she couldn't help herself. Kaine's Kitchen was her pride and joy, and being unable to do what she loved bummed her out. Between the medicine Synovi bought and letting her immune system build itself back up, she felt one hundred percent better and couldn't wait to get in the kitchen.

Gotta get my man back first, she thought, pulling up to her destination.

"It won't happen again, I know that. I'm about to run a few errands, so text me if you need anything," Torin said, finding a parking spot.

"That's my line," Mia laughed. "But okay. I will. Talk to you later."

The line disconnected, and Torin stared straight ahead at the living facility GiGi stayed in. Not knowing what else to do, she figured talking to the one person who knew him best had to count for something. While she could've called GiGi over the phone, Torin was damn near desperate at this point. The fact that Synovi had Racquel still doing daily check-ins meant he still cared in her eyes, so Torin wasn't giving up.

Exhaling, she pushed her nerves to the side and climbed out of her truck. She didn't know what apartment number GiGi lived in and hoped the front desk didn't give her a hard time. Torin already had a speech prepared in case they asked who she was. Fortunately, she wouldn't have to reenact it, as GiGi called her name from her porch.

"Torin," GiGi yelled out. "Girl, where you think you going?"

Smirking, Torin walked her way. She was sitting on the patio with a friend of hers. GiGi was dressed comfortably in a yellow sundress that came to her ankles and a cute pair of sandals. As she got closer, Torin noticed the marijuana pen on the table and what looked to be glasses of sweet tea and bowls of plain Lays chips.

"Hey, GiGi," Torin said, walking up the pathway.

"I knew it wouldn't be long before I heard from you. Carolynn, this is my grandson's little friend, Torin."

Carolynn gave her a warm smile. "Hey there, pretty. We were just talking about you."

Torin eyed GiGi. "Really? I hope all good things were said."

"Mm," GiGi grunted, pursing her lips as if she had nothing good to say. At least not right now. "Carolynn, let me catch up with you later."

Torin wanted to chuckle at her smooth dismissal but didn't.

"It was nice meeting you," Torin said.

"You too. I'll see you at trap karaoke later on, GiGi."

Somehow, GiGi had convinced the staff to let them have a karaoke night, and she couldn't wait to perform. When she finished gathering her things, Carolynn headed to her apartment four doors down. Torin took her seat and looked GiGi's way.

"Don't you say it. Acting like that grandson of mine," she fussed.

Torin giggled. "I wasn't going to say anything. Glad to know y'all are hanging out."

"Yeah, she's all right. What brings you by? I know you didn't come on this side of town to check on an old lady for no reason," GiGi said.

"I haven't heard from Synovi in days. Is he staying here with you?"

Torin got straight to the point.

"He told me what you did… or didn't do rather," GiGi explained, sipping from her condensed mason jar.

"And I apologized for my ex popping up at my house. I couldn't control that," Torin sighed.

"No, but you could've prevented disappointment from happening."

Torin's eyes widened. "H-He's disappointed in me?"

Her stomach toiled, and she couldn't imagine the thoughts festering in his mind over the days. Torin wanted to puke.

"Wouldn't you be if the shoe were on the other foot?"

"Yes, but to go missing and ignore me? I don't deserve that."

GiGi's curls shook as her head moved from side to side.

The tsk sound she made while doing so unnerved Torin. She knew right then that a speech would ensue.

"Trying to control how a person treats you after you mistreated them never ends well. It just turns into a bunch of hurt feelings on both sides when communicating to understand should've been the goal."

"I'm not the one who isn't trying to communicate," Torin huffed.

"And understanding? Do you see where he's coming from? Synovi doesn't trust easily, you know. I'm sure you know that; otherwise, you wouldn't have dragged your tail over here."

Torin stayed quiet. Her mouth was smart, and her feelings were hurt, so the last thing she wanted to do was come out of her neck disrespectfully. GiGi would cut their visit short in a blink of an eye right after she checked her.

"That boy of mine been feeling abandoned his entire life, and then that mess with that married Jezebel happened, and he thought the world was ending," GiGi scoffed.

Her entire face contorted at the thought of Jade. Torin didn't blame her.

"A person will settle being somewhere as long as they feel an inkling of love. You know that?"

Torin's head tilted forward as she mumbled, "Yes."

"Put up with any ol' thang believing that that's all their worth. And don't know any better 'cause no one ever showed them differently. But then, by the grace of God, someone does."

Torin swallowed the built-up emotions in her throat before they leaked through her watery lids.

GiGi glanced her way. "Don't you sit up here and start crying now. Your feelings are hurt, but so are his. And they matter," she said sternly.

"I know they do," Torin replied through shaky words.

"Knowing and showing are two different meanings. You can't consistently tell someone you care about them and then turn around and do something to hurt them. You think that's fair?"

Torin sniffled. "No."

"Synovi loves you."

Those words made Torin's heart lock up like a bad engine.

"Mhm," GiGi continued. "Boy, ain't ever expressed himself the way he do when he talks about you. Love, this and Torin that."

A chuckle fell from Torin's lips. "I can't believe he be telling you my business."

"Not everything, but enough to know that you're the closest thing to home for him besides me. You're supposed to always take care of your home and everyone in it. He trusts you, and that's saying a lot."

Torin felt honored one second and like a failure the next. To say someone felt like home was one of the greatest compliments; right now, Torin didn't feel deserving of the praise.

"So, should I keep apologizing? I don't know what else to do."

Her tone was defeated, yet hopeful. She hoped GiGi had an answer.

"Apologizing won't fix anything unless you mean it, and you've done that. I'm going to tell you this, and you do what you want with it." She cleared her throat and straightened out her dress. "Synovi is used to feeling like he doesn't belong anywhere or to anyone. People sticking around in his life is rare. So, once he gets a taste of that, he holds onto it. He doesn't know how to handle something or someone when they let him down, especially when he feels like things were going well. He's gotten better, I'll say that, but better doesn't mean perfect. Trauma doesn't heal itself overnight.

It's a constant journey of learning and relearning yourself and the people you invite into your world to share the experience with you. If that's not a journey you're willing to stick around for, please leave him alone."

For her grandson, GiGi was going to ride every time. Despite Synovi telling her about his strained relationship with his mama, hearing and reading between the lines from GiGi gave her much more clarity. Synovi felt like his position in her life was ending because Don popped back up, which wasn't the case. Torin thought she'd explained that, but now she needed to ensure he felt her. She needed to remind him that the moniker he gave her was for a reason.

The perk of setting up Synovi's website was having his schedule readily available to her. After her talk with GiGi, Torin pulled up his calendar and drove to the office building he was cleaning for the evening. She couldn't help but replay her and GiGi's conversation the entire drive there.

Gaining a new perspective on Synovi from someone who undoubtedly loved him and knew him better than anyone else was refreshing and heartbreaking at once. Torin didn't want to be on the outside looking in on his world when she'd already set up residence in his universe. So, that's why she stood outside the glass doors of the building. She tried the handle to welcome herself inside, but it was locked. Synovi walked the cord of the vacuum to the outlet in the lobby and plugged it in.

He shared his cleaning routine with her, and Torin knew that was the last thing he did before calling it a night. She hoped whatever song was playing on the wireless speaker on the desk didn't drown out her knocks against the door. Hearing faint taps over the Mozzy song playing, Synovi faced her direction.

Though he was shocked to see Torin standing there, he didn't show it. With a neutral expression, Synovi acted as if he didn't see her. Mouth dropping open, Torin banged against the glass, trying to keep her composure.

"I know you see me!" she shouted.

Not wanting her to cause a scene, Synovi hiked up the black sweats hanging low on his waist and strolled her way. A mean mug settled on his handsome face as he eyed her through the glass. Going days without being in her presence almost made him forget how pretty she was. She looked much more like the woman he was used to seeing compared to when she was sick. Torin had on a nude short-sleeved romper and some Yeezy slides. Her oily hair needed a good shampooing, so she threw it in a messy bun until she went to the shop.

"Can you unlock the door?" She asked, realizing Synovi was just standing there.

He made her suffer for a few seconds more before twisting multiple locks. When he pulled the door open just enough for her to slide through it, Torin took a deep inhale of his familiar scent. Without saying a word, Synovi locked the door back and went to power on the vacuum. Torin stood dumbfounded by his blatant rudeness, and she would've been offended had she been anyone else.

Walking over to him, she stood in his path. "I've been texting you."

He stared at her with a blank expression. "I know."

"You couldn't have responded to let me know you were okay? You had me —"

Brrrmmm

Synovi cut the vacuum on in the middle of her sentence. When he pushed the machine around her, Torin had the right mind to trip him. Instead, she hopped in front of him, forcing Synovi to stop walking.

"Really?" she pressed, popping a hand on her hip.

His eyes drifted there then back to her perplexed face. It was clear he wasn't trying to talk, but that wasn't going to work for Torin. Not in the mood to chase him around the lobby, she did something better. Walking over to the wall, she snatched the plug out of the socket, stopping all motion. When he faced her, Synovi watched the cord dangling from her hand. From the look in her eyes, he just knew she wanted to strangle him with it.

"I'm trying to have a conversation with you," Torin sighed.

"Talk then."

The bass in his voice hadn't changed, but the way he said those two words shook her like he'd spoken them in a different language. She exhaled and squeezed her eyes shut, praying tears didn't fall. When she opened them, Synovi was closer to her than she expected him to be.

"Why you about to cry?"

Her chest hiccuped as wet lashes dabbed her cheeks as she looked up at him. "Because… I hurt your feelings, and that's not what I was trying to do. You didn't have to leave. You don't ever have to leave. No one is taking your place, and I hate that me not telling you about my ex put this distance between us. I don't like it. I miss you so much, and everything just went wrong because of me."

Synovi gently gripped the front of her neck. His smoldering gaze blanketed her, letting Torin know exactly what he needed her to do. She was rambling, and he hated that shit, but her words… they sounded different from before. They were strung together in a panicked cinquain that could've gone beyond five lines. Torin merged them together as if she were trying to etch every syllable in his head. Spoken as if she didn't want to lose him.

"You love me?" Synovi asked, lips brushing against hers.

Torin took that as her opportunity to touch him, wrapping her arms around his waist. "Yes."

"Then don't ever make me feel like you don't."

"But I—"

Synovi quieted her with a peck to the lips. "Sshh. It's my turn now. I wasn't responding because I needed to clear my head before I cut you off."

Her body tensed against his.

"But then, you wouldn't let up. I had to tell myself that not everyone is out to do me wrong. That your past, like mine, shouldn't be held against you. I had a lapse in judgment, but that was me battling my own insecurities. Childhood traumas I'm still working on getting through," Synovi divulged.

GiGi's words about taking this journey with him floated through Torin's brain. She didn't know if she had permission to speak, but she did anyway.

"Why'd you leave?" She asked as he caressed the side of her neck.

Synovi missed her too, and the feel of her head resting against his palm was enough to tell her the complete truth.

"Felt like that's what you wanted me to do. So, instead of waiting for you to hand me my walking papers, I saved myself the embarrassment."

Torin pulled him tighter to her, wanting to mesh their bodies together. "I didn't want that, but I see why you thought I did. There won't be a next time, so I'm sorry for not being more cognizant of your feelings. Why would I want to give you away? I thought you were mine to keep?"

Synovi smirked. "Shit gets chaotic with me sometimes. You sure that's what you wanna do?"

"Mhm. It's peaceful in your world, too. The perfect balance. We don't ever have to leave."

"We don't. But know this…" he said, forcing Torin to peel her heavy lids open. She was relaxed as ever in his embrace. "I want you all to my-mothafuckin'-self. If I sound selfish, it's because I finally can be. Especially with you."

"Okay," Torin said softly as if in a daze. "Yours. I don't want nobody else but you."

"Good. 'Cause I'm a nigga worth keepin'. Now, plug my vacuum back up."

Torin grinned as he spanked her ass cheek. When he finished his duties, the two walked out of the building, and Torin squinted. Her truck was the only vehicle in the lot, and she wondered how he was about to get to wherever he'd been staying.

"You going back to GiGi's?" Torin joked, knowing he'd probably been about to call a Lyft.

"That ain't where I been staying."

Her heart sank. "Oh. Well, where have you been staying?"

"Mr. K put me up in a hotel."

Her eyes expanded. "What? When did you and my daddy get cool?"

"The other day. He wanted to make amends, so I guess this was his way of doing so."

Torin would've never thought her daddy would keep something like that from her. Mr. K's nosiness with Tracee had come in handy while Torin was sick. As her parents, no matter how grown she was, they still discussed her well-being. Racquel spilled the beans about Synovi taking care of her, but leaving her in charge to give him updates.

Amid fighting her cold, Torin told her what happened, and Racquel relayed it to Tracee, who, in turn, got her baby's daddy up to speed. As a man, Mr. K knew what it was like to need a break from his woman sometimes. As a married man, that meant he went to his mancave or office for some hours.

Knowing Synovi's background and all he'd been through, escaping somewhere where there was no pressure and space to think was right up his alley. He reached out to Synovi personally and gave him advice as a man but also as the father of the woman he was with. An apology was given during their thirteen-minute conversation before Synovi agreed to check in at the hotel. One wasn't needed, but Synovi appreciated it.

"I guess he's keeping secrets from me," Torin fussed. "I'm glad you were somewhere safe, though."

"I miss your bed," Synovi said, putting his supplies in the trunk.

"That's all?"

He chuckled, pulling the passenger door open for her. "Nah, Love. You know better than to think that. I miss you, too."

Torin blushed. "Thank you for taking care of me, even though you weren't physically there."

"Did she do a good job and rub your feet?"

"Hell no." Torin laughed. "She made sure I was able to pull up on you today, though. Let another day had gone by, and we didn't speak."

Smirking, Synovi stepped closer. "What were you gon' do?"

"The last resort was calling GiGi. We had a nice conversation before I came here."

"Good. 'Cause I was coming back to the crib today, anyway. We got some important business to handle tomorrow."

"We do?"

Synovi bobbed his head. "Yeah. SB's Cleaning Service is about to expand, and I want you right by my side when it does."

He closed the door, and Torin sat with a silly grin on her face. If her man wanted her by his side, that's where she'd be. The day's mission was to get her man back, and Torin had done just that.

nineteen

Synovi's absence had indeed made Torin's heart grow fonder, and it seemingly made her mouth wetter. His breathing grew ragged as she deep-throated him right by the garage door. What was supposed to be another quick congratulatory speech for his upcoming meeting with Bostyn turned into Torin's lips wrapped around him. Synovi wasn't complaining as his dick grew harder with each bob and suction she delivered.

"L-Love… we gon' be… fuck," he groaned, gripping a handful of her hair.

Torin moaned, loving when he got rough with her. It made her wetter, and the more turned on she was, the nastier she got. Saliva dripped from her mouth as she slurped him with fervor. They had almost a week's worth of sex to compensate for, and Torin was putting in overtime.

"I love you," she cooed, gliding her tongue along the thick vein on his underside.

Synovi heaved. "I know."

Torin shook her head and made her tongue do laps around his sensitive tip. Synovi hissed under his breath. His fingers curled around the back of her neck, and her eyes gleamed. She was waiting on his command, but he didn't give one right away. Using both hands, Torin stroked him in a weaving motion.

Seeing his jaws clench yet still seem completely relaxed made her stomach tingle.

"And you taste so good." Torin moaned, taking him into her mouth again. This time, she took him down her throat. Synovi pulled his bottom lip between his teeth. His dark orbs smoldered with a possessiveness that made her leak.

"Come here," he urged, swooping her up before she could process his request.

Torin moaned and melted as his tongue invaded her mouth. He gripped her ass in the dress she was wearing before turning her away from him. She knew to assume the position before he said it, but she loved hearing the roughness in his tone.

"Bend over."

Synovi always instructed; never asked unless necessary. In this case, he was running shit. Torin rested against the small entry table and whimpered as he filled her.

"N… Novi." She creamed his dick immediately.

Throwing her ass back, Synovi pounded into her. Lifting one of her legs, he stroked her at a different angle. Her warm walls and snug grip comforted him like her hugs, but better. Synovi couldn't decide which one he loved more. Wrapping his arm around her chest, he brought her back to his chest, making her practically sit on his pole.

"You was trying to give all this dick up?" He hissed in her ear, suckling on her earlobe.

Torin gasped as her eyes rolled. "No, baby. I swear I wasn't."

"I'ont believe you," he groaned, hitting her G-spot.

Her body began to tremble as he fucked her harder. Synovi's heart thumped wildly in his chest as he kissed all over her neck and face. Torin cried out in pure bliss when he pinched her left nipple and toyed with her clit.

"Yeah… that's it. Relax and nut on this dick since it's yours," Synovi coached.

Her body obeyed him like always, and Torin climaxed so gently and forcefully that she felt like she was floating. Her skin tingled as Synovi's warm, swift breaths tickled her flesh. Her head rested against his shoulder, and he couldn't help but wonder what it'd be like to witness the look on her face for the rest of his life.

The state of euphoria Synovi had her in was mind-boggling to him. He hadn't gotten used to it yet, but wouldn't stop taking her there. Feeling him pulse and thicken inside of her, Torin peeled her eyes open. A lazy, satisfied grin covered her face as her walls clenched.

"You feel my love?"

Synovi's nostrils flared as he nodded.

"Let me feel yours," Torin moaned.

It was a reckless request, but he fulfilled it. For that moment, Synovi gave Torin control, allowing her to be the boss, as he released inside her. His body stiffened, and Torin rubbed the back of his neck and kissed his jaw.

"Let's get cleaned up and go get this money, Mr. Black."

"This contract states my client will make approximately $124,800 a year if he enters a contractual agreement. Why the rough estimate?" Rianne, Torin's lawyer, asked.

She had her meet them at Bostyn's office to ensure they knew what Synovi was signing himself up for.

Bostyn cleared his throat. "With twelve suites getting cleaned weekly at two hundred dollars, that's an exact amount. No matter if the suites are occupied, which is highly unlikely, he'll still get paid. The extra cash flow comes in if the tenants request his services beyond what is already agreed upon," he explained.

Rianne glanced at Synovi. "Are you okay with those terms?"

"Yeah. I expected that."

"Great. And the upfront payment of fifteen thousand

dollars isn't included in the above numbers?" Rianne questioned.

"No. Think of it as a sign-on bonus," Bostyn said.

With excitement flowing through her, Torin squeezed Synovi's thigh underneath the table. He did his best to keep a neutral expression, but it was hard. Going from trying to figure it out to an opportunity like this falling in his lap was a reminder to never think about giving up again.

"I 'preciate that more than you know," Synovi said gratefully.

"It's nothing. I told you I'd be the one thanking you. It's an extra storage closet around the back of the suites you can use, too. India, be sure to grab that key for him," Bostyn told his assistant.

She stood from the table and tugged her blush pencil skirt down. "I'll get that now. Should I grab the basket as well?"

"Yeah. Get both," Bostyn said.

Torin smiled her way and focused on him as Synovi and Rianne talked. "What is it you do again?"

"Get money and put my people in positions to do the same."

His entire persona screamed boss ass nigga, exactly like his name. Torin wasn't blind to his handsomeness and assumed that Bostyn was just the type of man who possessed the power to make a woman lose all logic.

Hmm. Beautiful, dark skin like Onyx. Crisp, low-cut fade. Tall and has money. Just my friend's type, Torin thought with a smirk.

"That's always a blessing," she said.

"Indeed," Bostyn agreed. "Everything straight?" he asked, noticing Rianne give him her attention.

"Yeah, it is," Synovi answered, putting the cap onto the pen. He'd signed his signature in all the spots requested. Stacking the papers, he slid them across the table.

Bostyn grinned. "Welcome to the family."

The men stood and dapped one another up before giving a brotherly hug. India entered the room with a welcome gift basket filled with the best presents. Behind her was the receptionist, who held a chilled bottle of Veuve Clicquot and wine-glasses for five. India handed Synovi the bottle as Bostyn scribbled his name on the blank lines.

Pulling her phone out, Torin opened the camera app. There was no way she would miss this moment. The light in Synovi's eyes matched the one radiating from his face. His chest swelled as he popped the cork. Bubbly spilled onto the wooden floors. Once their glasses were filled, they raised them in the air.

"You have a speech?" Torin grinned.

Synovi went to shake his head no, but stopped. He had been bereft of speech since they arrived, but had something to say right then.

"Yeah, a lil' somethin'. This toast is to you," he said, nodding his head her way. "Thank you for seeing the greatness in me, despite fighting through the darkness. You've pushed me to want more out of life and saw the potential in me that everyone else overlooked. SB's Cleaning Service is what it is today because of you, and I'm so thankful for you, Love. Everyone needs a you on their team, but that's too bad 'cause I'm keeping you all to myself."

Torin's bottom lip poked out as she rapidly blinked her eyes. She was not expecting him to say that. "I'm so proud of you." She grinned. Going to stand by his side, she kept recording and hugged his waist.

Bostyn couldn't help but soak up the love in the air as the other women present smiled. You could feel their energy throughout the entire room.

"Boss," Synovi started, lifting his glass. "For putting a young Black man in a position to win... thank you," he said humbly.

Bostyn lifted his glass. "To new money, more opportunities, and Black wealth!"

Glasses clinked, and life as Synovi once knew it was no longer the same.

One Month Later

"Aye, bruh," D'Marco said, walking through Synovi's empty condo. "This crib is fly. I ain't even gon' hold you."

While he'd been on the waiting list for the apartments Mrs. Minnie had gotten him approved for, Synovi changed his mind. Not just because he wanted something different, but because he had the option to do so, and no one could stop him. Being told what to do, how to act, and what to say for most of his life no longer applied. He finally had control over his life and was indeed the boss people professed he acted like.

"It is, huh? Bitch cost a grip, but it's worth it," Synovi said.

The two-bedroom, two-bathroom, loft-style home wasn't what he'd told GiGi to pray for, but it was his. Her prayers and more had been answered, and they wouldn't stop because he'd gotten what he deserved.

"Money ain't an issue now. It ain't gon' ever be long as SB's keeps doing numbers like it is."

Joining the cleaning crew on weekends, D'Marco meant what he said that day in the car. He was just waiting on Synovi to see the results for himself. Having more businesses reach out than he could handle, Synovi had to hire employees. With that came a responsibility he was still adjusting to, but it was a good change. Synovi was willing to learn whatever to keep his business thriving.

Watching how the people around him handled their staff, Synovi took notes and applied them accordingly. Holding off an extra month had placed more money in his pockets. When he presented his bank statements and verified his income with the leasing office, they queried him about his business.

Not because they didn't believe he could make that kind of money but because they were interested in his services. In their eyes, he had to have a reputable company and wanted to contribute.

"Novi! We have to go back to Walmart. We forgot to get a shower curtain for the guest bathroom," Torin shouted from downstairs.

"You hear that?" Synovi chuckled. "She thinks I'ma have guests staying over long enough to shower."

She even tried to convince him to have a housewarming party, but Synovi wasn't going for that.

D'Marco cracked up. "Still a moody ass nigga. Where I'ma stay if I get too drunk or need to crash once Nikki puts me out of our place?"

"You the only nigga allowed up in here," Synovi stated. "I ain't got no friends but you."

"Shit, I was barely that," D'Marco joked as they headed down the steps.

Torin exited the bathroom with trash in her hand. "Did you hear me?"

"Yeah, Love. Who you think staying over here?"

Her shoulder lifted. "I don't know, but someone might. We'll get one, just in case. What time are the mattress and furniture people supposed to arrive? We don't want to miss them just in case they mess something up."

Synovi glanced D'Marco's way, and he smirked. Torin was indeed running shit today.

"They come tomorrow. Relax."

Torin turned on her heels and visibly calmed down, but gave a rebuttal. "How can I relax when this is such a milestone for you? I'm always going to be excited."

Synovi smirked and patted her ass as she walked by him. "Whatever you say. You almost done? I'm ready to go eat."

"Mhm. Give me five more minutes, and we can leave," Torin said. She walked away, then turned around to add, "Are we driving my truck or yours?"

"You can drive mine. I know that's what you wanna do."

Torin smirked. "I'm glad you know."

A few days after his contract with Bostyn was finalized, Synovi hit the car lot and copped him a clean black Chevy Tahoe. The big body-style SUV was right up Torin's lane to drive, and she was behind the wheel almost more than the owner. Being handed his first set of keys to a home and vehicle and seeing his name on documents was an unexplainable feeling.

D'Marco and Synovi chopped it up while Torin added her finishing touches to the bathroom. It was the first one you saw when walking in, so she wanted to make it presentable. With promises to link up later, D'Marco hopped in his fixed-up car that Nikki paid her uncle to fix and left. He'd moved out of Solace Place, and they were staying together for now. Seeing Synovi get his life together encouraged him to do the same, and he hoped Nikki kept her hands to herself this time. He was trying to do right by her and their daughter moving forward.

"What yo' mama cooking?" Synovi asked, getting comfortable in the passenger seat.

"I don't know. She wouldn't tell me. I hope it's some chicken. Ooh, or a roast. I could go for either right now."

While she didn't mind cooking, Torin was grateful Tracee also knew how to throw down in the kitchen and invited them over for dinner. Synovi's stomach growled in agreement just as his phone rang. The incoming call from Unique was one he was looking forward to.

"What up, Unique?" He greeted when the call connected.

"Hey! What's going on? How's moving going?"

The elation in her tone made Synovi crack a small grin. She was just as excited as Torin was, and that meant more to him than he'd ever reveal.

"Easy when you ain't got nothing," he joked, finally able to make light of his once unstable situation.

"Well, that's okay. You have a good heart and an unmatched drive about you. That's more than enough."

Torin grinned. "Tell him again."

"Oh, hey, Ms. Torin. I should've known you weren't too far

away." Unique chuckled. "How are you? I hope he isn't working you too hard."

"I'm doing fine, and he's not at all. I wish he'd let me do more," she said, cutting her eyes his way.

"You know how he is… a lil' stubborn, but that's why we love him."

"That's exactly why," Torin concurred.

Unique cleared her throat. "A lawyer came to see me today?"

"Yeah? Who?" he asked.

Synovi hadn't gotten around to hiring her one yet. He wanted to get himself situated before he did for anyone else, but it was on his to-do list.

"She said her name is Rianne Matthews. You ever heard of her?"

His head snapped Torin's way, but she kept her eyes on the road. Synovi licked his lips, trying to decipher what he was feeling. His nonchalant answer was given to hide his true emotions until they got off the phone.

"Nah. Never heard of her. I'ma have to look her up," he said.

"Real knowledgeable, sweet young woman. It sounds like she knows her stuff, so that's a plus. Thank God for whoever sent her," Unique praised.

Synovi reached for Torin's hand that wasn't on the wheel. Intertwining their fingers, he gave her hand a squeeze. The simple gesture let her know he was thankful.

Torin wasn't sure how he'd feel about putting money up for Unique, so she didn't ask. Like he did when he entered her life, she fulfilled tasks she knew needed to be taken care of, whether they were asked of her or not. Synovi needed his mama regardless of what they'd been through.

"Yeah… thank God," Synovi said. "He be sending His angels on earth to look out for us."

"Sure does," Unique expressed. "Now, tell me about this truck you got. GiGi said it's too big."

Torin chuckled as she pushed the Tahoe through traffic.

Synovi caught his mama up on everything happening in the free world, hoping that Rianne worked her magic to get her free. He almost couldn't believe Torin had gone to such extremes for him, but Synovi should've been used to it by now. Understanding a person with a good heart was hard to comprehend some days. He had to train his mind to know that she didn't want anything in return; just him.

When their call ended, Synovi exhaled. He had so much he wanted to say. There'd never be enough words to express his gratitude, but he wanted to. His quiet disposition forced Torin to see where his mind was at.

"I know what you're probably thinking, but it's really nothing. You and Unique deserve a fair chance at this dramatic thing called life together, so I hope you're not mad at me. I mean, it's too late to get my money back, plus—"

"I love you," Synovi declared.

Torin's heart flipped inside her chest. "Aww, baby. I love you more."

They came to a red light, and Synovi sat up in his seat. Leaning her way, he grabbed her face. "Nah, listen to me. I love the fuck out of you. You feel this?" He said, placing her hand against his chest.

Torin's eyes watered as she nodded her head. His heart was beating so erratically, she thought it'd leap from his chest.

"I ain't never shared this with anybody. I'm trippin' right now 'cause I can't believe you really rocking with a nigga like this." His words came out in a choked-out manner, making Torin want to sob.

When the light turned green, Torin quickly merged into the left lane. Pulling over into a grocery store, she parked and faced him. She leaned over the console, needing to be in his space.

"Believe it, okay?" she cooed, brushing a hand over his creased brow. "I'm not going anywhere."

"I know that now," Synovi breathed.

His hand lingered on her neck, massaging it with constraint. Synovi wanted to yank her onto his lap and make her feel his love. Everything she gave him only intensified when it was time for him to reciprocate. Instead, he gently kissed her lips, pressing his forehead against hers. Their intense lip lock was interrupted by the ringing of Torin's phone.

Huffing, she pulled away and dug inside her purse to retrieve it. "Yes, Racquel?"

"Are you on your way to Mommy's?"

"Yes. We're on our way there now. What's up?"

"She said can you stop and get a pack of Hawaiian rolls and a case of Sprite?"

Torin shifted gears so she could pull closer to the door. "Yeah. Anything else?"

"Nope. I think that's all. See y'all when y'all get here."

Telling her okay, Torin hung up. Unclicking her seatbelt, she said, "I'ma run in here right quick."

"We going in together," Synovi said.

The couple climbed out and headed into the store. Synovi followed Torin's lead, not knowing what she came to grab. He was grateful she pulled over so he could get himself together, but quickly regretted it when they turned down the aisle with the drinks.

Running into Jade and her daughters was the last thing Synovi expected to happen today. Torin spotted her first and didn't miss a step as she strolled right on by her. She expected her man to do the same, only Synovi's feet faltered. He'd seen pictures of her daughters before, but seeing them in person now, knowing they were his little sisters, brought upon an onset of emotions he hated feeling.

"H-Hey," Jade uttered.

Kalie's head of braided ponytails swung his way, and she smiled while waving. "Hi!"

Synovi couldn't even offer the little girl a head nod; he was stuck. Not far from them, in case something popped off, Torin exhaled. She knew this was an unexpected moment, but if Jade tried anything slick, she was going to forget all about being the bigger person. A shopper pushing their cart past them broke his focus.

"What up," Synovi finally spoke.

"Nothing much. Just getting some groceries. How are you? You know, after everything?"

She wanted to ask much more, but her kids were there.

"Better."

"That's good," Jade mumbled.

Synovi knew her answer wouldn't have been the same, so he didn't bother to ask. Jade was going through it, and it showed. Mentally, physically, and emotionally, Jade would never be the same. Her skin no longer glowed, dark circles pooled underneath her eyes, and she'd lost so much weight from not eating. She was suffering from depression and a host of other self-diagnosed conditions. Living with her mother hadn't made it any better, but at least she had help with the girls.

"Mommy, who's he?" Skylar questioned.

The words registered in her brain, but Jade became tongue-tied when she went to spit them out.

"H-He's your… Um, one of Mommy's old friends," she somewhat lied.

"Oh," Skylar said and went right back to minding her business.

Jade blinked back tears, knowing she'd possibly never be able to tell them who Synovi really was and how she knew him. But that didn't mean it couldn't happen.

"Do you… would you want a relationship with them?" she asked meekly.

The entire situation had changed Jade. She'd never been meek, but death and reality would do that to you. Her question shocked Synovi. He didn't know if she was serious or just trying to get a reaction out of him.

"Do you think that would be appropriate while you're healing?" Torin asked, overhearing her.

She wasn't trying to be mean; only honest. There was no way she thought Synovi could have a healthy relationship with her children; it didn't matter who their father was. This entire ordeal was messy, and Torin wasn't about to allow her to pull Synovi into her dark hole.

Jade's mouth opened slightly before quickly closing. She didn't know what to say. Synovi scratched the bridge of his nose. He knew whatever Jade was insinuating had to be because she still wasn't thinking clearly. That was the only logical answer because Synovi's loyalty was with Unique.

Regardless of her absence, he was her child. He'd battled with the thought of introducing himself to them if there ever came a time, and now that it was here, Synovi stuck to his first mind.

"I'ont think anything good will come from that," he said, breaking Jade's heart.

Truthfully, she didn't know if she asked because her girls deserved to know their brother or because she missed Synovi. She was in a mental tug of war, and before she could fly off the Richter and do something to land her in jail or worse, Jade decided to walk away once and for all.

"I'm truly sorry about everything. I know you wish you never met me," she said sadly before pushing her cart away.

Synovi swallowed the lump in his throat and watched as Kalie waved goodbye. Similar to his trauma as a kid, they had no clue how the sins of their parents would one day affect them.

"You okay?" Torin asked.

His head bobbed. "Yeah. What drink Racquel say get?"

Just like that, Synovi pushed Jade, his sisters he'd never get to know, and all the drama from his past to the back of his mind. It had no room to grow where he was and planned on going.

epilogue

Torin hated being late.

Being punctual and arriving at places, especially the airport, in a timely manner, had always been a priority to her. Panic settled in ten minutes into their drive when Leighton didn't answer her phone call.

"What is she doing?" Torin fussed, dialing her number again.

"She probably trying to pack the car, Love. Relax. She'll be there."

Synovi's words didn't calm her erratic nerves at all. For months, they'd been planning a trip to Panama City, Panama, and Torin would be damned if they missed it. Huffing, she sat back in her seat.

"She just had to be difficult and drive. We could've picked her up."

Synovi chuckled. "You gon' fuss the entire drive?"

"I can, but I won't. Are you going to miss me while I'm away?"

He licked his lips, rolling his tongue around his mouth. He could still taste her from his morning indulgence between her thighs.

"Rhetorical question," he answered, then told her what she wanted to hear. "I always miss you."

Torin smirked. "It's just for a week. You said I needed a break, so I'm taking one."

"You do. Remember what happened the last time you didn't listen."

Her eyes rolled. Too much occurred the previous time she hadn't listened to her body. This time, she listened to her man and cleared her schedule. She asked for a trip out of town, and that was exactly what he gave her.

"Don't remind me," she sighed as his phone rang.

Synovi eyed the number, not recognizing it. "Hello?"

"Hello. Can I speak with Mr. Black?" a masculine voice said.

"This is he. How can I help you?"

Torin damn near creamed her panties, seeing him get into business mode. There was absolutely nothing sexier than watching her man handle business on his boss shit.

"This is Mike Dendrite with Dendrite Homes & Construction. How are you?"

"I'm good, Mike. I'm assuming this call is regarding that email I received?" Synovi asked.

Mike chuckled. "Indeed, it is. We have new construction build on the northside and are in search of a reliable cleaning company. The last ones we hired did a horrible job. I'm sure you know wasted money is worse than no money."

Synovi disagreed but kept his opinions to himself. Being broke meant you ain't have shit to spend to consider it a waste. He knew that very well.

"Absolutely. When do you need a definite answer?"

"Today?" Mike chuckled. "That'd be great, but by next week if you can. Pay is in the two hundred range; a little more, a little less. We'll discuss that in the future."

"We will," Synovi said, liking those numbers. Adding another six-figure account to SB's would be just what he needed. "I'll give you a call next week."

"Sure thing. Take care."

Synovi pressed the end button on his wheel and exhaled. He was waiting for Torin to say something, because she always did, but her muteness was new. He glanced her way, finding her staring him down like she wanted to swallow him whole.

"What?" Synovi questioned.

"You don't even understand how sexy you are conducting business. Makes me wanna do some real freaky shit to you in this truck."

Synovi chuckled and glanced at the time. "How freaky? We got a good twenty minutes before we make it to the airport."

Unbuckling her seatbelt, Torin made her way across the console and pulled his dick out of hiding. She grinned and inhaled his scent that she wished she could've bottled up and taken on the trip with her. "I can make you bust in ten."

When they arrived at the airport, Torin had kept her word and was right back in her seat, chewing on a piece of gum like she hadn't just sucked the soul out of Synovi. She was grateful the ride was a straight shot and traffic flowed because he easily hit one hundred on the dash as she pleasured him.

"You know what… maybe she's already here and has no service," Torin concluded.

She couldn't understand why Leighton was playing games right now.

"Yeah, maybe," Synovi said.

"Wait. Why are you going toward the parking garage?"

Synovi smirked. "If I tell you now, will you relax?"

"Probably not, but I'ma say yes because what the hell is going on?"

"You and Leighton aren't going on a trip, Love. We are. I booked us flights and acted like it was for y'all to enjoy, but nah. It's for us. Leighton was never coming."

Torin teared up immediately. "Novi… are you serious?"

Her whining made his dick jump. "Yeah. This is our first of many dates out of the country. Look in the glove box and grab that envelope."

She eyed him with skepticism, but did as he said. "I can open it?"

"Yeah," he said, finding a parking spot. Reversing into it, he parked and watched as she broke the seal.

Torin's eyes shot to him. "Shut up," she whispered. The tears she'd been holding in clouded her vision as they dripped from her face. "You didn't," she cried.

"I did. You deserve that plus more, and I'ma make sure you get it," Synovi stated.

For months, Torin had been telling him she wanted a bigger kitchen. As Kaine's Kitchen continued to grow, so did her clientele. Mia had been searching but came up short. As her man, Synovi didn't want her stressing about a thing if he could prevent her from doing so. The connections he'd made over the months had come in handy, and he was able to score her an unused commercial kitchen from his old boss, Mr. Fred's, brother.

Freddy's had reopened, and they attended the grand opening. As always, Mr. Fred talked Synovi's ear off, even with there being tons of guests there. The conversation shifted to Torin, and how they were looking to expand, and just like that, he had a property with her name as the owner. He figured she could rent her other one out and still make an income.

Sniffling, Torin reread the deed and tucked it back inside the envelope. "Wow. I really can't believe you did that for me."

"Believe it, Love. Now, you trying to miss this flight or what?"

Giggling, Torin unbuckled her seat belt. "Absolutely not. You and Leighton are sooo sneaky. Let me guess; your suitcase is in the trunk?"

Synovi nodded with a grin. "Yeah. That's why I had to put yours in the backseat so you wouldn't be asking questions."

Torin shook her head. "You know me."

Leaving their businesses to D'Marco and Tracee to run for a week was just what the couple needed. Synovi didn't know if his plans would fall through, but he exhaled once they boarded and took off. Some days, he was still unsure how the universe blessed him with someone so selfless. Someone who genuinely loved him from the top of his thick, black hair down to his size twelve feet. Torin cherished everything about Synovi and reminded him daily that he deserved everything light and love in this world... especially her. Finally, she turned him into a believer.

Getting served breakfast in bed wasn't something new for Torin. When they were home, Synovi made her stay upstairs on the days he spent the night so he could cater to her. It was refreshing to be served in another country, on the top floor of one of the best hotels, overlooking the city. The corner room with floor-to-ceiling windows and a deep soaking tub were the main reasons the couple was still in bed.

Synovi made love to Torin right up against the window for the city to see, washed her body after she soaked, and gave her a massage that put her straight to sleep. This morning, she couldn't move from the plush, king-sized bed, and Synovi didn't blame her.

"I just want to lay here for another hour," she said, rubbing her hands up and down his tattooed arm.

She'd finally gotten one of her own from his childhood friend, Lito, and Torin was amazed by his raw talent. Sitting three hours for one tattoo that stretched down her side had been painful but worth it. Detailed flowers spelled out the word LOVE. She had Lito shade them with vibrant colors, so whenever Synovi saw it, he was reminded of what he deserved. The body art was for her, but for him more than anything.

"You can. Our tour of the city doesn't start until two," Synovi yawned.

Torin relaxed to the sound of his steady breathing. Her body draped his, snuggling against him as if he would disappear.

"You ever thought this is where we'd end up?"

Synovi kissed her collarbone, making her shiver. "In this city? Nah."

"Not here." Torin giggled. "I mean, here in this stage of life?"

He marveled over her words, trying to follow where she was going with the conversation. "I think deep down I knew I'd make it… just didn't know when or how."

"I knew the day I met you."

He cracked a grin. "You sound cliché as hell."

"I'm serious. Even though we met unorthodoxly, my gut told me whatever you were going through wouldn't last long."

Synovi scratched his cheek, where her hair had tickled him. "And I was paranoid about the way everything came together."

"You really were." She giggled. "It was weird, but I believe in coincidences. Being at the right place at the right time. Some people are just blessed."

He lifted in the bed, and Torin sat up with him. "Aye. Promise me something," he said.

Torin's chest heaved. "Anything."

She was willing to do whatever he asked of her.

"Promise to never turn your back on me, no matter how chaotic it gets."

She caressed his face and pecked his lips. "I promise. I'm here to stay… here for you to keep to yourself and ride through the waves with."

Grinning, Synovi stuck his hand out. Torin chuckled, remembering how he left her hanging on her couch that day.

"Should we shake on it?" Synovi asked.

Smiling, Torin gripped his hand and shook it. "Mhm. It's a deal, Mr. Black."

"It's a deal, Love."

The End